# CRASH TACK

## A MIAMI JONES CASE

### AJ Stewart

Jacaranda Drive Publishing

Los Angeles, California

www.jacarandadrive.com

Cover artwork by Streetlight Graphics

ISBN-10: 0985945591

ISBN-13: 978-0-9859455-9-6

Books by AJ Stewart

Stiff Arm Steal
Offside Trap
High Lie
Dead Fast
Crash Tack

To Heather: You are the wind in my sails and the sun on my back.

And to all the early readers. It is so much more because of you.

# CHAPTER ONE

**I stood on** the dock of the Palm Beach Yacht Club, thinking about the America's Cup. I was a small boy growing up in Connecticut, only a couple hours from Newport, Rhode Island, where in 1983, an Australian crew beat the United States for the first time, after more than 130 years of America's Cup racing, the longest winning streak in sports history. I recalled later my father talking about that day as if the Aussies had stolen the Declaration of Independence and used it for wallpaper. And I watched the television with him when in 1995, the Australians tried to win it back again in San Diego, only for their boat to break in half and sink into the Pacific. My father didn't rejoice. He just sat in our living room with a sense of bewilderment that such a thing could occur.

The same sense of bewilderment now hung over the dock in Palm Beach, as we waited for a yacht to return from the Palm Beach-Nassau race with a trophy but without its captain. My mentor, friend and boss, Lenny Cox, paced along the dock to the end and back, and his labored action took me back to my coastal New England roots, and stories of widows pacing around railed platforms atop their Victorian mansions, waiting with a sense of growing dread, eyes cast toward the sea, searching vainly for vessels that had left but never returned.

This wasn't a cold New England morning, but it was mild for South Florida in the spring. The breeze had shifted around from the north and a chill had arrived with it. Banners along the dock that read *Palm Beach-Nassau Classic 2008* had flopped around to the south, making the writing appear backwards to me. I stood in chinos and a shirt with small pineapples all over it, hands in pockets, watching faces both familiar and not, as they in turn watched each other and me and the gray Intracoastal Waterway. A couple of paramedics leaned against their truck, while a collection of law enforcement folks, county sheriff and two sets of local police swapped their gallows humor in whispers. A number of yachtie types, some dressed too well to truly be seaworthy, others as salty as the ocean itself, waited for updates from the Coast Guard cutter that had made its way down to West Palm from the station in Jupiter Inlet. A woman brought hot coffee out from the yacht club rooms, and it was being passed around when one of the Coast Guard personnel called *there she is*, and we all looked east at the yacht motoring toward us.

A Coast Guard crewmember shepherded us away from the edge of the dock to allow the paramedics first access. There had been no reports of injury, but the expectation of shock. The sleek, comfortable-looking yacht pulled alongside the dock under the hand of a man who had the face of a walrus. He wore a mustache the color of smoke-stained walls, and a blue cap bleached streaky white by sun and sweat. Fenders were tossed over the side by a petite, dark-haired woman and the welcome sight of my friend and colleague, Ron Bennett. Ron's silver hair matched the color of the water and looked suitably windblown, but his face was starved of emotion. The paramedics balanced on the stanchions, skipped across the guardrail and inspected each of the six crew, all of whom looked tired but otherwise unharmed. I made eye contact with Ron and he offered me a weak smile, the kind that said he was glad to be home, but somehow embarrassed by that fact.

I felt a body brush my shoulder and noted the gray polyester suit that could only belong to Detective Ronzoni of the Palm Beach Police Department. I had crossed paths with Ronzoni a handful of times in my brief career as a private investigator. To say he was my nemesis would be to vastly overstate his impact on the world, let alone on me, but he was an occasional thorn in my side. No doubt the feeling was mutual.

"Surprised to see the Palm Beach PD slumming it on this side of the bridge, Rigatoni," I said.

"It's Ronzoni, smart guy, and the boat and its owner both reside in Palm Beach, so it's professional courtesy."

I nodded. Professional courtesy was very big with the Palm Beach PD. The cities of Palm Beach and West Palm Beach shared two words in their names, and that was about all. Palm Beach was one of the most exclusive communities in the country, where exclusive is code for very, very rich. It sat on its own barrier island, separating the rest of Florida from the Atlantic Ocean. The bridge that crossed the Intracoastal Waterway between the well-heeled island and the regular Joes on the mainland was some kind of physical metaphor. Unlike Ronzoni and his colleagues, the West Palm Beach PD didn't do professional courtesy quite so much. They were busy dealing with crime.

"Why's the yacht coming here if it lives on the island?" I asked Ronzoni, as we watched a twenty-something guy who looked like a Ralph Lauren magazine ad that had been crumpled in the mail get his blood pressure checked by the paramedics.

"It just lives at the Biltmore. It races out of the yacht club here."

The club was called the Palm Beach Yacht Club, but it occupied a long dock off the promenade in West Palm. I had no idea why that was the case.

"So no case for you. Shame."

"No shame, Jones. Whatever this is, it's going to be a jurisdictional nightmare."

"How so?"

"Coast Guard says the skipper went overboard just west of the Biminis, which is Bahamas territory. The Coast Guard was called in to search because it's a US vessel, so they're all over it. But they don't investigate boating mishaps in foreign waters. If that's anyone, it's the FBI. The skipper was, *is*, a resident of Palm Beach, but the boat has landed here in West Palm, so maybe that's West Palm PD, maybe it's the sheriff. That's a lot of paperwork for nothing."

Ronzoni had a pathological aversion to paperwork and, it seemed to me, a similar aversion to every other kind of work. What he didn't have was an aversion to taking credit for the work of other departments, and that I guessed was more the reason for his attendance than any kind of courtesy.

It seemed that the county was taking lead on events, because it was a tall, blond investigator whom I recognized but didn't know who took control. He spoke to a deputy whom I certainly wouldn't have minded knowing, but didn't. She made the green uniform of the sheriff's office look like *haute couture*. Her brown hair was tied back and it gave her face a determined look that did all sorts of things for me. I watched her talk to the woman who had brought the coffee from the yacht club, and then she began ushering the crew off the yacht and into a room in the club. I moved toward Ron as he stepped over the guardrail and Lenny met me there. Lenny gave Ron a hug. He was that kind of guy. I followed with a hug of my own. If it was good enough for Lenny, it was good enough for me and Ron looked like he needed it. The attractive deputy didn't move us along, waiting for me to pull back from Ron before giving him a tap on the shoulder and shooting me a smile that I suspected was supposed to convey compassion, but actually made me feel like the sun had just burst through the clouds. I watched the petite, dark-haired woman from the crew lead the others toward the clubroom. She was followed by another woman, a thin blond with mousy features, and the preppy guy. Another guy, perhaps thirty or so, with coal-black hair and a Roman nose kept his eyes to the ground. The walrus who had been at the helm brought up the rear. We dropped in step with Ron as he walked toward the clubroom.

"What happened?" asked Lenny.

Ron shook his head. "I don't know. I really don't know." He moved his eyes to us but his vision was somewhere else, recounting events perhaps, trying to make sense of it all. He walked like a robot into the clubroom with the others, and the sheriff's investigator put up a palm to tell us that we weren't invited.

"What's happening?" I asked him.

"Just a few questions, that's all. We've still got a missing person out there."

I nodded and Lenny remained mute, and we watched the attractive deputy step inside and close the door. Lenny wandered over to the paramedics, and I headed for the Coast Guard cutter. One of the men was coiling a rope on the deck, and I threw him a nod.

"You guys find anything?"

He shook his head. "Nup. We've got boats and choppers still looking. If he's out there, we'll find him."

"When did they call it in?"

"Far as I know, they didn't. We called them."

"How does that work?"

"The guy was wearing a PLB."

"A what?" I asked.

"PLB. Personal locator beacon. It's a satellite beacon that can be triggered in an emergency. Helps us nail down where he is."

"So you know where he is?"

The guy shrugged. "We know where the signal is." He nodded to end our chat, and returned to his rope coiling. I wandered back to Lenny. The paramedics had packed up and headed off, and Lenny leaned against the rails where the dock met the promenade. There were some impressive yachts in the slips, a lot of *mine is bigger than yours.*

"Coast Guard says the skipper's still out there. They're tracking some kind of beacon," I said as I leaned my back against the rail.

Lenny nodded. He was wearing a shirt with lots of bikini-clad women on it, each leaning against a long surfboard. It wasn't the most PC of garments, but Lenny wasn't the most PC of guys.

"Paramedics said they're all okay, just tired and shaken," Lenny said. "It's not easy to lose someone overboard." Lenny said the last part staring out beyond the throng of masts and rigging, across the island and ocean to somewhere a long way away and a long time ago, somewhere I had never been and would probably never go. Somewhere he too had lost people. Lenny ran his hand through his thick mane of red hair, let out a deep breath and shot me a wink from his creased, well-tanned face. I wasn't sure if the wink was for my benefit or his.

We waited in silence, which was okay for both of us. Lenny could wax poetic with the best of them when he was in the mood, but he was equally comfortable with silence, and I was generally the same. I thought about Ron, how he seemed to have aged a decade in a week, and how it must feel to lose someone at sea. I didn't know the guy who was out there, but I felt a chill as I pictured him floating in the deep black Atlantic, no land in sight, watching his yacht sail away. It made me shiver and I shook the sensation out through my shoulders, and then I looked along the dock to see the door to the clubroom open and the attractive deputy step through. Then six weary sailors shuffled out, each looking in their own way like they were living a nightmare.

# CHAPTER TWO

**We took Lenny's** pickup and delivered Ron home. He didn't speak on the drive, preferring to stare out the passenger's side window. Lenny piloted us down I-95 past the airport and pulled onto Forest Hill Boulevard. We drove by the entrances to a stream of homogenous housing subdivisions before we turned off to the apartment complex that Ron was calling home.

As far as apartment developments go this was a nice one. Two levels of condos surrounded the ubiquitous man-made lake, with well-tended St. Augustine grass and tropical plantings. It wasn't the down-at-heel bachelor hotel one usually associated with a freshly divorced man. But the inside of Ron's apartment couldn't have said divorcé more if it was lit in fifty-foot neon in Times Square. Although tastefully painted and furnished in a business hotel style, it bore the empty walls and takeout food scent of a single guy who wasn't designed to be that way.

Ron dropped his sailing bag inside the door and flopped onto a microfiber sofa that was too red to be his. I asked him if he wanted a drink and he said it was a bit early, even for him. I hadn't meant an alcoholic drink, but I decided he wasn't firing on all cylinders so I let it go, and poured a glass of water from the faucet and handed it to him. He nodded thanks as if the previous question had never been asked. Lenny leaned against the wall, clearly not planning on hanging around. I had a whole list of questions to ask Ron, but was mindful of the ordeal he had been through.

"You should get some rest," I said, motioning to Lenny.

Lenny bounced his butt from the wall. "You be okay?"

Ron looked around the room. It was a one-bed apartment, so that didn't take very long, and then he looked at Lenny.

"I won't sleep right now. Why don't we go to the office?"

"You sure?" said Lenny.

"I might not be up for a pop quiz, but I can pack boxes."

We waited for Ron to change from his sailing gear into a fresh polo shirt and a pair of blue trousers, and then we jumped back into Lenny's truck. He cut up North Military Trail to Okeechobee Boulevard. Just after Cross Country Mall Lenny pulled into a seventies vintage strip mall of faded blue stucco with a parking lot that had been bleached gray by years of tropical sun and rain. He stopped in front of a store that had the vertical blinds pulled despite the cloudy day, and we got out. The air was heavy with incense and spices emanating from the Indian grocery next door. Lenny pushed the door with his name stenciled on it, and held it open for Ron and me. We stepped into the air-conditioned front office, where our receptionist, Lizzy Staniforth, sat waiting for us to appear.

"Big night, boys?" She scowled through her heavily painted red lips. Lizzy looked like she had just wandered in from a goth nightclub, lots of black clothes and attitude, but she was in fact incredibly organized. She had been working for

Lenny when he invited me to join his firm eighteen months earlier, and she was yet to offer me a smile.

"Ron was sailing," I said. Lizzy shot me a look like that was a likely story, until she recalled that he had indeed been away for the week sailing in the Bahamas. Ron offered a weak smile and stepped through into the inner office that was separated only by a partial wall. Lenny gave Lizzy a wink and she beamed like he'd just offered her a raise. I tried not to take it personally and leaned across the desk, speaking softly.

"They lost a man at sea," I told her, and her jaw dropped before she spoke.

"Oh my, Lord," she said. "Is he gone?"

I shrugged. "They're still looking."

"He must be distraught," she said, glancing at the wall between her and Ron.

"He's been better."

"Is there anything I can do for him?"

I looked around at the half-packed boxes. "Just keep this place going, like you always do."

I thought it was a nice thing to say, and I gave her a smile and got a nod in return. She turned to her computer and began typing, and I took that as my signal that I was dismissed.

The office beyond was actually one large room that in a previous life had been a video library, and there was still a box of random VHS tapes in the storeroom that was there when Lenny arrived and would be there when he left. Two desks punctuated the office space, along with a sofa, a coffee station and a water cooler. We never chatted over the water cooler. Most of our conversations happened with Lenny sitting on the edge of his desk, me sitting behind mine and Ron kicked back on the sofa. I found them both in those positions, and I took my seat.

"You wanna get it off your chest?" asked Lenny. He had a disarming personality that made a lot of people open up when they acted like clams with everyone else. Ron propped his head up on the arm of the sofa and looked at Lenny.

"Like I said, Lenny, I just don't know. We had done the race—it should have all been smooth waters."

"How did you do in the race?" I asked.

"We won our division."

"So what happened then?" Lenny asked.

Ron shook his head. "We were on our way back from Nassau and had just crossed the Great Bahama Bank. I thought we were going to anchor for the night at Bimini or Cat Cay, but I was down below and Drew came down and said Will had decided to keep going since we had a sou'easter, and Drew divided us into shifts. Will, Felicity and Drew were going first watch, so the rest of us hit the hay. We were pretty darn tired."

"Which one was the skipper?" I asked.

"That's Will. Will Colfax. He owns the boat."

"So who is this guy? Will Colfax?" I asked.

"He's pretty well known around the club. Businessman. Import-export, that sort of thing."

"You didn't know him that well?"

"Well enough, but you know with things like sailing. Probably the same when you played baseball. You kind of know people within that environment but not necessarily out of it. He was one of those guys. Big, loud. Charming in a boorish sort of way."

"But you sailed with him anyway?"

"Sure, he was okay. In small doses, you know. And he had a very nice boat."

"So who were the others on deck with him?" asked Lenny.

"Who? Oh, Felicity and Drew? Felicity's the blond girl, nice girl. She's works at the *Post*. Drew's a boat builder and sailor."

"The walrus with the mustache?" I asked. Ron nodded.

Lenny leaned forward on his desk. "What did they say happened?"

"They don't know. Felicity said she was on deck and Will told her that the water was as flat as a bath, so she might as well go below and rest. Drew had spent a good few hours eyes on the water getting across the bank, so he must have been pretty tired, and I think Alec offered to take his place on deck. Alec said he fell asleep waiting down below."

"Which one was Alec?" I asked.

"Young guy, smart dresser," Ron said.

I recalled the Ralph Lauren wannabe. "What was he waiting for?"

"No idea."

"So this guy, Will, was on deck alone?" asked Lenny.

Ron shook his head like he had let his skipper down. I knew the look. I'd had a few occasions in my previous life playing minor league baseball, when I'd done something, thrown a bad pitch or not followed the catcher's call, and I'd been thunked out of the park and felt bad about letting the team down. But what I didn't see was how this was Ron's fault in the slightest.

"He was up there, and somehow he went over," whispered Ron. I could see him kicking himself for not being there, up on deck, even if it wasn't his watch.

"Sounds like this Felicity or Alec guy weren't doing their job, not you," I said.

"Was it rough?" asked Lenny.

Ron shook his head again. "No, not really. I mean, it's the Gulf Stream, right, so it's no Lake Placid, but for the Stream it was darn good. Like I say, there was a light sou'easter, so we had the breeze at our back. There was just enough roll to put me off to sleep. The weather didn't turn at all until after."

"After what?" I asked, standing and pouring Ron a glass of water from the cooler.

He took the water and sipped. "The radio call. I woke a little because I felt the wind change, and it can't have been more than a few minutes later the radio call came. I was sleeping in the galley. There were only three cabins, each a double, so I bunked on the sofa in the galley. You know I can sleep anywhere."

"Exhibit one, that sofa," I said, nodding at Ron.

He gave a little smile, which was encouraging. "I took the call. It was the Coast Guard. They had been alerted by Will's beacon."

"His PLB," I said. Lenny lifted an eyebrow at me.

"That's right. They were new. Not many sailors have them," said Ron, sipping his water.

I frowned. "I would have thought they were mandatory." You wouldn't get me out in the middle of the ocean, even on a cruise ship, without some kind of tracking device.

"No, they're not. It's race rules that the boat has an EPIRB, but not individual sailors."

"EPIRB?" I asked.

"An emergency position indicating radio beacon," said Ron. "It's a beacon that's registered to a specific boat. As opposed to the PLBs, which are newer, and sailor-specific."

"So you didn't have one of these PLBs?" asked Lenny.

"I did. We all did. Will got one for everyone."

"So the Coast Guard knew he'd fallen off the boat?" I asked.

"They got the signal, and they were calling to confirm if it was a false alarm. I ran up on deck and found no one, and Alec had woken up by then. He was in a galley chair opposite, and he checked Will's cabin and found he wasn't there."

I felt my skin prickle. "Where was this?"

"Eighteen nautical miles west of Bimini."

"So what did you do?"

Ron shook his head again. "We did the only thing we could do. We kept sailing."

"You didn't look for him?"

"The wind turned," said Lenny. "Right?"

Ron nodded. "It was the middle of the night in the Gulf Stream, and the wind was turning to a nor'easter. And the boat has an EPIRB but it doesn't have tracking systems, so we can send the signal but we can't receive or track it. We'd be looking for a needle in a haystack. We had to make sure no one else was endangered, so we kept our westerly heading to get closer to shore before things got too choppy. And the Coast Guard was in the air before we ended the call. They had the signal, they knew where he was."

"So why haven't they found him yet?" I asked.

"I don't know," said Ron, not for the first time. "I just don't know."

# CHAPTER THREE

**The Coast Guard** search and rescue team lost the signal thirteen hours after it first alerted them. They called Drew, the walrus who knew the Coast Guard guys best, and he spread the news. They had a last position, they knew the direction the beacon was heading, and they planned to continue the search in the triangulated area. Twenty-four hours after the first alert, a front moved across Florida and drove the winds in hard from the north. Lenny told me that was the worst possible wind in the Gulf Stream, but I had no idea why.

Forty-six hours after the first alert, and sunset on the second day, the Coast Guard pulled its boats and birds in. There was no signal, and nothing to see in the dark. The next day a cutter headed out into the rough seas, and a fixed-wing search plane swept the sky, and at sunset on the third day a Coast Guard officer called Drew to say they were suspending the active search and informing the next of kin.

The next morning we left Ron to pack up his files in the office. He had the most files of all of us, since he did the most corporate work, and companies liked paperwork more than divorce or missing persons cases, who generally wanted a yes or no. He was quiet when we left, seemingly resigned to the bad news. Lenny decided we needed some time at the range, but more than that I think he wanted to give Ron some space. I was okay with that plan, because I was at a loss to know what to do for Ron. I couldn't feel his pain. Sure I'd seen approximations of it, times when I'd come face to face with my own mortality. The death of my mother, and to a lesser extent my father. I'd seen guys get injuries on the ballpark that I just knew, right there, would be the end of their careers. And all that the players knew to do was slap them on the back, tell them *chin up, you'll be all right*, and then leave them to work through the demons of opportunities lost, all by themselves. They were hollow words and hollow feelings, and if I couldn't do more than that for Ron, I didn't really want to do anything at all.

Lenny drove down to west of Hollywood, which was a bit of a hike from West Palm, but closer to Miami, where his buddy Lucas lived. The range looked like a set from a zombie apocalypse movie. We drove in through a rusted gate to a steel-sided structure that appeared to have been abandoned years ago. I saw Lucas's Tacoma pickup in the lot. The steel-sided building housed an office where a man in a white-fronted trucker's cap that had the remnants of a peeled-off logo on it stood behind a wooden desk, chewing gum. His T-shirt proclaimed in loud letters, *over my dead body*, which seemed overly ominous for a rifle range. We checked in, and the guy gave us our lanes and handed me safety glasses and bright orange earmuffs, and then he collected my handgun from the gun safe. Lucas was laid back on a bench, watching a couple of women firing pistols at targets of very ugly-looking men. He smiled as we approached. He had dusty, sand-colored hair and a deep tan that made his teeth glow when he smiled. We shook hands and his skin felt like hide. He wore yellow anti-glare goggles and subtle camo earmuffs.

"All right?" he asked loudly in his broad Australian accent.

Lenny and I both nodded, and we headed for our lanes. Lucas took a spot where he could lay down on one of the longer ranges, which were still way too short to test him. I'd seen him hit a can at eight hundred yards in the Everglades, and I got the impression that wasn't just a good day out. Lenny had served in the US military, and Lucas in the Australian Defense Force, both in capacities that they chose not to talk about much. Their paths had crossed somewhere in the Middle East years before, or as Lucas had called it, a red-hot dung heap of a place. It was my impression, gathered from piecing together fragments of conversations and filling in the gaps, that Lenny had also done some work for the National Security Agency. I liked Lucas. He was laid back, like I imagined all Australians to be, and despite his past, like Lenny he seemed to be at ease with the world. Despite that I couldn't say I really knew him. There were depths there that hid dark monsters.

Both men could pop a coconut off a tree with a rifle from a distance that most of the rest of us would struggle to see the tree. Lucas made his practice interesting by trying to make only one hole in his target, regardless of how many rounds he shot. I, on the other hand, just tried not to shoot myself in the foot. I hadn't grown up with guns, and preferred that they stay in the hands of the Army and the cops, and off the streets. But Lenny said in our line of work you could hope for that, but you could never be sure, so better to be prepared. Lenny also drilled into me the idea that if I was to handle a gun, I'd better be darn good at using it, so our visits to the range had been semiregular since my retirement from baseball.

I placed my empty pistol, a 9mm Ruger, on the table and opened a fresh box of ammunition. I unclipped the magazine and pulled the slide back to confirm the chamber was clear, loaded seven rounds into the mag, and then I looked at Lenny, who gave me a nod. I picked up the Ruger in my right hand and slid the magazine home into the gun, then used my left hand to draw the slide and allowed it to snap into firing position. A loaded gun is surprisingly heavy, although some of the heft comes from the weight of knowing that I am holding something that is designed to kill. I pointed the gun down the range, spread my feet slightly and then lifted the weapon to the target. I looked down the barrel at the round target at the other end of the range. I never chose a target printed to look like a person. I understood the logic for law enforcement or military. If you were ever going to have to shoot at another human being, you wanted to have plenty of practice behind you aiming at something approximating your target. I hadn't reached a point where I was that comfortable with either the weapon or the idea of pointing it at a person, and I couldn't see that day coming, so I went for the old-fashioned archery-style target.

I pulled back on the trigger, felt the resistance and then pulled a little more. Even through earmuffs, the sound of close gunfire was loud. The gun recoiled some, and I quickly took aim again and pulled off another six shots, until the chamber and magazine were empty. I realized I had been holding my air, so I let out a long slow breath, and then took another, in through the mouth, out through the nose. I released the magazine, placed it on the table and then pulled the slide back to reveal an empty chamber. As I put the empty pistol on the table before me, I felt Lenny lean across my shoulder and hit the button to return the target. It flapped as it was pulled toward us, and then with a thunk Lenny released the button and the target hung before us. There were seven holes. One was on the edge of the circles numbered nine and eight. The other six sat neatly within the red center circle. It wasn't a long range, but I turned to Lenny like a Little League kid who had just hit a humdinger beyond the diamond. He nodded and smiled, and gave me a wink. Then he stepped away and took his own stall, and we all practiced until our boxes of rounds were done.

Later we sat in a small Cuban *taberna* and shared a few beers. Neither Lenny nor Lucas lauded their ability with guns over me, and once they had both congratulated me on my good effort, they didn't usually mention it again. It occurred to me that to these men, guns weren't a lifestyle choice—something to enjoy—but rather tools of the trade, and they didn't feel the need to discuss it, like a dentist wouldn't captivate a dinner party with his latest toothbrushes. But as we sat around in a cinderblock bar, the smell of *carnitas* wafting out onto the street, Lenny frowned at me.

"You need another gun. It's time."

I returned his frown. "Another gun? I would have thought one was deadly and two was superfluous?"

"Different jobs require different tools. The one you have is your main tool. It's permitted and all above board."

"Of course," I said, moving to sip my beer but not.

"There may come a time when you need another. A job that might require, how can I say it? For you to go outside the lines."

This was not news to me. I'd known Lenny since I had met him in Miami while at college, and he had gotten me out of and into a few scrapes since then. I knew that he had a strong sense of right and wrong, and sometimes his sense of the world didn't quite match up with that written down by the legislature in the state capital. Sometimes he went, as he called it, outside the lines. And I was generally comfortable with that. But I didn't see where he was going now, so I deepened my frown, which must have given him an eyeful of furrowed brow.

Lenny sipped his beer and then put it down on a beer mat. "I'm talking about something off the record."

"You mean an illegal gun?"

"Untraceable," Lucas added, not really helping me all that much.

"Why?"

"Just in case. You never know when it might be important that something not be linked back to you," said Lenny.

"Do you have one?"

Lenny glanced at Lucas, and Lucas smiled and took a long drink of his beer.

"What would I use it for?"

Lenny leaned into me. "Insurance. The plan would be that you never use it. But you know what the Boy Scouts say."

"I don't think they mean have an illegal cache of weapons when they say *be prepared . . .*"

"Sure they do."

I leaned back and sipped my beer, and looked at the two men. I trusted Lenny with my life, and Lenny trusted Lucas with his. So I didn't take what they were saying lightly, even though I didn't understand.

"I wouldn't even know where to get one."

Lenny sipped his beer and raised an eyebrow. "What about your friend, Sally."

"Sally runs a pawn shop."

Lucas smiled again. "And the queen lives in a house."

"You think? Sally?"

Lenny shrugged. "If I'm wrong, you let me know and we'll sort something out."

We spent the next hour chatting about the weather and baseball and nothing at all. There was no mention of guns or Ron or sailing boats, or men lost at sea. But I was thinking about all those things. Of how the things we took for granted could be swept away from us in the blink of an eye. By a gun, or by a slight change in the wind. And I resolved to visit my friend Sally Mondavi, and catch a baseball game and eat a hot dog and drink a warm beer, and chat about batting averages and ERAs and unconventional forms of insurance.

I shook hands with Lucas and he gave Lenny a hug that reminded me of brown bears, and Lucas took off back to the marina in Miami that he managed. Lenny and I turned north and headed back to West Palm. The office was deserted when we got there. Lizzy's stuff was all neatly packed and ready to go. Lenny's was all over his desk and in piles beside. He looked at it, and around the empty space until his eyes hit mine, and he smiled.

"Longboards," we both said at the same time.

# CHAPTER FOUR

**Longboard Kelly's was** the kind of place tourists happened upon only if they were horribly lost. It didn't appear in any online review sites of the best dive bars, or haunts with local flavor, and if it had we would have all gone online and left a string of one-star reviews to keep the flocks at bay. And we would have done that with the blessing of the owner. Mick was a barrel-chested man who spoke as few words as possible to get his message across, and used facial expressions when he deemed words unnecessary. He didn't care for strangers, and it took me a good couple years before he offered me a nod as I walked in through the rear courtyard. Lenny and I got such a nod as we wandered in, the warm evening offering a hint at the summer that was brewing, the cloud front of the day giving way to a clear blue sky, lighting the courtyard tables with golden hues from a falling sun. The beer-labeled umbrellas had been opened on the tables in the courtyard and a light breeze wafted in, making them slow dance like lonely kids at the prom.

We headed for the outdoor bar that sat under a palapa shade to the side of the courtyard. Ron was waiting, beer in hand, chatting with Muriel behind the bar. Muriel wore her trademark tank top, hands on hips, ample breasts bursting at the seams. She wore a sly grin, as she often did, and I was happy to see that she had brought Ron's smile out of him. She saw us wander in and bounced her hips off the bar that opened to the inside of the place, to the dark interior bar that we never bothered with, and she was already pouring two beers before we got under the shade of the palapa.

"Gentlemen," said Ron, holding his beer aloft.

"Mr. Bennett," said Lenny. "How goes it?"

"All good. My files are packed and ready to go. You? Still a straight shooter?"

"Whenever possible."

Muriel passed us our drinks, and we said cheers and I put my arm around Ron's shoulder and drank silently to the color that had returned to his face.

I sat down on a wobbly stool that had been in vogue when Armstrong did his tap dance on the moon. "How ya doing?" I asked him.

"Good, better."

"New office digs, soon you'll get a new place to live. You just need to get a new case and you'll be set."

He held his beer up. "To new beginnings."

I smiled and took a drink. I was looking down my glass at Ron and I saw the smile in his eyes dissolve before me. I frowned and dropped the glass from my mouth. Ron was looking past me, across the courtyard, where the entrance was from the parking lot.

I turned on my stool, and almost fell off. The fragile nature of the stool was partly to blame, but I was also taken aback by the sight of the attractive sheriff's deputy from the day Ron and crew had returned. She was in full uniform, still making forest green look like a fashion choice. The gun on her hip bounced ever so slightly as she strode across the courtyard. Another deputy, a far less attractive guy with a buzz cut and hard face, marched one pace behind her. It didn't seem very chivalrous to walk behind her, but she didn't seem to need the help. The investigator from the day at the dock brought up the rear in a blue suit that looked like it was the latter half of a buy one, get one free. The deputies came straight to us. The woman held my eye, but didn't smile. She stopped before Ron, Lenny and me.

"Deputy," said Lenny.

"Mr. Cox," she said, all business.

"Can I offer you a cool beverage?"

"No, thank you. This isn't a social call, I'm afraid." She turned her gaze on Ron. "Mr. Bennett, I have to ask you to accompany us to the sheriff's office."

"Why?" asked Lenny. The investigator stepped forward.

"We have some questions," he said.

I looked at him. "Why not ask them here?"

I glanced at the female deputy and noted she was shaking her head, ever so slow, like my mother used to do when I was just about to do something stupid.

"It would be better to not be here," said the investigator.

"Is he under arrest for something?" asked Lenny.

"No, sir," said the investigator. "Not at this point in time."

It was the last part, the throwaway line, that gave us all pause. But if there was one thing Lenny had taught me in my short career, it was that messing with the law might sometimes be necessary, but you'd better have a good reason to refuse a direct request to attend questioning. That usually resulted in an arrest, and watching Ron walk out of Longboards in cuffs was not something anyone wanted. Especially Ron. He slipped off his stool and put his unfinished beer on the bar,

"If anything, I'd like to know what the heck is going on," said Ron.

I watched the female deputy nod and offer Ron a little smile. The deputy stood aside and Ron walked away. The two deputies dropped in behind him, one standing just off each of Ron's elbows.

"Where you taking him?" asked Lenny.

The investigator handed Lenny a card. "Gun Club Road."

"How long?"

"Come down in a couple hours. We'll see then."

"Is this trouble?" I asked.

"That depends on the SA." He tipped his head like he was wearing a hat, which he wasn't, then turned and walked out of the courtyard. I looked at Lenny and he held the guy's card up for me to see. It read: *Gene Moscow, Investigator, Palm Beach Sheriff's Office.*

"What on earth could they want?"

Lenny slipped the card into his red palm tree print shirt. "They think Ron pushed his skipper overboard."

# CHAPTER FIVE

**We didn't wait** a couple hours. We got straight in Lenny's truck and headed down around the airport to Gun Club Road. The criminal justice complex housed the headquarters of the Palm Beach Sheriff's Office, as well as outposts of various other law enforcement bodies, and it was the main detention center for the county. I had spent a bit of time there, fortunately as a visitor, but Lenny knew the place like the back of his hand. He drove in and parked at the back of the lot, and we walked across the large space and headed inside. Lenny asked about Ron and the civilian at the desk checked through his papers, and then told us that he was in an interview, and it could be a while.

Lenny nodded. "Tell Moscow that we're here anyway, will ya, Hank?"

"Sure thing, Lenny. Still might be a while."

Lenny winked. "We'll grab some coffee."

"Go to Dunkin'. I wouldn't feed the coffee we got here to my dead cat."

We went to Dunkin' Donuts. There's one for every ten snowbirds in South Florida. I got a juice that could have used a hit of vodka, and Lenny grabbed a coffee and a donut. We wandered back to the waiting area, and Lenny was just finishing the last of his coffee when the door to the offices buzzed loudly and Gene Moscow appeared. He had loosened his tie, but he still looked uncomfortable.

"That was quick," I said.

Moscow put his hands on his hips. "You guys know a lawyer?"

"Why?" asked Lenny.

"Your buddy needs one."

"You're arresting him?"

"A formal charge has not yet been laid, but Ron is refusing to answer any more questions without an attorney present."

"There must be dozens in this building," I said.

"We offered him a public defender to sit in. He declined and said to talk to you."

Lenny ran his hands through his thick hair. "Why won't he talk?"

"I can't speculate on what's going on in his mind, Lenny."

"Quit that, Moscow. You know what I mean. He was talking, right? To begin with. All helpful like. And then you drop something on him that makes him think twice about where this is all going, and he clams up. What was it?"

Moscow shuffled his feet and inspected the shine on his shoes. "I can't get into that with you—you know that, Lenny. But I'll tell you this much. There is a suspicion of foul play with the Will Colfax disappearance."

"Of course there is," said Lenny. "You've got to rule that out. But why Ron? That's crazy."

"It might be crazy, but we got motive."

"What motive?" I asked. I couldn't believe what I was hearing.

Moscow just shook his head. He wasn't sharing. "If he doesn't want a public attorney, then we have to hold him over until tomorrow morning. You think you can find him a lawyer by then?"

"Sure. He's not going in the main pen is he?"

"He'll be in minimum custody for pretrial, unsentenced males. He'll be all right."

I wasn't sure how spending the night in prison was all right, but I guess it was all perspective. Compared to being in maximum security with an ax murderer called Big Bubba, it was probably a dream.

"Can we see him?" I asked.

"Not tonight."

"Then we're done," said Lenny. "We'll sort something out and be in touch." We shook hands with Moscow and turned to leave. I had a last thought.

"Moscow, who's the state attorney on it?"

Moscow's face was granite. "Edwards. Eric Edwards. You know him?"

"The tall guy? Dresses like an Italian mobster?"

Moscow said nothing in reply, but his raised eyebrows and firm set mouth told me that the SA wasn't Mr. Popular with the PBSO. I nodded and we headed outside into the last of the twilight. Palm trees swayed in silhouette, and one could be forgiven for thinking all was right with the world.

"You got a lawyer in mind?" I asked Lenny as he started the truck.

"Yeah. Let's just hope he's around."

Lenny pulled out onto Gun Club Road and headed back around Palm Beach International. As he joined the traffic on Route 1, I looked toward the water I couldn't see. With the window down I could smell the salt air. A little burr had lodged itself in my brain, and it was scratching at my mind. I turned to Lenny, who was leaning one arm on the windowsill and using the other to steer with one finger.

"There's something I don't get," I said. "If we are talking a murder investigation, and that seems to be what we are talking, then I always thought that momentum was everything. Aren't most cases solved in the first forty-eight hours?"

"That's more about kidnapping, when someone's life is on the line. A dead guy is a dead guy. He'll wait," said Lenny. "But yeah, often useful intel is gathered pretty quick."

"So I'm wondering why the PBSO is so calm about waiting to interview Ron tomorrow. Surely that kills their momentum? And Ron doesn't get to delay the investigation because he can't choose an attorney. Either they interrupt his lawyer's dinner and get him out there, or they provide someone already in the building. So what gives?"

Lenny grinned. "Not bad, *Kimosabe*. Why do you think they're okay with that?"

I looked back out the window as I pondered that. Why would the state attorney want to delay an investigation? Unless he wasn't delaying it at all. I spun in my seat back to Lenny.

"They don't have enough to lay a charge. They brought Ron in to try and shake him, and he didn't shake. So now they are trying to get more on him. I bet they're investigating the hell out of it, but they want Ron on ice, so they can back up what they know, and formally charge him tomorrow."

Lenny nodded. "Like I said, not bad."

"So what do we do?"

"Get him a lawyer."


Lenny parked the truck under the gaze of the massive Palm Beach County courthouse. We walked away from the huge arch of the court, down First Street, to a newer office building that housed a bank, some companies whose owners had cleverly given them names that give no clue as to what they do and are utterly unpronounceable, and the law firm of Croswitz and Allen. I ran my finger along an empty space on the list of tenants, and Lenny smiled. He took out a key and opened the front door and we left the elevator alone and took the stairs. We stopped by the law offices and were pleased to see a light on. Lawyers, more than most folks, do love to brag on the long hours they work, as if this were the reason our species existed. Lenny tapped the glass and opened the door, and we wandered into a small front office. The computer on the reception desk was turned off, so Lenny called out.

"Anyone home?"

There was some rustling from behind the inner door, and a thin balding man with an even tan and a winning smile poked his head out. Allen was the rainmaker of the firm, although it was a generous use of the word. The firm consisted of just the two partners and their secretary, and Allen got most of their business on the golf courses around Palm Beach. Hence the tan.

"Lenny Cox," he smiled. "And young Miami. You boys moved in yet?"

"Not yet. Just finishing some internal walls and a lick of paint. Few days."

"The rental agreement is all done, right?"

"Yeah, it's all sweet. Thanks for looking that over for us."

"Happy to have you join our little family here in the building. What brings you here now?"

"Ron's in jail."

Allen lost the smile. "Do tell."

Lenny gave him the back-of-a-baseball-card synopsis, and Allen listened intently. When Lenny was done, Allen nodded to himself several times.

"You want me to sit in on the interview."

"If you wouldn't mind."

"Let's make a call."

Allen led us into his office. It was what you expected a legal office to look like. Lots of thick leather-bound legal tomes, a polished hardwood desk that was neat and dusted. The chairs were old but well cared for. Allen and his partner, Croswitz, were like the odd couple, and Allen was the fastidious one. He picked up the phone and hit a button and waited for the call to connect, and then he told the other end who he was and who he needed to speak with. He waited again and I looked at some of the photos on the walls. Most of them were of Allen with people unknown to me, and almost all of them were either on golf courses or in bars I assumed to be on golf courses since everyone wore polos, chinos and hat hair. Allen announced himself again, and said he would be representing Ron Bennett. He gave a couple of ahas, and then told the other end *until then*, and he hung up. He clearly didn't bill his clients by the word.

"That was Detective Moscow. He says we will resume the interview at 8 a.m. tomorrow. I shall be there."

"Thanks," said Lenny. "We appreciate it."

"I have a tee time at eleven, so hopefully it doesn't run too long." He smiled and walked us out. "I shall call you once we're done."

"Will you see Ron before?" I asked.

"Of course."

"Tell him . . ." Suddenly I couldn't think what I wanted to tell him. It will all be okay? We'll get to the bottom of it? Hell, we didn't even know what was going on. Allen put his hand on my shoulder.

"I'll tell him. Don't worry."

But I did worry. I worried about what I didn't know, and I worried about it all the way back to Longboard Kelly's.

# CHAPTER SIX

**The umbrellas at** Longboards were all folded up like flowers that had closed their blooms with the setting of the sun, but the party lights were on and cast a joyful rainbow of colors across the tables. The courtyard was about half full, and the vibe sounded light and easy and didn't suit my mood at all. There were two guys sitting in our spots at the bar, dressed in fishing shirts with more pockets than a pool table. Muriel saw us and gave a shrug, and nodded to a table. Lenny gave her a face like a sucked lemon but sat, and Muriel brought two beers out to us.

"Sorry, wasn't sure you'd be back," she said.

"Where else would we go?" said Lenny, matter-of-factly and without expectation of a response.

"Who are the fancy shirts?" I asked as I picked up my beer.

"Keyboard punchers from Michigan. They saw the party lights from the road."

"Mick needs a bigger fence," said Lenny, smiling as he sipped his beer.

"How's Ron?"

"They're keeping him overnight," I said.

"In jail?" she whispered.

I nodded. "They're going to interview him in the morning."

"Can they do that? Put him in jail like that?"

I nodded again. "They can."

"Has he been arrested?" she asked.

"No, but he asked for a lawyer and that won't happen until tomorrow. And the sheriff is within rights to keep him for a reasonable amount of time without a formal charge, so given it's Ron's lawyer who is the delay, an overnight stay becomes reasonable."

"Can't you get his lawyer out there tonight?" Muriel frowned with concern. It wasn't a great look on her. But it was a fair question and I turned to Lenny.

Lenny shrugged. "Ron didn't ask for a lawyer. He asked us to find him one. That means he didn't expect to get out, regardless."

"Why?" I asked. "What does he know that we don't?"

Lenny shrugged again.

"Poor Ron." Muriel glanced away and then did a double take. "Is that who I think it is?"

I looked at Lenny, who had broken out in a devious smile. "I believe it is," he said.

I turned in my seat, back toward the parking lot, and saw the female deputy who had taken Ron away, sauntering back into the courtyard. Only this time I was fairly confident she wasn't planning on arresting anyone. She had changed out of her uniform, and was making a white T-shirt and denim jeans look like the crown jewels. She had already seen us and it was clear where she was headed, so we waited for her to arrive. When she did, she gave me a smile that made my belly flip around like I hadn't eaten for a week.

"Hi," was all she said to me, but it was enough.

"Hi," I returned, with much less assurance.

She looked at Lenny and said, "Hello, Lenny."

"Deputy," he replied, the cheeky grin not moving from his face. "What can we do for you?"

"I heard you'd probably be here, and I just wanted to stop by and say I'm sorry about Ron." She looked at me again and the smile had gone.

"We all are," said Lenny. "Would you like a seat—we seem to have some spare."

"Thanks," she said, taking a seat between Lenny and me.

"Would you like a drink?" asked Muriel, coolly.

"Thanks. Vodka tonic would be great."

Muriel left to procure the drink and I watched her go, for reasons I didn't understand but had something to do with not wanting to face the deputy until I had something clever to say. And if something clever eluded me, then anything at all would suffice. I lingered a little too long on watching Muriel round the bar and start pouring vodka, and my mind was a blank, so I gave up and turned back and took the chicken's way out and looked at Lenny.

"I'm sorry—I don't think we were properly introduced," she said, making me turn to her. She had her hand out, long fingers and neat nails. "Danielle Castle."

I took her hand and shook it. Her skin was softer than I expected a deputy's skin to be, but then I hadn't really done a scientific study on it. She gave me another smile, this one from only half her mouth, but the effect was inversely proportionate. We shook hands for longer than was necessary, and then she let my hand go and I returned the favor. She lifted an eyebrow by way of inquiry, but as I didn't understand the nature of the inquiry I remained mute.

"And you are?" she asked.

I realized that I was as quiet as a church mouse, but with a Laurel and Hardy kind of face. "Oh, sorry. I'm Miami. Miami Jones."

She gave me the full-watt smile again and it made me grin like an idiot.

"Pleased to meet you, Miami Jones."

Muriel saved me from myself by delivering the vodka and tonic.

"So what's the deal with Ron?" said Lenny.

Danielle took a sip of her drink and then returned it to a coaster. "Let me start by saying in an unofficial capacity, I don't think Ron did anything. I've met Ron. There's not a mean bone in his body."

"So why is he in jail?" I appeared to have found my voice. She looked at me with concern.

"I can't say too much because it is an open investigation, but we had to notify next of kin, and in the process of doing that it became apparent that there might be a motive for the missing man's disappearance."

"Will Colfax," I said.

"That's right."

"A motive for what? Ron to push him overboard?"

"Yes. That or worse," she said, taking another sip.

Lenny leaned back in his chair. "And can we ask what this motive is?"

"Like I said, it's not my place to say too much, I just wanted you to know."

"To know that you don't think he did it," I said. "We got that. But he's still in jail."

"And I'm sorry about that. But the motive has to be investigated."

I didn't say anything more. I just frowned, which gave Deputy Castle a front row seat to the furrows in my brow that were deep enough to sow potatoes. When you spend every possible opportunity from age seven to present outside, playing football, or later baseball, and later still enjoying the sun in Florida, you end up with a tan and wrinkles. My uncontrolled blond hair might have gotten darker as I got older had I taken an office job in Stamford or New York City, but I didn't, so the sun had kept it as fair as it was as a toddler. Deputy Castle didn't look at my hair, though, keeping her gaze on my eyes. I'm not sure what she saw there, but it made her speak.

"Look, you'll find this out tomorrow when Ron is interviewed, but you didn't hear it from me. We discovered that Ron's wife was having an affair."

"Ron's wife?"

"Yes."

"An affair?"

"Yes."

"With whom?"

"With Will Colfax."

I glanced at Lenny but he was hiding behind his beer. I looked back at the deputy.

"There's one little problem," I said.

"What's that?"

"Ron isn't married."

Deputy Castle hid her surprise well. I wasn't sure if that was something that law enforcement types trained for, or if law enforcement just attracted the kinds of people who naturally hid themselves well. But her face gave nothing away. It was her eyes that sold her out. Her pupils shrunk and her eyes moistened, and I saw the uncertainty in them.

"We do have a source that claims to be his wife, and another source that corroborates that fact."

"Who's the source, the one that claims to be his wife?"

Deputy Castle hesitated, but again I guess she figured we'd find out in the morning, and we had no way to notify Ron while he was in the pen.

"You can't go harassing witnesses in an investigation, okay?"

"The thought never occurred," I said. I thought about adding a grin, but something felt wrong about it, so I didn't.

"Her name is Amanda Bennett."

I leaned back in my chair, picked up my beer and took a long pull on it, all while keeping my eyes on the deputy.

"You know her," said Deputy Castle.

I nodded slowly, and glanced at Lenny.

"She's not Ron's wife," said Lenny. "Divorce papers were served about four months ago."

Danielle took this in, and frowned. "Not sure that makes it better. If it can be shown that the divorce was a result of the affair."

"It wasn't," said Lenny.

"Are you sure, Lenny?"

"Totally. Ron and Mandy didn't work because . . . well, let's just say Mandy hitched her wagon to the wrong train."

We finished our drinks and Lenny made to get another round, but Deputy Castle stood.

"I need to get home. Thanks for the drink."

Lenny nodded and turned away to the bar. The deputy looked down at me.

"You driving?" she asked.

"No, ma'am. My bike's in the shop. I'll get a ride."

"All right then. I'll be seeing you."

"Thanks for letting us know. About Ron I mean."

She didn't answer. She just shot me another smile and strode away. I didn't watch her go. My back was to the exit, and the picture I had in my mind was more than good enough. I must have been smiling when Lenny returned, because he was standing at the table, watching me.

"What?" I frowned as he passed me a beer.

"That was different," he said, sitting.

"What?"

"Getting a visit from a deputy."

"Why was that different?"

Lenny took a long drink. "In all my years I've never had a deputy stop by after hours to update me on a case."

"This isn't a case—this is a friend."

"Never had a visit to update on anything, friend or otherwise."

"Never?"

"Not once."

"Huh. What do you make of that then?"

Lenny gave me a sheepish smile and a deep shrug, then leaned back in his chair and put his beer glass to his mouth.

# CHAPTER SEVEN

**Mandy Bennett had** taken up residence in a three-thousand-square-foot, four-bedroom home in a gated community on the edge of Lake Mangonia, across from the President Country Club. Although Deputy Castle had suggested we not harass their witness, we felt an early morning visit to the ex-wife of our good friend was well in order. Lenny pulled his truck into the paved driveway next to an Audi convertible. Divorce was clearly hard work for Mandy. We walked down a palm-lined path to a set of double doors that look like they had been pilfered from a Scottish castle. There was a huge iron knocker in the middle of each door, and I was reaching for one when Lenny hit the little plastic button to the side and the doorbell chimed *take me out to the ballgame*. I felt embarrassed for the door.

We waited for a good long moment before one of the doors opened with a sucking sound like on a refrigerator and Mandy Bennett stood before us. She had tied-back blond hair, thin in the legs and arms but not the chest. She was a good ten years younger than Ron, but she worked hard and passed for fifteen years less and dressed like she was twenty years his junior. She was in some kind of yoga gear, gray tights and a pink shirt, and I wasn't sure if she was mid-workout or if she just hung out like that.

"Lenny, Miami, what a surprise."

"Hi, Mandy," I said. It wasn't that much of a surprise given we were checked in by the guard at the gate of the community.

"How's Ron? I heard one of his crew was missing. Did they find him?"

"That's why we're here," said Lenny. "Can we come in?"

"I was just headed out, but sure."

We followed her into a large great room with high ceilings and a stellar view across the lake. All the furniture looked new and the art on the walls looked mass-produced.

"A rental, Mandy?" I asked.

"Yes, Miami. I'm still finding my feet."

I should be so lucky, I thought.

"Can I offer you boys a drink?"

She didn't mean apple juice and I saw Lenny giving it some thought.

"No, thanks, Mandy. It's a bit early," I said, replying for both of us. We sat on flat leather sofas that looked like upholstered coffee tables and were just as comfortable.

"So, you were going to tell me about Ron," said Mandy.

I nodded. "Yes. I'm not sure how to put this. He's in jail."

"What!" Mandy's mouth dropped open in a most unbecoming way, and I noted that her eyes moistened up, but no tears came. "H-how?" she stammered. "Why?"

"We're not completely sure, and we hoped you might be able to shed some light on it."

"Me?"

"The sheriff told us that they had a motive for the disappearance for the guy lost at sea. And they said that motive was you."

Again Mandy looked shocked, such that lines appeared on her smooth forehead for but a second, then the years of moisturizer and spa treatments kicked in and it all smoothed over, in a way that made me oddly envious. She took a breath that raised her chest but didn't seem sufficient, yet it appeared to help her gather herself.

"I don't understand."

"Some sheriff's detectives came and spoke to you yesterday."

Mandy looked hard at the glass coffee table between us, as if thinking, maybe recounting events the previous day. "I still don't see how that puts Ron in jail."

"You were in a relationship with the man that went missing, Will Colfax," I said.

Mandy did the little breath thing again, and then spoke to the coffee table. "Yes. But . . ." A sheen of moisture covered Mandy's eyes as she showed as much emotion as she ever really did. I just wasn't sure whether the emotion was for Ron or Will Colfax.

"The sheriff believes that your relationship gives Ron a motive to kill Will Colfax."

"That's crazy—Ron wouldn't hurt a fly."

Everyone agreed on that point, except the people keeping Ron in prison. Lenny leaned forward and rested his arms on his knees. "Mandy, did you tell the sheriff's investigators you were Ron's wife?"

"I don't know if I did or I didn't."

Lenny cocked his head. "Mandy, did you tell them you were Ron's wife?"

Mandy lifted her gaze to Lenny and jutted her chin defiantly. "So what if I did, Lenny. I was married to the man. So what if I don't want to appear like soiled goods."

"You're certainly not soiled goods," I said. I was referring to her situation, nice house, nice car, not short of a dollar and not working as far as I had heard, but she seemed to take it as a comment on her physical appearance because she gave me a cutesy smile and the pretense of a blush.

"Mandy," said Lenny, drawing her attention back to him. "Were you involved with this man before your divorce?"

"What kind of a question is that, Lenny?"

"It's the question the detectives are asking Ron as we speak. If you were having an affair prior to your divorce, then they will argue that the affair wasn't a by-product of the divorce but rather the reason for it. And that's a big motive."

"No, Lenny. I was not having an affair when I was with Ron. I never did the wrong thing by Ron."

I was going to make a comment about that, but decided to hold my powder. Mandy had met Ron at the yacht club, and as many women did, had fallen for his gentlemanly charms. I didn't get it myself. Ron was a good-looking fellow in a sunburned, windblown kind of way. He had a few skin cancers removed here and there, which seemed to add to his allure, and women of all ages were drawn to him. Mandy, however, made a fateful miscalculation in her estimation of Ron's net worth. Ron did quite well for himself, working in banking and insurance, eventually ending up in fraud detection, where he pored over company accounts and sniffed out financial shenanigans. He had an apartment on the island, not waterfront but on the island nevertheless, and drove a very nice C-class Mercedes. He was a member of the Palm Beach Yacht Club and the Palm Beach Country Club, and was known by name at the bastion of all that was monied and good in Palm Beach, The Breakers Hotel. Mandy saw a fish worth catching, and Ron was happy and willing to take the bait. What Mandy failed to realize was that it was by and large a charade. Ron's memberships were paid for by his insurance firm, not only to provide the pretense of a mover and shaker, but also because much of the fraud they discovered was committed by rich folks hitting hard times and was uncovered not by forensic analysis of balance sheets but rather by loose tongues at the bar. When Ron fell victim to the stress of being the mole in the bunker and retired, the company-supplied memberships and cars went with it. It was at this point that Mandy was left with the reality of living in a small apartment with limited income, a used Camry for transport and no access to the ritzy clubs to which she was looking forward to growing accustomed. The divorce was more like a dissolution of a failing business, and there were no public spats or harsh words. Ron sent his bride on her way with a good chunk of his limited funds, selling his apartment and moving onto the mainland. And Mandy, it seemed, set off in pursuit of a better standard of husband.

"Mandy," I said. "How did the sheriff know about your aff —, your relationship with Colfax?"

"I don't know. Probably that witch of a wife."

"He was married?"

She pursed her lips at me. "Don't judge me, Miami."

"No judgment, Mandy. I just didn't know."

"Yes, well, he was. But it was a sham. He wanted to be with me."

"Indeed," I said.

Lenny stood and brushed out his chinos. I followed suit, not bothering to brush out my cargo shorts. Mandy showed us to the door and thanked us for visiting.

"If the sheriff asks again, please tell them that the divorce was amicable and you weren't in a relationship at the time," Lenny said.

"I will, Lenny. Please tell Ron I'm thinking of him."

"Will do."

We left Mandy and got back in Lenny's truck. Lenny pulled out and away, and then spoke.

"Thoughts?" he asked. He had a habit of asking me questions to get my deductive juices flowing.

"She does care about Ron, say what you will."

"I always thought so."

"Can't say the same about Colfax."

"How so?" Lenny asked as we crossed the channel between Lake Mangonia and Clear Lake.

"She looked pretty shaken by the news about Ron being in jail, and granted she had a night to process it, but she didn't seem so moved about Colfax."

"No, she didn't. What do you make of that?"

"She's cold. I knew the way she discarded Ron there was a touch of ruthlessness there, but I always thought she was a nice person, underneath. But the Coast Guard has only just given up the search, and she's moved on. Did you note the way she referred to him in the past tense."

"You did as well."

"I wasn't smooching the guy."

"True. So?"

"So if she's telling it like it is, then she was done with Ron before hooking up with Colfax and that hurts the motive."

"As long as she's telling the truth," he said, turning onto Route 1.

"Exactly. If needs be we could talk to the wife, Mrs. Colfax."

"If needs be," said Lenny. "First let's find out what's happening to Ron."

# CHAPTER EIGHT

**Lenny parked in** the open lot next to our new building and we went up the stairs to the new office. The contractor was there, putting the finishing touches to the place. They had put up an internal wall to create a small second inner office, giving Ron and me somewhere to hang our hats. Fact was we didn't spend a lot of time behind desks, and most of our debriefs happened at Longboard Kelly's, but the extra office was Lenny's nod to the fact that his firm was now much more than just him. We left the contractor to his business and headed further up the stairs to see Allen.

Lenny knocked on the door and we stepped in to find a young woman dressed in a knee-length skirt and long-sleeved blouse watering a potted banana palm. The little tree didn't look happy about being indoors, but the woman gave us a warm smile.

"Mr. Cox," she said, walking to her desk, picking up her phone and letting Allen know we were there. She didn't put the phone down before telling us to go in.

"Gents," said Allen as we opened the door. "Come in, take a seat."

"How'd it go?" asked Lenny as he dropped into a chair in front of Allen's polished desk.

"In short Lenny, it's a play. They don't have a lot, and they're fishing."

"So you're saying there's nothing to worry about?"

"I'm not saying that. Sometimes when you go fishing, you catch a fish. Here's where it stands. The skipper of the yacht, a Mr. Colfax, went overboard about one-third of the way between Bimini and Fort Lauderdale. The weather was fine and the ocean was flat. This is all according to the sheriff, of course. We would dispute this with data from the National Oceanic and Atmospheric Administration."

"What if the data says the ocean was smooth?" I asked.

"One man's ripple is another man's wave. Anyway, their point is that it is unlikely Mr. Colfax just fell off the boat. So they claim that Ron's wife was having an affair with Mr. Colfax, and that Ron took the opportunity to dispose of Mr. Colfax by pushing him into the Atlantic Ocean. Now Ron at this stage has only answered questions directly related to events on board. He says he was asleep at the time of the incident because he was not on watch. The sheriff has obviously checked the fact about being on watch because they do not contest it. The individuals who were on watch . . ." Allen leaned forward to look at his notes. "Ms. Felicity Havill and Mr. Alec Meechan." He leaned back in his chair. "Both claim to also have been asleep. Why they were asleep, we do not know, as yet. But the sheriff claims that Ms. Havill was the last to see Mr. Colfax alive and well on deck."

Allen took a moment to look at the ceiling and collect his thoughts. It was a long pause, and I looked at Lenny and he at me, wondering if Allen had lost his train of thought. Or maybe this was how he padded out his billable hours. Either way he came back to us and continued.

"Now, in conference just between us, Ron confirms that he is no longer married to the woman in question, a . . ." Allen leaned forward to look at his notes again.

"Mandy," I said.

"Yes, that's right. He also claims no knowledge of the affair at any stage. He claims he and Mr. Colfax were friends. Not particularly close, but friendly around the club."

"Sure, but how does any of this help Ron get out?"

"Well, it doesn't, I'm afraid. At the conclusion of the interview the sheriff placed Ron under formal arrest. They can keep Ron under arrest without arraignment for twenty-four hours, and they can apply for additional time from a judge, and given this is a murder investigation they will probably get it. So that puts us out to tomorrow morning at best. If they get more time, maybe we're looking at another couple of days. At that point, they either play their cards or release him."

"And if they release him, is that the end of it?" I asked.

"I'm afraid not. They can and will investigate further, and at such time as they have enough evidence, they can arrest again at any time."

"What about the body?" asked Lenny. "How can they charge him without a body? Technically the guy could still be floating out there."

"It makes it difficult for them, but far from impossible. Once upon a time a person could not be found guilty of murder without a body. There was a case back in England in the sixteen hundreds, the Campton Wonder case, where three individuals were convicted of murder without a body and duly hanged, and then the murdered fellow promptly reappeared. The law was changed as a result. But with advances in forensic technology and so on, the laws have changed and even of recent times defendants have been found guilty on the basis of forensic and circumstantial evidence. The burden of proof is high though, so the SA and the sheriff will need something quite compelling to prove their case."

"Surely an alleged affair is not enough," I said.

"Quite right, it is not. It provides motive, nothing more. Now opportunity is obvious, the fellow was alone on the deck in the middle of the sea. But they will need more, and they know it, but that is what an investigation is for."

We sat looking at each other for a while. Perhaps the other two were thinking things over, but I was waiting for someone to say something, like suggesting a way forward. It didn't come, so I went looking for it.

"So what should we do?" I asked.

"If the SA wants to keep Ron longer than tomorrow morning. they will have to present a prima facie case to a judge. If that happens, our job will be to muddy the waters, to make it look like the state has no basis for an arrest, let alone a conviction. You gentlemen are investigators. I suggest you investigate what happened out there."

# CHAPTER NINE

**Felicity Havill had** been the last person to see Will Colfax alive, according to the PBSO. And Ron had told us that she worked at the *Post*, meaning the local rag, the *Palm Beach Post*. If she was a reporter, she might have the kind of memory and eye for detail that could help us clear Ron. Lenny called the main switch at the *Post* and was put through to Felicity, where he explained Ron's predicament, and Felicity told him she liked Ron a lot and would do anything to help.

The *Palm Beach Post* came out of a bunker-like building on South Dixie Highway on the east side of I-95 from the airport. The harried air of ink and cigarette smoke was absorbed in its walls, so Felicity suggested we meet at a bar around the corner. The bar was as white as a hospital bathroom, with flat white sofas and white bar stools that looked as comfortable as tractor seats. Despite being close to the *Post's* HQ, there were no reporter types in the place. It really didn't seem to be my idea of a reporter hangout, and I knew I was right when I saw Felicity Havill bounce into the bar. She had looked like a print journalist when I had seen her getting off the yacht that day, but now she looked anything but. She was far too attractive— pretty enough to be on television. She had blond hair that fell across her shoulders like a shampoo commercial, a button nose, soft features and pert breasts that were covered by a pink twin set that gave her a certain Sandra Dee look. What Sandra Dee wouldn't have worn was the tight skirt below it that accentuated shapely legs. It seemed she was playing down her looks, wanting to appear cute rather than sexy. Perhaps a professional trade-off, perhaps just personal preference. She wasn't a Florida native, not by my reckoning, because her fair skin was still fair, and yet to be crisped up by the Florida sun. She was everything Mandy Bennett was still trying to be twenty years later. Despite it all, she wasn't my type. There was something just too darn delicate about her, like you'd spend your whole time making sure she didn't get cracked whenever you went out.

"Felicity Havill," was the first thing she said. She offered her hand and both Lenny and I shook a firm grip that made me reassess how delicate she was before I even sat down. She ordered a white wine, Lenny a margarita on ice and I got a rum and cola. It was a fancy drink kind of place.

"I'm so sorry about Ron," she said. "It's surely a mistake. Ron's one of the good guys."

"We think so," said Lenny. "So, Felicity, what is it you report on at the *Post*?"

"Oh, I'm not a reporter." She smiled like that was the funniest thing she'd heard that day. "I'm senior executive of advertising sales."

That made a whole lot more sense to me than reporter. Reporters usually look hassled and flustered and permanently close to a deadline. They talk fast and listen hard, and there's usually some kind of ballpoint ink on their fingers. Felicity had none of that. I bet she sold a lot of advertising, though.

"How did you come to be on the boat for the race?" I asked, and it occurred to me as I spoke that I didn't even know the name of the vessel.

"I wanted to learn to sail. It's Florida, right? So I went down to the club and took some lessons, did a few twilight series, and one night after a race I met . . ." She stopped for a moment and put her hand to her mouth and gulped back emotion. Our drinks arrived, giving her some time to collect herself.

"Sorry," she said. "I met Will. He invited me to sail on his yacht, and I did a few races, a few day cruises, then this race came up and it sounded like fun."

"Where are you from, originally?" I asked.

"Why not Florida?" She smiled with her eyes as she sipped her wine. It felt like a trick question, one of those testers that women throw out and men drown in like quicksand. I had nothing to lose and no skin in the game, but years of practice made me give her the answer that I had ready.

"You said, *it's Florida, right*. Suggests you are from somewhere else." I kept the flawless skin thing to myself. That felt too much like flirting, and I didn't think that was the right way to go with this one.

"You're good. I grew up in Montana. Billings to be exact. I went to school at University of Georgia."

"A Bulldog."

She nodded. "Fortunately, this far south they let being a Georgia alum slide. Living in Jacksonville would be a nightmare."

I nodded. I went to college in the same state as Jacksonville, and being a Miami Hurricane didn't go down that well there either.

"By the way, what's the name of Will's boat?" I asked, ticking a box.

Felicity gave an eye roll, fished out her purse and pulled out a packet of photographs. She licked her finger, flicked through the prints and selected one, and then slid it across the table to me. It was a photo of what looked like the crew, some standing in the cockpit of the yacht, a couple on the dock. They all looked fresh and happy and ready for adventure, and for a moment images of young men preparing to go off to the First World War came to mind. The name of the yacht was written across the back of the boat.

"*Toxic Assets*?" I frowned and Felicity raised her eyebrows.

"Will's sense of humor, I guess. I took that picture just before we headed out from Palm Beach for the start of the race."

"And this is Will Colfax?" I pointed at a man in a new-looking ball cap, red sailing shirt. He was a little pudgy around the jowls, but wore a smile the camera loved.

Felicity nodded and sat back in her seat. We all sipped our drinks and then Lenny got to the point.

"Can you tell us about that night?"

Felicity dropped her smile and nodded again. "We came across the Bahama Banks during the day. It's shallow and you need to keep an eye out for shoals and reefs. Drew had the helm most of the day. When we got to Cat Cay, that's just south of the Biminis, it was sunset, and the decision was made to head across the Gulf Stream overnight. It's deep water after you drop off the banks, and safe, and they said the weather was good to push us home, so we kept going." She took a sip and continued.

"We had raced over to Nassau without sleep really, so we were all pretty tired, and Will said we'd do shifts. First shift was Will, Alec and me. The others were below and went to sleep."

"So you three were on deck," said Lenny.

"Yes. No. I don't remember Alec being there. No, he wasn't, for some reason. I was on deck with Will, and now I think about it, when I went below, Alec had fallen asleep in the galley."

"So you went below?" I asked.

She nodded slowly, and I could see her weighing that decision, knowing it was the wrong call, as things turned out.

"Will and I were on deck for a while. It was dark, and pretty smooth sailing. We were making good time, the breeze at our backs, and Will said I looked tired and I said I was, and he said I should get a few winks in. I wasn't sure I should. We were taught to always have at least two crew on deck at all times, but he said it was like a bath out, and he'd wake me if anything changed."

"So you went down?"

"Yes. Will said I could crash in his cabin. He had the stateroom, it's his boat, so I did. I fell asleep in seconds, I think. I didn't wake until someone started banging on doors, and I found out Will had gone over."

"Felicity, how do you think that could have happened?"

"I don't know. The weather was a little choppy by the time I got on deck, but it wasn't a big sea or anything."

"Had Will been drinking?" asked Lenny.

Felicity hesitated and in doing so gave Lenny his answer. "We were tired, it had been a pretty hard race and he wanted to relax a little."

We nodded but said nothing. It was often the best way to get people talking. Most interviewers just kept asking questions, and talked right over the answers. But the majority of folks are uncomfortable with silence, and sooner or later feel the need to fill it. Felicity was one of those people.

"He had a bottle of rum. I don't care for it much, but it seems to be a sailor thing. Like from pirate days. So we shared a couple of rums. Just a couple. He wasn't drunk or anything."

"Where was Ron when you woke up?" I asked.

"He was on the radio, to the Coast Guard. I think he took the call."

"Was anyone else up?"

"Everyone. I think they banged on my door, Will's door, last, because they assumed he had been on deck, not asleep. So I got up and everyone was on deck, looking out at sea."

"For Will?"

She nodded.

"Felicity, do you know anyone on board who might want harm to come to Will?"

She shook her head instantly. "No, no. Certainly not Ron. But none of the others either. I mean, I didn't know them all well. I'd sailed a couple times with Drew, and I knew Alec and Amy from the club. But everyone seemed to get along pretty well."

"So you think it was an accident."

She stared into middle distance for a moment, maybe picturing that moment in her mind, the moment Will went over. Perhaps she was replaying it, each time slotting one of the other crew members into the scene, showing them pushing the skipper over the side. I had played the same scene in my mind, trying to see Ron doing it. Somehow the image of him never formed properly. Felicity may have had the same problem.

"Yes," she said, almost to herself. "I don't get it, but yes. I think it was an accident." She looked up at me, tears welling in her eyes. "I think he fell overboard."

# CHAPTER TEN

**Our investigation took** a hiatus as we made our way to the courthouse adjoining the county lockup on Gun Club Road. As predicted by Allen, the state attorney had to put up or shut up if he wanted to keep Ron in custody, and he had opted for the former. Ron's preliminary hearing was held on minimal notice but Allen was there, sitting opposite the state attorney for the Florida 15th Judicial Circuit, who had decided to make the appearance himself. Allen suggested this was not a great sign for Ron. The SA was seated at a plain table and had a large file box next to him, behind which sat one of his minions. The file box seemed to have a lot of paper in it, and I was surprised they had so much paperwork already. Or perhaps it was all blank and he used the technique to psych out his opponents. Or that might have been my mind getting the better of me. Despite sitting, the SA looked tall. He sat erect, spine against the back of the chair, which accentuated the effect. He was lean too, and had the tight cheeks of a marathon runner. I watched him stare at the judge-less bench, like a quarterback before a big game, and I wondered if he was visualizing how his plays would work out. He kept his gaze ahead, and ran his hand down his tie, in a subconscious move that I didn't think he even knew he was doing.

The judge came into the court and we all stood, and then we sat again and a guy in uniform announced the first docket. Ron was led in. He was dressed in an orange jumpsuit despite not having been charged with anything until that morning. He looked gaunt and withdrawn, and the orange suit did nothing for his complexion. In short, he looked guilty. Guilty of anything and everything.

"Does he have to wear that jumpsuit?" I whispered to Lenny.

Lenny nodded sagely and whispered back. "The court says it isn't prejudicial if there isn't a jury present."

"But the judge is human, too."

Lenny shrugged. "Everyone they see is in orange. They believe they're above it."

"Are they?"

Lenny shook his head and directed his attention back to the bench. The prosecutor stood and proved to be taller than I thought. I was a lazy six-two, and he beat me by a good couple inches. He looked like a well-dressed string bean.

"Your honor, Eric Edwards for the People. In the matter of the People versus Ronald Anthony Bennett, charge of first-degree homicide, we ask the court that the accused be held in custody until formal arraignment due to the nature of the crime."

"I understand the alleged crime took place at sea?" The judge looked over thin glasses at the prosecutor.

"Yes, your honor."

"And no body has been recovered?"

"That is correct, your honor. The incident occurred in the Gulf Stream, and the Coast Guard believes the body was swept away in the current. We will provide expert testimony that proves the deceased would have been dragged out into the Atlantic and that survival is not possible."

The judge nodded and looked at his documents. I leaned to Lenny again, who had seen a lot more courtroom action than I had.

"Why isn't Allen objecting? Surely they have no idea where the body ended up."

"This isn't *LA Law*. Allen will get his chance." I let the reference to a show I vaguely remembered as a kid slide, and turned my attention back to the courtroom.

"What do you have for me?" asked the judge.

The prosecutor, Edwards, flipped over a page on his table and then looked up as he spoke. "Considerable circumstantial evidence, your honor. The accused had motive, as outlined in the court documents before you, as well as means."

"Means?"

"He was conveniently situated on the yacht, your honor. All other crew members had been assigned cabins, twin cabins, with one other person. The defendant elected to sleep in the galley, alone, where he had access to the deck without being seen by any other crew."

"I see."

"The sheriff's office has also found physical evidence, which is being analyzed as we speak, and we fully expect such evidence to prove the state's case."

"Okay, Mr. Edwards, thank you. Mr. Allen, it's been a while since this court has seen you."

Allen stood when addressed. "Yes, your honor."

"You disagree, of course. What do you have to say on the matter?"

"The state is fishing, your honor. The alleged motive is paper-thin and we can show it to be so. As for opportunity, there were six other people on the yacht, apart from the alleged victim and my client, your honor. Furthermore, the state cannot even prove that Mr. Colfax's disappearance wasn't an accident."

"Mr. Edwards?" The judge turned his gaze back to the prosecutor.

Edwards stood. He was a good six inches taller than Allen, and that seemed to give him some kind of unfair advantage. I always felt a little smile cross my face when a short batter took the plate back in my playing days. It made me feel like I had the physical edge, before I ever threw a pitch. Never did it cross my mind at the time that a smaller batter meant a smaller strike zone for me. The mind works in mysterious ways.

"As I said, your honor, we have collected considerable physical evidence that we believe will show foul play. There is also the matter of the victim's considerable experience at sea, and the calm nature of the water at the time."

"Okay. Anything else, Mr. Allen?"

"Your honor, there are no grounds for this matter to be heard in your honor's courtroom. The alleged incident occurred in the territorial waters of the Bahamas, and as such should be the domain of the Bahamas Maritime Authority."

The judge looked at Edwards, who had remained standing. "Your honor, there is considerable precedent here. The vessel is registered in the state of Florida and the victim is a resident of Palm Beach County."

The judge nodded and turned back to Allen. "Anything else?"

"Your honor, the state has nothing but thin, circumstantial evidence, and the promise that they will find proof. That simply isn't good enough. They are, of course, welcome to continue their investigation, however frivolous, but not at the expense of my client's liberty."

I thought the client's liberty thing was pretty impressive, but this wasn't my ship to steer.

"Mr. Edwards, I'm inclined to agree with Mr. Allen. Without formal arraignment I see no reason not to release the defendant. You are welcome to lay charges and arraign at a later date."

"Your honor, we believe the defendant is a flight risk."

That was news to me. I'd never known Ron to vacation outside Florida, let alone be a flight risk. I couldn't see Ron leaving Florida if the only other option was to be thrown into the fires of hell, and not just because the fires of hell were mild compared to South Florida in summer. Ron was the poster child for the Florida life. He loved everything about it: the sun, the sea, the heat driving one to beat a hasty retreat to the bar.

"How so?" asked the judge.

"The defendant is a dual national, your honor."

That stopped the room. I frowned and saw Allen freeze in his standing position, and then glance as surreptitiously as he could at Ron. Ron looked up with a look of wonder, and nodded to Allen. I turned to Lenny, who didn't look at me. He just nodded as well.

"Explain," the judge said to Edwards.

"The defendant was born in Jamaica, your honor. He is a Jamaican national, and later became a citizen of the United States. This fact, combined with his expertise as an open ocean sailor, suggests he presents a significant flight risk."

The judge pursued his lips as he considered this news. I didn't take that as a good sign. He turned his attention to

Allen. "Mr. Allen?" It was as simple a loaded question as I had ever heard.

"Your honor, may I conference with my client?" asked Allen.

The judge leaned back in his chair and looked over his glasses at Allen. "You may, Mr. Allen. In the county lockup. I am going to agree to Mr. Edwards's request to hold the defendant in custody. Mr. Edwards, I shall demand a greater burden of proof at arraignment, and I expect such hearing to happen as promptly as possible so as to not impinge the accused's liberty unnecessarily."

The judge wrapped up proceedings and Ron was escorted from the courtroom. Lenny stood and wandered out of the gallery, but I stayed seated. I was having a hard time processing what had just happened. I had expected Ron to walk from the court a free man. I wasn't naive enough to expect the SA or the sheriff to give up the investigation, so I expected Ron to remain in the frame, but I was also confident that Lenny and I would find enough evidence ourselves to clear Ron of suspicion. But it hadn't panned out that way. Ron was staying in the slammer, and that was unthinkable. I was roused from my rumination by a hand on my shoulder. I looked up to see Allen standing in the aisle, briefcase in hand. The courtroom was moving quickly to the next case, so I stood and followed Allen out into the hallway. Lenny was waiting for us. Allen dropped his case on a seat alongside two men waiting to appear in the court, and turned to us.

"Did you know about the Jamaica thing?" he asked.

Lenny nodded. "His father was a US diplomat, based in Jamaica when Ron was born. But to suggest Ron is anything other than American is ridiculous."

"It might be ridiculous, but it was an effective tactic today."

"Will it work at an arraignment?" I asked Allen.

"No. The state will have to show more for trial, and more than a passport for flight risk. Push comes to shove, Ron could surrender his passport."

"I don't think he even has a Jamaican passport," said Lenny.

"That might have been useful to know, but bygones are bygones. That brings us to the future."

"What about it?" I asked.

"You need to know that I can't represent Ron if this goes to trial. I'm not a criminal trial lawyer. I can do a hearing, but defending a murder case is outside my scope. If things go beyond arraignment, you'll need to find someone better qualified."

"How do we stop this going to trial?" asked Lenny.

Allen thought for a good long moment. "Same plan. We muddy the water. The state needs to show evidence that a crime has been committed, and then that Ron committed it. The first part is usually self-evident, but that's not the case without a body. So your job, gentlemen, is to find plenty of alternate explanations for events."

"Felicity Havill says Will was drinking before she went to bed," I said.

Allen nodded. "Good, good start. That's what I'm talking about. If we can show that an accident is just as likely as foul play, then reasonable doubt becomes unreasonable. But there is more. Alternative hypotheses mean even if they establish that there was foul play, we show the possibility that any of the other crew could have committed the crime."

"How do we know who did it, though?" I asked.

"Irrelevant, Miami. We don't have to prove who did it, we just have to show that there is equivalent probability that anyone committed the crime."

"Everyone else on the yacht had means, didn't they? So what we need is a motive for each of the rest of the crew."

"Precisely," said Allen.

"So where do we start?" I asked Lenny.

Lenny nodded to himself and then looked at me with a firm set jaw.

"We start at home."

# CHAPTER ELEVEN

**The next morning** brought one of those days that tell a South Floridian that the joyous few weeks of spring are done, and the heat is about to ramp up and fry them like a Thanksgiving turkey. The sky was as clear as Polish crystal everywhere except the eastern horizon, where the fog banks clung to the Gulf Stream that seemed to be so important right now. We drove toward it as Lenny pointed us across the bridge to Palm Beach. When he said we should start at home with our ongoing investigation to free Ron, he didn't mean his home or my home. He meant the victim's home. Which, as Detective Ronzoni had conveniently pointed out, was at the Biltmore.

The Biltmore was opened in 1925 as the Alba Hotel, and during the seventies was renovated and turned into condos that overlooked the Intracoastal Waterway and now started at a cool million bucks, shooting all the way up to ten million or so. This was how the other half lived, at least in the Palm Beaches. We decided that a drop-in visit to Mrs. Colfax was the best, so Lenny parked on the street and we walked up the raised driveway. About halfway up we saw someone walk out in a sun-bleached cap and shorts. It was the walrus from Will Colfax's boat, Drew Keck. He didn't stop for a chat, striding away down the circular driveway in the opposite direction.

We told the building concierge we were investigating Will Colfax's disappearance, but neglected to mention we were investigating for the defense. A maid met us at the elevator and walked us into a plush living room with expansive views of the Intracoastal. This was not one of the cheaper pads in the building, and from our vantage point I thought I might be able to see the Gulf of Mexico. The condo was directly across the water from the Palm Beach Yacht Club, and I wondered if Mrs. Colfax had stood at the window like a New England widow when her husband's boat came in without him. I turned away from the sparkling view and took in the room. It might have been called a condo, but the word had a different meaning from where I lived. The living room was twice the size of my entire apartment. The dining room was half as big again. It was furnished tastefully but richly, heavy fabrics that looked expensive but didn't really say Florida to me.

Celia Colfax came in, wearing a simple blue dress that wouldn't have looked out of place on a red carpet. She was a little too thin, and her cheekbones pushed at her skin like they were trying to escape. The sleeveless dress showed off toned but sinewy arms, and the blue fabric played off her auburn hair in a way that suggested great consideration had gone into the color choices. She wore a string of pearls around her neck, which seemed overkill for midmorning, and which drew attention to her neck, which was the one part of her that was truly showing her age.

"Mrs. Colfax, my name is Miami Jones, and this is my colleague, Lenny Cox." We shook hands as she looked us over. We had independently both decided that a trip to the island demanded trousers, so we wore matching chinos. I wore a solid blue Tommy Hilfiger shirt, but Lenny had stuck with a print, a conservative number with fifties-style cars all over it. Mrs. Colfax seemed neither impressed nor unimpressed by us.

"How can I help you, gentlemen?" She pointed toward a linen sofa and took a wing-backed reading chair for herself.

"First of all, please let me say I am sorry about your husband," I said. "There's still hope."

"Not according to the Coast Guard. They said he'd be halfway to Africa by now." She said it matter-of-factly, as if it were a verbatim quote, and I found it hard to believe that it was the kind of image the Coast Guard would use with the family of someone lost at sea.

"Be that as it may, there are questions about events out there."

"I heard the police made an arrest."

"The sheriff, yes. One of Mr. Colfax's crew, Ron Bennett. Have you met Ron?"

She nodded as she glanced out the window toward the shining water. "Yes, once or twice. I didn't spend a lot of time with the boat people."

I left the boat people reference alone. "Do you have reason to believe Mr. Bennett would wish to harm your husband?"

She glanced back at me and raised a well-sculpted eyebrow. "I thought he seemed nice enough. Perhaps charming to a certain set. But anyone is capable of anything, are they not?"

I had to admit, in my experience, that this was true.

Lenny leaned back in the sofa, looking as comfortable as he did at Longboard Kelly's. "Celia, did you tell the sheriff that your husband was having an affair with Mandy Bennett?"

Mrs. Colfax's lips tightened, and I wasn't sure if it was the question or the use of her first name by the likes of Lenny that caused it.

"I answered their questions."

"Was your husband having an affair with her?"

She smoothed the fabric across her thigh. "Probably. William had many *excursions*."

Excursions. That was a new one.

"Did that upset you?" Lenny continued.

Mrs. Colfax smiled. "Mr. Cox, if you are inching your way to asking if I had a motive to make my husband disappear, the answer is no."

"This looks like a pretty nice place," he said, glancing around the room.

"I like it. And I own it, Mr. Cox. It's in my name."

"Nice," said Lenny. "What did your husband do for a living?"

"William bought and sold things."

She made it sound like he was the owner of the general store in Carson City.

"What sort of things?" I asked.

"All sorts of things. William found companies that were in trouble, and he bought them and sold off their assets. Or he bought whatever they had left in their warehouse, and he found a buyer for those things. It really wasn't my interest."

"Looks lucrative," said Lenny.

"Putting the right people together often is. Look, gentlemen, please excuse me, but I have a lunch date that I do not wish to be late for, so let me get to the point for you. My husband was lost at sea. Do I think Ron did it? No. I suspect he just fell overboard. But who knows? Like any successful businessman, William had enemies, both within and without.

So could it have been murder? Possibly. I suspect we'll never know. And you may find me cold, but frankly, I don't care." She stood and we stood with her, and she smoothed out her dress again. Then she looked us both in the eye, stopping on Lenny.

"I loved my husband, Mr. Cox. I just wasn't in love with him anymore. And he felt the same. But neither of us wanted a divorce, so we agreed to give each other a long leash. I know William had dalliances. I don't care. You may find it hard to believe, but I liked my life. Unlike most marriages, I knew exactly where I stood. There were parameters, and there was absolute trust. I didn't wish my husband harm, and I don't benefit from it. This home is in my name, not William's. So is our estate in Pound Ridge. And yes, William had life insurance, we both did, but with no body recovered, I can't access it until he is declared legally dead. And how long does that take without a body? Seven years? Mr. Cox, if that were my motive, I assure you a body would have been found."

She lifted her chin and took a long breath. It was quite a speech, but I believed every word of it. We could and would check the facts of ownership and so on, but I expected them to be exactly as Mrs. Colfax had presented them. What I was struck by wasn't the lack of grief over her husband. I suspected she had done her grieving many years before. What struck me was that she didn't seem lonely. She was alone, but appeared comfortable with that fact, as if she had been that way for a long time. An image of a human heart flashed across my mind, and there I watched it slowly transform into granite, then crack and crumble and blow away on the wind. I shivered at the thought, shook it out, and offered my hand to Mrs. Colfax.

"Ma'am, do you know Drew Keck?"

I saw her eyes narrow. I got the feeling she was calculating whether it was a stab in the dark, or if we had seen Drew leave the building.

"Not really," she said. "He did some work for my husband. Boat maintenance, I think."

She walked us to the door. As we were about to leave I turned to her.

"Can I ask, what will happen to Will's yacht?"

"It was registered in Cyntech's name, so I really don't know. I certainly don't want it."

"Cyntech?"

"My husband's company. Now if you'll excuse me."

We thanked her again and took the elevator down to the lobby. The concierge wasn't at his desk, so instead of turning to the street, Lenny headed for the rear of the building. We walked out into the sunshine along a path, by grass that might not have been putting green smooth, but it would have made a wonderful fairway. There was a swimming pool and tennis courts overlooking the Intracoastal. We wandered out to a small dock, where a collection of motor and sail boats waited patiently for someone to take them out. Several of the docks were empty, and I suspected some of the owners had moved their boats out of the water and into storage when they headed back north for the summer. One dock had the nameplate *Toxic Assets*. It sat open. I assumed the boat itself was still moored across at the yacht club. I looked back up at the building, a grand feature on the Palm Beach skyline, and wondered what kinds of happiness and what kinds of loneliness hid behind its gilt-stained walls.

Lenny looked long and hard across the water back toward West Palm, and I wondered what was going through his mind.

"You were pretty direct with Mrs. Colfax," I said.

He nodded. "What is it Lucas says? She's just not my cup of tea." He looked at his watch and then ran his hand through his hair.

"It's visiting time," he said, striding toward the street.

# CHAPTER TWELVE

**Visiting hours in** a jail deliver the best and worst of humanity. There are all sorts of inmates, from those who are actually innocent, or those who made mistakes they are paying for, to those who killed in cold blood, and everything in between. And there are all sorts of visitors. Attorneys, some who wear their cases on their sleeves, others who are jaded and can't remember their clients' names. There are wives and girlfriends who blame everyone: the system, the guards and especially the inmate they are visiting. And there are families, torn apart but holding together as best they can, small children who get to see Daddy once a week or once a month, or maybe less if it's a federal prison and the family lives in another state. Entering the visiting area is like going through airport security in the worst airport in the country. The guards eye everyone with suspicion, their firm-set jaws and pinched brows setting the tone for the whole place. I felt like a criminal just for being there, and it wasn't a feeling I enjoyed one bit. We sat and waited for Ron to be led in. He was still in a section with other men yet to go to trial, so not the worst population, but not a church picnic either. The fact was that all of the men in with

Ron were yet to be tried, but when they were, most of them would be found guilty, because most of them were.

Ron looked like he had developed kidney disease. He shuffled in, the gray pallor of his face matching the institutional walls. He was in need of a shave, and his hair looked like it had been combed with his fingers. That was my method, and it suited me well, but then I had spent the majority of my life underneath a ball cap or a football helmet. Ron's grooming was of a higher standard altogether, and it pained me to see him that way. He sat with a forced smile and as he did a flicker of light came into his eyes. I looked around me and watched similar embers spark around the room. Hard-looking men walked in, but the façade was broken by the sight of loved ones. The guys who had little kids were the best and worst. Their metamorphoses were complete, and more than one broke into tears. It was beautiful, and tragic, and I wondered what the men must think as they transformed back, led away into the concrete bowels of the prison, to become hard again.

"How's digs?" Lenny smiled.

"Could be better, could be worse," Ron replied.

"How's the food?"

"Worse than your cooking."

Lenny grimaced.

"We're gonna get you out," I said. It sounded hollow and false, as if I didn't have anything better to say. Fact was, I didn't. I wasn't sure if I should get to the point, or tiptoe around it. Fortunately I had Lenny.

"Allen says they'll have to prove a case at the next hearing, and our job is to muddy the water."

"Show it was an accident," said Ron.

"Right."

"Or show one of the other crew could have done it," I added. Lenny turned slowly and creased his brow at me.

"I don't like that idea," said Ron. "Those people are my friends. I know they didn't do any such thing. This is just a horrible, horrible accident."

"Understood, but MJ's right," said Lenny. "We're not going to try to frame anyone, just show that it is possible someone, anyone could have done it."

"Alternative hypotheses, Allen called it," I added, helpfully.

Ron nodded. "What do you need from me?"

"Background. Who are the crew, how they know the deceased."

"Okay, I can do that." I noticed that doing something proactive had given Ron some color, and I realized that for most people tied up in the legal system the battle wasn't just against the system—it was a battle against hopelessness.

"Start with Felicity Havill. She's the only one we've spoken to so far."

"Nice girl. She came to the club to learn to sail, and did. I think she met Will at the club, and he invited her onto his boat."

"They involved in any way?" asked Lenny.

"Will didn't mind having pretty girls crew his boat, but there's nothing wrong with that. I didn't mind crewing alongside them. But no, I wasn't aware of anything more."

"Okay. Next?"

"There's Amy. Amy Artiz. She's a lovely girl too. She's actually a pro sailor. Even done an around-the-world race, did you know? She teaches at the club."

"How did she know Will?"

"Again, just through the club, I think."

"More eye candy?"

"Knowing Will, probably. But there was more to it as well. This was an ocean race, and while it's not the wildest part of the ocean, you need to take it seriously. Amy was experienced, and I think that mattered to Will."

"She works at the yacht club, you say?"

Ron nodded. "She's always there."

"Okay. Who else?"

"Well, you talk about experience, there's Drew. Drew Keck. He's the guy with the big mustache. He's also a professional sailor, like Amy. He's the one Will deferred to most times when it came to sailing. He was the navigator and tactician on the boat."

"Tactician?" I asked.

"He basically looked at the weather and the wind and decided which way we should go."

"Was he any good?"

"We won our class, so, yeah, he did all right."

"How does he know Will?" asked Lenny. "Through the club?"

"Yeah, but he's also a boat builder. Or you might say a boat repairer. I think he did the maintenance on Will's boat, and I heard something about them working on a project together. Maybe a restoration thing? Not sure."

"What's he like?"

"He's okay. A bit gruff at times, and he doesn't suffer fools, but I know a few people like that." Ron shot Lenny a look which Lenny chose to ignore.

"Okay, good. Who else?"

"There was Alec Meechan."

"He was the one who was supposed to be on deck with Will but wasn't?"

"I believe so. Originally it was Will, Felicity and Drew who were on first watch that night, but I heard that Alec offered to swap with Drew."

"Why would he do that?"

"It was a nice thing to do. Drew had been on watch all day as we crossed the Great Bahama Bank, making sure we didn't run into anything. Staring at water like that for hours on end, it's hard on the eyes. When I think about it, Alec should probably have taken first watch to begin with."

"Who decided who was on watch and when?" I asked.

"There was no fixed plan. We just agreed a schedule on the fly. I guess the only real rule was that Amy and Drew didn't watch together."

"Why?"

"They were the best sailors, the most experienced in open water. It made sense to have at least one of them on deck at all times. Other than that, we just divided up the hours, three on, three off."

"So who made the decision that night?"

Ron shook his head. "I don't recall there being a meeting or anything. I think Will must have just made the call. We were all pretty tired at that point, so I for one didn't want first watch."

"So, what about Alec then?" asked Lenny.

"He's a young guy—you know how they are," said Ron. Alec had to be around thirty, give or take, a similar age to me, but Ron either didn't make the connection or didn't consider me the same sort of young.

"What's he like?"

"He's harder work than I generally prefer to put in."

I frowned and Ron elaborated.

"Everything's a competition with him. He never gives a straight answer. It's always a throwaway line, or he's trying to one-up everything anyone else says. I don't think it's malicious —he's just one of those ones that never listens to what other people are saying because he's too busy coming up with his own next comment."

"He sail?" I asked.

"Yes. Not much open water stuff, I don't think, but on the Intracoastal, sure. He actually skippers sometimes."

"You've sailed with him?"

Ron nodded. "Yes, but only as crew, not with him as skipper. Like I say, he's young."

"Meaning?"

"Meaning young guys often sail like they drive. A little too close to the wind."

"What does he do with his days?" asked Lenny.

"He sells sports cars. I think Will used to buy his cars from Alec. Will went through sports cars like most folks go through Kleenex."

"Where's the dealership? On the island?"

"No, on the mainland. Palm Beach Gardens or thereabouts."

"All right," said Lenny. "Is that everyone?"

"No," said Ron. "There's Michael. Baggio I think is his last name."

"You don't know him?" I asked.

"No, not well. He's a nice guy. Didn't know much about sailing, but was ready and willing to chip in, happy to listen and do what he was told. He was pretty nervous about being on the open water, out of sight of land, but he got through all right."

"How did he know Will?"

"I don't really know. I never recalled him being at the yacht club. And I've certainly never sailed with him before."

"Why would Will have someone who didn't sail on his crew in an open water race?"

"Not sure. Maybe they did business together. I couldn't say."

"You didn't talk to him on the boat?" I asked.

"A little. I think he said he was from Michigan, or was it Illinois? Came to Florida for his partner's work."

"What does he do for a living?" asked Lenny.

"I want to say he said he was an architect. It was something like that. Some kind of professional job."

"Got it," said Lenny. "So, how did you all end up on this crew? It's a mixed bunch. Not exactly an America's Cup crew."

"No, but the Nassau race is like that. Most of the boats are cruisers rather than straight-up racing yachts. They're designed for comfort as much as speed. These are owners who take their sailing seriously, but it's also social. Crews are stitched together around the club. Most guys will get at least a couple of really experienced hands, and then fill in people they know from the club."

"Okay. That gives us something to work with," said Lenny. "We'll have a chat with them and get everything squared away."

"I don't want to cause any trouble for any of them," said Ron.

"Understood."

We asked if Ron needed anything and he said no, and we tried chitchat for a while but, unlike the constant banter of our office, it felt forced and stilted, and I think Ron picked up on it because he suggested he didn't want to keep us, and we said we had plenty to do and we'd be in touch.

Before he turned to be led away, Ron stopped. "If you see her, tell Mandy there's no hard feelings."

Lenny nodded without speaking. We left the facility under the scornful eye of the guards, and wandered back out to the lot.

"Ron's in jail and is worried about whether the love of his life, who left him high and dry, is upset with him," I said. "How can the SA think a guy like that committed murder?"

"The state attorney isn't paid to think about Ron—he's paid to win cases and make everyone feel safer," said Lenny.

I shook my head.

"And Mandy wasn't the love of Ron's life," he said, stepping up into his truck.

"I wasn't being completely serious," I said. Lenny pulled out of the lot onto Gun Club Road and turned onto Australian Avenue. "So who was the love of Ron's life? Or should I ask how many have there been?"

"There's been one, as far as I know. He was married before, long time ago. I gather they were too young and headed in different directions."

"Ships in the night," I said.

"Quite. But she wasn't it either. Lucille was the one."

"Lucille?"

"Lucy, yeah. She was one for the ages. A free spirit, that one. She didn't care about the money, the big house. She was one of those few folks who actually just enjoyed the now." Lenny smiled at the thought of her, or maybe at the thought of enjoying the now.

"So what happened? Why did they get divorced?"

"They never got married. Ron says she told him on their first date that they were soul mates, but she was never going to marry him. And she didn't. They were together fifteen years and they never got married."

"So what happened?"

The joy in Lenny's eyes disappeared as quickly as it arrived, the thought of this Lucy bringing sadness as readily as joy.

"She died. Cancer. One day she's dancing circles on the beach, three months later she was gone."

"Oh, man," I said, poetically.

"Aha. Six months later he met Mandy."

"So she was his rebound girl."

"Maybe. On the surface Ron looks like a player. The ladies certainly enjoy his company. But deep down, maybe he's a serial monogamist. He's like a swan. He needs a partner."

"Right now he looks like an ugly duckling."

Lenny nodded as he pulled into the lot next to our soon-to-be office. "Let's fix that. You feel like a walk?"

"I could use some air."

"Let's wander down to the yacht club."

# CHAPTER THIRTEEN

**Things were quiet** midweek at the yacht club, and we asked for Amy Artiz, and got a lot of frowns and closed mouths, until we mentioned that we were working for Ron. That brought a lot of *oh, no* and *is he okay* type comments, and fingers pointed down the dock. We followed directions and found Amy Artiz in the cockpit of a white yacht, looking skyward at a man who appeared to be attached to the top of the mast. Amy couldn't have been more than five-one, and not much more than a 110 pounds, but it was all toned muscle. She was stocky in a feminine way, strong arms and firm legs and a trim waist. I wondered if she lifted weights or some such. She had brown hair that she tucked behind her ears but didn't reach within a few inches of her collar, and she had perfect white teeth that hid behind a smileless visage. She seemed vaguely Latina to me, but the barking at the guy up the mast had no accent to it.

"Just yell when it's connected," she yelled herself.

"Amy Artiz?" asked Lenny as we watched from the dock.

"Busy," she replied without turning around.

"We're here about Ron Bennett."

"What does that mean?" She kept her back to us and her eyes up.

"We're trying to get him out of jail," I said, a little impatiently.

Amy glanced back at us with a frown, gave us the quick two-second appraisal, and then turned away. "Give me five."

The guy up the mast called down, words lost to me between the wind and the tinking of rigging, but Amy yelled *okay*, and she dropped down into the cockpit and started pushing buttons on a display of some kind. She did that for a minute or two, and then she stepped back up to the deck and yelled *all good*. She grabbed a rope that was tied off on the mast and wrapped it behind her buttocks, and as she fed it through the guy up the mast slowly came down. He was in some kind of chair assembly, a wooden plank and rope that looked like a child's swing.

"How's it look?" said the guy.

"Better. I think we got it."

"Good. I've got to get into town, but if you need some help to take her out and test it . . ."

Amy turned and looked at Lenny and me on the dock. With his crazy mane of red hair and tanned face, Lenny looked like a boaty kind of guy. My sandy blond locks blowing in the wind usually got me pegged as a surfer or beach bum, and only the latter was remotely true.

"You guys wanna chat about Ron?"

"Yes, ma'am," said Lenny.

"You sail?"

"Yes, ma'am."

That was news to me. I'd never seen Lenny sail, but then what I knew of his shadowy past wouldn't have filled the prologue of his biography.

"All right, then. Let's go," said Amy, and she thanked the guy and he stepped off the rear of the yacht as we stepped on.

It was a nice yacht, not that I was any kind of expert. I didn't sail. It wasn't that I didn't like it, or I didn't have the opportunity. Ron was always trying to get me to come down and crew, but I always suspected what he really wanted was for me to meet some of his younger women friends, and I never really warmed to that idea. So I knew a little about sailing, but not enough to get the thing up and running.

The cockpit was a big depression in the deck, like a large built-in sofa. A crew of eight could have sat either side comfortably. There were two large wheels, one either side at the back, and a bank of screens and buttons nearby.

Amy dropped behind the wheels and fired up the motor, and gestured for me to step down and take a seat in the cockpit. I offered my hand and she took it. It was a good firm handshake, but unlike Felicity Havill, Amy's skin wore the patina of someone who spent a lot of time in sun and salt water.

"Miami Jones," I said.

She arched an eyebrow at me. "Amy Artiz. Miami Jones?"

I nodded. I got that a lot. No, I wasn't related to Indiana. No, I wasn't born there. No, I wasn't conceived there.

"You part Native American?" she asked.

That was left field, so I blinked hard. "Do I look Native American to you?"

"Not in the slightest, but I thought you might be named after the Mayaimi people."

I nodded at the idea. It was an educated guess, with the emphasis being on *educated*, which was different from the usual remarks I got, where the emphasis was on the *guess*.

"No," I said. "I went to school there. UM."

"Shame," she said, like carrying a name from your alma mater was fratty juvenile.

Lenny untied us from the dock and then stepped deftly onboard and Amy pointed the yacht out of the tight space. As she turned to the Intracoastal Lenny pulled the fenders from over the side and dropped them onto the floor of the cockpit area.

"Lenny Cox," he nodded, as he plopped down onto a cushioned bench.

"Amy Artiz." She nodded back. "You're the guy Ron works for?"

"With, I'd say," said Lenny.

Amy nodded and put her eyes to the water. There wasn't much traffic on the Intracoastal, but she seemed to be aware of every vessel. I got the impression that she was a very confident sailor, not just because she was happy to go out in a big yacht with two guys who to her knowledge might not know how to tie a knot, let alone sail. She had that casual assurance of someone who knew her craft so well she could do it in her sleep. I didn't know anything about Will Colfax other than what I'd been told, but if I were sailing into open water, Amy was the kind of person I'd want to have holding the wheel.

"So how can I help you?" she asked, as she punched some buttons on a console beside her.

"We're trying to get Ron out of jail," I said.

"I would hope so."

"So we are trying to get an idea what really happened that night."

"Procedures were not followed and someone lost their life as a result," she said, looking up at the top of the mast.

"What procedures?" asked Lenny. "How did Will Colfax run his boat?"

"Like a cruiser," she said, and it didn't sound like a compliment. We waited for her to expand on her answer, and she took her sweet time. Amy didn't seem at all uncomfortable with silence, or at least not talking. She played with the console again, and then looked up. We were getting perilously close to the Flagler Memorial Bridge, which was not open and which our mast was way too tall to get under, but Amy didn't seem fussed by it. She gave the wheel a gentle tug and the yacht spun on a dime and turned away. She pointed us north up the Intracoastal before speaking again.

"Sailing in open water isn't the same as here on the Intracoastal. Here the weather's always good and help is always a minute away. There are lots of other boats to assist if you have problems. In open water, it's just you and the ocean. And there's only one rule out there."

"Which is?" I asked.

"Ocean wins. Ocean holds all the cards. Even if it's dead calm and the water is azure, the ocean wins. It can go from idyllic to deadly faster than any boat can get to safety, so you can't be cocky."

"And Will was cocky?"

"You didn't know Will?" She raised the eyebrow again.

"No, but I'm forming an impression."

"Will was a type. They believe they can beat anything, anyone. You get a lot of boat owners like that. They're successful guys, they do these big deals, think they're the kings of the world. But you can't beat nature."

"So why sail with him?" asked Lenny.

"Look, what I'm saying is, it's a mentality. It didn't make him a bad guy. Lots of people thought him utterly charming. I'm just painting a picture."

"You weren't on deck that night," I said.

"No," she said firmly. There was no regret in the word, just disappointment.

"You think it would have happened differently if you had been?"

"Maybe," she said. "Like I say, ocean wins. If it wants you, it takes you. But I would have followed procedure."

"You mentioned. Like what?"

"There should be two crew on deck at all times. No exceptions. We had a big crew for this boat. Three can sail it easy enough. We had seven. Plenty of eyes to go round. There should be no alcohol on the open water. In dock, go crazy, but not out there."

"There was drinking on the boat?" I asked. Felicity had confirmed there was, but I wanted to hear Amy's take on it.

"Of course. Some bright spark always stashes a bottle of rum. Like we're a bunch of pirates."

"So you think it could have been an accident? Even though it was calm?"

She frowned. "Who said it was calm?"

"The Coast Guard, and the state attorney for that matter."

"The Coast Guard goes out when no one else will, so anything less than a ten-foot swell is calm to them. And I bet the state attorney's sailing logbook features a lot of time on Carnival cruises."

I nodded. I was inclined to agree about the state attorney. He looked too tall to function on a yacht as anything other than the mast. "So it was rough?"

"No," she said. "Not really. But it was the Gulf Stream. Things change, wind, the swell. A rogue wave."

"But this cockpit seems pretty safe," I said.

"It is. But what if Will got up to check a sheet?" She pointed to the deck, where some ropes were coiled up, like the

Coast Guard guy had done the day Will disappeared. "All it takes is a small wind shift. If the lines are lax, the boom moves a little, whack, you're over the side. Or guys like to pee over the transom." She pointed to the back on the boat. Behind her there was a platform, where the name of the yacht was written.

"Guys are always stepping over the guardrail and peeing off the back. Will could have done that, a wave hits the boat, even a small one, and he could lose his balance. It's too easy. Like I say, the ocean wins."

Lenny spoke but kept his eyes on the water. "So you knew he was gone when the Coast Guard called?"

"Yes. I felt the motion of the boat change, clearly the wind had shifted, so I was awake, and I heard the buzz, but Ron was sleeping in the galley and took it. I came out and he said something like *the Coast Guard is saying Will's in the water*, and I jumped up on deck and there was no one there. Not a soul." She seemed lost for a moment, maybe out at sea, maybe on that night. Then she snapped back.

"Let's get this main up," she said. "Grab a winch handle in that bag there," she said to Lenny. He pulled a plastic handle from a mesh bag, and slotted it into a hole in the middle of a gleaming chrome winch. Amy turned the boat as he was getting in place and pointed us back toward the south, and I noted for the first time that the wind was coming from that direction, where it had definitely been coming out of the north the day *Toxic Assets* came home one short. Amy pointed the yacht into the wind and told Lenny to winch. He started winding the handle around, and the sail that was wrapped up on top of the boom reached skyward.

"Put some effort into it," she said, and Lenny responded by winding harder, and the sail went up, up, up, until it hit the top of the mast. "Going round," she said, and she turned the wheel and the yacht spun back toward the north, and the wind collected into the sail and it whipped across the deck, right above our heads, and I saw what she meant about getting hit by it. In the cockpit it went safely overhead. Up on the deck was a different matter.

"Trim the sheet," she called to me, and I gave her a blank face like she had just said *batter up* to a Masai warrior. "The sheet," she repeated. "The red one. Uncleat it and let it out."

The red rope was wound in a figure eight around a cleat, so I unwound it, and as soon as I did the wind drove the sail out and pulled the rope through my fingers.

"Don't let it go," called Amy, calm but forceful.

I grabbed the rope and it slid through my fingers, burning me, until Amy pulled the wheel back and the sail flapped loose and the rope went lax.

"Use the winch to wind it back in," she said. I found a winch handle like Lenny had used and I slotted it into the winch and turned, but the rope didn't move. Amy leaned over and grabbed the tail end of the rope and pulled on it, then I wound again and it bit, and the sail stopped flapping. Amy pointed the yacht back up the Intracoastal and the wind pulled the boom back away from the side of the boat, but my rope stopped it going too far.

"Okay, now take hold of the sheet first, then ease it out."

I did as I was told, and the boom eased out over the side and the sail opened flat against the wind that was coming from behind us. We seemed to stop moving.

"Feels like we've stopped," I said.

Amy looked at the screen on the console beside her, and smiled. "That's relative velocity. We're moving with the wind and the waves, so it feels like our motion has slowed. In fact, we're doing ten knots."

"Is that good?"

"Pretty good." She smiled. "And it means the new telemetry is working."

I frowned and she nodded toward the top of the mast. "We just installed new electronics on her. Upgraded GPS, vane."

I nodded like this all sounded very nice, when in fact it all sounded like babble. But Amy looked pleased and Lenny looked like a Labrador with its head out a car window, so I figured all was good.

"So you think it was an accident. Will, I mean," I said, slipping back into my seat.

"I guess. Yes."

"You guess. What does that mean?"

She moved the wheel ever so slightly and glanced at me. "It never occurred it could be anything but an accident. A failure of procedure. But then Ron got arrested and it got me thinking."

"About what?"

"Our heading."

"What do you mean?"

"Heading. The direction we were sailing." I must have given her another blank stare because she explained. "The shortest distance between two points is a straight line, right?"

I nodded.

"Except in sailing that's only true if the wind is directly behind you. From any other direction the wind is partly driving you forward, but partially driving you to the side. You're leeing. Imagine a river with current. To cross the river to a set point, you need to start upriver from that point because part of your motion will be across the river, but the current will be pushing you down river. You can't go across in a direct line."

"Okay, I see that. So?"

"So the Gulf Stream is a current. Biggest current in the world. It's like a river in the ocean. Water warms up in the Gulf of Mexico and off the coast of Africa, and is pushed through the Caribbean and meets up in the Florida Straights, and then it rushes up the east coast, south to north. The flow is driven through what is essentially a massive channel, between the Florida coast and the Bahama Banks."

"So?"

"So like the river, you can't cross the Gulf Stream directly. It pushes you north. If the prevailing wind is in the same direction, a southernly, then you have wind and current working for you and you can go very fast on a northerly heading. But if the wind is from the north, then it is going against the current."

"And you go slow."

"More than that. The wind against the current means big waves. Bad seas. Some of the worst. Crossing the Gulf Stream in a predominant northerly is a bad idea. Yachts this size sometimes wait weeks for the right window to make the crossing. East-west wind is hard. South is easy. North can be deadly."

"So how was it blowing that night?"

"South, to southeast, as we came across the banks. Moving southeast as we got to the western edge of the bank."

"So good?"

"Yes, good. Will made the call to keep going." She pursed her lips.

"You wouldn't have done that?"

"It was a judgment call. We had all been on for the best part of two days to race over to Nassau. We had a night partying in Nassau, and the plan was to take it easy going back.

We were going to call in to the Biminis, moor there, get some rest. Everyone was very tired, and tired crew make mistakes."

"But Will wanted to keep going?"

"He said he had business to attend to."

"But you didn't agree?"

"I didn't disagree. Maybe I should have. But the weather was in our favor. A sou'easter, and we were heading northwest. Like we are doing now, the wind at our backs means we get home faster. So from that point of view it made sense."

"So what was the problem?"

"When the Coast Guard called, Ron gave our coordinates. From Bimini we were on more of a westerly heading."

"So you were crossing the river in a straight line?"

She smiled and nodded, happy I had gotten the point of her story. "Right. We weren't using the prevailing conditions well at all. It was like we were trying to make way to Miami, rather than heading to Palm Beach."

"And that's bad?"

"Not bad, just not smart. In another wind, sure, you might just try to get across the Stream as quick as you can, and then head up the coast or even inside the Intracoastal, if the weather's bad. But we had almost optimal conditions to head straight for Palm Beach."

"It didn't seem optimal to me, the day you came in. It seemed cold and rough."

She nodded. "Let's go about. Get ready to pull in your sheet." She turned the wheel and the yacht moved around on the breeze until we were heading back down toward the yacht club, roughly to the south. The mainsail flapped a bit until I wound the rope, or sheet back in, and it snapped tight against the breeze.

"So the day we came in," Amy said, continuing where we had left off. "You're right, it wasn't that good. About the time of the Coast Guard call the weather started to turn from the southeast to the northeast. Anything with a north in your wind direction means rougher seas across the Stream. So we cut northwest, got across as far as Hillsboro Inlet, then we came the rest of the way under motor up the Intracoastal."

"When did the weather turn?"

"I think the wind shift was what woke me. The boat was under autopilot, and the trim was off when the wind shifted, and I felt that."

"Autopilot? Boats have autopilots?"

"Sure. There's a couple of variations, but in this case, it's linked to the GPS system. It essentially keeps you heading toward a predetermined point via GPS, but if the wind shifts significantly it won't work—you need to reset and retrim."

"Why would the autopilot be on if Will was on deck?"

"Best guess, laziness. People put it on so they don't have to pay attention to the trim so much. Okay, guys, let's pull the main down. Lenny, is it? Can you let the halyard out, and Miami, can you jump up there and fold the sail over the boom as it comes down?" Amy pointed the yacht into the wind and the life went out of the sail. Lenny dropped the rope, which in my yachtie knowledge I assumed was the halyard, and the sail dropped down. I folded like a madman in a laundry, securing the mainsail in a very sloppy fashion across the top of the boom. Amy motored us back into the dock and expertly reversed the boat into its slot. Lenny and I dropped the fenders over the side, and then Lenny stepped onto the dock and tied us up.

"Can I ask you—the state attorney thinks Ron had good opportunity to push Will overboard because he was sleeping in the galley. Was there a reason he was sleeping there?"

"Luck of the draw. All the cabins on the Oceanis 523 are doubles, and for that race there were only three. So technically that meant one odd man out."

"Technically?"

"Like I said, there should have been two, preferably three bodies on deck at all times. That means only four bodies asleep in six bunks. But it doesn't always work like that. Michael and Drew took one aft cabin, Felicity and I the other. Will had the stateroom, the fore cabin, but being Will he had it to himself. So that meant Ron and Alec shared the sofa in the galley, so they'd always be on opposite shifts."

"So not really Ron's choice."

She shook her head as she jumped off the yacht onto the dock. "Ron liked a good bed like the rest of us. But he could sleep anywhere, was my experience."

I nodded.

"Is it normal to have more crew than sleeping berths?" asked Lenny.

"No, it's not. On a racing yacht, sure. I've been on some that use hammocks, and some guys sleep on folded-up sails. But not this kind of boat."

"What do you mean *this kind of boat*?" I asked.

"You haven't been on Will's boat?"

We both shook our heads.

"Come with me." Amy walked us down the dock to another boat and stepped across a small gangway onto the transom. I followed, and noted the name of the boat painted there was *Sudden Thunder*.

"I thought Will's boat was called *Toxic Assets*?"

Amy gave a guttural laugh. "It is." She took out a new-looking phone and brought up a photo on the screen. It was a picture of the crew at the back of *Toxic Assets*, except someone had put a large orange bag on the transom, so the name read *Toxic Ass*.

"*Toxic Ass*?" I asked.

Amy looked at the picture and frowned. "Huh, I hadn't noticed that. Fitting for Will."

"Where was this photo taken?" I asked.

"Nassau, just before we came back. But you see how it looks like this one?"

"Aha."

"Well, this isn't Will's boat, but it's the same model. A Beneteau Oceanis 523. This, like Will's, is the latest model, the 2007." She opened the hatch at the rear of the cockpit and stepped down the ladder-like steps. I followed her down, and Lenny brought up the rear. Below there was lots of polished wood. On the right was a small kitchen area, and forward of that a couple of plush cream-colored seats. On the other side was a long lounge, also cream, with a table set up like a banquette. Forward of that was a small desk, where someone could read charts, or use the marine radio.

"Behind us there are two double berths, one either side," said Amy.

I opened one of the doors and looked into the cabin. There was a wedge-shaped mattress and room for not much else. It was enough space for two people to sleep, but they would want to be pretty good friends. Amy took us forward, to a door at the front end of the boat.

"This is the main cabin," she said, flicking the door open. This one had more space, enough to stand up and swing a very tiny cat.

"Each cabin has an en suite head," she added. "There is another cabin further forward of the main cabin, but it is only accessible via a hatch on the foredeck. For the Palm Beach-Nassau race Will pulled the mattresses out and used that cabin for sail storage."

"Is that usual?" I asked.

"Usual enough," she said. "Like I said, sometimes crew will sleep on top of the sails, but that's usually on a longer race."

"It's fancier than my house," said Lenny.

"Mine too," I added.

"Mine also," said Amy. "They're really cruisers, for pleasure sailing. But the Beneteau is a good enough boat to do a decent race as well."

Amy led us back up onto the deck, locked up the hatch and we stepped back onto the dock.

"So where is Will's boat?" I asked.

"Impounded. It got moved to the boatyards in Riviera Beach, I believe."

We thanked Amy for her help, and for the sailing lesson in my case.

"One last thing," said Lenny. "You said the autopilot was set. Who would know how to do that? Apart from Will."

"It's not that complicated, but I suppose in that crew? Probably just me and Drew."

"Drew Keck?"

"That's right."

"You have any idea where we might find him?" he asked.

"Funny you should ask. He has a boat maintenance business. Runs it out of the boatyards."

"Which boatyards?"

"Riviera Beach."

# CHAPTER FOURTEEN

**The boatyard in** question sat next to the Port of Palm Beach, tucked in behind Peanut Island. Lenny pulled in off Route 1 and drove down a short street flanked on one side by shipping containers and on the other by what looked like a boat graveyard. Rusted hulls, discarded anchors and the broken bones of ocean vessels littered the view through the hurricane wire fences. Lenny parked on the street and we walked into a wide concourse that housed an assortment of large boats up on stands. If we had ambled into an upmarket shopping mall in Palm Beach, we would have had a team of security guards following our every move, but in a boatyard we looked the part. We wandered down to the water, where a motorboat that was a good fifty feet long was being lifted out of the water by a large crane. A group of men stood around watching, cigarettes in hand. I thought Lenny might ask after Drew Keck but he didn't, choosing to take a good look around unfettered before questions earned us quizzical looks and an invitation to leave.

We wandered around a large warehouse where several more boats stood, their hulls being cleaned or sprayed. At the end of the warehouse was another hurricane wire fence, with several boats on the other side, like sleeping lions in a zoo. One of the yachts up on a stand was a blue-hulled beauty, and I noticed a ladder alongside it. As my eyes reached the deck high above, I realized it was *Toxic Assets*. Yellow police tape of the *Do Not Cross* variety was strung around the yacht. As we looked the yacht over, a man in a dark suit and red tie appeared on the deck. It was like some kind of modern art installation: a yacht up on dry land, being helmed by a man dressed like a banker. I couldn't even begin to guess what that kind of thing might mean. But the man paid us no mind, carefully stepping over the guardrail and climbing down the long ladder to the ground. It was once he hit *terra firma* that he noticed us.

"Help you?"

Lenny nodded. "You from the sheriff's office?"

"No," he said. He was in a nice suit that wasn't expensive but fit well, and his hair looked like it had been cut that morning. "Who are you?"

"Lenny Cox. And you?"

The guy looked Lenny over nice and slow, and then he gave me the treatment. It was one of those conversations where everyone holds their cards close and no one wants to give away anything, and I couldn't figure out what the purpose of it all was. We weren't looking to buy a damned boat. The guy must have come to the same decision, because he reached into his breast pocket, pulled out a wallet and flipped open an ID.

"Special Agent Moss, FBI." He gave us a moment to look at his ID, and then he flipped it closed in a well-practiced move that saw it land back inside his coat pocket. "And your interest in the boat is?"

"We're investigators for one of the crew members. Looking into the disappearance of the skipper."

"Which crew member?"

"The one in jail," said Lenny.

Special Agent Moss just frowned, as if he didn't know what Lenny was talking about.

"Ron Bennett," said Lenny.

The FBI man nodded. "Right. The missing persons thing."

"That isn't your interest in the boat?" asked Lenny.

"That's a local matter."

"So why is the FBI crawling all over a local matter?" Lenny nodded toward the yacht.

"We have impounded the yacht."

"Why?"

"Can't say."

"Bud, we're talking about a guy in jail who, trust me, shouldn't be there."

"Like I said, that's a local matter."

"Did you serve a warrant to impound the boat?" I asked.

"Excuse me?" he said without a frown.

"A warrant. Who did you serve the warrant on?"

"The owner of the boat is dead," said Moss.

"No, the owner of the boat is Mr. Colfax's company, of which I am sure he is not the only corporate officer." I recalled Celia Colfax telling us that the boat was registered to her husband's business and that she was happy about that because she wanted no part of it. "So the question remains, on whom did you serve the warrant? Because if you didn't serve a warrant, then I think what we have here is illegal search and seizure. And everything you found after it would be, what do they call it in court? Fruit of the poisonous tree?"

The FBI man dropped the façade involuntarily. "What is it you want?"

"Why is the FBI involved in a murder inquiry?" I asked.

"We're not. Our case is completely unrelated."

"How so?"

Special Agent Moss shuffled his feet like he didn't want to tell, but I knew he would. He felt like he needed to placate me, then rush off and get that warrant he needed. Fact was *Toxic Assets* had been put in the impound by the PBSO, and they had every right to do so. But finally Moss arrived where I was already waiting.

"Okay, this is confidential. You can't tell anyone."

"What is this, high school?" I asked.

He gave me a look but continued. "We're investigating some financial irregularities within the Colfax businesses."

"Financial irregularities?"

He nodded. "We suspect someone was embezzling money from the company."

"I assume from inside the company?" asked Lenny.

"How else?"

"So as our client, Ron Bennett, doesn't work there, he is not of interest to your investigation?"

"Not at all. But I am serious. This is an ongoing investigation. You tell anyone what I told you, you can be charged with obstruction."

"Keep your pants on, special agent," said Lenny. "We're not going to tell anyone. So you're taking over custody of the boat."

"Yes. PBSO will be allowed to inspect further if they require it, but I think they already got all the samples they need."

"Samples?" I frowned.

"Biomatter. They found blood and other biomatter under black light," said the special agent, who had become way too chatty.

"Where?"

"On the deck, I believe. Now, I've done you a favor, you do me one."

"If anyone asks, you had the warrant in place," I said.

Special Agent Moss nodded, and we nodded in return, and goodbyes were said silently. Lenny and I walked away, and Lenny smiled at me.

"Nice move with the ownership of the boat thing—that really threw him off."

"Thanks, Lenny."

"You know, you might end up half decent at this caper." He slapped me on the back, and we wandered into the large, high-roofed warehouse, searching for a man who looked like a walrus.

# CHAPTER FIFTEEN

**There were a** lot of men who looked like walruses in the boatyard. Facial hair seemed to be a thing, as did sun-bleached polos and caps. Every boat in the space was being worked on, most around the hull. Some were being sanded, others painted. One seemed to be getting a coat of glue smeared all over it. We found our walrus polishing the chrome on a beautiful wood motorboat. It looked like the sort of thing you'd see on the canals of Venice in an old Sofia Loren movie. The materials could just have easily been used to build an expensive log cabin, lots of gleaming wood and leather trim.

"Drew Keck," called Lenny, above the noise of sanders and air compressors. Drew looked over the edge of the deck at us and grunted.

"Who's askin'?"

"Lenny Cox. I'm here about Ron Bennett."

"Don't know nothin' 'bout that."

"You were on the boat, weren't you?"

"Yeah. Look, I already spoke to the cops."

"And they've put Ron in jail. We're trying to get him out," said Lenny. I could see where he was going with it. Pretty much everyone liked Ron, and wanted to help get him out of lockup.

"Is there somewhere we can grab a beer?" asked Lenny.

The mustache poked over the edge of the deck again. I could see Drew was having a hard time passing up a beer.

"Gimme a couple minutes."

We waited while Drew put away his rags and cleaning polish, then packed up some other tools and put them inside the boat, and then he gingerly made his way down the ladder to the floor. It wasn't anywhere near as long a ladder as the one reaching up to *Toxic Assets*, because the yacht had a large keel under its stand, and the motorboat Drew was working on had no keel and a shallow hull, so was only up about five feet. Still, Drew made it look like a hell of an effort. My impression may have been tainted by his look, but he had the labored movement of a walrus too.

Drew washed his hands, which seemed to be the cleanest part of him, and took us in a truck that was in worse condition than Lenny's around the corner to a small, no-name bar. We were close to the water but couldn't see it. The place had a few outdoor tables, but Drew headed inside, nodded to the waitress who waltzed by with a tray full of empty beer glasses, and took a booth. The room had low false ceilings, the kind of removable squares one sees in older office spaces, and I would have put money on the fact they were filled with asbestos. There were pictures of boats on the walls, and a few buoys hanging from the ceiling, but these weren't the Disney-fied artifacts that hipster bars liked to use to add character. These items were the real deal; they were scratched and scraped and dented, pockmarked and nibbled at. The beer mats were soaked through and dried a hundred times over, so they were warped and rock hard. It was a total dive, and it was my kind of place.

We ordered beers and fish sandwiches, and Drew tapped his fingers on the table until his beer arrived. I wasn't sure if he was nervous about something, or just one of those people who had to have something in their hands all the time.

"That's a nice boat you're working on," said Lenny.

Drew nodded. "Yup, she's one of a kind. Wasn't too good when I found her, but I rebuilt her from the superstructure up."

"What sort of wood is it?" I asked.

"Superstructure is oak, the hull is mahogany over black locust, the deck is African mahogany."

I didn't know anything about wood, but it all sounded impressive, and it certainly looked fantastic.

"Bet she goes well," said Lenny. "What sort of horsepower you got in there?"

"Twin 330s."

Lenny nodded. "Nice."

"Yup." The beers arrived and Drew took a drink. I watched his mustache droop into it and get all wet. I couldn't quite see the point.

"So what do you think about Will Colfax?" asked Lenny. "Think they'll find him?"

"Nup. He'd be somewheres off the Grand Banks by now. But he's fish food."

"Can't survive that long in the water?" I asked.

"Nup. Without a raft you'd get hypothermia."

"Really? Isn't the water warm down here?" I asked.

"It's all right if you're from the northeast. And the Gulf Stream's warmer than most ocean, but still. What's it, eighty degrees on a good day? Plenty warm for a swim, but hypothermia sets in when you go below ninety-five. So it would take a while, but it'll get ya."

Our fish sandwiches arrived, and were so fresh mine practically winked at me. Florida is hardly the culinary capital of the world, but I've never tasted a finer fish sandwich anywhere. We all bit into our lunch, and then I tapped my lips with a paper napkin and looked at Drew.

"So do you think Will was an accident?"

He seemed to shrug. "Maybe."

"You don't seem positive."

"I wouldn't know."

I wasn't sure if Drew was being purposely uncooperative or if he was just uncommunicative in general.

"Why was Will on deck alone?" I asked.

"Who says he was alone?" Drew took a large chomp on his sandwich.

"Who else was up there?"

"I dunno," he said with a full mouth. "But if someone done him, then someone was there, right?"

"Do you think that person could have been Ron?"

He shrugged again, although it was more like a spasm in his shoulders. "Maybe."

"You didn't get along with Ron?"

"He's all right. But I heard his old lady was doing the number with Will, so who knows."

"They were divorced," I said.

"So?"

We ate in silence for a moment. Some guys came in from a fishing boat and ordered the same thing we were having without bothering with a menu. Then Lenny put his sandwich down.

"You were the tactician during the race, is that right?"

"Yup."

"And Will deferred to you on sailing matters."

"I guess."

"Amy Artiz is also a sailor, isn't she?"

"Yeah, you could say that."

"You didn't like her?" asked Lenny.

"Not saying that. But when push comes to shove, and you need a bit of muscle to get things done, girls don't cut it, do they?"

Lenny nodded. "Used to be they'd say having a woman on board a boat was bad luck."

"Women and bananas, yup. No business on boats, either of 'em."

"So what about the rest of the crew?" I asked.

"What about 'em?"

"What did you think of them?"

"I didn't. The girls were good to look at, for something different."

"Different than what?"

"Than staring at the sea all day."

"Felicity's quite the cutie," I said.

"Yup. But everyone knew that was off-limits."

"Why?"

"Will," he said, stuffing some fish in his mouth.

"They were having an affair?" I asked.

Drew stopped chewing and looked at me. "You do know where she was sleeping on the boat?"

"In Will's cabin," I said to myself.

Drew gave a nod.

"But she said Will offered it to her since he was on watch anyway."

"Yeah, that's why."

"What about Amy?" asked Lenny.

Drew shook his head. "She likes the girls, that one."

"Really?"

Drew nodded again, then took a long pull on his beer, finishing it off, and held it up to signal the waitress for another.

"I heard that you were working on a project with Will," said Lenny. I was still thinking about Felicity and Will.

"Where'd you hear that?"

"At the yacht club?"

"Well, they don't know what they're talkin' about."

"So you weren't doing something together? Like that beautiful boat you're working on back there?" Lenny nodded in the general direction of the boatyards.

"That's my boat. Anyone tells you different, they're lying. All I did for Will was the maintenance on *Toxic Assets*, that's all."

Lenny nodded and sipped his beer and looked at me. So Drew and Amy had different information on the boat he was restoring. I wasn't sure if we were double-teaming Drew, but I picked up the ball anyway.

"Did you know the other two guys? Alec and Michael?" I asked.

"Alec, yeah. He's around the club. He's young and stupid, you know."

"And Michael?"

"Didn't trust that guy."

"Why?"

"Something about him, just something off."

"Off?"

"He didn't sail. Knew nothin'. Had no business being there."

"So why was he?"

"No idea. Asked Will about him. I said he didn't know a sheet from a halyard. Will says *we all start somewhere*, whatever the hell that means."

"How did he know Will?" I asked.

"No idea. Never seen him before."

I finished my sandwich but didn't order another beer. "What will happen now, with *Toxic Assets*?"

"Did you see it, in the cage?" asked Drew.

I nodded.

"Depends. The cops often hold stuff there, until they move it to wherever. If there's no crime I guess the owner gets it back, but I don't figure Will will be needing it anytime soon."

"His company owns the yacht," I said.

Drew nodded and finished his second beer. "Figures."

"And if there's a crime?"

"If there's a crime, and the court decides the boat is ill-gotten gains, they'll take it to an impound auction and sell it off."

"Would you buy it?"

Drew laughed from deep within his throat. "Not my kind of boat. And even at ten cents on the dollar, I couldn't afford the upkeep."

I knew the feeling. I had a motorbike that lived in the shop, and the upkeep on it was making me think very seriously about ending our relationship. I paid the check and we all clambered back into Drew's truck, and he dropped us at the gate to the boatyard. I was going to ask him one final question, the old Columbo technique. People often let their guard down as they were pushing me out the door. Not Drew Keck. Lenny got out and I followed, and then I turned to close the door and hit him with my zinger, but in one movement he nodded, hit the gas and was gone like the wind.

# CHAPTER SIXTEEN

**They say home** is where the heart is. Or it's wherever you lay your hat. By those definitions I didn't have a home. My childhood home in Connecticut had fit the bill, but some people I had never met lived in that house now, and my parents rested in a cemetery in New Haven that I might never visit again. I had felt at home during my years at University of Miami, but no one ever considered the transient halls of college dorms home. Adventures, good times, great memories, yes. Home, no. Then I played baseball for six years, living in short-term rentals and rooming houses that weren't home because I was never there long enough. The team bus was more of a home. And after six years, three minor league teams and twenty-nine days in the majors, where I didn't throw a pitch in anything but batting practice, I hung up my cleats and moved from St. Lucie West to the Palm Beaches, and took up residence in another dwelling that didn't feel like home either.

My apartment was a two-bedroom, split floor plan, a one-bedroom place with a kitchen that joined onto a smaller second-bedroom unit with a kitchenette that could be closed off and rented separately. The idea was that a bigger group could rent the whole place, or smaller groups or individuals could rent each separately. The place was marketed at the budget golfing crowd, who flocked to South Florida in the season to play the many nice courses and drink beers during working hours, but who didn't have the cash to spend on the flashy resorts, and didn't plan on spending a lot of time in their rooms anyway. It was sound logic, except the place wasn't built on a golf course, or even that close to one, so it was the last to fill up in season, and even then rarely did. So I got a two-bedder for the price of a one, and I kept the door closed to the second bedroom and never went in there. Like the golfers, I didn't spend a lot of time in my room.

Lenny dropped me at the bike shop and I collected my increasingly expensive old bike. It wasn't a classic and it didn't run well, but I had figured at the time I bought it that I didn't need a car in Florida weather. One tropical downpour on I-95 showed me the flaw in my logic. But I just hadn't gotten up the motivation to replace it. I rode the thing home and wheeled it in under the stairs that wound up to the apartments above me, and then I went inside and grabbed a beer from the fridge. I looked around the room, the white-tiled floors that had been mopped in my absence, the eighties-style overhead fan, and the small television that offered basic cable plus the golf channel, if I were so inclined. I stepped out onto the back patio and sat down in a stackable plastic chair. The space was big enough for two chairs and one round table, and was screened in from the bugs that descended every night.

I couldn't stop thinking about Ron. About how he looked in jail, and how nothing more than circumstance had caused him to be there. It was all so tenuous, the invisible lines that pulled us in one direction or another. I sat for a long while thinking about Ron and his wives, and the love of his life who never married him. And I thought about Felicity and Amy and Drew Keck, and about Will. I closed my eyes for a moment against my better judgment, and I saw the transom of the boat slipping away from me, the words *Toxic Assets* the last I would ever see as the darkness stole my boat and the ocean closed around me.

I snapped my eyes open and realized I had nodded off. My beer was warm and covered in condensation, and the sun had fallen low in the sky. I rubbed my eyes and stood, and then I went in and poured the warm beer down the sink. It was a waste, but life is too short to drink warm beer. I resolved to learn how to make bread using leftover beer. I was watching the last of the amber liquid froth in the sink when the doorbell rang.

The community I lived in was gated, which kept out most door-to-door types, the salesmen and the evangelists, and the neighbors didn't drop by for a cup of sugar. I opened the door and found Beccy Williams standing in the evening light. She looked fantastic, and that didn't suit my mood at all. Her blond hair had been coiffed to perfection, and the dress she wore was simple and satin and sheer.

She smiled her orthodontist's dream. "You look terrible, sugar." She ran her hand across my cheek, a couple days' stubble.

"Mmm," she said. "Rough."

Beccy kissed the cheek she had just rubbed and slid past me into the apartment. I stood looking at the street, SUVs and full-size sedans returning from one golf course or another, and then I closed the door.

"Place looks clean," she said, spinning around on the living room tile.

"Maid's been."

"And you haven't, or it would be messed up."

"What can I do for you, Bec?"

"You could offer a girl a drink." She flopped down on the floral print sofa and crossed her long, thin legs. Beccy was beautiful in person, but even more so on television. The camera loved her, and it added the extra few pounds she needed. Her facial bones were striking, and her breasts pert, but her chest reminded me of a bird carcass. I always felt she was one decent meal short of good health. I took a shaker out of the cupboard and made her a martini, dirty with three olives. To Beccy an olive was the staff of life. I handed her the drink, but didn't take one myself.

"Mmm, good," she said, looking at me with her Caribbean blue eyes.

"So, what's up?" I asked.

"Can't a girl drop by for a visit?"

"No, not really. We broke up, remember? When that happens, people don't usually drop by for a visit anymore."

"Oh, there's breaking up and there's breaking up, sugar."

"And we did the version where you took all your stuff and left."

"Are you still sore about that?"

Fact was, I wasn't sore. I was lazy. Beccy had come into my life when there was still hope for my major league career, and she was covering the minor leagues for a local paper. But she was headed upwards onto television, where she now did sideline work on college games for a local affiliate, and had no intention of stopping there. So when my baseball career went south, so did the relationship. I didn't break up with her, but I wasn't sad she left. She was sure nice to look at, and energetic in the sack, but after a while I realized, like Drew Keck, that I couldn't afford the upkeep. There was never any downtime, always something to do. As if kinetic energy gave her life, and slowing down and smelling the roses would be the end of her.

"I'm sure I can make it better," she said, running her finger around the rim of the martini glass. I couldn't remember which movie I had seen that in, but I recalled it had been black and white and I hadn't seen it with Beccy.

"I don't think so."

"Come on, sugar, can't we still be friends?"

"Sure," I said, but I didn't really believe it. Ships in the night seemed to be the metaphor that kept making itself at home in my mind. That was Beccy and me. She was on her way someplace big, somewhere I wasn't going to go, and once she got there, she would do everything she could to forget the path that had taken her there.

"Friends with benefits?"

"Bec, I have to be somewhere."

"A girl?"

"A case."

"Right, the detective thing." When I'd hung up my cleats Beccy hadn't believed it. She said I'd be back in the spring, missing the boys and the action and the smell of the grass. But when spring came and went, and I graduated with a master's in criminology and joined Lenny full-time, she realized that I had moved on. Or quit, as she put it. You could have been great, she had said. And I realized at that moment that what I wanted more than anything, and had wanted all along, probably since the day the cancer took my mother, was someone who thought I was great already.

"You really think those guys will be there for you? Come on, Miami. I'm your Annie Savoy, and you're my Crash Davis. You know it's true."

I didn't appreciate the metaphor, or the reference to *Bull Durham*. Mainly because she had it all wrong. If she was Annie Savoy, then I was Ebby Calvin LaLoosh. I wasn't a catcher, or a hitter, or a sage on the ballpark. I was a pitcher. I was the meat. And in the end, Ebby Calvin went away. Beccy had the story all wrong.

"I really have to go," I said, picking up my keys.

"Did I tell you I'm looking at an apartment in Hollywood? Right on the beach."

"Sounds nice," I said, grabbing my helmet off a lounge chair.

"You're kicking me out? I haven't finished my drink."

"Feel free to finish the drink, Bec." I turned and walked away down the hallway.

"Will you be long? I could wait."

I opened the door and glanced back into the bland apartment, the only spot of color coming from Beccy Williams. She was bright, she was beautiful and she was a shooting star. A lonely shooting star.

"Don't wait," I said, closing the door behind me.

# CHAPTER SEVENTEEN

**The truth was**, I did have an Annie Savoy. There was a person who sat in the stands in St. Lucie West and passed notes to me about my pitching. Someone who watched pretty much every game, and gave me wisdom I couldn't comprehend at the time. The difference was that my Annie, my Susan Sarandon, was a balding old man with mob ties and a great eye for batters' weaknesses.

Sally Mondavi's Pawn and Check Cashing sat on the wrong side of the turnpike along Okeechobee Boulevard. I parked the bike in front of a Chinese restaurant that also claimed to specialize in *Amercian* cuisine. My headlight lit up the guy in the window and he gave me a savage look, and not just because I wasn't going into his restaurant. I suspect I had parked in the spot his delivery car usually occupied.

I left my helmet hanging on the handlebars and tried to smooth out my sweaty hat head. Riding a motorcycle in Florida wasn't that much different than having a personal sauna on your head. I wished I'd brought a cap, but it wasn't the first time Beccy Williams had put my thoughts all out of kilter. The little bell dinged as I opened the door and stepped into the cool of the store. I nodded to the girl in the check cashing booth, hiding in full view behind Perspex and chewing gum like a professional baseball player. I hadn't seen her before, and the look of disinterest she gave suggested we weren't going to become best buddies.

I wandered along the low glass cabinet that ran the length of the store, not looking at the rings and cameras and music players inside. I could hear some grunting coming from the aisles of shelving that made up the bulk of the space, and I followed my ears and found Sal Mondavi with a massive amplifier in his arms. He was trying to put it on a shelf above his head but he couldn't get the thing higher than his chest.

"Some help there, Sal?"

"Excellent timing, kid."

I grabbed the amp and Sal pointed to the top shelf, and I lifted it up into place.

"Why do you put the heavy things up top?" I asked.

"Do I tell you how to pitch?"

"As it happened, you did."

"Only when you done it wrong." He smiled his nicotine grin. "Which wasn't often." He slapped my back and led me to the rear of the store. Sal Mondavi had become an unlikely friend. We had met when he had sent a note to me during a game at Tradition Field. When the bat boy handed me the note, the entire dugout went silent, assuming a love letter from a fan, and then every guy with the single exception of the manager jumped up onto the grass to see who had sent it. The disappointment when the bat boy pointed out the old man in the Jets cap was palpable, and I was the subject of ridicule for weeks. But the note hit home, and after giving up five hits in the first two innings before getting the message, I pitched a clean sheet before I was relieved in the eighth.

"So to what do I owe this honor? Shouldn't you be out with the ladies or something?"

"Beccy came to see me at home."

"She's a feisty one. I thought that was done."

"It is."

"But she came to your home."

I smiled. "And that's why I'm here."

"Kid, if I'm the best option you got, you gotta work on your strategy." He stepped in behind the glass counter at the rear of the store. "You still in that tiny little holiday apartment?"

I nodded. "It suits my purpose."

"It's for divorcees and golf nuts. You need a real house."

"I have neither the time nor the money to go looking at houses, Sal."

"Balls. Time is right. The market is tanking, kid."

"Isn't that bad?"

He shook his head and gave a phlegmy cough. "Aach. You sure knew baseball but you don't know nothing about business. When the prices are tanking, that's the time to get in. I am."

"You? You're buying property?"

"Hey, Mr. Smart Guy, watch yourself. I get into anything that's profitable. Just because property is all aboveboard, doesn't make it a bad investment." To look at Sally's store anyone would think he struggled to rub two bits together. And that was how Sally liked it. He was a simple man, with simple needs.

"And just because property is a good investment doesn't make it all aboveboard," I grinned.

He raised his eyebrows, made a gun with his fingers and pulled the trigger.

"Here," he said, handing me a brochure. "This is how you get a house, kid. Foreclosure auction."

"I fear you're going to explain what that means."

"You know all these moron banks giving millions away to folks who can't pay it back? Well, eventually the math catches up with them. And when these folks can't make payments, the bank forecloses."

"But what does that mean? The bank takes their house?"

"That's it."

"That's rough, Sal."

"It is. But folks really need to do the math before they go taking all this money. It's not a giveaway, is it?"

"No, but still. Seems everyone gets nailed except the banks."

"That's always true. The big end of town always comes out smelling like roses. But here's where you get your pound of flesh. Because the market is tanking, no one wants to buy the property for what is owed. So the court auctions the property, and the bank gets whatever they get. Sometimes cents on the dollar. There are some bargains to be had."

"But I don't want to be part of a system that kicks folks out of their homes, Sal. Even if they have made dumb choices."

"I thought you'd say that, kid. Take a look at page three."

I flipped the brochure open, where Sally had circled a listing for a property. It sounded like a standard house, three bedrooms, one bathroom, built 1973.

"It's older than me," I said.

"Most good things are. But I checked the title history on it. It's not a family home."

"It sure sounds like one."

Sally shook his head. "It's on Singer Island. A developer bought the house when the owner passed on, with a plan to knock it down and build one of those ugly minimansions we see everywhere now. But the bottom fell out of the market and they couldn't afford to develop it, so they walked away."

"Walked away? I thought banks were believers in the *until death do us part* thing. How do you walk away?"

"Don't return calls. Don't pay the property taxes. Don't pay the mortgage. So the bank takes it back. If you bought the property, you'd owe about two large in back property taxes. You should go take a look."

"If I take a look, will you stop going on about it?"

"It's your best chance. And you'll need to pick me up to go to the courthouse for the auction."

"Why on earth are you going?"

"To make sure you don't do something stupid. And I might pick something up."

"You're not going legit on me, are you, Sal?"

"Stranger things have happened, kid."

I shrugged. Strange indeed.

"There's one other thing, Sal."

"Name it."

"Lenny says I need a piece."

"A piece?"

"A gun."

"What's with *the piece*?" Sal frowned, giving a face full of wrinkles.

"Isn't that what you guys call it?"

"No, whitebread, that isn't what *we* call it. *We* call it a gun. Aach, Francis Ford Coppola has a lot to answer for. But yeah, Lenny's a smart guy. You need a gun in your line of work."

"Lenny suggested I needed a second gun, if you know what I mean."

"One on each hip? What are you, a cowboy now?"

"An emergency weapon. I have a registered handgun already, a Ruger, but he suggested it was worth having something off the books."

"Yeah, he's a funny-looking piece of work, but he knows what he's saying, does Lenny. Okay, kid. A spare piece. Let's take a look."

"I thought you didn't call them pieces."

"Just checking you're awake, kid. I am about to hand a gun to a Connecticut Yankee."

Sally reached into his cabinet and pulled out a boxy-looking weapon with hard edges. He pulled back the mechanism and looked inside, and then let it slide back. He handed it to me.

"It's a Glock. Austrian. Decent gun, if you like that sort of thing."

"What sort of thing?"

"Foreign."

I nodded. I had nothing to say to that.

I held the gun in my hand and felt it. "It's light."

"There's no mag or rounds in it, genius. Loaded it's heavier."

I nodded again and looked at the gun. I didn't like the feel of it, but then I didn't like the feel of any gun. If I ever pulled this baby out, things were not going well.

"I know you're not a gun guy, kid. So I gotta ask. You know how to use this thing? I don't want you hurting yourself."

"Lenny's been taking me to the range every week."

"Good. That's good. Is it comfortable?"

"Is it supposed to be comfortable? It's not a pair of slippers."

"I'll grant you that."

"So is this thing registered, or how does that work?"

"This ain't the one I'm gonna give you. I just want to see how it fits. I got another, same gun, untraceable. As you say, for emergencies only. But it's not here."

"Okay, thanks Sal." I placed the gun back on the glass countertop. "It'll do."

"Every gun's different, right? So when you get the other one, you test fire, make sure you know how it feels."

"I'll practice, don't worry."

"Not at the range. Those guys get pretty hinky about unregistered weapons on their premises. Take it out into the 'Glades. Go shoot a gator."

"I'm not shooting a gator, Sal. But I'm sure I can rustle up some old beer cans."

"As you wish."

"I appreciate this, Sal."

"Don't mention it."

So I didn't mention it. I didn't offer to pay, either, because that would have just got his blood pressure all out of kilter.

"Hey, the GM at St. Lucie offered me some seats in one of the corporate boxes, anytime. We should go catch a game, eat a hot dog."

"I sorta lost my enthusiasm for it, since they were too stupid to keep you."

"Come on, it'll be fun. Like old times."

"Old times? You gonna take the mound?"

"No, Sal. They got young guys for that."

"I bet you'd pitch 'em under the table. But sure, that sounds like a plan."

"All right, I'll give them a call. And this thing?" I asked, nodded at the gun on the counter.

"It will find its way to you."

"Thanks, Sal. I'll see you later."

"You bet, kid. And go look at that house."

"Sure thing, Sal."

I walked out into the evening light. There was no breeze this far inland and the air had a thick quality to it. The Chinese restaurant was still empty, save the guy in the window, who was still watching me with a look of disdain. For a moment I contemplated some Chinese food, but decided against it. I got on the bike, gave the guy in the window a wave, and then headed back to my little apartment, and only half of me hoped that it was empty.

# CHAPTER EIGHTEEN

**The morning brought** a glorious Florida day. The grass behind my apartment glistened with dew as I put on some coffee, and there was a coolness to the air that hadn't been there when I went to bed the previous night. It wouldn't stay cool; the heat was just there, lurking in the background, waiting to strike. But these mornings were my favorite, crisp and clear, the sky more blue than white. I unlocked the front door and sat on the back patio, watching squirrels rush about madly. Lenny arrived and helped himself to coffee, and then sat on my only other chair.

"So, what's the plan for today?" I smiled.

"You look chipper," he said.

"Chipper? What are you, Dick Van Dyke?"

"I get around," he said. "So."

"I'm feeling kind of righteous."

"Do tell."

"Beccy came over last night."

"Oh." He sipped his coffee.

"So I went out."

Lenny raised an eyebrow.

"Alone," I said.

"Is that growth?"

"I was hoping you could tell me."

"Don't look at me, MJ. That girl comes to my house, there's no way I'm going out." He raised both his eyebrows.

"Maybe I'm overthinking it."

"You are overthinking it. But that's what you do. And in my experience, you can't change that, so you have to learn to live with who you are. That's your way. You can't just have the fun—you gotta think about it later."

"You don't seem to have that problem."

"I'm not you, MJ. And you're not me. I have my own limitations. I can have the fun and not overthink it, sure. But I'm the wrong side of fifty and a bachelor. What does that say?"

"Footloose and fancy-free?"

"There is that. But sometimes ladies need a guy who does overthink it. And young Beccy, she just ain't that girl for you."

"This is a very depressing conversation."

"Ah, but there's a silver lining."

"You think?"

"I never had a sexy deputy come hunt me out at Longboards." He gave me a cheeky grin.

"Now you're overthinking it," I said.

"Time shall reveal all. Now, I've got an address on this Michael fellow. Let's get some breakfast, then pay him a visit."

We ate toasted sandwiches at a diner and then headed across the bridge to Cocoanut Row in Palm Beach. Michael Baggio turned out to be exactly what Ron had said, an architect. He was working for Shute and Marrow, an unlikely name for one of the most prestigious architectural firms in South Florida. They specialized in corporate and retail redevelopment—that is, taking old buildings and making them new, rather than knocking them down and starting afresh. It was a novel idea in Florida, where keeping historical buildings erect for history's sake was a recent and fairly unwelcome concept. Lenny had worn chinos despite the likelihood of heat, so I followed his lead, and we looked borderline professional when we asked at the reception desk for Michael Baggio. Michael came out to meet us. As with most of the crew, he looked better than the day I saw him arrive home on *Toxic Assets*. He was shorter than I had thought, but in great shape. He was probably late twenties, and his shoulders were broad and his waist trim, as if he had been a wrestler at college. He had Sicilian features, dark, slicked-back hair and heavy eyebrows, but his facial structure struck me as feminine.

"Michael Baggio," he said without a smile as we shook hands. Maybe it was the defining difference between architects and builders, but his hands were soft as satin. We introduced ourselves and told him that we represented Ron, and he ushered us back to his office. His space was neat and tidy and had a killer view of the water. We sat at a small conference table by the window and he asked us if we wanted ice water, and we both said yes.

Michael cleared his throat. "I'm afraid I really didn't know Ron," he said sitting down.

"He told us that you met on the boat," I said.

"That's right."

"We're more concerned about getting a feel for events on the night of Will's accident."

"So you think it was an accident?"

"Don't you?"

"I can't see why not, but Ron was arrested, so I don't know."

A young guy came in with three glasses of water, then left and closed the door. We all took a sip.

"So, how did you come to be on the boat?" asked Lenny.

"I was invited, by Mr. Colfax. By Will."

"And how did you know Will?" I asked.

He cleared his throat again. "Through a friend."

"And who was that?"

He took a sip of water. "Is that relevant?"

"I don't know what's relevant."

"A mutual friend."

Who had no name, apparently. "Did you know Will very well?" I asked.

"Casually, I guess you would say."

Lenny swirled his water around in the glass. "Do you have any idea why Will would invite you to sail in an open water race given you had never sailed before?"

"How do you know that?"

"Seems to have been the opinion of everyone on board. They all had considerable sailing experience, bar you."

Michael stood with his hands behind his back and looked out the window at the water.

"Well, I suppose that's true. I guess I expressed an interest and Mr.—, Will—offered me a place on board, in order to learn."

"It's not that common for a first-time sailor to go open water," I said, as if I was some kind of expert. "Usually you do a few races on the Intracoastal or in Biscayne Bay first."

He cleared his throat again. I wondered if he was coming down with something, and I hoped he wouldn't give it to me.

"I suppose there was a lot of experience on board and he figured it would be fine."

"Did you know anyone else on board?" I asked.

"Only a few, by reputation. I had heard Amy was a good sailor."

"And Drew Keck?"

"I heard he was doing some kind of boat restoration, but I didn't know he was a sailor until we were on board."

I nodded and sipped my water. Michael turned around but didn't sit.

"So where were you when Will went overboard?" asked Lenny.

"Asleep."

"Where was that?"

"In my cabin." He seemed to frown, but no lines appeared in his brow. He either moisturized a lot, or he was doing Botox.

"The cabins were doubles, weren't they?" I asked. "Who did you bunk with?"

Michael took a deep breath. "Drew Keck."

"Cozy," said Lenny. "Those cabins are small."

"Yes, they are. Most of the time we were on opposite watch or both awake, so only one of us was in there at a time."

"And the night Will went missing?"

"Drew was supposed to be on first watch, and I went to bed. But I heard later that Alec swapped with him, so he came down and slept too."

"How did that go?"

"It wasn't very comfortable, to be honest. He snores, loudly." Michael made a face like he'd eaten a bad olive. "And his personal hygiene is not all it could be."

I nodded. "I can see that. So did you get any sleep?"

"Yes, I was very tired. We all were. I thought we were going to stop in Bimini, and I wish we had. But the others decided to go on, and it wasn't my place to argue."

Michael moved back to his chair and stood behind it, hands on the back of the seat.

"So when did you know Will was gone?"

"Someone banged on the door, said there was a man overboard. Woke me up."

"Woke you both up," said Lenny.

"No, just me. Drew was up."

"He was up already?" I asked.

"Yes, he was up."

"When did he get up?"

"I don't have any idea. But only a couple hours had passed, so it can't have been long."

"How do you know the time?"

"I was disoriented. I checked my watch. I remember because I wasn't due to be on deck for another hour."

"So what happened?"

"I got up."

"And?"

"Well, I don't know. I didn't know what was happening. Ron was on the radio, to the Coast Guard, and Felicity was pulling on shorts and running through the boat, to go upstairs. So I followed."

"And?"

"Drew was at the wheel, and he said Will had gone overboard, and for me to look."

"Look?"

"Look for Will. Felicity and Amy and Alec were on the front of the deck, with flashlights. Alec might have had a spotlight of some kind. They were looking for Will in the water. So I looked too."

"For how long?"

"I don't know, maybe ten minutes. Maybe twenty."

"You're not sure on the time?"

"No, I wasn't looking at my watch then. I was trying to find someone in the water." Michael pushed away from the chair and returned to the window. I wondered if he had a step count he was trying to achieve.

"Makes sense," said Lenny. "So why did you stop looking?"

"Ron came up and said the Coast Guard helicopter was en route, and he said something about the signal was moving away from us, and Drew said we had to keep heading for shore because the weather was turning."

"Was it?"

"It was certainly getting rougher, yes."

"And did everyone agree with Drew's decision?"

Michael nodded. "They did. Drew seemed to look at Amy, not so much for agreement, more to see if she would disagree. They didn't really see eye to eye. But she didn't disagree. She said the Coast Guard could track the signal but we couldn't, so it was the right call. I think Felicity and Alec were okay with it because Amy was."

"What about you?" I asked.

He looked me in the eye. "I'd never been on the ocean before. Honestly, I just wanted to be on dry land again."

"Reasonable," I said.

"What about Ron?" asked Lenny.

"What about him?"

"You said everyone else agreed with Drew's decision. Did Ron?"

Michael thought about it a moment, and then slowly shook his head. "You know, I don't think he did. Not immediately. He said Will couldn't be too far, and we had the last coordinates from the Coast Guard, so we could use the GPS to find him."

Lenny frowned. "But they didn't listen?"

"No. I think it was Amy. She told Ron that Will was a moving target in the Stream, and they didn't have the equipment to track him if he was moving. She said the weather was changing direction, I can't remember how, but it was going to get worse. She said they had to make sure no one else was lost, and that the Coast Guard would be over the spot within twenty minutes. I think Ron then agreed."

We took all that in, and then Lenny finished off his water and thanked Michael for his time. We stood and wandered out into the morning sun. Already the ground was warm and the moist air seemed to be rising from the pavement. We shook hands with Michael, and one more time Lenny thanked him, and said if he thought of anything useful, he should call. Lenny gave him a business card. We turned to walk to Lenny's truck and were almost knocked down by a guy in a suit who was running like a windmill trying to make a break for freedom.

"Michael!" called the suit.

We watched him run toward the entrance, arms flailing, to where Michael Baggio stood, mouth agape.

"Michael!" called the man again, somewhat unnecessarily. He had attracted every eye in the zip code.

"What are you doing here!" said Michael, in a whispered shout.

Lenny and I watched as the man in the suit screeched to a halt and tried to regain his breath.

"They're going to arrest me," said the man, more quietly but not quiet enough for Lenny and me not to hear. We took a couple of steps toward them.

"What are you talking about, Keegan? You can't be here," said Michael.

"Don't you hear me? The FBI, Michael, the FBI is going to arrest me. They think I've been stealing money from Cyntech."

# CHAPTER NINETEEN

**The mention of** arrests and Will's company reeled us right back in. Michael looked around as if the guy in front of him was a psycho, embarrassed by the whole episode. The guy seemed to be having a nervous breakdown. Lenny stepped forward to suggest we take a walk to Poinciana Plaza, a mall behind the office building. The guy having the breakdown stared at Lenny like he was wearing a hazmat suit, but complied when Michael nodded his agreement. It seemed Michael was keen to do whatever was necessary to get this crazy loon away from his place of work. We cut through a parking lot and Lenny directed us toward a grassed area, under the shade of a large tree that might have been an oak, but certainly wasn't a palm.

"Take a breath," Lenny said to the crazy guy.

"Who are you?" he replied. He frowned a creaseless frown like Michael had. He was average height, somewhere between Michael and me, maybe five-ten, and he had perfectly trimmed brown hair. He was an unusual sight in South Florida, in that he wore a pinstripe suit with clubby red tie. He would have passed for a Boston banker.

"I'm Lenny Cox, this is my partner, Miami Jones. We work with Ron Bennett."

"Who? What? Lenny? Miami? What kind of names are those?"

"They work with Ron, the guy who is in jail for Will's disappearance," said Michael.

The guy didn't look any less confused.

"Who are you?" asked Lenny.

"What?"

"This is Keegan Murray," said Michael.

"What?"

"Keegan," said Lenny, stepping in close and taking up the guy's full sphere of vision. "Take a breath. Do it."

Keegan took a shallow breath, like a sparrow.

"Again, Keegan. Deeper. Give me a good breath." Lenny spoke like he was praising his prize labradoodle, which he didn't have. But Keegan responded with a deep breath.

"Now, slowly. Tell us what happened. The FBI . . ."

"They're going to arrest me!" He started flipping out again, waving his hands like he was directing planes at JFK.

"Keegan, calm down. They're not going to do anything here. You're safe. Just breathe, then talk slow."

Keegan took another breath and nodded to Lenny. "My assistant called. He said the FBI is in my office. They have a warrant."

I gulped and wondered if I had given them the idea for the warrant. Then I brushed the idea away. The feds didn't really need my help to figure out how to serve a search warrant. Lenny nodded but didn't speak, and kept his full attention on Keegan.

"They're taking computers, files, whatever. He said they wanted to know where I was, that they had questions. My

assistant says he thought he heard one of them say I should be
arrested as soon as I arrive."

"Okay, Keegan, that's good," said Lenny. "And you work at
Cyntech?"

Keegan nodded.

"Will Colfax's company?"

He nodded again.

"What do you do there?"

"I'm the finance director."

I thought back to the FBI agent we had met at the
boatyards. He had said they were investigating financial
irregularities at Will's company. Now it seemed they were
swooping in on the culprit. Michael Baggio stepped forward
into Keegan's line of sight.

"I think we should go," he said.

Keegan looked at him. "Go where?"

"Home. So we can figure out what to do." Michael glanced
at Lenny, then back at Keegan. "And I don't think you should
be answering any more questions."

"We're not the feds," said Lenny. "But I can assure you,
they will be watching Keegan's home. Or is it your home, too?"
he asked Michael.

"Yes, we live together," said Michael. "Roommates," he
added.

"Well, going home isn't the right move."

"What is the right move?" asked Keegan.

"What do you think the FBI is after?" asked Lenny.

Keegan threw his hands in the air. "I don't know!"

"Keegan, calm down. Breathe."

The guy seemed permanently set to one second from
panic.

"I'm calm. I think they are interested in the offshore accounts."

"They do like looking at those," said Lenny. "Where does the company have offshore accounts?"

"All over. Will liked to fly close to the wind, tax-wise. We had accounts in Hong Kong, Nassau, Caymans. Dubai."

"And you worked closely with Will?"

"Yes, I told you, I was his finance director."

Lenny looked at Michael. "And he just happened to ask you on board his boat?"

"What are you saying?" Michael stood erect. He was a fit-looking guy, a good percentage of muscle. "That we engineered for me to be on the boat to knock off Will so Keegan could get away with embezzlement?"

It was an excellent theory.

"What I think doesn't matter. But the FBI will certainly wander down that path."

"Oh, my gosh!" yelled Keegan, losing it all over again. The hands went into the air, the pitch went up toward the territory that only dogs can hear, and Lenny spent several minutes calming him back down.

"Okay, Keegan," said Lenny. "Does the company have insurance against this kind of theft?"

"Yes," he said, on the edge of hyperventilating. "But it isn't valid if the theft was committed by an officer of the company."

"And who are the officers?"

"Will, of course. His wife, Celia. And there are two non-executive board members based in New York, but they have nothing to do with the day-to-day."

"And that's it? You're not an officer of the company?"

"I am."

"Okay, Keegan, listen to me close now. This is what you need to do. You're going to have to give yourself up to the FBI."

"Are you crazy!"

"No, no, I'm not crazy," Lenny said, calmly.

"He's not doing that," said Michael.

"Yes, he is," Lenny said to Michael. "And I'll tell you why. The feds will find him. He can't go home, he can't use credit cards or an ATM. He can't see anyone he knows, family or friends. They will find him. So it's going to look better for him if he turns himself in."

I wasn't sure why Lenny had gone all good Samaritan suddenly, but I let him run with it.

"It's a setup," said Michael.

"That's what they all say," said Lenny. "But the guilty ones run."

"So he just walks into the FBI office with his hands up."

"No, don't do that. That will end up looking like an arrest. It needs to be documented that you are coming in of your own volition." Lenny looked at Keegan. "Do you have an attorney?"

Keegan nodded.

"Not a company attorney, one of your own."

He nodded again.

"Who is it?"

"Curruthers Partners. Here in Palm Beach."

"Okay. You are going to go to them now. Tell them what is happening. Have them contact the FBI to arrange a time and place for your surrender. Doing it that way means it will have to be documented. You understand?"

Keegan nodded.

"You understand?" Lenny said to Michael.

"Yes." He didn't look happy but the logic of it seemed to hit home.

"All right, you should go now."

"I can't do jail time," said Keegan. Every man and his dog could see that was the truth.

"It's a white-collar crime," said Lenny. "Most likely you will have to surrender your passport and make bail, but it's unlikely you'll be held until trial."

Keegan nodded. He had gone pale, and I wasn't sure he had done all the flipping out he was capable of, but he and Michael strode back to the office, and climbed into a red Lexus convertible. They didn't say goodbye as they screamed out of the lot.

I watched them go and then looked at Lenny. "You think they'll do it?"

"I do."

"You think he embezzled from Will?"

"No idea."

"He seemed pretty shocked."

"Yeah, the shock was real enough. But was it the shock of being accused of something he didn't do, or the shock of getting caught?"

"Which do you think?"

"Don't care," said Lenny. He turned and walked toward his truck. "Either way, Ron just got some serious reasonable doubt."

"Michael?"

"The FBI thinks Keegan embezzled money from Will's company. They think it enough to issue an arrest warrant. Will gets wind of it. To cover it up, Michael gets on board and pushes Will off."

"It's thin," I said.

"So is what the SA has on Ron. We just have to discredit his story, not prove this one."

"You think we're done?"

Lenny frowned and ran his hand through his hair. "I don't want to assume that. Ron's fate might depend on it."

"So what do we do?"

"I'm going to go see Allen, tell him about this embezzlement business. You need to check the final box. The last crew member."

# CHAPTER TWENTY

**The last box** to be checked ran a prestige car lot in Palm Beach Gardens. Lenny dropped me home and headed back downtown to see Allen, while I took my bike and headed north to chat with Alec Meechan. I parked the bike in the driveway and hung the helmet on the handlebars, and then pulled on a Patriots cap. The lot was full of low-slung speed machines. If you were in the market for a staid luxury sedan, this was not your place. Ferraris, Maseratis, Lamborghinis. A lot of testosterone waiting to tear up the pavement. I was looking at a red Ferrari when a preppy-looking dude sauntered out toward me. He didn't know it, but he was a caricature of himself. He wore pressed trousers and a double-collared polo, with one of the collars popped. But the kicker was the sweater he had knotted around his shoulders. It had to be ninety degrees in the shade.

"Chick magnet, my man," he called as he approached. "They'll be all over you with this baby."

He flashed a winning smile that complemented his perfect thick hair. He had chiseled features, and if he were wearing a kerchief around his neck I would have sworn he was Fred from the Scooby Doo cartoons I watched as a kid. He didn't offer a handshake. I recalled what Ron had said, that he liked to one-up everyone, never liked to give a straight answer, so I decided not to ask any straight questions.

"This car was made for you, brother," he said, slapping my back.

"It's very Magnum PI." I smiled. I could be Magnum PI. Except for the fact that I didn't have dark hair or a mustache, and my look was more Huey Lewis than Tom Selleck.

"What's Magnum PI?" he said.

I raised an eyebrow and wondered if the world was going to hell in a handbasket.

"You the owner here?" I asked.

"You better believe it," he said, finally offering his hand. "Alec Meechan."

"Miami Jones."

"Miami Jones." He smiled. "Miami, like Indiana."

"No," I said. "Miami is nothing like Indiana."

"No, I meant—"

"Don't hurt yourself, pal," I said. "Tell me about this car."

So he did. He rattled off top speeds and cubic inches of displacement and trim quality. I walked around the car like I had the cash in my pocket to drive her off the lot.

"So, enough chitchat," said Alec. "You need to take her for a spin."

That was true. I really did. I had ridden a bike for too long. I was sick of having to wear jeans that stuck to me like spray paint just to go out and get some milk. I was tired of having to borrow Ron's Camry for stakeouts. It was time to step up and get a car. And test-driving a Ferrari was as good a way to delay that event as any.

Alec backed the thing out of the lot like it was on fire, and slid over into the passenger seat. I dropped down, a long way down, into the car. It felt like a go-cart.

He smiled. "She's got serious grunt, so watch out."

I checked the mirrors and realized that the Ferrari was a stick shift. That made things interesting. I popped the gear into first, and then slowly pulled out, easing the clutch and praying that I didn't stall. I would have liked to have asked Alec Meechan some questions as we drove, but I was so fixated on making the gear changes and not crashing a quarter-million-dollar car, that I couldn't string two words together. Fortunately Alec suggested we get onto the turnpike and see what the car could really do, so I pulled north and I tightened the cap on my head, dropped the transmission into sixth gear and the little red car took off like a ballistic missile. Once I was at a steady speed, I relaxed a little.

"Feels good, huh?" Alec shouted above the wind whipping around us.

I nodded. "So I heard you were a sailor."

He did a bit of a double take, and then nodded. "Yeah, I sail. Down at the PBYC. You?"

"A bit."

"You own a yacht?"

This was a leading question. To answer yes, meant I probably had the resources to buy the car.

"A Beneteau. Oceanis 523."

He nodded again. "Nice."

"Didn't you do the Palm Beach-Nassau in one of those?"

Now he frowned. "How do you know that?"

"I do my research."

"You do, huh?"

"Wasn't that the boat that the skipper got lost on?"

"That's right."

"Lost at sea. That's gotta suck."

"I wouldn't know." He motioned for the next exit. "Let's get off here."

I did as I was told and pulled into the right lane to get off the turnpike.

"Word at the club was that you were supposed to be on watch when the guy went overboard?"

"Who says that?"

"Just the word about."

"That's baloney, man."

"Really? I heard you relieved the navigator, Drew Keck, wasn't it?"

Alec looked me up and down. "You know a lot."

"I keep my ears open. So is that true?"

"What difference does it make?"

"I like to know who I'm doing business with."

"Yeah?"

I glanced out of the corner of my eye and noticed him making an assessment. Was I worth the potential sale or not?

"Well, your sources need to get their facts straight, friend," he said. "I did relieve Drew, that's true. He'd been on watch all the way across the banks. There's lots of stuff to run aground on out there, you know? So I said I'd take his turn when it got dark."

"Makes sense. But you didn't do it?"

"Nah. The skipper, Will Colfax. You ever meet him?"

"Once or twice."

"So you know he's a bit of player, right? He's an older dude, but he likes to think he's got the moves. So he's putting the style on this chick on board, right?"

"Felicity Havill?"

"Yeah, you know her?"

"Cutie."

"Yeah, she's okay, if you like that sort of thing. But old Will thinks he got the stuff, right?"

"You weren't interested in Felicity yourself? Come on," I said, shaking my head.

"Nah, man. I mean I could do that. I coulda had her, sure. But it's Will's boat, you know? So I cut the old guy a break. Let him have his shot."

"So you didn't go up on deck because Will was up there with Felicity."

"You got it. Just giving the dude his space. So I waited in the galley. And what with the race and all, I was tired, I must have just fallen asleep."

"Wasn't there another girl on board?"

"Amy, yeah."

"You have a shot at her?"

"I coulda, but Hispanic chicks aren't my type, you know what I mean?"

"I've seen her around—she's attractive."

"You think? I don't know. She's hard work. I tell ya, she didn't like Felicity none."

"Why not?"

"Cause Will put the moves on Felicity. Girls get their noses out of joint over stuff like that."

"She was upset that Will chose Felicity over her?"

"Nah, man. She was upset because Felicity chose Will over her." He raised his eyebrows and nodded.

I got off the turnpike, then wound back onto I-95 and cruised around the speed limit back to Palm Beach Gardens.

"It's a bad business, anyway," I said. "You think it was an accident, or did someone shove him off the boat?"

"My guess is he sent Felicity down to his cabin for a little R 'n' R, you know, and while he was setting up the autopilot he was drinking too much and fell off."

"You know about autopilots?"

"I know what I'm doing on a boat."

"It's a grim way to go, lost out at sea."

"Yeah, that's for sure. That's why you gotta pay attention. Drinking out at sea is for fools, man."

I pulled back into the lot and stopped the car.

"So what do you think? Hot ride or what?"

"It goes nice," I said. That was the understatement of the year. It was like driving a bullet, just with better handling.

"So, shall I get some paperwork together?"

I got out and closed the door. "Tell you what, give me a day to think on it."

"This is one hot item, man. I can't guarantee it'll still be here tomorrow."

"That goes for all of us," I said, picking up my helmet.

Alec frowned like he had no idea what I was talking about, which was fine, because I wasn't a hundred percent sure myself.

"That's your ride?" he said with a look at my bike like he just caught me cheating at poker.

"Just borrowed it from the shop," I said, which wasn't a complete lie. I pulled the helmet on and revved up the bike, and I saw Alec's mouth move, but I couldn't hear him. So I waved and rode away.

# CHAPTER TWENTY—ONE

**Lizzy sent me** a text to say Lenny was at the new office, and when I arrived I left the bike in the shadow of the building and headed upstairs. Movers were hauling file boxes into the new space, and Lizzy was directing traffic, telling each where to deposit their load. A tradesman was measuring up the new wall that separated the two interior offices, preparing to install the drywall. Lenny sat at his desk, looking through a pile of boxes. The sofa was yet to make it in, so I sat on the edge of his desk.

"You talk to Allen?" I asked.

Lenny nodded. "I did. He thinks the Keegan thing muddies the water well and truly. He plans to ask for a hearing in chambers."

"How does that work?"

"He sends a brief to the judge, outlining the basis, and if the judge thinks it sufficient, he'll call in the state attorney for a chat in his chambers. Based on that he'll set a hearing, or maybe knock it out straightaway."

"Sounds long-winded."

"Allen says it can happen quickly, like all in a day, but the unknown is the FBI. The judge will want to verify the arrest warrant on Keegan, so that may take time to do. And he might want to speak to the FBI agents about their basis for the warrant. But he thinks it's a matter of when, unless the state comes up with something new."

"Like what?"

"I mentioned Special Agent Moss had told us there was some physical evidence found. He was curious about that."

"So we wait and see?"

"We do. What did you find?"

I told him about my discussion with Alec Meechan.

"So do you think he and Will were competing for the affections of the same ladies?" asked Lenny.

"Possible. He acts like the big man on campus. I don't see him doing the so-called honorable thing and stepping away from Felicity just because it was Will's boat."

"So-called honorable, you got that right."

"There's also Amy. Drew Keck said he thought she liked the ladies, and Alec backed that idea up."

"That's always interesting."

"Question is, do we have enough to get Ron out?"

"Allen thinks probably, but I don't want to leave Ron's freedom to probably. Let's not muddy the water—let's serve up a few of those alternative hypotheses on a platter."

"So what have we got? Michael Baggio pushes Will overboard because he's onto the roommate committing embezzlement."

"Or they were in it together," added Lenny.

"Right. Then there's Amy, who might have been keen on Will or Felicity, but either way was rebuffed."

"Thin, but muddy."

"Drew Keck had some kind of deal going with Will, which he denies but everyone else confirms. Maybe the deal goes south?"

Lenny frowned. "I'd like to know more about that."

"Right. Then there's Alec, who may have been in competition for Felicity's affection, but got beaten by the richer man."

"That always hurts."

"And there's the ex-wife, who has the houses, but what will she do for cash? The life insurance won't pay out without a body, not for years at least. And what was Drew Keck doing at her house if she didn't like the yachtie types?"

"Well, she wasn't on the boat, but any link to Drew makes her interesting," said Lenny.

"And I've been wondering, why did she tell the police about Mandy? There was no suspicion of her having done anything wrong—the sheriff was there to inform her that Will was lost at sea. And she said herself she was okay with Will's so-called dalliances, so why did she feel the need to point them in the direction of Mandy? To incriminate Ron somehow?"

"That's an interesting theory, but as likely as not, it's nothing more than coincidence."

"Isn't that exactly what we're trying to do? Make coincidence look like more than it is?"

"True enough."

Lizzy tapped on the frame of the wall and came in carrying a box wrapped in brown packing paper.

"Hand delivery for Miami," she said, handing me the box.

"We haven't even moved in yet," said Lenny.

"I must be ahead of my time." I looked at the box and saw no return address and no postage stamps or courier barcodes. As a rule I don't get many hand-delivered boxes, but if I did I wouldn't open them in public, so I put the package on Lenny's desk.

"I'm going to get office supplies," said Lizzy. "Do you need anything?"

"Ron?" Lenny gave her a solemn smile.

"Have faith. The Lord will look after Ron."

"Can he tell us what happened to Will Colfax?" I asked. The question earned me a look that would have turned a lesser man to stone.

"I'll be back," she said to Lenny.

"Me too," said Lenny.

"Where you going?" I asked.

"See Allen again. I want to update him. And see if he's heard anything more."

"Okay. I guess I'll stay here." So I did. I sat down in Lenny's chair and flicked my feet up onto the desk, and I watched the tradesman lift some drywall up and screw it into place. He did two sections, and then he stopped. Half the wall remained open on one side. He turned to me.

"Gonna need some more drywall."

"So it seems."

"Got some in my truck."

"Excellent."

I wasn't sure if he was aiming to get me to volunteer to go get it for him, or if he was just a master of stating the plainly obvious. He nodded like he'd come to a definitive decision, and he ambled out of the office. I watched him go, and then I looked around the room. It was much nicer than the old office, and closer to Longboards, which was a huge plus. Being across from the courthouse probably wouldn't hurt business either. And despite Lenny and me doing most of the boring, dirty work, it was all really possible because of Ron. It was his contacts in banking and insurance that were bringing in the corporate dollars, and it was Ron who did most of that corporate work. So it felt all wrong to be starting here without him. Beyond my feet I noticed the package Lizzy had brought in, and glancing around at the empty office, I picked it up.

It wasn't ticking, so I felt safe enough. I undid the paper and tossed it aside. Inside was a wooden box. It had no markings, just brass hinges. I opened the box up. Inside was something wrapped in a soft cloth. I looked around the office again like some kind of secret agent, and then unfolded the cloth, revealing a Glock handgun, an exact copy of the one I had held in Sally Mondavi's store. There was no note, and no ammunition. Just the gun, and a single magazine. I picked the gun up and felt its cold weight in my hand. I noted that the weapon had scuff marks on the frame, the side of the barrel and on the slide under the ejection port. Serial numbers long gone. It didn't make me feel better to have a gun in my hand, let alone an unregistered and unlawful one. I always considered myself to be on the side of the good guys, and this didn't feel like the actions of a good guy. But Lenny was a good guy, and Lucas was a good guy, and I trusted their opinions that this was an item of last resort, one worth having if I was going to continue spending time on the seedy side of the tracks.

The question that plastered itself all over my mind was where to put the darn thing. I didn't feel good about taking it to my apartment, and I certainly wasn't leaving it in a filing cabinet in the office. I knew Lenny didn't carry on a regular basis, but I didn't know where he kept his weapons, and my registered gun, the Ruger, remained in the custody of the shooting range. But they weren't going to hold a gun with the serial numbers removed, so I had to find a plan B. Then I saw it. I was staring at half a wall. The framing was in place, as was the drywall on the outer side. But in Lenny's office only half had been finished. I stood and looked at the space. There was enough room to place the box on the framing so the box would be hidden inside the wall once the drywall was put in place. The trick was getting the drywall up before the tradesman noticed what was behind it.

I wrapped the gun up and packed it back into the box, then put the box onto the wood frame on the floor, right up against the stud. I finished just as I heard a grunt at the front door. I stepped through into the outer office and found the tradesman carrying a couple sheets of drywall. He was straining to the point of turning purple.

"Can I help?" I asked, grabbing one end of the sheets.

"Couple of minutes ago wouldn't have hurt," he huffed. I ignored the barb, instead pulling the sheets into the doorway between the two offices. We picked up one of the sheets, and I took the side that would end up near my hidden box, and I directed the sheet of drywall up and into place. I held it there as the guy grabbed his drill and screwed the drywall into the studs. I helped the guy place the next sheet, and as we finished Lizzy came back into the office. She was sorting things on her desk and paid us no mind. I didn't fancy another stint of sitting behind Lenny's desk staring at the walls under construction, so I told Lizzy I was heading out, and she told me not to drink too much. I wanted to take offense but couldn't find any basis for it, so I just kept going. I ran into Lenny in the stairwell.

"You headed out?" he asked.

"At a loose end. Any news?"

"Yeah. The judge has asked Allen to meet with the SA in the judge's chambers first thing tomorrow, before the arraignment."

"That's good, right?"

"It is, it is."

"So Ron could be out tomorrow."

Lenny nodded and grinned sheepishly.

"What aren't you telling me?" I hated it when Lenny held back the punchline.

"The SA will have a sheriff's detective there to present the *fruits of the investigation*, is what Allen called it. He's big on fruit metaphors."

"He is. Maybe it's a lawyer thing. But what does that mean?"

"Allan said the judge might want to hear from the defense investigators."

"Meaning us?"

"Meaning you."

"Why me?"

Lenny winced, and it was most unlike him. He was always so confident in himself, in his opinions, even when he was stone-cold wrong. Now he looked like a choir boy who had been caught sneaking a sip of the altar wine.

"Lenny?"

He shrugged. "I have some history with the judge."

"History?"

"You've heard the one about the boy from the wrong side of the tracks and the judge's daughter?"

"Lenny, Lenny, Lenny."

"Yeah. What can I tell ya?" The mischievous smile widened.

"When was this?"

"About ten years ago."

"I take it you don't think he'll have forgotten."

"He might have forgotten the first time, but I doubt he's forgotten the second."

I shook my head. "How old was his daughter?"

"At the time, about thirty."

"So a grown woman? What's the judge's problem?"

"He had many, but I recall the first time his main issue was that it was the night of her engagement party."

I stifled a laugh. "And the second time?"

"It was the night before her wedding."

"That's classy."

"Not my finest hour."

"What happened to the marriage?"

"They're still together, far as I know."

"That's impressive. The groom must have really loved her, to forgive that. Twice."

"He doesn't know. The judge said he'd bury me except under two conditions. Never mention this to anyone, and you'll take it to your grave, won't you?"

"I will."

"And secondly, never set foot in his courtroom."

"Aha." The punchline. "So I'm flying solo tomorrow."

"You are. You might not get called in to the meeting, but then if it doesn't go well, you might get called into the arraignment. Or not."

"Okay. And if he asks where I work?"

"Right here. At your firm. LCI."

"But it's not my firm. Isn't that perjury?"

"Not really. I've been meaning to tell you, but with the move and all. I want to make you a partner."

It was a hell of a revelation to get in the stairwell, and my jaw dropped like a busted elevator.

"Lenny, you can't do that."

"I already did. You just have to sign the papers."

I looked at him. He was disheveled at the best of times, a mass of flowing rust-colored hair that had a mind of its own, and an easy manner that belied the eyes of someone who had seen and done things that would keep most folks awake at night for the rest of their lives. He was the kind of guy my mother would have called *the wrong sort of friend*, but after I lost her and later my father, and then nearly lost myself in the process, he was the best kind of friend a guy could ever have. You don't count the worth of a man by the cut of his suit, but by whether he'd give you the shirt off his back. Lenny had done that, quite literally. I hadn't always worn palm tree print shirts.

I thought about hugging him, then thought against it, then I stopped thinking and wrapped my arms around the big bear of man. He didn't recoil, he didn't move. He just reciprocated, and I felt his huge meaty paws land on the middle of my back. We hugged for longer than was necessary, and then we pulled away. Lenny had moisture in his eyes, as did I.

"I don't know what to say."

"Yeah, you do." Lenny nodded.

"Thanks."

"There you go."

"So," I said.

He smiled. "So. Longboard Kelly's, I think."

I couldn't have agreed more.

# CHAPTER TWENTY—TWO

**The next morning** I sat in the corridor outside the courtroom in my wedding suit. I'd never been married myself, never come close, but I had been to a few, and Lenny had recommended getting a decent suit for such occasions, rather than renting some other man's clothes. I had never worked in an office, so I had never worn such a thing to work. I did have what we called traveling clothes in the major leagues, a blazer and pressed trousers, but Lenny felt the Oakland A's logo was not really wedding attire. After attending a couple weddings, I had to disagree. The A's gear often started conversations, which were in short supply at the weddings I had sampled. Of course, those conversations usually ended up at the place where I was on the Oakland roster for twenty-nine days but never played an actual game, and was then sent back to the minors, never to see a major league park again, and that little tidbit usually shut people up quicker than a clam in ice water.

I never felt comfortable in suits. They were supposed to give one a sense of power—the well-dressed man—but I always found a well-drilled fastball was more of a rush. And in Florida, where I could feel the humidity rise from the collar of my shirt, they were borderline ludicrous. But Allen had donned a pinstripe and the state attorney, Eric Edwards, always seemed to be in a well-tailored suit. That man didn't seem to sweat. Same went for Detective Ronzoni, who despite having nothing to do with the case, was lingering in the halls in his wrinkled Sears special. Unlike Edwards, Ronzoni literally didn't sweat. The word out of the station house was that he didn't have sweat glands or something. He just couldn't produce the stuff. Which sounded ideal in Florida, where I could go through a selection of shirts just wandering around a golf course, but in reality was like a car with no radiator. He ran the real risk of overheating, so he always seemed to have a bottle of water in his hand.

I was sitting on my own section of polished wood, avoiding Ronzoni and practicing my lines, when Deputy Danielle Castle wandered by. I wasn't sure if she was appearing in court or not, but she was in full uniform. She slowed as she passed, looking at me as if she couldn't quite place me, and then she stopped and smiled.

"Look at you."

I nodded. "Weddings, funerals and court appearances."

She looked me over, not bothering to be furtive in the least. Law enforcement types do that. They looked you all over and make no bones about it, as if we're all carrying weapons or illegal something-or-others. Given their business, they probably found something as often as not, but Deputy Castle's eyes didn't seem to be searching for guns or drugs on my person. If I had to guess, and I wished I didn't, I would have guessed that she was undressing me with her eyes. But that might have been the suit talking.

"You look uncomfortable," she said.

I nodded.

"You here for Ron?"

I nodded again.

She smiled again. "You'll do great."

I believed her. On the back of that smile, I would have believed anything.

"See you later," she said as she marched away down the hall. I watched her go and hoped I hadn't lost the power of speech.

As it was, a bailiff came into the hall and called my name, and then asked me to follow him to the judge's chambers. It was a grandiose title, *chambers*, because it was really just an office, and not a very neat one at that. And it was surprisingly small. The judge was behind a messy desk, and I stood shoulder to shoulder with Allen, Edwards and Sheriff's Detective Moscow. Perhaps the judge had a bigger office in the main courthouse.

"So you are Mr. Jones?" said the judge.

"Yes, sir."

"And you are the investigator for the defendant?"

"Yes, sir."

"You licensed in that capacity?"

"Yes, sir."

"And you work for?"

"I'm a partner at LCI. Our offices are in the court precinct." Now I was doing it. *Our offices.* We only had one. But if this room was *chambers*, then anything was fair game.

"All right, Mr. Jones. The purpose of this meeting is to ascertain if there are grounds for arraignment of Mr. Bennett." I noted, belatedly, that Ron was not in the room. "The state attorney here has provided his grounds, which quite frankly, are pretty thin."

I glanced sideways at Edwards. He didn't shift his feet, he didn't clench his jaw. He was a cool customer.

"You can focus on me, if you like, Mr. Jones," said the judge.

I snapped back to the judge. "Yes, sir."

"And for future reference, since I can tell by your suit that you are new here, *sir* is just fine in my chambers, but in my courtroom, should you appear there later today, I prefer *your honor.*"

"Of course, your honor." Can I get you three bags full with that? I was all for process and fairness in our judicial system, but when these elected officials started acting like Marie Antoinette, I started to lose my form. Perhaps I should refer to him as my servant, since my tax dollars paid his damned salary. I was going off the deep end in my mind, and tried to pull it back. I had to suck it up and take one for the team. Take one for Ron.

"So, Mr. Jones. Mr. Allen suggests you have evidence of alternate hypotheses for events. Can you elaborate?"

There was that phrase again. So it wasn't just Allen. The whole legal profession was wrapped up in pompous phrases about hypotheses and fruit.

"Yes, your honor. I have interviewed all the crew and found that every single one of them has a motive that matches or exceeds that of Ron Bennett."

"Mr. Jones, leave the determination of whose motive exceeds whose to me and the jury, should one be appointed. Just tell me what you found."

So I told him. I told him about Felicity and Will, about Amy getting rebuffed by Will or Felicity, about Drew having a deal with Will that had gone south, and about Alec soliciting the attentions of Felicity but losing out to Will. I didn't have any proof of any of it, but Allen had said to muddy the waters, so that is what I did. Allen told me to leave the best to last. Get the judge thinking that anything could have happened, and then serve up one with some basis to it. So I left Michael Baggio to last. I told the judge that I spoke to the FBI, that embezzlement charges had been laid against Michael's roommate, Keegan. That Keegan had come to Michael prior to the arrest, and that my firm had advised them to turn themselves into the FBI. As instructed I left Lenny well and truly out of it. When I finished, the judge put on his reading glasses, and then looked at me over the top of them.

"Thank you, Mr. Jones. You could have led with that last part and saved us all five minutes that we'll never get back." *Score one, Judge.* "Nevertheless, Mr. Edwards, I think Mr. Jones has you trumped. Five motives to one, wouldn't you say?"

"Your honor, as I mentioned, we now have physical evidence as well."

"Mr. Edwards, you and I both know you are fishing. I gave you some line before, but I told you I would require more to arraign the accused. Your physical evidence suggests the possibility, even the probability of foul play, but it does in no way suggest that the accused was responsible. You yourself said there were no fingerprints on the alleged weapon."

"Your honor, we believe—"

"Mr. Edwards, you are better than that. You know I don't care what you believe. I care about what you can prove. And right now, I am doing you a big favor. If we were to go into my courtroom and you were to present what you have, Mr. Allen would move for dismissal, and although I rarely consider dismissal at arraignment, I would not only be forced to consider it, I would be forced to act on it. And I would do so with prejudice, Mr. Edwards. You do know what that means, Mr. Edwards."

"Of course, your honor."

"And it means?"

"It means we could not bring the same charges against the defendant if we later get further evidence."

"See, Mr. Edwards. I knew you were good at this. So this is what I am going to do. I am not going to grant Mr. Allen's motion for dismissal."

I couldn't believe what I was hearing. I'd nailed the case shut like Perry Mason, and the judge wasn't going to let Ron out? I tensed and looked down the parade line, and it seemed I was the only one who was shocked. Edwards looked duly berated. Detective Moscow looked duly bored. And Allen had the merest hint of a smile on his face.

"Instead, what *you* are going to do," continued the judge, "is drop the charges. You are going to let Mr. Bennett go free. And you are going to continue your investigation as you see fit, but you are not going to come back to me until you have something firmly resembling an open-and-shut case. Do I make myself clear?"

"Yes, your honor." Edwards was calm but the color was rising in his cheeks.

"Mr. Allen, what say you."

"Nothing, your honor."

"Good answer." The judge looked at me, but asked me nothing. He banged his hand on the desk like it was a gavel and stood. We were all already standing, so we didn't move.

"You'll take care of Mr. Bennett's release?" The judge looked over his glasses at Moscow.

"Immediately, your honor."

The judge nodded. "Then we all have work to do."

Allen gave me a nod like we were done and it was time to leave, and since no one could get by me to reach the door, I turned and went first. I was opening it when I heard the judge speak.

"Really, Eric. This is not like you."

"Sorry, your honor."

"I've come to expect watertight cases from you. What's got you so off your game on this one?"

"Nothing, your honor. A bad day at the office."

"Let's not have another."

"Agreed," I heard Edwards say, and then I walked out into the hallway and the conversation was lost on me. I got into the hall and stopped. Allen took a deep breath and smiled.

"Thanks," I said. "You did it."

"No, you did it. And well done on biting your tongue. The judge is well known for baiting newbies into saying stupid things. You did well."

"For Ron."

Allen looked over my shoulder. "Hmmm."

I turned to see Deputy Castle standing there. The coincidences were piling up.

"How'd it go?" she asked.

"Ron's getting out," I said.

She smiled. "Great, I'm glad." She stepped forward and put her hand on my shoulder. "Really great." Her hand rested there for a moment, and it sucked the speech from me. Then she leaned in. "Can you wait for a moment?" She didn't stop for a response, spinning on her heel like a Marine on parade and striding over to Detective Moscow, who looked completely nonplussed by events. Then my view was ruined by the string bean suit of State Attorney Edwards.

"Out does not mean forgotten," he said to me.

I stood tall but he was still taller. That doesn't happen often, so I pulled my shoulders back. I was almost twice as wide as him. "What is your problem? You know Ron didn't do anything. Michael Baggio has more motive that anyone."

"Baggio isn't a friend of yours." There was almost a snarl on his lips as he said it, but he stayed serial killer cool.

I gave him an eyeful of frown. I couldn't believe what I was hearing. "What the hell are you talking about?"

Edwards looked toward where Detective Moscow and Deputy Castle stood talking, and then he refocused on me.

"What indeed," he said.

I had no idea what that meant. I had barely even heard of Edwards, but he sure seemed to have a bee in his bonnet about me. "Look pal, a buck gets you two that this thing was an accident. The guy was drinking."

"It was no accident. That we know. And next time you won't get so lucky."

Edwards didn't wait for a reply. He stormed away, long strides and a bouncy gait making him look like he was on stilts. He may have been marathon runner thin, but he was no runner. I turned to Allen.

"What was that?"

"You made a friend," he said, poker-faced.

"What did he mean, they know it wasn't an accident?"

"Physical evidence."

"The FBI guy mentioned something about that. They found something under blue light?"

Allen nodded. "Blood, on the deck, and on the base of the mast."

"Whose blood?"

"Will Colfax's."

"So couldn't he have bumped his head and fallen off?"

"The blood is in the middle of the boat. The sea wasn't that rough. They think he couldn't have fallen overboard from that position."

"You ever had a head knock? Concussion?"

Allen shook his head.

"I have. It can make you spinny, unstable. Not hard to see a guy get up, maybe using the mast, then stagger and trip."

"There's more."

"What more?"

"Cerebrospinal fluid, it's the stuff that surrounds your brain and spinal column, acts as a cushion. It was found on a winch handle."

"That was the weapon the judge mentioned?"

Allen nodded.

"What does that mean?"

"It means his head was probably cracked open, via blunt force trauma."

"Brain fluid?" I'd never had that come out of me. "So could you get up from that?"

"I have no idea, Miami. That's something the defense would have to figure out."

"Where was this winch handle?"

"If I recall," said Allen, "in a pocket in the cockpit. I don't know what that means. I don't sail."

"So is Ron off the hook or not?"

"For now, yes. And Edwards lost some credibility today. He'll need more to get past the judge now."

"The guy seems so buttoned up. How did Ron—how did *I* get him so rattled?"

Allen looked beyond me and shrugged. "I think the winch handle shows it wasn't an accident and he was going after the most obvious option—the one he already had in jail. As for you?" Allen looked past me, nodded and said, "I've got to get going."

He walked away and I watched him go, then I noticed Deputy Castle behind me again, and I wondered how she kept doing that.

"Hi," she said.

"Hi. Crazy day."

"Sounds like it all went well."

"Except for a crazy prosecutor who seems to have it in for me."

"Don't mind him. He just gets a little zealous sometimes."

"You know him? Edwards?"

"Yeah, you could say."

"So what's going on?"

"I wanted to tell you. We found out something interesting about Michael Baggio and Keegan Murray."

"The roommates?"

"That's one way of putting it. They're married."

"Married? How does that work?"

"They were married in Boston in 2004."

"So they're . . ."

"Gay, yes. Does that bother you?"

"Me? Not in the slightest. Free country. But I didn't think they could get married."

"In Massachusetts, yes. Florida, no. That's why they probably kept it quiet. We're not quite so progressive down here."

"That's funny. I always thought we were. Live and let live, and all that."

"You'd think. And Key West is like gay paradise."

"Key West is just paradise, period. But it explains why Keegan came straight to Michael when he heard he was going to be arrested."

"It does."

"And it tightens them as suspects, doesn't it?"

"It does. And I asked around. Will was known as a bit of a passive-aggressive homophobe. Misogynist was another word I heard a bit."

"So he didn't like men and wasn't keen on women."

"Oh, he liked women. Just wasn't keen on their rights."

I nodded. "So you think Ron's out of the frame?"

"I do."

"Your prosecutor buddy doesn't seem to think so."

"He's not my buddy." She smiled, like this was amusing. "And the evidence doesn't point to Ron at all."

"Evidence is like baseball statistics," I said. "It can be whatever you want it to be."

"That's a lot of cynicism for a guy who just got his friend out of jail."

I nodded. "You're right. Sorry." I wasn't sure why, but I didn't want her to think me cynical. So what I didn't say was that I had just gotten my friend out of jail, but why the hell was he there in the first place?

"Look I have to go," she said. "But can I ask you a professional question?"

"Sure."

"You've spoken to all the crew. Do you think Michael Baggio did it?"

"With the FBI thing, and marriage. He's as likely as anyone."

"But what's your gut say?"

I thought it over for a second. I didn't want to give her a glib answer. Some people are worth a little thought.

"My gut's not sure. I didn't get a good vibe from Alec."

"Just because he's a slippery car salesman?"

"Maybe. But his story didn't sit right. Nothing more." I looked at her. "It's not much to go on."

"Moscow will look at everyone again. He's thorough like that."

Deputy Castle's attention was taken by something along the hallway. "I gotta go. Thanks." She smiled and turned away.

I smiled and watched her leave down the hall, where another deputy, a shorter guy, was waiting. I watched them walk around the corner. Then I looked at the people around me, some well-dressed, some just trying to be. Everybody moving somewhere. I watched the hubbub for a while, until I realized I was standing in the middle of the hallway in the court attached to the county lockup, with a stupid smile on my face. I shook my head and wandered outside to wait for Ron.

# CHAPTER TWENTY—THREE

**Ron looked like** he'd been in jail. He was out of the orange jumpsuit, which did wonders for his complexion, but he still looked terrible. He was gaunt, and he was a thin guy to begin with, besides his little beer belly. His clothes were wrinkled and his face was too, and the smile he wore when he came out suggested that he had reached the point where being kicked in the shins brought some semblance of joy, when the other option was being punched in the face.

I put my arm around his shoulder and gave him a pat. I didn't want to make too much of it, to move on as quickly as possible. I didn't know if that was likely, let alone the best course of action, but I was making it all up on the fly. I'd never been in jail. I'd spent time in interview rooms, sweating it out while investigators of one stripe or another turned the screws or played good cop/bad cop. But that wasn't the same thing, not by a long shot. Freedom was an assumption we all made, even if it was all smoke and mirrors. Politicians liked to do song and dance numbers about defending freedom, and on baseball fields around the country I'd sung about it more often than a kid in elementary school. But even in its illusory form, this freedom could be ripped from you at any time. Ron had done nothing wrong, and his had been stripped from him in an instant. And once stripped, I wondered if it was ever fully regained. A lot of guys at college and later in ball clubs ranted on about it, but my feeling was that if freedom meant the right to go where you wanted, when you wanted, and to do whatever you wanted without causing harm to others, then why was there a toll on the turnpike? And what happened if I didn't pay that toll? And this house that Sally was so keen for me to buy, that had property taxes attached to it. My personal property could be taxed for money I didn't earn from the property, and the property could be taken from me if I didn't pay it. That seemed the kind of freedom that wafted up the chimney pipe.

I tried to push such thoughts from my head as we got in Lenny's truck. Ron was out, and so was the sun, and Longboard Kelly's beckoned. If all was not right, it was a hell of a lot better than it had been that morning. Mick would have still been hosing down the courtyard at the bar so I headed for the office first. Lizzy practically jumped into Ron's arms, which was more animated than I'd seen her, but it brought a hopeful smile from Ron.

"I was praying for you," she said.

"And I thank you for it, my dear."

Lizzy let him go and her smile faded some, but she directed what she had left at me. "Good job," she said before she turned back to Ron. My day had been made.

Lenny ambled out of his office. The tradesman had finished and bar the smell of fresh paint, the office looked ready for work. He gave Ron a big hug, and slapped him on the back with a balled fist.

"Sorry I couldn't be there," he said.

"Miami explained." Ron looked at me. "But he did a great job."

"I never doubted it," said Lenny. "Come sit down."

Lenny's office furniture had been put in place. His desk remained where it was, but a small fridge and the sofa from the old office filled in the space. I took the visitor's chair by the desk, Ron took the sofa.

"Is it too early for a drink?" said Lenny.

"What time is it?" Ron said, looking at his watch. I realized he hadn't worn one for the past couple days. Then Ron shrugged. "On the inside, it's never five o'clock."

Lenny took a bottle of bourbon out of his desk drawer, cracked the seal and poured Ron a glass and handed it to him. Then he poured two more. I wasn't the biggest fan of bourbon, but that wasn't the point, and we saluted Ron's health and new beginnings.

"Place looks good," said Ron, glancing around the room.

"Not too bad, is it?" said Lenny, sipping his drink. "So, let's call this our first official staff meeting. We have no paying cases. How do we change that?"

"I have a few irons in fires," said Ron. "I'll try and rekindle them."

"Good," said Lenny.

"I'm working with a designer to build a website, get some search engine exposure," I said.

"I have no idea what that means, but also good," said Lenny. "That leaves us with unpaid cases."

Ron looked blank. "Being?"

"You," Lenny said.

"I'm out."

I shook my head. "Out, but in the words of the state attorney, not forgotten. We have to keep on it, make sure there's no chance that you end up back inside."

"Didn't we do that?" asked Ron.

"Only maybe," said Lenny. "Let's see where the feds take the Michael/Keegan thing, but be ready to move if it doesn't go our way."

"Plus we should keep our ears to the ground at the yacht club," I said.

"So that's that," Lenny said. "Meeting adjourned." He looked at Ron. "What would you like to do?"

"I'd like to sit at Longboards, and I'd like to take a shower by myself. Not necessarily in that order."

"I think we can accommodate that," I said. "I'll take you home. Pick you up later for a drink."

Ron nodded. "And I'd like to go see Mandy."

"Why?" asked Lenny.

"Just so she knows there's no hard feelings. I don't blame her for this."

"I don't think that's such a fabulous idea, pal," said Lenny. "The cops have her down as a witness, and though your intentions may be pure, I don't think they'd agree. We don't want to give them anything more than they've got."

Ron shrugged. "I don't feel good about her thinking I blame her."

I had to hand it to Ron—he really did look for the best in folks. He didn't feel used by Mandy—he just saw their marriage as a mistake she made, one that anyone could have chalked up. Gold digger wasn't in his vocabulary. But all the same, his dropping in on someone the state attorney might use as a witness against him didn't feel like the smartest move.

"Tell you what, Ron," I said. "I'll drop you home, and then I'll spin past her place and let her know you're out, and pass on your message."

Ron shrugged again like that was a passable if not preferable alternative. We stood and I took Lenny's keys from my pocket and waved them at him, and he nodded and sent us on our way. The sun was high in the sky by the time we headed out, and I stayed off the freeway so Ron could travel with the window down. He was like a superpowered Labrador that regained its energy by sticking its head out the window and taking in the cosmic rays of the sun. I swore his skin browned a shade or two on the drive to his apartment.

"You got your keys?" I asked as he got out, and he jangled them in the air. Then he stopped and looked at me as if he had something more to say.

"No, you don't," I said. "You don't owe anybody a damned thing, least of all me."

He smiled and nodded and headed for his apartment.

I stopped at the gatehouse for Mandy's community and the guard called her and then let me in. I pulled Lenny's truck to a stop a couple doors down from her house on Lake Mangonia and walked along the nice sidewalk. There were no other cars parked on the street, and I wondered if that was against community rules. Lenny's truck certainly didn't fit the ambiance they were going for, but I figured I wouldn't be there long enough for them to do anything about it. I noticed that Mandy's garage door was open and her car was inside. The garage was surgically clean. It wasn't a well-lived-in space, and certainly not used by a man, who would have filled it full of the crap that men seemed to collect: old tools and random cables and fishing tackle. There was nothing but her nice little Audi convertible. The top was down, and I noticed that the space that passed for the backseat was packed full of water bottles. Perhaps Mandy had taken up running along the lake and had done a bulk buy at Sam's Club. I tried to picture her pushing her cart around a warehouse store and the image wouldn't fully form in my mind.

I rang the doorbell and heard the slap of bare feet on tile, and Mandy opened the door. I could see what Ron saw in her.

She was still, or again, in yoga-type clothes, skintight black pants and a lime green top, and she was in great shape. She didn't carry an ounce of anything she didn't need, including cash. She was a credit card kind of gal. Her hair was tied up, and I could see a parallel with Felicity Havill. Felicity was still at an age where she wanted to play down her physical attributes; Mandy was the same woman having reached the age where she wanted to play every card she had. And she had more than most.

"Miami," she said, with a smile. "Unexpected."

"Yeah, was in the neighborhood."

"Well, come in, you look hot."

I thought she meant it was warm out, but I was still in my fancy suit so I couldn't be sure.

"Can I offer you a smoothie, some water?"

I thought about making a remark about the stash of $H_2O$ in her car, but didn't.

"No, I'm good. I just wanted to let you know, Ron's out of jail."

She spun her head to me, surprise etched across her face. Perhaps she really did have some semblance of feelings for the old dog.

"He is? Oh, Miami, that's great, really great." She stepped forward and hugged me, as if I were Ron's representative for news *and* physical contact. It was the real deal, and she crushed herself hard against me. I wasn't sure where to put my hands, so I touched them briefly on her shoulder blades, and then removed them, but she held on. After longer than was necessary she let me go, and stepped away.

"Is he okay?" she asked.

"As good as can be expected. He wanted me to pass on a message."

She frowned. "Really?"

I nodded. "He wanted you to know that he doesn't blame you. For talking to the cops, I mean. Or your relationship with Will Colfax." I wasn't completely sure on that last count, but it felt like the right thing to say. "He didn't want you thinking that he thought badly of you."

She dropped the frown and smiled.

"I've never thought badly of him. Not ever."

"I know." I didn't know that, and I didn't really believe it, but I was on a roll saying things I didn't actually believe.

"So, where is he? Why didn't he tell me this himself?"

"Lawyer's orders. The cops aren't through with their inquiries, so it's best he doesn't see you right now."

"Have they found another suspect?"

"Maybe. There's a guy who worked for Will—he's been charged by the FBI for fraud, embezzlement. The cops are looking at his partner for Will's death as well."

"Good."

"Not that good for him."

"No, not good for him. But Ron, I mean. Good for Ron."

I asked if she was okay and she said she was great, so I made to leave. As I turned, my eye caught briefly on a large mirror on the lounge room wall. It looked back toward an empty bedroom, the doors of which lay open but out of my direct view. I stepped to Mandy and gave her a goodbye hug. I didn't go quite as hard as she had, and she didn't either. Perhaps she thought I had read too much into the first one. But I held on long enough to look into the mirror and confirm that I had seen a brown Louis Vuitton duffel bag sitting by the open door. I could easily move into a new place and leave a bag on the floor, living out of it until everything was worn and in severe need of a laundry. But that wasn't Mandy. She would

have everything put away in the closets before she even
stocked the fridge.

I let her go and she gave me a cute little smile, and I told
her I'd see her later. Then I walked back to Lenny's truck and
took off. I wondered where Mandy could be going. Her former
husband was fresh out of jail and her former lover was in
Davy Jones's locker less than a week, but she was headed off
somewhere, and it didn't look like back to Mom's for a
shoulder to cry on. There was no doubt in my mind. The
pursuit of a life of leisure was hard work.

I drove through the gates of the community, and then
pulled into the parking lot of the Lakeshore Club condos to
wait. About thirty minutes later the little Audi zoomed through
the gates. Mandy had the top down, and was heavy on the gas.
The car sure was zippy, and I almost lost her in traffic, but I
noticed her pull up onto the freeway and was able to follow by
pushing through the red light. Her little car went like a bullet,
and the old truck labored to keep up. Slow and steady was its
mantra, and the hare nearly broke away. I was saved by traffic
just after Fort Lauderdale, and by the time we reached the
Miami Beach exit I was tucked in three vehicles back, with a
nice view from my high ride of the sleek Audi.

It was the perfect position to see the little red car zoom off
into the distance. Mandy didn't take the exit—she sped on
south toward downtown Miami as Lenny's truck gave a series
of knocking sounds, and then the pedal beneath my right foot
gave up and I looked madly around, my eyes settling on the
dashboard where the fuel gauge offered me a resounding red.
The truck lost all momentum and I drifted to a stop on the
side of I-95 as Mandy Bennett sped away, ever southward.

# CHAPTER TWENTY—FOUR

**The following day** dawned another bright one, a hot breeze
easing across the state, swirling around so it hit us from the
northwest. Ron and I spent the day arranging our shared
office. There was only room for one desk and piles of boxes,
so we arranged the boxes along a wall, and then changed our
minds and put them all on the desk, so there was room to
move around the desk, but no room to work.

Lenny had laughed himself hoarse when I had told him
about running out of gas on the freeway while following
Mandy, and he suggested that I keep the Mandy thing to
myself, lest it set Ron on a train of thought we wanted him to
avoid right now.

Ron started making calls to drum up some business, so I
played lunch boy and wandered down Clematis Street and
returned with hoagie rolls and sodas for everyone. I even
remembered to get whole wheat for Lizzy, which earned me
the raised eyebrow of admiration. Or was it shock?

By late afternoon Ron had finished his calls and I was at a
loose end. Lenny had gone, as he called it, to see a man about a
dog. It was a phrase he had picked up from Lucas, and like
most *Lucasisms*, it made no sense to me whatsoever. Ron leaned

back in his chair and ran his finger over his wall calendar, tapped it twice, and then looked at me.

"There's a twilight race on at the yacht club this afternoon," he said.

"Aha."

"Do you think it's too early to go? Or should I keep a low profile?"

"I think you should get on with your life. You wanna sail, sail."

That brought a smile from him. "Care for a walk?"

I didn't care for a walk. It was hot out. But I went anyway. Partly to support Ron as he rejoined his group after being accused of killing one of them, and partly because I was just curious to see how they responded to him. We left Lizzy in the cool office and headed out into the hot sunshine. It was only a tick over a half mile from our office to the yacht club, but I was melting by the time we reached the docks. The water was right there, looking all sparkling and inviting, but the breeze was coming from the other direction, making even the docks swelter.

There were more people around than I suspected there would be. Ron got a lot of looks, but he also got a lot of hugs and handshakes. The general consensus was that if the state attorney for the 15th Judicial Circuit thought Ron capable of murder, then the state attorney was barking wildly at the wrong tree.

Felicity Havill made a beeline along the dock toward Ron with tears forming in her eyes, and practically jumped into his arms. They hugged each other, and then she pulled back and ran her hand across his cheek.

"I'm so glad you're back," she said.

"That makes two of us."

"It must have been awful."

"Like you say, I'm back. Now I just need a boat to sail on."

"You'll come with me. I'm on *Off Your Rocker*. Jim and Denise would love to have you onboard."

"Just let me stop in the office and say hi," said Ron, and he stepped away. Felicity was about to bounce back along the dock when she noticed me.

"Hi," she said. She looked good in a blue polo shirt and matching shorts. The heat didn't seem to affect her, even if she was from Montana.

"Felicity," I said.

"You must be glad Ron's out of trouble." She smiled.

"Out of jail, not out of trouble."

"What do you mean?"

"The state attorney reserved the right to lay charges at a later time. They're still looking at Ron."

"That's crazy. Ron didn't have anything against Will."

I shrugged. "Except that Will was sleeping with Ron's ex-wife."

I watched the air in Felicity deflate some.

"What about you?" I asked.

"Me?"

"And Will?"

"What do you mean?"

"You were sleeping with him, too."

She pinched her eyebrows together. She was going to rule the roost over some guy one day, because her angry face was drop-dead gorgeous.

"Excuse me?" was the best she could come up with.

I didn't feel good about bringing it up, and I felt even worse about having a beautiful woman hate me, which is exactly what Felicity would do after this conversation. But I brought it up anyway, and I really didn't know why. Ron was out, there were other suspects. Maybe I just didn't like people lying to me. Or maybe I expected them to lie, and didn't give a damn if they did, but still wanted to know what they were hiding.

"You had an affair with Will."

"Listen, I don't know where you heard that—"

"Here," I interrupted. "It seemed to be common knowledge among your crewmates."

The air was sucked from her a little more. I could see she wanted to fight it, to deny it, maybe even go back and make it not so. But life ain't like that. Once the pitch is thrown, it's either a hit, or it's not a hit. There is no do-over.

"Look, I'm not proud of it, okay."

"I know."

"How do you know?" She pinched her eyebrows together again. It was really something.

"I know because you lied about it. You're a smart girl—you know that on a small boat like that, everyone knows everything. There are no secrets. But you lied anyway. Because the whole thing gives you a bad feeling inside."

She lost the frown and nodded. "It was just in Nassau. Just a race thing. Just one time."

I nodded but said nothing.

"He was a charming sort of guy. And we'd spent this time close together, and a few drinks, you know?"

I nodded again.

"I knew he was married, but . . . Well, you know what they say."

"What?"

"What happens on the boat stays on the boat."

"They used to say the same thing in baseball. What happens on the away stand, stays on the away stand. The thing is, it doesn't. What happens on the away stand always finds its way back home. Because you always return home."

Now she nodded. I gave her a moment, and then I spoke again.

"Can I ask you something?"

She nodded again.

"Did anyone else on *Toxic Assets* ever put the moves on you?"

She blushed. I found it hard to believe that on a little boat, far away from home, with a few rum and colas going down that more than one hadn't made a play for Felicity.

"I don't want to talk about it."

"I don't either," I said. "I just want the answer."

"There may have been one."

"Who?"

She looked away down the dock, and then back again.

"Alec. He had a few drinks and asked me to dance at the bar where the post-race party was. I said no, he kept at it. Will told him to go away, cool off."

I listened and then watched Ron come out of the office. I wasn't sure if it was the ocean air, or being around friends, but the life had returned to him. He came over and Felicity offered him a smile that was tinged with regret.

"You guys have a good sail," I said.

"You're not coming?" asked Ron.

"Nah." I didn't want to come. I wanted Ron to return to his element. And I didn't want to look at Felicity, she having made a mistake that I had made her share. I didn't want to see her eyes looking at mine, seeing me as the physical embodiment of something that she could have gotten past if I wasn't there to remind her of it. I wanted to find the bar, somewhere cool, and watch the sailboats fly their white wings across the azure water.

"Come on," said Ron, again. "Come out with us."

I shook my head, but the words didn't make it out.

"He can't," said a voice behind me.

# CHAPTER TWENTY—FIVE

**I turned to** see Amy Artiz standing on the dock, dark and tanned and potential energy. "He's coming out with me."

I stood in place, looking at her and she at me, and then she glanced at Ron and winked. Ron and Felicity disappeared up the dock, leaving me looking down at Amy. She threw a sailing bag at me and I caught it.

"I need another crew member." She smiled, dropped the smile and strode by me. I followed. I don't know why I did. I had just resolved to find a bar, which was usually a determination I could not be dissuaded from, but this little pocket rocket of a woman had me following like a Grand Canyon mule. We walked far out on the dock, to a yacht that wasn't as long as *Toxic Assets* but had a wide open deck. It looked built for speed, not comfort. Another two men and one woman were already on board, coiling ropes and setting up winches. Amy stepped over the guardrail onto the deck, turned and put her arms out. I put my hand out in return.

"The bag," she said.

I snatched my hand back and lobbed the sailing bag to her, and then she turned away to stow the bag below. I stepped over the guardrail all by myself, no help required, and waited on the deck. Amy reappeared, having tucked her dark hair under a ball cap. I had no such respite from the sun. She stood behind the wheel, and I sat in the cockpit by the winch, so I had to look up at her.

"You know I don't really sail, right?"

She nodded. "You've been out with me before, remember. Don't worry, I just need an extra hand on a winch."

"You need me as a hand on a winch?"

"Yeah. I was a body short for the twilight race. Now I'm not. Good timing. Just do what I tell you."

Evidence suggested I had no problem with that. We prepped the boat and Amy fired up the motor and expertly steered us out of our mooring. She didn't mention Ron. In fact, she didn't speak to me at all. As we reached the midpoint of the Intracoastal Amy directed for the headsail to be hoisted, and the fleet of boats grew thick. They seemed to be coming from all directions, seemingly without any order. Amy looked around as she steered with the big wheel, calm but alert.

"Is it every boat for himself, or is there method to this chaos?" I asked.

"Starboard tack has right of way," she said, glancing at me. She must have seen the blank look on my face, because she continued. "There are two sides to a boat, starboard," she said, pointing to her right, "and port." She pointed to her left. "Your tack is determined by which side the wind is coming over your deck. If it is coming anywhere over your starboard side, you are on starboard tack. You have right of way. If it coming over the port side, it's port tack, and you must yield to all boats on a starboard tack."

"Okay, I think."

Amy pointed ahead. "You see that boat coming straight at us? Who has rights?"

I had no idea. It was a head-on waiting to happen. I was sitting on the left side of the boat facing forward, so that meant port side. The headsail was on the other side of our boat, so I assumed the wind was coming across my side, which meant port tack.

"We have to yield," I said, like the schoolkid with his eye on becoming teacher's pet.

"Why?"

"We're on port tack."

"Good," she said. She didn't smile and she didn't look at me, which seemed a smart move given we were sailing straight into another boat.

"So what do we do?"

"Yield?"

"How?"

I searched my memory for a term that Ron might have used. "Bear away?"

Now Amy looked at me. "We might make a sailor out of you yet. Bearing away."

She jinked the wheel ever so slightly and as we reached the other boat our bow turned away from the wind a touch, and the woman working the headsail winch eased the sail out. I noted that she took the winch handle from a mesh pocket between her legs on the side of the cockpit, and clipped it into a hole on the winch itself. The handle was heavy-looking chrome, and I thought of Will Colfax getting that in the head. It would be like being hit with a hammer.

We passed the other boat only feet apart, but everyone seemed okay with that. I noticed that it was Ron's boat, and he was standing right at the front, doing something to the sail. He waved to me and I waved back.

"Let's get the main up," said Amy, and she pointed the boat close to the direction of the wind. I pulled the halyard as the other woman winched, and the big sail slapped in the wind like a whip as it filled with air. The woman tied the halyard to a cleat and smiled at me.

"Miami Jones," I said, offering her my hand.

She took it with a glove that had the fingers cut off.

"Dakota," she said. "Ain't that something?"

I nodded. She was a heavyset girl with a bird's nest of hair, but she moved about the boat like a ballerina.

We jostled around with other boats until an air horn sounded, and Dakota hit a button on a display in the cockpit and a timer started counting back.

"Five minutes," she called. She did the same with each minute, and then at thirty seconds. From ten she counted down each number, and I watched Amy positioning the boat for the best possible start. Dakota called *one* and I heard a loud air horn again, and the guy standing on the bow of our boat looked back with his thumb in the air.

"Perfect," said Dakota. Amy gave no reaction. She was all business. As we headed away I noticed much of the fleet dropping behind. We must have had a fast boat.

"Quick boat," I said to Dakota.

"Quick skipper," she replied.

I looked at Amy. "How come Will Colfax deferred to Drew Keck on sailing decisions and not you?"

Amy glanced up at the mainsail. "Bring it in a touch." Dakota winched the sail in a little.

"You see those little red tags on the sail?" Amy said to me. "Those are called telltales. If they're flying straight back the sail is more or less trimmed right. If they flap, you're off and the sail needs to come in or out." Dakota was looking up at the sail as we went.

"You didn't answer my question," I said.

"Because he was an idiot. And a chauvinist dinosaur."

"You a better sailor than Drew?"

Amy shrugged. I glanced over at Dakota, who nodded emphatically.

I looked up at Amy. "So were you okay with him doing that?"

"I was paid to be there, so I did what I was paid to do."

"I didn't realize you were paid."

She nodded. "Me and Drew."

We sailed on until we came upon a marker buoy in the water. Amy called the mark, and told me to swap sides with Dakota, and to watch the boom. She spun the wheel on her call and the boat whipped around on a dime, and the sails flapped angrily and the boom went zooming over my head. Dakota eased the sails out wide so the main was way over the side of the boat.

"Wind's behind us?" I asked.

Amy nodded. "This is where we'd run a spinnaker, you know the big colorful sail at the front?"

I nodded.

"But this is a non-spinnaker race."

We were booking. The yacht seemed to move faster than the wind, which defied physics but not my logic. It felt like there was no breeze at all, and the sun beat down hard.

"I heard Felicity Havill was having a thing with Will," I said to Amy.

She shrugged.

"Did you know that?"

"Everyone knew that."

"I also heard you were keen on him, but he chose her."

Amy stared down at me. "You heard that, did you?"

"I did."

"Let me ask you a question. You're a private eye, right?"

"That's right."

"You any good?"

"I solve more than I don't."

"Well, what do you make of that idea?"

I thought about it. Was Amy Will's type? My deduction based on available evidence was that she was, because she was female and had a heartbeat. Moreover, she was attractive. She had the fit strong body of someone who worked hard, and I figured that was about all Will was looking for.

"I think he'd be interested, yes."

"I'm not talking about him."

She was talking about herself. Would she give the likes of Will Colfax the time of day? She was a strong, confident woman, who clearly didn't suffer fools and was still on the fence about me. Would she be a sucker for Will's fraternity old boy charms? I didn't see it. And then there was the alternate hypothesis.

"I heard another suggestion."

"Let me guess," she said, looking up at the headsail but saying nothing about it. "I'm a lesbian."

Score one, Artiz. She could see my questions coming a mile away. But that didn't mean the answers were wrong.

"Something like that."

"And what if I am?"

"Makes no difference to me."

"Really? No difference?" She had a raised eyebrow like she wasn't buying it.

"No. You are who you are."

"That's very poetic."

"I'm a regular Walt Whitman."

"You'd look terrible as a sweaty-toothed madman. And for the record, I'm not a lesbian. Not that you care."

"As a detective, no, I don't. Doesn't tell me much about you as a person. But if you're not, it tells me plenty about the people spreading the rumor."

"Yes, it does."

"You want to know who said it?"

"You don't have some kind of PI confidentiality?" Now she was mocking me.

"This wasn't a client."

"I know it wasn't."

"You suspect."

"Let me guess, Drew Keck," she said.

"He might have mentioned it."

"Yeah."

"But there was another source."

"Okay, guess two. Drew Keck was passing on a rumor he heard, because he wouldn't own up to it himself. He got the story from Alec Meechan."

I sucked in some sea air and looked hard at Amy. I hoped she didn't decide to become a PI, because I'd be out of job if she did.

She grinned without joy. "Well, what do you say?"

"Something about nails and heads."

She nodded.

"So you weren't interested in Alec, either?"

Amy screwed up her face at me. "Seriously?" She looked over at Dakota, who was still looking up at the sail. "*Kotes*," Amy said. "Alec Meechan."

Dakota looked down at me, rolled her eyes and poked out her tongue like she was gagging on battery acid, and then turned her eyes back to the sail.

"Okay, ready for the mark," said Amy, back to business.

She counted down the mark and spun the boat around again, and Dakota and I worked together on the sails. Amy pointed us toward the island.

"Where we going?" I asked.

"The mainland side is in the lee of the wind, so we'll get more breeze out here, plus we'll be on starboard tack when we hit the mark." She looked at me. "And that means?"

"We have right of way."

"Finally, something out of your mouth that isn't complete garbage."

I looked out across the water and smiled. For some reason I didn't want Amy to see. As a rule, I didn't take kindly to being belittled, by women or men. I didn't think it was a good look on anyone, even myself. But from Amy I kind of liked it. Not in some warped masochistic way. I just liked the way she got to the point. Maybe it was a fair comment. Maybe what I was asking was complete trash. I could see that from her point of view. And maybe if I was better at my job, I wouldn't need to ask such questions. Or maybe in my job I had to ask such questions because I got lied to a lot.

We neared the island and Amy called us to get ready to tack, then like a well-oiled machine we did just that, the boom slipping across the deck in an orderly fashion, the sails repositioning as if they knew where they needed to be.

"Nice tack, team," called Amy. "Very nice."

I smiled even though my major contribution had been swapping sides of the boat. We headed back across the Intracoastal. The guy up on the bow said we were on a good line for the mark. We sailed into the wind in silence, and the breeze across the water cooled us somewhat. Dakota passed around a bottle of water and we all took some. No one seemed worried about catching something. There were no parents of preschoolers on board. I watched across the water as another boat that had banked away in the opposite direction tacked back, so it was headed in a criss-cross pattern to us. It also looked quick, but not quite so sleek as ours. More a cruiser, I guessed. I was starting to see how people fell in love with this caper. The fresh air, the patter of the water. There was an odd sense of camaraderie in working as a team despite my not even yet knowing the name of the two other guys on board. I had missed the dressing room camaraderie since I had retired from baseball. A group of guys, each required to perform as individuals but also as a unit. On bad days we were only as good as our weakest member, but on good days we were better than the sum of our parts.

"Okay, guys, we're nearing the mark, get ready to bear away," said Amy. She looked at me. "We're going to bear around the mark and ease the sails out gradually, okay?"

"Got it. What about that boat there?" I pointed across the deck at the boat I had been watching. Its crisscross path was going to bring it mighty close to us.

"What tack are they on?"

I looked again. "Port."

"So?"

"So they have to yield."

"Right. They'll have to bear away and go behind us, then ease all the way around. They made a bad choice."

I got ready to do my thing, which wasn't much, and the guy on the bow called the mark ahead and said Amy was right where she needed to be. I kept looking under the boom at the boat to our port side. These guys liked to run things close. It seemed to me we were on a crash course, but I knew these big boats turned way faster than I gave them credit for, and these racing skippers liked to test the limits.

"Nearing the mark," called the bowman.

"Ready team," called Amy.

"Those guys look close," I said.

"They'll turn," said Amy.

We were doing a good clip, even into the wind.

"Ready," called Amy.

"Amy, they're not bearing," said Dakota.

"They're just trying to scare us off our game. Focus."

I was focused. On the boat heading to a point right in front of us, a point we were about to hit.

"Amy," said Dakota, this time with a nervous edge to her voice I hadn't heard before.

"Focus."

"Amy!"

Amy glanced at the boat headed for us and yelled. "Rights!"

They either didn't hear, or didn't care. But they didn't make to move behind us. I gripped a cleat with one hand and a handrail with the other and prepared for impact. The other yacht sped directly at the midpoint of our side.

"Crash tack!"

I heard Amy scream the command but I didn't know what she meant. I figured it out pretty quick. She spun with the wheel hard, and the rudder bit and the boat jerked back to starboard. Our speed died and the boat lost control, and the world turned side on as the boat fell sideways and the sail dove toward the water. The boom dropped toward me like a torpedo, but I was looking right at it so I got lucky.

For a second, anyway. I threw myself down as the boom whooshed overhead, and I hit the deck hard. Then as the yacht lurched sideways I slid down, down toward the side of the boat. The edge of the deck was submerged in the water, the guardrails gone from view, and I flailed wildly for something to grab hold of, but nothing came. I plummeted into the water, and was up to my waist, about to join Will Colfax in the great deep, when I came to a screeching halt. Suddenly the world stood still. The boat didn't move, it didn't lurch further and I didn't slip any deeper into the water.

I looked up across the deck, toward the sky, and saw Dakota. She was holding on to a cleat above her head with one hand, and my shirt below her with the other. She winked. Then I saw Amy crawl up the deck and pull the wheel around. It didn't have much effect as we were dead in the water, and even I knew that we needed to be moving for the rudder to work. Dakota pulled me up. She was stronger than I gave her credit for. I got my foot onto the guardrail and pushed myself up further, and then we crawled toward the high side of the boat.

Gradually, like a slow-motion tree falling in reverse, the weight of the keel pulled the bottom down, and the mast moved skyward, gaining momentum, until the sails spat out the water they had collected and the mast sprang upright, and then continued past vertical and the boat leaned the other way, and I thought we were going to dip into the water on the other side, but the boat only went a little way, and then flopped back toward equilibrium, and settled upright.

"Everyone okay?" called Amy.

"Man overboard," returned the guy who had been working the middle of the boat. The bowman had gone over. We cast our eyes over the water and I spotted him.

"There!" I pointed.

He wasn't wearing a life jacket, but he was treading water with a huge grin on his face. The guy by the mast grabbed a life buoy and threw it out, and the one in the water grabbed it and kicked his way over to us. He swam around to the stern and Amy dropped a ladder and he climbed up onto the transom.

"I needed a bath," he said.

"Who was that?" asked Dakota.

Another yacht pulled alongside and the skipper yelled at us.

"You all right?"

"Yes, all accounted for," called Amy. "Did you see that?"

"I did. He would've t-boned you. Put your protest flag up."

"Who was that?" Amy called back to the other skipper.

"*Burnside*."

"A charter yacht?" Amy said to herself. She directed her attention back to the other boat as it began to ease away.

"Who's skipper on that boat today?" called Amy.

The other yacht picked up speed as the wind gathered in its sails, and the skipper turned back and cupped his hands around his mouth to yell.

"Alec Meechan."

Amy looked down at the guy sitting on the transom, getting his breath back, and then she turned to look at me.

"You still think he's my type?"

# CHAPTER TWENTY—SIX

**Alec Meechan was** unapologetic. Amy attended the protest meeting after the race, where she told me Alec had claimed that he had eased to go behind our boat and that Amy had panicked, crash tacked and cut off his line, so he had to continue forward to avoid an impact. None of the other boats who witnessed events agreed with him. The protest was upheld, and Alec's boat was disqualified from the race. He dismissed the whole thing with a shrug and a *whatever*, and then headed for the bar. There was talk of barring him from future races, but Amy said nothing would come of it because there wasn't an actual accident. The whole thing was of no consequence to us, since we had crawled to the finish line near the end of the field, having been in first place at the final marker. Amy shrugged it off.

"It's just a twilight. It's not the America's Cup," she said.

"Still," I said. "Can I buy you a drink?"

"Really?" she said. "That's your best line?"

"No, that's what I say when I offer to buy the crew a beer."

Amy gave a sheepish nod. I got five beers and the guy from our crew who didn't go overboard helped me carry them.

"I'm Miami, by the way."

"Jeff," he replied. "I saw you play ball."

"You did? Where?"

"At Roger Dean Stadium."

"So you're a Cardinals' fan," I said.

"Yeah. Sorry."

"Don't sweat it."

"You were good."

"Thanks."

"You mind if I ask you something?"

"Shoot," I said, delivering the beers to our crew. Everyone shared a cheers, and the guy who had ended up in the water joined us with a towel, and told me his name was Rob.

Jeff took a sip and looked at me. "You beat Palm Beach every time I saw you pitch. So how is it that you didn't make the majors?"

"You played baseball?" asked Amy.

"I did," I said. "And I did make the majors, sort of. Back when I was playing in California. With the A's."

"I didn't know that," said Jeff.

"Yeah. I got on the squad in '04, but never actually got to play."

"That sucks."

I nodded to him and sipped my beer. "You're right, it did. But that's life. I got traded for the next season, to the New York Mets, and they sent me down here to St. Lucie. That's where I played out my career."

"That's sad you never got to play," said Dakota.

"Sad? Nah, I don't think so," I said. "It was a joy to play baseball for so long and get paid to do it."

"So you weren't good enough?" asked Amy.

"Geez, Amy," said Jeff.

"What? I just wondered why."

I looked her in the eyes. "I don't mind. I don't know why. Sometimes it's timing, sometimes another guy takes his chance at the right time when you don't. Why I didn't get my shot? I can't tell you. The people who made the call never explained it to me."

"So were you good enough?" she asked.

I shrugged. "I think so. I think I could have matched those guys. But it's easy to say you could win the America's Cup if you never get to board a boat."

I drank my beer quicker than I had planned, but then I noted all my crew mates were matching me. I'd heard stories about how sailors drink. Rob and Dakota got another round, and I tried to slow down a little. I found it hard, and I wondered if it was the result of the adrenaline in our bodies after the near crash. But everyone seemed to chill and the place developed a nice easy buzz. We sat in the corner and Amy kicked back and I noticed her relax. She had a nice smile when she got around to dropping the frown. But she never lost the look in her eyes, an intensity as if she were analyzing the folks in the room like they were wind shifts. It was the kind of focus that would have burned Longboard Kelly's to the ground. Even as she relaxed and enjoyed the company of her crew, her body stayed ready, like a coiled spring.

I saw Ron across the room, a genuine smile in his eyes, so I excused myself and weaved my way through the crowd to him. He introduced me to a bunch of people whose names I instantly forgot, and they asked me about *the incident*, as it seemed to have been dubbed, and I gave them the *Reader's Digest* version. Then I slapped Ron's back, and told him I'd see him the next day at work. He winked, which told me that jail time was the furthest thing from his mind.

I walked outside and stood on the dock and leaned on the steel balustrade for a moment. The sun had fallen and an almost full moon was out, lighting up the water. It was still balmy, but it was an ice bath compared to the earlier day, so I let the cooler breeze glide over me. The light from inside the yacht club lit the dock up for a moment as the door opened and then closed. I saw the silhouette of a man with a familiar shape walk away toward the promenade and then stop. Under the light of the canopy, where the yacht club valet did his thing, I saw the face that belonged to the shape.

It was Drew Keck. I hadn't seen him inside, but there were so many sailors in there it was like *Where's Waldo?* I followed Drew to ask him about his boat project with Will, but I stopped when I realized that he wasn't waiting for the valet. The nosey part of me wanted to see who he was waiting for, so I pressed up hard against the railing on the dock and slid as close as I dared to get. Drew lit a cigarette and sucked on it hard, once, twice, three times. Once was nothing. Twice was a habit. Three times was anxiety. He inhaled the cigarette almost literally, and then turned to a trash can with sand in the top where he crushed the butt. I had to give him props for at least not tossing the damned thing into the water. As he turned around from the trash can a conservative silver Mercedes pulled into the valet station. I saw the driver wave the valet away, with the flick of a toned, feminine arm, but I couldn't make her out in the dark car. Drew Keck leaned into the passenger's side window as it dropped down. I couldn't hear what was said, but the driver passed Drew something, and he stood back and tapped what appeared to be papers on the sill of the car. He made to turn away, and then I heard the driver call to him.

"When, Mr. Keck?" she asked.

"Soon. Days."

"You drive a hard bargain."

"Not for what I had to do," he said, and then he did turn and walk away. I stepped down on a jetty between two large motorboats so Drew didn't see me, but he was looking at whatever papers the woman had given him, and he paid me no mind. He headed back to the bar and I stepped back toward the valet to get another look at the Mercedes, but it was gone.

I wandered back along the dock, thinking about whether to ask Drew who he was meeting, but I decided the yacht club, where he was a known quantity and I was not, was not the place to do it. Instead I resumed my position on the railing, looking out across the boats.

I was watching a radar or some such thing spinning slowly on the top of a motor yacht, when I felt someone brush against my arm and join me leaning over the edge of the dock. I glanced aside and saw Amy. She had removed her cap when she had gone into the clubrooms and had not put it back on, so the breeze was playing with her short hair. I just watched her as she looked at the water. I wondered about the chip she carried around on her shoulder, and how that hardened her some. And I wondered if I would be like that if I had been met at every step of my baseball career by people telling me I wasn't strong enough because I was a woman, or I couldn't play because I was a woman. Or worse still, telling me I could be anything I wanted to be, and then never giving me my shot. We had some stuff in common. Everyone has baggage. I'd struck out some of the best batters in major league baseball, but I'd only ever done it at batting practice. Amy had been told by the likes of Drew Keck that she was too weak, so she had gotten strong. She'd been hired as a pro sailor by Will Colfax, and then he had deferred to Drew on all sailing matters. He probably paid her a fraction of what Drew got, too. She was told by the likes of Alec Meechan that she must be gay if she could rebuff his advances. No one's life is a picnic, and a person deals with adversity or they don't—it's their choice. I just knew if I had lived through those comments, there'd be a few more busted noses around the Palm Beach Yacht Club.

After the longest time Amy took her eyes from the water and put them on me. It felt like a retinal scan. She was soft and hard, strong and vulnerable. We looked at each other without speaking for a time that would have made most people itchy. She didn't smile, but she wasn't frowning. Then she spoke.

"You should take some sailing lessons," she said.

"You teach?"

She nodded, gently. "Talk to Ron. He knows the guy who runs the sailing school."

I nodded in return, but said nothing.

Then she touched my arm. "Nice sailing with you today." And she turned and walked back into the club.

# CHAPTER TWENTY—SEVEN

**Balmy evenings bring** heavy days in Florida, when the whole place turns into a massive *bain-marie*, and the moisture rises from the wetlands that lie beneath the entire state to slowly braise everyone and everything. I woke early in a sweat, with a sense of unease that I couldn't quite place. I got up, drank some water, and then stood on my balcony in the first light. The clouds hung like a false ceiling, and the wind had all but gone. It was the kind of day you prayed for rain, to drive away the humidity, and when that rain came as it inevitably would, you would regret your prayers as the fresh moisture did nothing but ratchet up the stickiness.

I got in some shorts and an old Mets T-shirt and went for a run. The streets around my apartment were quiet at this time, the golfers and business types still working off their booze and all-you-can-eat seafood buffets. There was no traffic inside the community, and my footfalls echoed off the blacktop, bouncing off the apartment buildings and back at me. I jogged down to the community pool, and stopped. I just wasn't feeling it. I wanted to open up like a gazelle and run, and something about the canyons of buildings made me feel closed and small. I took off my T-shirt and wandered into the beach entry pool, the incline slowly taking me deeper and deeper, until nothing was above water but my head. The pool wasn't officially open until later, but that rule was only as good as the people who enforced it, and the complex owners didn't pay for staff to wander the pool area at five in the morning. I wasn't making any noise anyway. I was like an alligator, eyes and nose above water. I floated around for some time, thinking random thoughts, the kind that shoot into your mind like meteors, seem to take hold, and then get bounced out of the way by the next random thought. Except such thoughts were rarely random. I just didn't know how they were connected.

I was, like many Floridians, the product of another place and time, drawn here by cosmic forces and great weather. I had loved New England as a kid, snow days and summers at the lake. But the older I got, the less I wanted to stay. It wasn't until I played in a baseball carnival in Orlando during high school that not wanting to stay developed into wanting to leave. I chose University of Miami not because it was as far away from Connecticut as I could get, but because it was Florida, and they offered me a scholarship. I wondered at the time if I had gotten a scholarship at Stanford, whether I would have fallen in love with California. Then after college I got to test the theory, when I was recruited by the Oakland Athletics organization, and I spent the better part of four years in Modesto. I enjoyed it. It was a great club, a fun time and damned hard work. But when I got traded to the Mets, and they sent me down to their minor league team in St. Lucie, it felt like I was being sent home. And now it felt like a crossroads. Time to go or time to leave. Sally wanted me to buy a house, Lenny wanted me to buy a car, Ron wanted me to join the yacht club. There was a big world out there, unexplored by *moi*. I stood on the cusp of my thirtieth year on the planet, and I couldn't help but feel like the universe was forcing me into a corner. What I didn't know was whether the universe was telling me to stay or telling me to leave.

I walked home, showered and put on a red shirt with gold desert islands all over it and a pair of jeans, and I headed out. I generally didn't like to wear jeans but made the exception when riding my bike. Coming off a motorbike was too easy, and the fall too hard. But there was little traffic as I drifted up toward Riviera Beach. I zoomed past the port, and the dockyards where Drew Keck had been polishing his beautiful boat, and crossed over onto Singer Island. I wound down past the older, low-slung homes on the canals, following the map in my mind and the brochure in my pocket. I got down near the Intracoastal and crawled slowly along, looking for the right number. I didn't need a number. The house I wanted stuck out like a beacon on a rocky shore. The street was lined with new-build minimansions. Four-, five- or six-thousand-square-foot homes, more cinderblock and stucco than the eye was capable of taking in at one glance. They were all the same, yet unique, as if their owners were still in high school, trying desperately to fit in with the cool kids, while simultaneously proving they were individuals. They were mostly two stories, a couple three. Some had white pillars and some had arching palms and some had huge double doors, but they all wore the pastel colors of Florida.

I stopped the bike in front of the house that was the ugly duckling of the street. It was a single-story rancher, low-roofed and painted wood siding the color of shallow Caribbean water. To the side of the front door stood a royal palm, the tree of trees. It was thick-trunked and leaned over like a drunk at a bar. I got off the bike and wandered around. Sally said the owner had bought the place to knock it down and complete the matching set of luxury houses along the waterfront, but when the market plummeted they walked away. It was still early and the suburb was barely stirring, except the pickup full of guys who had arrived to continue work on the monstrosity next door. It looked like they were constructing a giant Greek wedding cake. They were quietly moving around, sharing a flask of coffee, waiting for the clock to tick over so they could begin banging and sawing in compliance with city regulations.

I turned away and peered in through the window at the front of the old home. Certainly no one was living in the place. It was as empty as a banker's soul. I wandered around the side of the house and stood in awe of what I found. I could see what the developer was about. The rear of house was nothing more than a few palms and a roughly paved patio by a rear sliding door. But it looked out directly onto the Intracoastal Waterway. The water was ebbing from black to dark blue as the cloud reflected its mood. A couple of yachts were moored just out of the channel, and their rigging softly tapped against their masts, sending a *tink, tink, tink* across the water. On the mainland stretched the city of Riviera Beach, the last of the night lights doused, the town waking to another day. It was one hell of a view. I turned away from it to look at the house. It was a seventies original, like me, and like me, it seemed in reasonable if not spectacular shape. I pressed my nose to the sliding glass door to look inside. With the sun rising on the other side it was hard to make anything out.

"How you doing?" I heard someone say. I turned around to see a Cuban-looking guy in long sleeves and jeans ambling toward me. He had the thickest black hair and an easy smile.

"Good," I said. "You?"

"Very good. You looking at this place."

"Yeah. I heard it was for sale."

The guy reached me and we both looked at our reflections in the glass door.

"Yeah, man. The guy who owned it, he went bust."

"It happens, I guess."

"Third one on this street."

"That right?" I looked over to the building site he had come from. "You working on the place next door?"

"Yeah, we're lucky. That guy lives in Argentina, Brazil or somewhere. This is gonna be his Florida place. He paid cash, so no bank to take it away from him."

That sounded good to me.

"Still," continued the builder. "It'll be worth less finished than what he paid for it. But I guess what goes up must go down."

"Let's hope the opposite is true, too." I smiled and the guy shrugged.

"You wanna look inside?" he asked.

"It's locked up."

The guy frowned and grinned at the same time, then turned and ambled over to a palm tree and yanked one of the fronds off it. As he walked back to me, he pulled a piece of fencing wire from his pocket, and then he set to work on the door. With the foliage and wire he took less than thirty seconds to open the door. I considered hiring the guy as a consultant.

He slid the door open and ushered me in. The inside was like the outside: old but in decent repair, and oh-so seventies. The living room was sunken, and covered in orange shag carpet. The walls were wood-paneled, right around the rear door until the kitchen on the opposite side, where a floral wallpaper took over. The kitchen counters were brown laminate and the counters orange Formica. All the appliances were in place with the exception of a refrigerator, which left a large empty space between the cabinets and a pantry. I wandered through the place, looking in each of the three bedrooms, which all met my basic criterion of being big enough to fit a bed. There was one bathroom, a shower in the bath and a basic tile, nothing too grotesque. I turned the faucet but got nothing but thumping pipes.

"Everything's turned off. The power, the water, everything," said the builder from the bathroom doorway. I nodded at his deductive reasoning.

We walked back into the living room and I took one more look around. It had been a home, a real home, to someone. Someone probably of a vintage not unlike my own. A couple, with kids who grew and left and found colleges and lives in Seattle or Boise or London. A couple now no longer of this zip code or maybe no longer of this earth. There were memories here, and I glanced at the sliding door we had left open as if those memories were wafting away on the breeze, lost forever.

"You could really do something with this place," said the guy. "Do it cheap, you could just go up, second story, redo this kitchen, add beds and baths upstairs. Or you could just knock down and do it good."

I nodded and took one last look, and then we stepped outside. The guy used the palm frond and the wire to lock the door. He was a master at break and enter, but he was no criminal. He threw the frond away and put the wire in his pocket, and then handed me a business card. It said, *Ernesto Anaya, Contractor.*

"You get the place, you wanna fix her up, you call me." He smiled and nodded.

"Thanks, Ernesto," I said, and he ambled away toward his work site.

I took one more look at the water, and then I walked back around the side of the house. I threw my leg over and slipped my helmet on, and then I checked my watch to see how long the drive was to the office.

# CHAPTER TWENTY—EIGHT

**I made it** to the office in twelve minutes. I left the bike under the eaves of the building, a vain attempt to shelter it from the rain that would surely come sooner or later. Then I bounded upstairs. No one was in and I didn't yet have a key, so I wandered back down to Banyan Street and grabbed a coffee and a bagel breakfast sandwich. I walked down to the water and watched the comings and goings, looking over to near where we had almost crashed a boat the previous evening. I didn't fancy ending up in the Intracoastal. I heard the bull sharks were something.

By the time I made my way back, the downtown was alive and Lizzy was in the office. I said good morning and she said it back, which was nice, and then I mentioned I didn't have a key, and she opened a file drawer, took out a large envelope and handed me two keys on a keychain that read *And be not drunk with wine, wherein is excess; but be filled with the Spirit; Ephesians 5:18.* I had plenty to say on that, but kept it to myself. Lizzy made me sign for the key, and then I went into Lenny's office and lay on the sofa to wait.

Lenny and Ron came in together, offering good mornings to Lizzy and getting chirpy responses.

"Top of the mornin' to ya," Lenny said to me as he ambled into his office.

"Did I miss something? Is it St. Paddy's day?"

"Luck of the Irish, my boy." He smiled. Ron offered raised eyebrows.

"You're not Irish." Then I looked at the mane of rust-colored hair and spotty complexion and reconsidered. "Okay, maybe you are."

His smile deepened. "Ron got a client."

"That so?" I flipped my feet off the sofa and Ron sat down.

"Last night at the yacht club. One of my irons caught fire," said Ron.

"Is that how that saying goes?" I asked.

"It is now. He's an insurance guy. We do a good job, there could be plenty more work."

"Good work, Ron."

"When are you meeting them, Ron?" asked Lenny.

"He wants to see me this morning."

"All good," said Lenny, and he looked at me. I knew what he meant. It wasn't about the client. Clients always found us, and we were rarely out of cases for long. It was about Ron getting back on the horse and moving on. Then the horse turned around and came to a stop, refusing to budge, as the phone buzzed. Lenny picked up and said hello, then held the phone up and looked at it like it was busted, then put it to his ear again and said hello once more. He was staring at it again with a frown when there was a tap at the door and Lizzy stuck her head in.

"You need to press the button," she said to Lenny.

"What button?"

"The button that lights up on the phone. It's the intercom."

He looked at the phone's console. "What light?"

"It's not lit now, Lenny. I've hung up, haven't I?"

He replaced the handset. "How about you just open the door like you are, and come in if you want to speak to me?" He smiled and she shook her head.

"There's someone here to see you."

"Someone?"

"A new client."

"Well, send him in."

"I will. His name is Mr. Baggio. Mr. Michael Baggio."

Lenny's eyes opened wide and he looked at me. I turned to Ron, who looked at Lenny. It was like a Three Stooges routine, without the physical violence.

Michael Baggio stepped into Lenny's office. He looked as well-presented as he had before, if a little tired. He wore pleated trousers and a pressed Oxford shirt that tucked into his tight waist. He was a fit little unit, and I could imagine him in another life being a mob enforcer.

"Mr. Baggio," said Lenny, sounding like a schoolteacher.

Michael nodded at Lenny, and then glanced at Ron and me.

"Ron," he said in surprise. "I heard you were out."

"Michael, yes, back on the streets." Ron smiled, but Michael didn't. Suddenly he didn't look so sure of himself. He turned back to Lenny.

"Mr. Cox," he said. "You're a hard man to find."

Lenny shrugged. "I'm in the phonebook," he said. I wasn't sure anyone used phonebooks anymore, but I took his point.

"Your listing has you on Okeechobee Boulevard. It looked empty."

"That was our old place. We just moved."

"You might want to stick a note on the door," said Michael. It was a fair point, and a good idea. I made a note to drop by and do just that.

"What can I do for you, Mr. Baggio?"

Michael half-glanced back at Ron, and then turned back to Lenny. "I need your help."

"How so?"

"You told Keegan to give himself up to the FBI."

"I did."

"He's been charged with embezzlement."

"I would have expected so," said Lenny, leaning back in his chair.

"He didn't do it."

"I recall he said that at your office. If that is the case, I'm sure that will come out."

"Now the sheriff is looking into Will Colfax's death. He's suggesting the two are linked."

"But he didn't have anything to do with that either," said Lenny.

"No, he didn't. Nor did I."

"Did you speak to your lawyer?"

"Yes, and he thinks he can get Keegan off, but he says it might be a drawn-out process. And there's the link to Will. They say the sheriff might come after me for that."

"Keegan didn't get bail?"

"The federal prosecutor said they can show funds being transferred from the company to accounts abroad, so they claimed Keegan was a risk to leave the country. The judge agreed."

"I'm sorry to hear that," said Lenny. "But what is it you want from me?"

Michael glanced at Ron, and then back to Lenny. "You got Ron out of jail. I want you to get Keegan out, too."

Lenny took a deep breath, and then sat forward in his chair. "Michael, we found enough to get Ron out where the state attorney had nothing to go on but limited circumstantial evidence. We just showed that evidence could have applied to anyone. This is not the same."

"Why?"

"I don't know what the FBI has, but I'll bet there's something that links Keegan to the money. Signatures, passwords, account access. Whatever. Stuff that only he could do. We might find enough to muddy the waters at trial, maybe, but that would still be at trial. It might help get him off, but it won't get him out early."

Michael propped his hands against the desk and leaned over. For a second I thought he might be sick all over the new carpet, but he wasn't. He was just spent. He'd come here as a last resort, hope overriding logic. And Lenny had set him straight, as he must. Michael was short and stocky, and bent over like that he resembled a dying rhino.

He didn't look up when he spoke. "Mr. Cox, I don't know what else to do."

"Your attorney probably has investigators they use. They'll look into it."

"They'll look into that and a hundred other cases. I don't have much faith." Now he stood, slack-shouldered, beaten. I didn't know if Keegan Murray was innocent, but I knew Michael Baggio believed he was. Lenny saw it too.

"Look, Michael. I don't want to give you false hope, or take your money doing what your attorney may already be doing."

"He's not looking into Will's death, Mr. Cox. So can I retain you to do that? Keep me out of jail."

Lenny took a deep breath. "There's a problem, Michael. A conflict of interest."

"What conflict?"

Lenny looked at us on the sofa. "Ron," he said. "Ron remains in the frame for Will's death. As our colleague, and quite frankly our friend, he is our first priority."

Michael looked at Ron and me. He looked pretty close to the end his rope.

"Lenny," said Ron. "I didn't hurt Will. And I don't believe Michael did, either. So if you continue looking into this, I think you'll help us both stay out of jail."

"There's more," said Michael, looking back to Lenny. "The sheriff told Keegan he has physical evidence that shows someone hit Will, dragged him across the deck and threw him overboard."

"The sheriff might be overstating his hand," I said. "They found blood and some kind of brain fluid on a winch handle. It suggests that someone did hit Will, but there are no fingerprints, so it doesn't say who did it."

"I'm not surpised there are no fingerprints," said Michael. "Pretty much everyone wore sailing gloves. But the rest till suggests someone is trying to set up Keegan and me."

Lenny put his hands behind his head, and then ruffled his hair. "All right, Michael. Here's what we'll do. We'll look into this. If we can show that you didn't or couldn't have killed Will, we'll provide such evidence."

"Thank you, Mr. Cox."

"There's a but. What we won't do is take you on as a client. If we find something that shows you did hurt Will Colfax, we will turn that over to the sheriff, because as I said, our first priority lies with Ron. If we find in your favor, something that helps you, then we can agree to terms for our work."

"You mean hold me over a barrel? Not release information unless I pay up?"

"Mr. Baggio," said Lenny. "You don't know me that well so I'll let that slide. You do yourself a favor and ask around. If you find one person who tells you I'm not a man of my word, then I'll do your case for free."

Michael nodded. "I apologize. You're right. I did ask around. And I agree to your terms."

"Good. In that case, Michael, sit down and tell us your story."

# CHAPTER TWENTY—NINE

**Ron made his** excuses to get to his meeting with the insurance client, and Lizzy brought iced tea in from goodness knows where. Michael took a seat and Lenny came around and sat on the sofa. I sipped my tea and Lenny gave his a suspicious look as we waited for Michael to talk.

"So where do I begin?"

"At the end," I said. Lenny glanced at me and raised an eyebrow.

"Okay," said Michael. "So, I guess, why Keegan was arrested. He works for—worked for—Will's company."

"Cyntech?"

"Yes," said Michael. "He's the finance director. In charge of the accounting, financial planning, cash flow, that sort of thing."

"So he had his hands on the till, so to speak," said Lenny.

"Yes, I suppose."

"Who else had access to the finances?" I asked.

"Not many. There were a couple subsidiaries that had their own finance people, but they reported in to Keegan. Then I think there were the directors. I think they had limited access. Keegan had a couple people working for him, so they had some access. That's about it."

"And how does this link to you?" I asked, although Deputy Castle had already filled me in on the likely reason. I just wanted to hear it from Michael.

"I think someone was stealing money from the company, and I think they killed Will, or arranged to have him killed, and set Keegan and me up to take the fall."

"So why were you on the boat?" I asked. "You said before that Will just invited you, even though you had never sailed before. That doesn't smell right, does it?"

Michael coughed into his hand. "I think it was part of the setup."

"Go on," I said.

"There are certain things, personal things, that I'd rather keep out of this, if possible."

"You mean the being gay thing?" said Lenny.

Michael's jaw dropped, and then he gulped and closed his mouth. "How do you know that?"

"I don't think you're as clever at hiding it as you think you are," said Lenny. "I doubt anyone at the yacht club is buying that roommates story."

"Oh."

"And the sheriff knows that you guys were married back in '04," I added.

"They know that?"

"It's public record, Michael," I said. "It might have been all the way up in Boston, but it's still public record."

"So why the ruse?" asked Lenny. "It's 2008. Why lie about your relationship?"

Michael analyzed the carpet, and then looked up. "Because it's 2008. And it's Florida." He rubbed his face and then put his hands together, fingers on his chin so it looked like he was praying. I wondered if he knew he was doing it.

"Look, we didn't plan on it," he said. "We got married when we were in Boston, and we had every intention of being open about that when Keegan got the job down here. But it took all of five minutes to know that Palm Beach isn't South Beach, let alone Massachusetts. People were more conservative. Our marriage isn't recognized in the state of Florida. We decided that for the sake of our careers that we would keep it low-profile."

"You ever go down to South Beach?" asked Lenny.

"Yes," said Michael, matter-of-factly.

"Good spot down there. I used to hang down there a lot."

"You did?" Michael frowned. "You're not . . . you know."

"I'm the one who's supposed to find it hard to say the word gay, not you. But no, I'm not. But a lot of good guys I know are. I'm all for it."

"You are?"

"Of course. Leaves more ladies for the rest of us." Lenny smiled wide. I contemplated the idea that if a certain percentage of men weren't interested in women, then it was possible a similar percentage of women weren't interested in men, but I kept that thought to myself. I didn't want to harsh Lenny's mellow.

"So, you decided to hide in plain sight, so to speak. And as you say, Palm Beach might not be South Beach, but it's not the Appalachian backwoods either. What gives?"

"There was one more thing."

"Which is?"

"It turns out Keegan's boss was a bit of a homophobe."

Lenny and I looked at each other.

"Will Colfax?" I asked.

Michael nodded.

"Okay, I get that." I said. "From all reports he was a bigot and a sexist. So not a stretch."

"Except," said Lenny.

"Except what?" said Michael.

"Except he hired Keegan. They obviously met before the hire, right?"

"Sure, Keegan interviewed in Michigan, and then he and I came down here to check it out before he committed. We had dinner with Will and his wife at their place in the Biltmore."

"You met Celia?" I asked.

"I did. She's intense," said Michael.

"You could say that," I said.

"And Michigan?" asked Lenny.

"Will's business was originally based in Detroit. Keegan's first job was closing that business down."

"Ouch," I said.

"But my point is, they met before he was hired," said Lenny.

"Yes, several times," said Michael. "Why?"

"Not to put too fine a point on it, but your husband is a bit of drama queen."

"You didn't see him at his best," said Michael.

"I'll concede that," said Lenny. "But does his best still involve a lot of hand waving and high-pitched yelps?"

"Occasionally. What's your point?"

"My point is, Will would have to have been blind to not think that Keegan was gay. But he hired him anyway."

"Maybe," said Michael.

"So Will either hired him because Keegan was gay, or he didn't care. And we seem to have ruled out not caring."

Michael frowned. "I don't see where you're going."

"I don't either," said Lenny. "Continue. We'll see if I can figure it out."

"You know, now that you mentioned Celia, it made me think. She was pretty pro-Keegan."

"How so?" I asked.

"At the dinner we had, she had a few drinks, we all did, and she said more than a couple times how she loved Keegan and how Keegan was the right guy for the job and how the island needed more guys like Keegan."

"You don't mean finance guys?"

He shook his head. "I didn't think anything more of it, but now I wonder if she was a fruit fly."

"A fruit fly?"

"A woman who likes to hang out with gay men. Ladies like Celia love stuff like that."

"Ladies like Celia?" I asked.

"Bored rich housewives," said Michael.

We all sipped some tea while we digested that thought, and then I prompted Michael to continue.

"So you're in Florida, hiding in plain sight, and you meet Will, and despite his reputation he asks you to sail on his boat. Why did he do that?"

"I don't know. I mentioned at a function that since we were in Florida, we should do some sailing. Sometime later Will says he needs an extra hand on his boat for a race, and wonders if I am interested."

"Did you tell him you didn't sail?"

"I might have said I wasn't that experienced. He said there was lots of experience on board. Now I think about it, I wonder if someone was setting me up by getting him to invite me."

"Who would do that?" I asked. "Who would have that influence?"

"Drew Keck," said Michael. "Drew was essentially skipper of the boat, in all but name. He could have convinced Will."

"Let's not jump at shadows," said Lenny. "There's another simple reason. Will needed an extra hand on board, but he didn't want another crew member who would be competing for the attention of the ladies."

"That does fit what we know about Will," I said.

"But he could have recruited another woman," said Michael.

"Now that is something that would have upset Drew Keck," I said. "He wasn't keen on women being on board at all. Bananas either, apparently."

"This is really a bunch of stand-up guys," said Lenny. "Alec Meecham starts to look like a class act in comparison."

"He was," said Michael. "He was the nicest one on board, to me at least."

"Did he hit on you?" I asked.

Michael did a double take. "Have you met Alec?"

"Yeah, okay. Was he trying to sell you a car?"

"No, nothing. He was just friendly. I could see the girls thought he was a bit too smooth, and I've heard stories around the place, but that wasn't my experience."

"What about Ron?"

"I didn't speak to Ron that much. He was nice too, but it didn't work out that we were teamed together."

"All right. Is there anything more you can add?" asked Lenny.

"I don't think so. Where do we go from here?"

Lenny stood. "We'll take another look at all these goons, and dig a bit deeper. If you can get any details on what Keegan was doing, the financials, anything, we can look into that too."

"I think the FBI took everything, but I'll ask him."

"Just be aware that anything you say to each other in lockup can be recorded."

We walked Michael out and then I flopped back down on the sofa. Lenny sniffed his ice tea and then put it down.

"So what now?" I asked.

"Start at the end, is that what you said?" Lenny laughed. "How about we do that. Are we convinced it wasn't an accident?"

"If the sheriff's evidence is accurate, and I'm sure it is. The brain fluid on the winch handle kind of nails it. Someone hit Will Colfax in the head."

"It's definitely Will's fluid?"

"According to the state attorney it is."

"Why wouldn't the killer throw the winch handle overboard?"

"Not sure. Panic? Mistake? Trying to set someone else up?"

"But not an accident," Lenny said.

"No, but more than that. I wasn't completely sure Will was even dead. I mean, no body, right?"

"You think he swam through the Gulf Stream?"

"I didn't have a working theory, but it doesn't matter now. It's foul play."

Lenny leaned back in his chair. "So foul play. Who benefits?"

"The wife, usually."

"So we look at Celia first. See if we can find any connection to the crew."

"Business partners are usually second. So Michael and Keegan."

"And the FBI will do the hard digging on them," said Lenny.

"So other business partners?"

"Who were?"

"Drew. Everyone says he and Will had something brewing, but he blew it off. He did meet someone last night, late at the yacht club, but I don't know who, or if it's even connected."

"So let's find out what that was. And the girls?" asked Lenny.

"No business as far as I can tell."

"Just funny business," said Lenny.

"Yeah. And that leaves Alec."

"Links?"

"Will bought his cars through Alec, apparently. Nothing more that I know."

Lenny nodded. "You've met him. Why not go see what he's about?"

"What will you do?"

"I'll go check out Celia Colfax."

I frowned over reading glasses that I wasn't wearing and gave him a look.

He just smiled.

# CHAPTER THIRTY

**Lenny left in** his truck to visit Celia Colfax, and Ron was out with his new insurance client, so I took my bike out to Alec Meechan's car lot. I decided to watch things from a distance for a while. I parked my bike in front of a taco shop on the opposite side of the road, then went in and sat at the window. There's a limit to how long you can sit in someone's restaurant without ordering anything, and in this case that limit was only fifteen minutes. There was no table service so I didn't get hassled by a waitress, but the guy behind the grill was a dark-looking unit with a meat cleaver, so when he started grunting in my direction I ordered a couple tacos and a soda.

I learned a few things about the automobile business. One, it wasn't a volume business. As I watched, only two people actually entered the lot. One took a look at the Ferrari I had driven with Alec, but left before Alec could get out there. The other stayed long enough to speak with Alec but left without a test-drive. The second thing I learned was that working in a lot would be a pretty boring job. Alec spent most of his time sitting in the goldfish bowl of an office, punctuating the time with sporadic walks into the customer-free lot. It wasn't that different from being a security guard, and I began tossing around ways one might combine those two jobs for greater efficiency.

It takes a particular kind of person to do stakeouts well. You have to be okay with sitting around doing essentially nothing for long periods of time, but be ready to jump into action at a moment's notice. I was generally fine with that. I had spent a lot of downtime in ball club locker rooms. Some guys almost went insane during a rain delay. I just cleared my mind and waited for the clouds to clear. Lenny was a master at it. He dropped into a trance of sorts, not speaking, barely breathing, but always watching. I wondered if it was something he picked up back when he was in the military. I could have stayed in the restaurant all day and waited for Alec to do something, but after a couple hours my taco and soda tab hit fifty bucks and I realized my wallet couldn't hold out much longer, let alone my stomach. I resolved to get proactive. I also resolved that if I was going to do stakeouts on my own in the future, I really needed a car of my own.

I pulled out the card Alec had given me and called the number.

"Palm Beaches Luxury Auto," was how he answered.

"Alec, this is Miami Jones. I test-drove the Ferrari with you the other day."

I saw Alec sit up straight in his office chair. "Jones, yeah. I didn't think you were serious."

"Why wouldn't I be serious?" Clearly he didn't think much of my motorbike.

"No reason. How can I help?"

"I'm still interested in it. Do you still have it?"

I watched Alec stand and look out from his office at the car in question. "I'm not sure. I don't see it on the lot. There was a lot of interest in that one."

I tried to hide the smile in my voice. "Oh, that's too bad. Well, perhaps another time then."

"Hang on, Jones, let me check something for you." Alec held the phone to his chest for a few seconds, and then he came back on the line.

"Looks like a customer had a hold on that one, but they didn't come through with the deposit yet. There is a waiting list on it by the looks of things, but since we know each other, I think I can bump you to the top. But we'd have to take care of it quickly, you know what I mean."

"Gee, Alec, you'd do that for me?"

"I always look after my friends." So it had taken only two minutes to go from a time-waster on a bomb of a bike to best buds forever.

"Well, that's swell," I said. I frowned at the *swell*. That might have been pushing it a tad far. "I'm in New York, at the Ritz Carlton tonight, and I won't be back in Palm Beach until late tomorrow. Can we do something then?"

"Sure, Jones, sure. I'll take care of it."

"Thanks, Alec. Appreciate it. Hey, interesting news about Will Colfax, wasn't it?"

"What was that?" he asked. "There's a lot going on there, I can tell you."

"I heard the feds raided his office."

"Yeah, I knew that."

"A golf buddy of mine who knows says the sheriff has let that other guy out."

"Ron Bennett? Yeah, that's old news."

"Yeah, but my buddy says because of the feds thing, the sheriff is going to raid everyone who was on the boat. Hey, hang on, you were on the crew, weren't you?"

"Yeah," said Alec, the confidence dropping from his voice.

"Did they raid you yet?"

"No. No, they didn't."

"Well, I'm sure you've got nothing to worry about, but if I were you, I'd clean up anything I didn't want the sheriff getting his nose into. We've all got stuff we don't want big brother getting into, right?"

"Yeah, right."

"All right then. I'll see you tomorrow."

"Yeah, tomorrow."

I hung up and paid my bill. I figured either Alec was going to do something, or he was going to do nothing. Doing nothing seemed a long shot. It was what he did that would determine whether I was interested in him. He didn't waste any time. He made another call, then he collected his keys, locked the office, pulled a chain across the driveway to his lot and put a padlock in place. Then he got in a Porsche hardtop the fluorescent orange color of a life preserver and took off. I was sitting on my bike, waiting for him to go, and I pulled across the road, got a couple horns sounded at me and resolved to never do that again.

I followed Alec onto I-95 south, and he opened the afterburners and took off like a rocket. He changed lanes without signals or regard for the presence of other vehicles, and it was only the garish color of the car that allowed me to see it pull off a couple exits later. As he headed east I almost lost him again, but the lights stayed red long enough for me to catch up, and I was two vehicles behind as we crossed the bridge onto the island. I could hear Alec revving the engine through the helmet and from five car lengths behind as he slowed and pulled onto Bradley Place. It was then I knew where we were going. I stopped a half block back and watched him pull up on the other side of the street from the Biltmore apartments, home of Will Colfax's widow, Celia. Lenny was already staking her place out, and was parked on the apartment side and down a touch, and he sunk lower in his seat as he gave me a little wave. I ran across the road and pressed myself against the hedgerow that ran around the grounds of the Biltmore and the Royal Poinciana South apartments next door. I called Lenny.

"Interesting development," he said.

"Indeed."

"Celia's not home."

"Where?"

"Lunch at The Breakers."

"How do you know that?"

"Doorman."

"They're not very discreet, are they?"

"If you ever live in a building with a doorman, tip generously. Their lips tend to loosen for a twenty."

"I'm gonna go up for a closer look."

"Don't let him see you."

I stuffed my phone away and crawled under the hedgerow and jogged past the Royal Poinciana, and came up on the side of the Biltmore. I pressed close to the building, which would have looked awfully suspicious to anyone who saw me, but I was more worried about being seen by Alec. I waited in the shade of a palm tree on the corner of the building and watched the front entrance. It took only a minute for Alec to come out. He looked agitated and was pacing up and down in front of the building. The doorman strode out under the canopy that extended out onto the driveway, which was raised above the street level.

"You can't just stand here, sir."

"You don't own the damned sidewalk!" Alec was on the phone but clearly getting no response as he started banging the buttons with his fingers, as if it were the technology at fault. He turned to the doorman.

"Just tell me where she is," he said.

"Sir, I told you. I don't know where Mrs. Colfax is, and I don't know when she will be back. Now it would be best if you left."

So old Alec was too cheap to blow a twenty to get the same intel Lenny had. Alec paced for a bit more, and then he strode down the driveway past me, toward the sidewalk. There he turned away from view. I wasn't sure if he was taking off again, so I called Lenny.

"What's he doing?" I asked.

"He's just standing under the canopy out the front. Looks like he's waiting for her to come back."

"Then I guess we wait, too."

I moved away from the front of the building, back to the lawn in front of the Royal Poinciana. The entrance to that building was actually around the side on Sunset, so I guessed I would only be disturbed by a gardener. As it was I didn't even see that much. The hedge blocked my view of the street, and Alec was out of my eye line, so I leaned against a palm tree. There was no sun, which was a blessing, but the air was so thick it was like drowning. Breathing came harder than it should, and I was sure the clouds were reaching down to the tops of the trees. After about a half hour Lenny called.

"I see a car coming."

I dashed back to the side of the Biltmore, and saw a conservative silver Mercedes pull up into the driveway. It looked very much like the car that had met Drew Keck late at the yacht club. That got me thinking about their conversation. She had said he had driven a bargain, and he had replied not for what he had done.

I pushed the thoughts from my mind and crept up the front of the building and pressed myself in behind a small palm tree. The doorman ran out and opened the door, and Celia Colfax stepped out.

"Celia!" called Alec Meechan as he ran up from the street level.

"I'm sorry, Mrs. Colfax," said the doorman. "He's been here for some time."

"Can't you do something about that?" she snapped at him, and I understood what Lenny had meant about looking after your doorman.

"Yes, ma'am," he said. "I'll call the police right now."

"No, damn it. Don't call the police. We don't want a scene." She left out an exasperated sigh, and then turned toward the approaching Alec. "I'll handle this."

Alec was puffing when he reached her. This was no weather to be running anywhere.

"Celia," he repeated.

"I told you to stay away from here."

"I need the papers," puffed Alec. His hair was dropping over his red face, and his suave appearance was lost.

"I don't care what you want, Alec, and I don't care what you were up to with Will. That's done now. We're done. Goodbye."

Alec stood straight and brushed back his hair, and spoke to Celia as she walked away.

"You walk away from me, then you're done too." He'd gotten his wind back because the words struck Celia like bullets. She stopped. She must have been considering her options because she took her time turning around, but eventually she did.

"Are you threatening me, Alec?"

"Those papers are mine, Celia."

"Those papers are Will's."

"They're no good to Will, and they're no good to you."

She thought about that for a moment. "If I give you what you want, this is the last time I see you."

"The last time, Celia."

She turned away again. "Come on, then."

I watched them walk away, toward the building entrance. I figured I wasn't going any further myself, so I retreated to my bike and called Lenny.

"Celia has some papers Alec wants, something he was doing with Will. She wasn't too keen, but she seems to be getting them."

"Your sheriff raid story seems to have lit a fire under him."

"It does, and there's more. She didn't want to do it, but he said if she didn't, she was done."

"Done how?"

"No idea. And there's more. I'm almost certain I saw Celia's Mercedes at the yacht club last night, meeting with Drew Keck." I explained the hard bargain and Drew's retort.

"So what is it that Drew did for the widow Colfax?"

"Someone more cynical than me might suggest he murdered her husband."

"That would be cynical. I'll keep on Celia," said Lenny. "See if she goes out again. You keep on Alec."

"Roger Wilco," I said.

"What?"

"I saw it in a movie."

"Goodbye."

# CHAPTER THIRTY-ONE

**I got on** my bike and waited about ten minutes, and then saw Alec jog down the driveway and back to his car. He looked to have his mojo back. He was carrying a large manila envelope, which he tossed onto the passenger seat, and then he dropped into the sleek car and powered away. I followed, shooting a quick wave at Lenny as we passed. We did a loop of the block and headed back to the mainland. Alec didn't head back to the freeway, instead turning onto Route 1. The traffic was heavy and clearly frustrating the hell out of Alec, because he constantly revved the engine, pulsing an annoying whine out into the ether. I followed him up toward Riviera Beach, but before we got there, Alec pulled off into the parking lot of liquor store. I kept going, not sure if I was made, or if he needed to buy a fifth of off-brand whiskey. I pulled into the next side street and walked back, helmet in hand, and stood outside the office of an insurance agent. I glanced around the corner at the lot. Alec was sitting in his car. He didn't appear to have gotten out, and he didn't appear to be doing anything but waiting. I looked around me. Just north of me the houses and stores stopped, and the road lifted into the air, as it passed by the open lots and container storage of the Port of Palm Beach.

It reminded me that I needed to visit Drew Keck, whose boatyard was nearby.

I watched a shiny Dodge Ram pull into the parking lot and stop on the far side of Alec. The two vehicles could not have been more mismatched for a clandestine meeting if they sat down and planned it that way. Both were nose in, so the drivers weren't window to window. The Dodge truck stood so high off the ground it should have been marketed with a free stepladder. The Porsche on the other hand was practically a go-cart. The drivers might have been contemplating who was going to come to whom, and they did it for so long I decided that they had nothing to do with each other. Then the driver of the truck got down and walked around to Alec's window. Alec didn't get out. His window came down and Alec handed the manila envelope to the other man. Before he took it, the guy from the truck looked around the lot, appearing to check if they were alone. But it was all for show, or because he'd seen it in a movie. If he had really looked, he would have seen me standing on the corner, watching him. But he didn't. He swept his eyes across the scene so quickly he would have missed a Sherman tank. He took the envelope and stuck a hand inside. He pulled out some papers, white and blue and yellow sheets, if my eyesight was all it should be. He gave them a quick look, slid them back in and pulled out something else, holding it close. I wasn't sure what it was until he flicked the end of it, and ruffled through a wad of cash. If they were ones, there must have been a thousand bucks. And I was betting they weren't ones. The guy dropped the cash back in the envelope and returned to his truck, and then he pulled out and drove away. I pretended to look at the interesting material in the window of the insurance agent, and then I turned back to the lot. Alec still wasn't moving. He turned the engine on to keep the AC working. I, on the other hand, was sweltering. My jeans were sticking to me like an abrasive second skin, and the sight of a liquor store I couldn't visit was something from the demented dreams of an explorer lost in the Sahara. After thirty minutes I was ready to throw in the towel. I certainly needed one. I saw Alec take a call, and then he pulled the Porsche out of the space. I ran back to the bike, and was putting my helmet on when he zoomed past. By the time I got onto the road, he was gone. I rode up the overpass, and as I headed down I noticed the orange Porsche below me, on the surface street, turning into the port offices.

I pulled my bike over to the side of the overpass and watched Alec park the Porsche in the lot and stride into the customs office. He was clearing something through the port, and if I knew one thing about the customs office, like all good government agencies, it was that bureaucracy moved like a glacier. I figured Alec would be a while, and I had no intention of standing in my helmet, the humid skies baking me from within like a microwave oven. So I jumped back on my bike and zoomed down to Riviera Beach.

I parked just inside the lot for the boatyard, left my helmet and wandered down to the water. I was looking for any breeze to cool my overheating core, but there wasn't a breath of wind, so I gave up and took my time getting to the large boathouse. I slipped inside and walked over to where Drew Keck had been working on the polished wooden boat. The boat stand remained in place, but it was empty. There was no boat. There was no Drew Keck. The area had been cleaned, and his tools were gone. I stepped around a patchy-looking white barge in the next space and found a guy who looked like Drew Keck's cousin, same hat, same mustache, bigger belly. The guy was sanding the hull of the barge and I waited for the buzz to stop before I could be heard.

I was going to try *ahoy*, but figured I'd better check the cred on that with Ron before I used it in public.

"Hey, there," I said.

The guy looked up through thick plastic safety goggles. He nodded.

"I'm looking for Drew Keck. He was working next door." I pointed in the general direction of the next slot in the shed.

"Gone," said the guy, which was really helpful.

"Yeah, I see that. You got any idea where?"

The guy shook his head. "Think he was headed north."

"When did he leave?"

"Put her in the water this morning." The guy turned the sander back on and that was the end of that productive conversation.

So Drew was into something with Celia Colfax, possibly involving the demise of her husband, and now he had taken off. It was suspicious, but I had no lead to follow, so I figured I'd better get back to the port office before I lost Alec as well.

But I didn't lose Alec. I stood out by a shipping container for another half hour, and then I saw him come out of the customs office. He strode out to the access road to the port, as if he planned on hitching a ride. Within a couple minutes, a convoy of trucks appeared from the port and stopped on the road. The drivers stayed in their air-conditioned cabs, and Alec walked alongside, looking up at the shipping containers that each semitrailer held. I grabbed a pen out of my pocket and scribbled down the container numbers on the back of Alec's business card. Alec walked the length of the convoy, turned back to the lead driver and spoke to him for a few seconds. Then with a collective grunt and sigh, the trucks pulled out.

Alec wandered back to his car, and I followed him away from the port.

East-west driving in South Florida is a drag. The Florida turnpike and I-95 run side by side down the east coast this far south, and they make getting north-south a breeze. But the east-west roads are like a fat man's arteries. We crawled west, out past the turnpike, until we got onto the Beeline Highway and the traffic fell away and we sped that last few miles to a warehouse near the raceway. Alec pulled in the gate and I stopped on the roadside. The whole area was just west of civilization, halfway to Lake Okeechobee. It was surrounded by lush vegetation, and even though it was only a few miles from Palm Beach Gardens, it felt like the middle of nowhere. The trees and scrub and low clouds and silence were claustrophobic. It didn't feel like a place man belonged. But men were there, in a convoy of trucks, lined up one after the other. I watched through the hurricane wire fence as one at a time the trucks entered the warehouse, and then one at a time they left, bare naked, their shipping containers gone. The whole process took an hour, and by the time the last truck pulled away, I was seeing unicorns. Unicorns drinking steins of beer. Beer that was delivered by Scandinavian wenches. And I had no idea what a Scandinavian wench was, or if such a thing even existed. I shook my head at the thought, and shook it again at the thought that the idea of unicorns hadn't fazed me at all. I was dehydrated and my head was pounding. I wondered if sunstroke was possible when there was no sun.

I saw Alec come out of the warehouse, get in his car and pull out. I wasn't sure I could follow. I was worried about keeping the bike in a straight line, but I had no intention of being out here after dark, so I got on and followed Alec back toward town. I lost him pretty quickly. He shot off into the distance, and it was a pace neither my bike nor my brain could match. I drifted into Palm Beach Gardens, and I figured I'd try the car lot. It was an educated guess, and as it turned out, the education paid off. I stopped in front of the taco shop again. The chain on the driveway was lying across the pavement, the Porsche was back in place, and Alec was sitting in his office, doing what appeared to be absolutely nothing.

# CHAPTER THIRTY—TWO

**I had an** idea that there must be some kind of place where I could check the container numbers I had written down, but I had no idea where that might be. Fortunately I knew a guy who always knew a guy, and I happened to be meeting my guy that evening. I turned up at Sally's store looking like a reconditioned zombie. I had made it home, drank a couple gallons of water with half a dozen ibuprofen, and then stood under the shower until I resembled an old man. The humidity had sucked the hunger from me, and I could feel the water sloshing around inside, so I just put on a fresh shirt and pair of chinos, and headed for Sal's. The girl in the check cashing booth was gone, and Sal recoiled as I walked in.

"What the heck happened to you?"

"Nice to see you, too," I said.

"Seriously, kid. You look like you just crawled out of Dachau."

"I'm not sure that's an appropriate reference."

"Then you haven't looked in the mirror. You sure you can drive to PSL?"

"We'll make it."

"That's encouraging. Give me a second." He disappeared into a back room, and then came out with an ill-fitting Mets cap on his head. "The car will be here in a few minutes."

"Okay."

I had gotten tickets for the baseball game up in Port St. Lucie, and given my lack of a suitable vehicle, we had agreed I would drive Sal's car to the game.

"You get anywhere with those containers?" I asked.

"Got a kid looking at it now. He'll have something by the time we get back."

We chatted for a bit, then a horn blasted twice outside and we walked out and Sal locked the front door. In the parking lot sat his classic '67 Cadillac Eldorado coupe. The car was the size of the Titanic, but didn't handle quite as well. A young guy sat behind the wheel. I made for the driver's side door, but Sal called me around and flipped the front seat forward and we both bent low and dropped onto the rear bench seat.

I looked at Sally. "I thought I was driving?"

"Like I said, take a look at yourself. I wanna make it there and back. Besides, young Christopher doesn't mind driving us, do you son?"

"Not at all, Mr. Mondavi."

"You gonna do some study while you wait?"

"Got my textbooks right here, Mr. Mondavi."

"Good boy."

The kid pulled the mammoth car out toward the freeway, and Sal and I leaned back and enjoyed the ride. It took about five miles for the Caddy to reach top speed, but once it did it floated above the blacktop with a grace that belied its age. We reached St. Lucie West inside an hour, and the kid dropped us by the entrance for the corporate boxes.

"See you in a couple," said Sally, to the kid.

"I'll be here, Mr. Mondavi."

I walked up to the stadium gate where the GM had left our names. The guy checking the names looked familiar, and when he glanced up from his sheet, he smiled.

"Say it ain't so. Miami Jones."

I pointed at him. "It's Pete, right?"

"Yes, sir, Mr. Jones."

"It's Miami. Mr. Jones was my dad."

He smiled. "Miami. Great to have you back here."

"Rex said he would leave some tickets here."

"Yes, sir. You gentlemen are up in the sponsors' box. Take the elevator right here."

Sal and I waited for the elevator, and were joined by some more Mets fans who didn't recognize me. I was okay with that. Even when I was a professional I always found it strange when folks recognized me. Most people would recognize the guy who cuts their hair every three months before they recognized a minor league baseball player. But in the small towns where teams were often based, there were always plenty of folks who did. I didn't mind people wanting to chat or grab an autograph, even though I never understood why, but the part I found disconcerting was the familiarity. People acted like you'd been college roommates, or shared a trench on the beaches of Normandy. Fame distorted our sense of familiarity, and the sense of access and entitlement that came with it. One time on the mound I was abused from the stands by a spectator for not turning up to the bar mitzvah of his son, who I couldn't recall ever meeting.

We got off the elevator and walked along the concrete concourse until we found the box. Inside white leather sofas and flat screen televisions greeted us. A lovely young lady in a white blouse and black skirt asked us if we cared for a drink, and we ordered two beers. Sal took a seat on a sofa that sat before a cutout in the wall that allowed a view down at the field. It was like looking through a giant flat screen. Sal looked at me like he'd sat on broken glass.

"All right?"

"Is this seat made of ice? I keep sliding off."

The girl came back and handed us beers, and then offered us access to the buffet of hot dogs and burgers. We each took a china plate and looked over the chafing dishes at the hot dogs. Sal was looking at the whole setup like he'd just been introduced to food.

"You know what I'd like?" asked Sal.

I looked down at him. "Yeah, Sal. I think I do."

So we left the box and found some seats in the stands. I handed Sally a plastic cup of beer and a hot dog wrapped in foil and he looked as happy as a pig in the proverbial. Sally was a man of considerable means and even more considerable connections, but his wants were simple. We ate our dogs as the players took the field, and as the Mets pitcher took the mound, Sal dropped into analysis mode.

"Kid needs to stand up—he's losing a good five miles an hour on his throws."

"He should curve it, though."

"Not much point curving it if the batter has all day to adjust."

The Mets dropped to three-zip to Fort Myers by the fourth inning, and Sally suggested I get my uniform on.

"We all have days like these."

"Aach."

I got Sal another beer and he nodded his thanks.

"So how's the PI business?"

"Can't complain. Keeps me in beer and shrimps. Lenny offered to make me a partner."

"So he should. You paid off that degree yet?"

"Yeah, that's done."

"What the hell is a master of criminology anyway?"

"I thought you were."

"Wise guy. You take a look at that house, the one in the brochure I gave you?" asked Sally.

"I took a look around."

"You took a look around."

"Yeah, nice view. The house is decent."

"It's on the auction block tomorrow, you know that," he said.

"I did."

"Good. You can pick me up."

I smiled. Some conversations with Sally were a *fait accompli*.

"That's reminds me. I saw your young lady on the TV."

"Beccy?"

"The blond one. She's gonna go far."

"I don't doubt that for a second. You know we're not together anymore, right?"

"I'm old, not senile. I'm just saying she was on TV."

"Fair enough."

The Mets batters faced only eleven pitches for the innings, and headed back out to the field.

"Sal, you know many of the folks in the sheriff's office?"

"A few, for better or worse."

"You heard of a Deputy Castle?"

"Not sure. Describe him."

"Her. Long brown hair, athletic build. Not bad-looking."

Sal looked at me from under his cap and gave me his full nicotine grin. "Not bad-looking? Yeah, I know the one. And *not bad-looking* is like calling Texas *not that big*."

"What do you know about her?"

"Good cop, smart. I think she was a triathlete or some such garbage at college. Why do you ask?"

"She's been involved in this thing with Ron. Just trying to understand who's who."

"That right?" He shook his head and turned to a crack of a bat as the Fort Myers catcher smacked one over the right field fence for two more runs.

"I'll tell you one other thing I know," he said.

"What's that?"

"Deputy Castle. She's married."

I nodded. Sal didn't look at me and I sure didn't look at him. I shouldn't have been bothered, and I shouldn't have been surprised. But I was. For all Lenny's joking, she was just doing her job. And it hit my pride, my ego more than I thought it should. We watched the game for a while in silence, sipping our beers. Finally I asked the question I shouldn't have cared about but did.

"So, who's she married to? Do you know?"

Sal nodded. "A lawyer."

"A lawyer? Really? Who? Do I know him?"

"Yeah, I think so." His smile turned into a chuckle that he tried to suppress but failed. "She's married to State Attorney Eric Edwards."

If I had eaten cinderblock I wouldn't have felt as heavy in my guts. I suddenly felt like I'd been played. The state attorney who was after Ron was sending his wife the deputy to feed us intel that was probably misleading. I wondered how Lenny didn't know that. But then I recalled his jokes, and I realized he had to have known it. Which meant he would have seen through the ruse, if there was one. Which meant it was possible that the state attorney's wife was telling us stuff behind her husband's back. Which really made no sense to me at all.

Sally was ready to leave after the seventh inning stretch. St. Lucie was going down in flames, so we wandered out to the lot. The Caddy wasn't that hard to find. It practically had its own zip code. The kid, Christopher, was sitting in the front with a textbook open and notepad in his lap. He seemed to be preparing for an exam in microeconomics, which I would think about later that night to help me get to sleep.

"How was the game, Mr. Mondavi?"

"The hot dogs were good, kid."

We drove back down to Sally's store, and he asked Christopher to wait for ten minutes, as he needed a ride home. We went inside and Sally led me into the back room. It was an office-cum-storeroom, like a slightly less orderly version of the store itself. Another young guy was sitting at a laptop at the desk in the room.

"Did you find anything, Jordan?"

"I did, Mr. Mondavi. I found that most of the shipping containers coming through Port of Palm Beach are owned by the shipping companies. But your containers are different."

"How so?" I asked.

"This is Miami Jones, Jordan," said Sally. "Jordan's a junior at the college. He does a bit of computer work for me to pay for his books."

The kid and I offered each other nods. We both knew he earned more than a little to buy schoolbooks. Sally didn't know much about new technology, but he was okay with that. He often hired smart kids from the college to do *odd jobs* for him, like computer work or chauffeuring him to ball games. And he had a habit of helping those kids finish college with no student debt whatsoever.

"So your containers are owned by another company, not a shipping company," said Jordan.

"What company?"

He clicked a key on his computer. "Cyntech."

"Will Colfax's company," I said.

"That's right. He's the CEO and major shareholder."

"So do you know where these containers came from?"

"I do. They came from Guangzhou, China, via the Suez Canal."

"Guangzhou? Where is that?" I asked.

"It's the provincial capital of Guangdong province, that used to be known as Canton," said Jordan. "It's mainland China, just north of Hong Kong." Maybe this kid was a geography major.

"Okay. So do we know what's in the containers?"

Jordan shook his head. "No, there's no way to access that without hacking into the Cyntech system." He looked at Sally. "And that might take a day or two."

"That's not necessary," I said. I didn't want the kid breaking into systems that the FBI might be looking at right now.

"But I can tell you what Cyntech does," said Jordan.

"Go on."

"It's kind of arbitrage. They buy failing companies in China, often the Chinese offshoot or joint venture of a foreign company, or they buy the excess and remainder stock of companies that have gone bankrupt for cents on the dollar."

"What sort of stock?"

"Anything and everything. Past shipments have included athletic socks, cheap MP3 players and even those little plastic American flags that they hand out at parades."

"So what happens to the stuff?"

"Cyntech sells it for cents plus a percentage, often to dollar stores, pop-up stores, other businesses."

"And that's it?"

"That's it?" Jordan frowned at me. "Dude, you don't get it. The stuff might be garbage that people don't really need, but that garbage is worth hundred of millions every year. Any given shipment could net them between one-half and five million."

"Dollars?" I asked, shocked.

"Not yuan."

"In little plastic flags?"

"You know how many of those things get sold every fourth of July?"

"A few?"

"About three for every American. That's close on a billion."

I nodded. "That's quite a few."

"It is. Plus they then break up the companies they buy, auction their stuff. The desks, the cubicles, the light fixtures. Or they sell the whole lot to the next joint venture starting up. They make money right down to the pencils. In one example I found, they sold the furniture and fittings to a company, and when it failed, they bought the same stuff back at auction for pennies on the dollar, then sold it to the next company. They've so far sold that same block of furniture and fittings four times to four different companies that have all failed."

"Nice business. So why is Alec Meechan delivering these containers for a guy who is now dead?"

"I don't know who that is, but I'll tell you something. From what the public data says, the containers are going back to China empty."

"So?"

"So a shipping company would never do that. They take up space on the ship and don't earn any money if they're empty. For a company that's pretty crafty about the business they're in, paying for freighting empty containers seems pretty dumb. There are plenty of brokers who will fill empty containers, for a cut."

The kid was right. That did seem pretty dumb. And he was right again. To make millions out of the business they were in not only meant that Will understood business fundamentals but also meant he had plenty of contacts to find the deals.

I thanked the kid for his efforts, and Sally walked us all out and locked up again, and then offered Jordan a ride home. Sal got in the back again, and Jordan slipped in beside Christopher.

"I'll see you tomorrow. Thanks for the beer and the dog," Sally said with a wave.

"Thanks for everything else," I replied as the huge car made its wide turn and headed away. I put on my helmet and sat on my bike for a while, talking myself out of going where I really didn't want to go, and failing.

# CHAPTER THIRTY—THREE

**I hopped onto** the turnpike for a bit and the traffic was light. By the time I pulled off at North Jog Road the traffic signals were my only companions. I rode back over the turnpike and as I turned onto the Beeline Highway I dropped into another world. It was like *Jurassic Park* or *Journey to the Center of the Earth*. There were no other vehicles on the road and the sad yellow headlight on my bike was the only source of light. I was riding through a tunnel of foliage and atmosphere, the barely tamed trees and shrubs either side of the road arching inward, their nightly coup underway as they attempted to reclaim the state from the asphalt and the cars and the people. Above me there was no starlight, no moon. A celestial blackout, a dreadful blanket thrown over the Everglades.

I pushed the bike further and faster. While there was no traffic at all, if any kind of animal wandered onto the road it would end badly for the both of us. The dark tunnel sent shivers down me, a supernatural force at work that pushed my bike forward despite what should have been my protestations.

Stopping didn't make anything better. As I pulled over and wheeled my bike into the thick-grassed water catchment channel beside the highway, I was assaulted by the noise. The night was alive, and the whining of the bike was replaced by something loud and organic. A trillion bugs sang a tuneless chorus, competing with frogs for the audible bandwidth. I wanted to know what was going on with the containers, and why Alec had collected them when they belonged to Will and Will was dead. But standing in the darkness observed by a million little eyes, I wondered how badly I wanted to know. But I shook it off, hung my helmet on the bars and grabbed a couple tools from the small pouch that every rider who had a bike with the reliability of mine learned to carry.

Then I saw a single light in the distance, like an oncoming train. I tensed and waited, transfixed by this singular source of light, as a sailor alone at sea would be on sighting a lighthouse. The light grew closer, and as it did it broke apart, one cell becoming two, life dividing and multiplying, until it became two distinct lights. Then the bank of light on top of the cab showed itself, orange from the white of the headlights, and a big rig bellowed through, the sound of the truck not hitting me until it was almost past. I watched it flash by, a roar and gone, swallowed by the cacophony and the night.

I rolled out the tension in my shoulders and stepped up onto the edge of the road. No points of light in the distance, so I walked along the strip of blacktop toward the warehouse where Alec Meechan had delivered the containers. I reached the main gate of the warehouse as a light appeared behind me on the road, and I pressed myself into the scrub and waited for another lonely truck to pass.

The warehouse was lit with sodium lamps, casting an amber tint across the low cloud and the lot. There was no sign of life. Human life at any rate. The swirls of amber made the building appear like an apparition, and then the lights petered out before they reached the edges of the lot, where the trucks had waited in line earlier that day, and where in the darkness the army of the night waited to take over, if given half a chance.

I noted the sign for the security company that patrolled the facility, attached to the main gate. The gate was locked tight, and coils of razor wire wound across the top of the wire gate and fence. I put my left hand on the fence and moved right, away from the gate, away from the light, from the solidity of man-made ground. The fence dove into the foliage and I followed. I kept my hand on the wire, as if it were my last tenuous grasp on civilization. I hit the corner of the facility, a thick steel pole folding the wire ninety degrees, across to the side of the parking lot, as far from the warehouse as one could get.

The trees and scrub had been cleared beyond the fence line when the facility was built, but after that had been left to encroach into the space against the fence. Keeping the tropical fauna at bay was a necessary task in South Florida, whether it was a warehouse on the outskirts of town or a gated community by a golf course. Even the lawns spoke of a desire to reclaim the state, and it was never more than a few months away from doing it. I swear some nights I could hear the grass outside my apartment growing. But the battle was also an expensive one, and in facilities like this, where aesthetics were of minimal concern, the wilds were left to themselves until they promised damage to the expensive security fences, at which point they would be hacked back again.

I stopped about one-third of the way along the far side of the square lot, and halfway between two of the poles holding the fence in place. I took out the pliers I had grabbed from my bike's tool bag, and I unclipped a series of ties at the base of the fence. When I thought I had enough, I returned to the center between the poles and lifted the wire. It was taut and solid, but with a bit of grunt and a few muffled profanities, I managed to lift it a few inches off the pavement. I got on my back and wiggled like a beached dolphin under the wire fence.

It took a lot more energy than I thought it would. I was puffing when I was done, and badly needed a drink, of the *agua* kind. But I brushed myself off and moved at a slow jog, away from the gate further, following the fence line beyond the gaze of the sodium lamps. In a couple of minutes I stood behind the warehouse. Here at the back there were more lamps, and with only five feet between the structure and the fence, I was bathed in amber. Fortunately there were no human eyes to see me. I checked the length of the building for a way in. It would be tricky. The fence was for show, and to keep flora and fauna at bay. The warehouse would have alarms, probably silent. No point putting in a siren out here, where there was no one to hear it. But the security company would, and at this time of night they could be here in as little as ten minutes. Unless a patrol was in the area, when that time could be cut in half.

The only option I could see was a window about ten feet above my head, and it would be locked or alarmed, or both. But it got me looking at a pile of pallets that had been lazily dumped on the back side of the building. They were in a bad shape, many missing slats, the wood discolored by old rain. But they were piled seven feet high, in an unsteady mound under the eaves of the warehouse. I figured the roof might provide the only way in, but climbing a makeshift ladder of unstable pallets didn't strike me as a genius of an idea. They were heavy and jagged. The cuts I could handle—having a pile of pallets land on me was another story. I tried pushing them into an orderly stack with no success, and I searched for another way but found none. I resolved to climb, genius idea or not. I spat on my hands for reasons that eluded me, and then grabbed the pallet above my eye level. The pile wobbled but held. I stuck my foot into a lower pallet and levered myself up, then reached for the top pallet. Then Jack came tumbling down. The piled pallets groaned and leaned, and I knew I was done for. I kicked away from the pile like a swimmer pushing off the end of a pool, and flipped in midair. The pallets dropped like a house of cards, crashing and splintering into the pavement. I landed and rolled and hit the fence, but did so just clear of the collapsed pile. I put my hand to my hip. There was blood, but not a flow. I had torn my pants and grazed my skin, but I'd done worse before, and would again. I stood gingerly to check that I could walk, and found that I could. I was canvasing the idea of getting the hell out of there when the paved lot exploded in light.

I pressed myself against the side of the warehouse and peeked around the corner. A truck beamed its lights across the lot, and someone dropped down out of the cab and unlocked the gate. Then they pulled the gate open and the truck drove into the lot. The truck edged along the fence that I had cut to get under, and there it waited, throbbing and hissing. The figure at the gate ran across the tarmac to the door. I saw them unlock a small door, person-size, and then step inside. Seconds later the main door creaked to life, winding around itself and curling up, like the yawn of a sleepy lion. Only a soft glow came from inside the warehouse, emergency lighting. The person who had gone in stepped just outside, soft light from behind, bright amber light from outside. And I saw Alec Meechan. Alec waved the truck forward. But the truck didn't move forward. It pulled further into the lot, then stopped and hissed again. Then it shuddered and moved backwards, curling around to point the back of the trailer at the door. It got about half in, and then stopped. The driver killed the engine, leaped out of the cab and ran inside.

I moved around the side of the warehouse to the front, and then edged along until I was but a few feet from the truck. It was an auto transport, loaded full with cars. Luxury cars. I glanced around the door to the warehouse. The driver of the truck was dropping steel ramps out the back, and before he got the last into place, a sleek black car moved back on the trailer. The ramp gave a hefty thunk as it dropped into place, and the black car raced down the ramp at a pace that implied both practice and confidence at the task. The black car, which I now recognized as a Maserati, zipped backwards, stopped on a dime and then turned and drove deeper into the warehouse.

I wanted a better look, so while the truck driver was pulling the next car down off the rack, I ran inside and around the edge of the warehouse. There wasn't a lot of light, but there was plenty enough for me to be seen. The warehouse was heavy with shipping containers and wooden crates, so I hid behind them and followed the throb of the Maserati. It was loud inside the confines of the warehouse, and then it became deeper and more resonant, and then stopped altogether. It was replaced by the sound of another car, also a deep muscular sound, but different. It moved into the warehouse and I pushed further in toward it and caught a silver Ferrari slow and then move inside a shipping container. The engine was doused, and the space again became quiet. I saw the two men stride back toward the truck in silence. Neat rows of pallets loaded with boxes were lined up alongside the empty containers. I watched from behind a shrink-wrapped pallet. As the two men walked away I glanced at the boxes. Fireworks, product of China. One of Will Colfax's deals. Cheap fireworks from a bankrupt Chinese factory. Heaven help us.

I stayed behind the boxes while the process was repeated. Another two cars, another shipping container. So Alec Meechan was shifting luxury sports cars in the dead of night. It didn't make the whole exercise look aboveboard. Quite the opposite. It felt, as Sal Mondavi would say, on the contentious side of legal. Why the cars were going into containers I suspected were headed for China was a mystery. The next two cars slipped into a container, and the two men returned to the truck. I heard the sounds of the ramp being pulled, then the sound of chains being removed and a hydraulic hiss. They were rejigging the trailer to get the cars off the top rack, so I took my chance.

I slipped into the nearest container. I wanted to know how legal this caper was. Inside the container was a Mercedes that didn't look like any Mercedes your father would drive. It was shaped like a bullet. I took out my little point-and-shoot camera to take a picture of the license plate but there wasn't one, so I slipped around the side of the car and looked through the windshield at the vehicle identification number plate. The VIN was a unique number assigned to each and every car produced, detailing in numbers the who, when, where and what of the car's manufacture. I tapped the flash on, and took a couple of shots.

The inside of the container lit up like New Year's Eve, and I stopped and held my breath, listening for Alec and the driver running back to investigate. All I heard was the hydraulics and clanking of the ramps as they were maneuvered into place. I ran further back into the container and repeated the trick on the car there, another sleek piece of work that I couldn't discern in the darkness of the container. I took a couple shots and edged my way out. I was at the mouth of the container when an M series BMW coupe grumbled toward me. I froze against the wall of the container, and then slipped back into the shadows. The BMW cruised by me and into another container, and another Ferrari followed suit. The two men strode out and back toward the truck, and I breathed again, and then ran out of the container and back down the side of the warehouse.

I heard another car come down off the ramps, and as I reached the front of the warehouse I saw what might have been an Aston Martin roll back off, turn and head away. I didn't wait to see any more. I broke for the outside. I figured I had ninety seconds—while Alec and the truck driver got the last two cars in place—before they came back and might see me. I sprinted across the lot, not bothering with the darkness at the fence line. I wanted the gate that was gaping open.

I'm not a great runner, not in the grand scheme of things. I'd kept up the odd bit of jogging since I retired from baseball, but I hadn't sprinted hard in eons. It hurt, and combined with my previous dehydration and that day's diet of beer and hot dogs, I was spent by the time I hit the dark foliage beyond the gate. I bent over to vomit, but it didn't happen, so I just sucked in as much as moist air as I could.

I stayed pressed into the trees for what felt like forever, but was probably six or seven minutes. As it was, I could have taken a leisurely stroll across the lot, and I cursed Alec Meechan for that. I wondered what was taking so long, and decided they must have been chaining the cars into their containers, readying them for shipment. Finally the truck roared to life and pulled out, the large door dropped slowly, and then Alec came out of the regular people-sized door and jogged across the lot.

The truck pulled to a stop just beyond the gate. If the driver had looked down past his left shoulder, and if he had the eyesight of a cat, he would have seen me there, holding my breath in the bushes. Alec pulled the gate closed and locked it, and then jumped up into the cab. The truck gave one last hiss and roared out onto the lonely highway, leaving me with the deafening silence of a million years of life on earth.

# CHAPTER THIRTY—FOUR

**I was woken** by my phone. It was Sally, making sure I was up and ready to come get him. I told him I was, and then I lay back down to go to sleep. But I had slept fitfully and ended up angled across the bed, so I dropped back to a pillow that was actually at my feet and I missed the bed altogether, dropping with a thud onto the floor. I dragged myself up and splashed some water on my face. My mind was a fog, lingering between the previous night at the warehouse and whatever it was I was supposed to do today. I contemplated some week-old strawberries in the fridge, but went with a glass of water. I wasn't sure how it was possible but it seemed to have gotten more humid. There wasn't a wisp of wind and the cloud acted as if it had heard bad things about the Bahamas and had no intention of heading that way. I wore my jeans again despite the steaminess, and I was sweating before I even got on the bike. Putting my helmet on was like sticking my head in a pressure cooker, and I felt my ears clog. Then I jumped on the bike and headed up to get Sal.

He was at the store already, and he left the girl in the cash checking booth in charge, which she seemed excited about, as exhibited by the emphatic nod of her head. I drove Sal's Caddy down to the courthouse and he saw a spot on the street, but I

didn't fancy reverse parking the huge car, so I drove on to a lot.
As we were locking up I told Sal about the cars I had seen the
previous night, and he agreed that they were most likely stolen.
I showed him one of the photos I had taken, one that clearly
showed the VIN of the Mercedes.

"You know how I can check out that number?" I asked
him. I suspected he knew a kid who could access a database or
something.

"Easiest way? Ask the sheriff."

"They'll tell me?"

"Depends who you ask. Surely you know someone you
could ask, don't you?"

I gave him a look, one he thoroughly deserved.

There was a small gathering on the courthouse steps,
people gathered in tight groups or standing alone, eyes hidden
behind Wayfarers that were completely superfluous with the
dark clouds overhead. At precisely five minutes to nine the
comptroller for the county came down the steps and handed
out a sheet with a running order of the auctions. Everyone
scanned it, some making notes. A few of the properties had
been pulled from the auction, marked as removed by order of
the court, I assumed because the owner had made good on his
debt to the bank. A couple of people looked at the list and
walked away, the property of interest to them having been
removed from proceedings. My Singer Island place was listed
as being fifth on the block. The comptroller started by telling
us that a certified check of approximately ten percent of the
purchase price was required immediately to secure the
property, with the remainder due before close of business that
day. I frowned at Sally but he gave me the palm of his hand
and a nod. *Don't worry.*

We watched the first two auctions take place. The whole process took four minutes, most of which was taking down the details of the winning bidder and collecting their check. Sally bid on the third property, a multifamily building in Wellington. One other guy was bidding, a cool-looking customer in aviator sunglasses and more hair product than a Texas debutante. They traded bids, the numbers going up by a thousand each time, the guy eyeing Sally through his shades, Sally returning the favor with a look that one generally reserved for those times when one was scraping dog poop off their shoes. The guy made a bid, and then the comptroller looked back at Sal, who must have grown bored of the whole thing, because he upped the bid by ten thousand and blew the other guy out of the water.

My place came up fifth. Sal suggested that I not bid straightaway, as there was every possibility the starting price might go down on this one, because the costs of redeveloping it in a falling market were too high.

"What about me?" I asked.

"You're not looking to develop, you're looking to live in it, and there aren't too many other home buyers who can pay all cash."

"I can't pay all cash."

Sal frowned at me. "Yeah, you can."

The comptroller called the auction number, residential property, and gave the particulars. He called out the starting offer and got no takers, and as Sally has foreseen, he began backpedaling, until final the price got too good to refuse, and the guy in aviator glasses got in. The comptroller asked if there were any other bids, and Sally gave me nudge and I put my hand up. The guy in the aviators put in another bid, maybe to see if I was serious, and I countered, and he quit. The comptroller called the property sold, and in four bids and forty-five seconds, I was a home owner.

I signed my name on a sheet and wrote my current address down, then Sally passed me a cashier's check and the comptroller's assistant wrote down the amount, the amount still owed plus the outstanding property taxes, and gave me a final amount to be paid that day. It was a much smaller amount than any standing house was worth in my estimate, and a tiny fraction of what a waterfront property would have sold for only six months previously.

"I don't have that much money in the bank," I said to Sally, and he handed me a document. Two sheets of paper, and I read it as we walked down the street to the bank. It was a loan agreement, between Sally and me, for the loan of monies for the purchase of said property. I didn't read the entire document. I didn't need to.

"Sal, I don't know if I'm comfortable having money come between us."

Sal frowned. "Aach. First, I never loan money I can't afford to lose or aren't prepared to hurt to get back, and I ain't planning on hurting you. Second, you will pay me what you currently pay for rent, and at that rate this debt will be done within three years."

"I'll own the house in three years?"

"Free and clear."

"What's the interest rate? That doesn't seem long enough."

"Prime plus zero point two five, as of yesterday."

"Sally, I don't know what to say."

"So shut up and sign."

I shut up and signed. Sally got two cashier's checks and we wandered over to the office of the comptroller, where he passed over the checks, and we each signed a document, taking possession of our respective properties, and then the lady at the counter handed us two sets of keys.

"Have a nice day," she said, returning to paperwork.

I looked at Sal. "That's it?"

He nodded. "That's it, kid."

"Seems somewhat anticlimactic."

"It ain't nookie, kid. Let's get back to work."

I drove Sally back to the store. The girl looked up at the tinkle of the bell on the door, and seeing us, folded up the magazine she had been reading and returned to the check cashing booth without a word. I thanked Sally again, and he grunted me away, and I made to leave and then noticed something in his store out of the corner of my eye. It was old aluminum baseball bat. I held it up.

"How much?" I asked him.

Sally appraised it like it was a Fabergé egg. "You get the hot dogs at the ballpark next time."

I smiled. "Deal."

I strapped the bat to my bike and headed toward the office, but my radar dragged me off course and I found myself wandering onto Singer Island. I didn't feel excited, but something in me wanted to see this property, this house that was now my house. My home. I took the bat, and put the key in the front door and opened it. The house was just as I had seen it before, when the contractor from next door had let me in, but now it felt different somehow. It wasn't a sense of ownership per se, rather a feeling that this house and I had wound our way through the previous three decades always destined to meet. I sat on the edge of the sunken living room and glanced around. It had been a long time since I had called somewhere home. I had lived in many places, places I had loved being. College in Miami, Modesto, Port St. Lucie, Palm

Beach. And while I had always felt at home in Florida, right from my first visit as a teenager, there was, I realized, a difference between feeling at home and being at home. I wasn't sure why I had bought the house. As much as anything it was to stop Sally hassling me about it. But that man knew things that maybe I would learn as an old man, or maybe he held wisdom I would never earn, but he knew. He knew I wasn't in need of a house. I was in need of a home.

I patted the bat in the palm of my hand, the soft metallic *tink* ringing through my bones, and then I stepped over to the sliding door. I dropped the bat into the track of the door, such that it couldn't be slid open, even if the lock were picked by a palm frond. I wandered into the kitchen and looked at the space where a fridge should have been. I resolved to order a fridge, *pronto*. I also resolved to call Florida Power and Light and get the power turned on.

I put my hand in my pocket to check I had both sets of keys, then walked out, locked up and went looking for the state attorney's wife.

# CHAPTER THIRTY—FIVE

**I drove out** to Gun Club Road, to the criminal justice complex that was becoming too familiar. I parked in the large lot and called Lenny.

"How'd it go, MJ?" asked Lenny, without a hello.

"I am officially a property tax payer," I said.

"Excellent news. I'm sure you got a deal."

Of the century, I thought. "What's Alec doing?"

"Nothing. He's in his office, staring at a computer. Not a single customer this morning. The only thing more boring than watching him work would be doing his work."

"Sally suggested I speak to someone at the sheriff's office about the VINs on his cars."

"Yeah?" I heard the smile in his voice. "You know anyone at the sheriff's office?"

These guys were having too much fun at my expense. "I thought you might."

"I know a young deputy who might be willing to help." He was having trouble stopping himself from laughing.

"You know she's married, right?"

"Is that so?"

"That's what Sally told me," I said.

"That so."

"Yes, so you can quit with the jokes."

"Jokes? What jokes? I'll call if anything happens here." He hung up on me.

I looked at the phone, and then got out and walked into the sheriff's office reception. I asked the civilian at the counter for Deputy Castle, and he made a call and told me to wait. I waited about ten minutes. The door buzzed, and Deputy Castle sauntered through. I was ready. I had practiced. I don't mess with married women, or other men's dogs, unless either are in grave danger. She was not in grave danger. I suspected she could handle herself in more situations than I could concoct.

"Miami, this is a nice surprise."

"Yeah, I'm here in a professional capacity." I was setting the ground rules firmly in place.

She smiled and broke my heart. "Of course you are. How can I help you?"

Let me count the ways . . . no, professional, that's what this is. I outlined the situation with Alec and his cars, and showed her the photos of the vehicle identification numbers.

She lowered her eyebrows. "How did you get these photos?"

"The door was open. I walked in."

"Trespassing?" Her voice was stern but her eyes were soft, and I really needed her to stop looking at me like that.

"There was no sign. I was just looking for the guy in charge."

"Did you find him?"

"No, I didn't. So I left. I don't know how these guys run a business like that."

"Indeed." She smiled again. "Let's go upstairs and run these."

I followed Deputy Castle into the building, and then up some stairs. The floor we came out on didn't look like any kind of police station from television. It looked like an insurance firm. Lots of cubicles, and the low-level hum of conversation. Danielle found a cubicle and sat down. She logged onto the system, not bothering to hide her password from me. But I was too busy watching her type to look at the screen.

"Do you have the first one?"

I handed her my camera and she touched my fingers as she took it, and smiled again. It was totally professional. She did some more typing, and then she frowned at the screen.

"This car is registered to a company. The address is in Palm Beach Gardens."

I leaned over her shoulder to look at the screen. Law enforcement officers should not smell that good. "I know that address. It's Alec Meechan's car lot. But that company isn't his car business."

"And the registration isn't a dealer tag." She hit a button and printed out a copy of the registration information, and then she moved onto the next photo.

"This is pretty fuzzy," she said.

"It was dark."

"Dark?" She frowned at me, the kind of frown that made me want her to be angry at me more often.

I shrugged. "It's a warehouse, you know. Not very well lit."

"Okay," she said, not buying it for a second, but letting it lie. I liked that about her. "What's this symbol on the tag?"

"I've been looking at it. It's sort of a stylized T, but I don't recognize it."

"Let's try these numbers." She took her time deciphering each number, and hit enter.

"What's it say?" I asked.

"Hmm. It says the car is called a Tesla."

"Never heard of it."

"It's new, I think," she said. "Not many around. But it's registered to the same company. Same address."

"So Alec owns the cars?"

"Someone using his address owns the cars, but they don't look stolen. Hold on."

"What?"

"This one is a salvage title."

"A what?"

She spun on her office chair and strode away. I wanted to follow, but I figured she would be back. She returned with a sheet of paper. She held it up to me.

"The other car is also a salvage title."

"What does that mean?"

"When a car is in an accident, and the insurance company determines the damage is too expensive to repair, they write the car off. The car is issued a salvage title, which tells any future buyer that it has been badly damaged."

"Why would anyone buy it?"

"Some people buy these titled cars and repair them. But even then, the salvage title remains, because often the damage is structural, like a bent chassis. But some people are prepared to take the chance on a salvage title, in return for a much cheaper car."

"Is that safe?"

"That's the question, isn't it? But here's another question. Did any of these cars look damaged to you?"

I shook my head. "No, they didn't. They looked brand spanking new, if you ask me."

"This is fishy," she said. "Let me make a call."

She did that. She spoke to someone on the other end, and gave them details about the company on the registration papers, and then she listened for a good time. Then she hung up and turned to me. "The company that has title on these cars is itself owned by a Bahamas corporation, registered address in Nassau."

"Nassau?"

She nodded. "And the US company director? Will Colfax."

"Huh. So Alec and Will were doing something together. But what exactly were they doing?"

"I know who'll know."

She jumped and nodded for me to follow, which I did willingly. The view from behind was all good. She glided down the stairs, onto another floor of cubicles, and turned to an office at the side of the room. She knocked and entered.

This was a real cop's room. There were file folders everywhere. The latent stench of cigarette smoke hung in the air. The guy behind the messy desk looked the part. He wore a wrinkled suit and short haircut, and his tie only came halfway down his belly, despite being loosened around his neck.

"Danielle," he said gruffly. He didn't seem quite as taken with her as I was.

"Neitz," she said. "This is Miami Jones, he works with Lenny Cox."

"Oh, yeah?"

"He's found something you might be interested in."

Neitz leaned back in his chair and put his hands behind his head. I assumed this was his listening position. Deputy Castle outlined what I had found, and showed the photos and the printouts to him. He gradually leaned forward in his chair, and dropped the hands, and became interested.

"What do you think, Neitz?"

"I've seen this before. They get people, straw buyers in other states—usually states with no sales tax like New Hampshire—to buy the car with money they supply as a cashier's check. They pay those people a few hundred bucks to make the buy and deliver the car. They do this because it's against the law to buy a car from a dealer in the US for export purposes."

"It's against the law?" I asked. "Why?"

"Them's the rules. Manufacturers don't want people buying cars cheaper here in the States and then shipping them overseas where they charge more. So the government's on it, the FBI is seizing cars and freezing bank accounts."

"But why is it against the law?"

The detective shrugged. "Because big companies with lots of money and lobbyists in DC don't like it. So the dealers make buyers sign a non-export agreement. That means there's a breach of contract if the buyer does, and it's that the FBI is enforcing, because the courts are saying that the practice itself is otherwise technically legal. But there is no rule against exporting a used car, so the company buys the vehicles as used from the straw buyer, then ships it overseas. But it's the salvage titles that interest me."

"How so?"

"It's a red flag. See, these guys get the car, then claim they were in an accident. They'd need someone on the inside on the insurance side, someone who would confirm the car was a write-off. They issue a salvage title, claim the insurance money."

"But if they bought the cars, they don't make any money from the insurance."

"That's where your containers come in. You say they came from China?"

"That's right."

"So I'll bet dollars to donuts that the cars are headed back to China. See, they claim the insurance, then they sell the cars on the black market in China. There are massive tariffs on luxury cars in China, as much as thirty to sixty percent. Plus all the luxury manufacturers charge big dollars for their cars there, much more than they charge in the US."

"Is the return worth the risk?" I asked.

"Never," said Neitz. "The risk is jail time, so when is that ever worth it? But there's certainly money in it. See, a luxury car that might cost $60,000 here in the US, might cost $140,000 in China. A $200,000 Ferrari might go for $600,000."

"Wow, that's some markup."

"That's a rich elite. The poor are dirt poor, but the rich are very, very rich. But being stingy is in their nature over there."

I raised an eyebrow at his social commentary. "You've been to China, have you?" I asked.

"Why would I want to go to China? Anyway, they make money both ends. You say these cars are in their containers?"

"In a warehouse up on Beeline."

Neitz stood. "I think I should go take a look." He picked up his jacket off the back of his chair and flung it over his shoulder. "How do I get in touch with you?" he asked me.

"Call Deputy Castle." I wasn't sure why I didn't just give him my cell phone number, but there it was. He ambled out and we followed as far as the elevator. He got in and left us standing there.

"You had lunch?" Deputy Castle smiled.

"Huh?" I was nothing if not an exercise in articulate communication.

"Lunch?"

"Ah, no."

"Does that mean, no, you haven't had lunch, or no, you don't want to join me?"

It meant all of the above.

"Lunch sounds great."

She drove a patrol car around the airport to a small taqueria. None of the menus were in English, but no one was speaking English anyway. The smells coming from the grill were to die for. Deputy Castle ordered for the both of us, and despite the threatening skies and growing wind we took a table by the street.

"They do great food here," she said. "Plus not many law enforcement types come here, so it's a nice place to get away."

"Smells great."

We sipped *agua fresco* and waited for our food, which came quickly.

"I hope you like fish," said Deputy Castle.

"Love it." My fish tacos were delicious.

"So how's Ron?" she asked.

"Better," I said. "You guys still looking into Michael Baggio?"

"Think so. It's not my area. I'm not an investigator—I'm just a deputy."

"You seem pretty well connected, through."

"You mean Neitz? He's one of the old breed." She bit into her taco with gusto, and I watched her eat. There's something about women who love to eat.

"I'm thinking more about downtown," I said.

"Downtown?"

"At the court complex."

"I know quite a few folks down there, I suppose."

"Lawyers?"

"One or two."

"Any state attorneys?"

She sat back in her seat and dabbed her lips with a napkin. I wasn't trying to surprise her, or catch her off guard. At least that's what I told myself. It was just an itch I had to scratch.

"What do you think you know?" she asked with an arched eyebrow. Suddenly I felt like I was the one under interrogation, which wasn't how this was supposed to go down.

"Tell me about Eric Edwards."

"What do you want to know?"

"What do you want to tell me?"

She smiled. "Nothing." She took another bite of taco. I didn't watch her eat this time, because she was watching me. I looked out at the lazy street instead.

"You're married," I said to the sidewalk.

"Is that what you heard?"

I turned back to her. "That's what I heard."

"Your intel's somewhat dated."

I frowned at that, and was about to follow up when her phone rang. She picked it up and listened.

"He's here," she said looking at me, and she listened again. Then she held the phone away and spoke.

"Neitz is at the warehouse. He says the containers are gone."

"They must have headed back to the port."

She relayed my words and listened again.

"He says he'll need a warrant to get access to the containers at the port. He wants you to make a written statement and for me to fax it to the judge."

"Okay."

She spoke back to the phone. "We'll do it now. The judge will have it within twenty minutes."

We left our lunch and I dropped some cash on the table, and Danielle said thanks to me and *gracias* to the cook and we headed back to her office. She typed the statement by memory, and she typed fast. I wondered if sheriff deputies took a typing course. It would be a useful skill for them. They certainly did more typing than shooting. When she was done she printed it and gave it to me to read, which I did. I signed it and she faxed it away.

We stood in the office without anything to say. I didn't want to ask why my intel about her was so out of date, but then that was the only question on my lips. Then her phone buzzed and she read a text.

"He got the warrant. He's headed in now."

I nodded and looked around the office. "What do we do now?"

"I've got work to do," she said, "but . . ."

The thought was never completed, as my phone rang. It was Lenny.

"Something's up," he said. "Alec just got a phone call and now he's heading out in a hurry."

I turned to Deputy Castle. "I gotta go."

"What? What is it?"

"Alec Meechan's on the move."

I made to turn but she grabbed my hand. It was like a velvet handcuff, soft but unyielding.

"Don't do anything silly, okay?"

"I won't."

"And if there's trouble, call me."

"I will."

She gave me the smile again and almost made me not go, but she dropped her hand from mine and I turned and ran down the stairs. As I hit the daylight I put the phone back to my ear.

"Where are you?"

# CHAPTER THIRTY—SIX

**Lenny was following** Alec on I-95, headed south from Palm Beach Gardens. I was already south of there on Gun Club Road, so I zoomed up onto the freeway. I couldn't see them, so I kept going. I didn't have a hands-free system on my phone, and talking on a phone through a helmet while riding a motorbike was a recipe for futility if not disaster, so I stuffed the phone up inside my helmet, tight against my ear, and I resolved again that I really needed a car. I screamed south and got disconnected from Lenny, so I had to pull over near Fort Lauderdale to reconnect the call.

"He's getting off toward Miami Beach," said Lenny, so I stuffed the phone back into my helmet and took off. When I got to the Miami Beach ramp I took it. Then I heard Lenny again, garbled through my helmet. I thought he said he was at Miami Beach marina, which was to my way of thinking really the back end of South Beach. I headed across the MacArthur Causeway and cut down Alton Road to the marina.

I pulled into the parking lot and headed for the rear, where Lenny was grabbing something from his truck in the lee of the swaying palm trees. I didn't think it possible, but the weather had gotten darker as I rode south, and the wind was whipping across the large lot. Something was about to give. Either the clouds were going to get blown away, or they were going to get blown apart. And the latter would mean a real dumping. I ripped my helmet off and my phone went flying, arching up into the air and then dropping with a shattering crunch on the pavement. The screen was smashed and pieces of plastic fell away as I picked it up. I tossed it with a shrug into the bed of Lenny's truck, and we jogged across the lot to the marina.

The office was three deep with vacationers looking to rent boats, but Lenny stepped around them and leaned across to the kid behind the desk.

"Where's Lucas?" said Lenny.

The kid glanced up and away, and then back again when his brain kicked in. "Lenny," said the kid. "He's out on the water."

The guy in the front of the line turned to Lenny like he was going to make an issue of the interruption, so Lenny gave him a ice-cold stare that dissuaded him from the idea.

"I need a boat, now," said Lenny.

"All I've got is the tender."

"That'll have to do."

"You know where it is."

Lenny did, and he didn't wait for directions. He yelled *thanks, kid* as we ran out the door and down toward the dock.

"Where's Alec?" I asked as we ran.

"He got on a speedboat, on the first dock. He was untying the lines when I came back to the truck."

"Why on earth did you go back to the truck?"

Lenny lifted up the back of his shirt to reveal his gun, the holster tucked into the back of his pants.

We got to the end of the dock, and dropped down the unseen ladder into a small tender that was tied up below. I pulled the lines away and Lenny fired up the motor and

zoomed out of the marina. He wasn't paying too much
attention to the no-wake rules, and I hoped the Coast Guard
on Terminal Island opposite the docks didn't see us. Lenny
pulled out into Government Cut and opened the motor right
up, and with a whine we took off.

"What kind of boat was he in?" I shouted.

"Fast one," said Lenny.

Lenny cut right across the path of a container ship coming
into port, and pulled hard back around through Fisherman's
Channel, past the ships being unloaded at the dock, and then
out along the south channel and under the Rickenbacker
Causeway, out into Biscayne Bay. There were plenty of craft
out, fishing boats and sailing yachts and jet skis. I trained my
eyes for a speedboat, one that was probably using that speed to
its fullest. Lenny kept to the Key Biscayne side of the bay, but
we saw nothing that drew our interest.

"We'll go to the end of the key," he yelled above the
whipping wind and the whine of the motor. "Then we'll come
back around past Grove Island."

"He might be going further south," I screamed back.

Lenny nodded. "And if he has, we've lost him. We can't go
that far in this."

It was true. Alec could speed down into Card Sound and
beyond. With a decent tank of gas he could make Key West,
and on a fine day maybe even Cuba. We were at risk of getting
stranded in the middle of Biscayne Bay in a boat designed to
take people to and from their moorings. Lenny kept the speed
up, though, until we hit Bill Baggs Cape, and the end of Key
Biscayne. He turned west, and pulled back on the throttle, and
the day fell silent. We both looked south, out into Biscayne Bay
and toward Card Sound further on. Then I felt a fat drop of
rain smack onto my head. It was like a water balloon. Then

another, and another. Huge globs of rain hit us. Then Lenny put his arm up and pointed.

"There," he said.

I saw nothing, and looked up at the clouds and got another drop right in the forehead. Going back to the marina felt like a good idea to me, but Lenny hit the throttle and banked around again and headed south. This time he didn't go quite so fast. He was watching the water, the ripples making it hard to see what I realized were sand banks.

The rain began properly with the sound of a machine gun hammering the aluminum hull of the tender. Lenny didn't take his eyes off the water, even as he was doused from head to toe. Then, in the middle of the bay, we passed a house. Not a houseboat. A house. It looked like a beach cottage, faded yellow from the years of wind and salt and rain. A house in the water. A house on stilts in the middle of the sand banks.

"Stiltsville," I said to Lenny.

Lenny nodded. "Have you been before?"

"No," I said. I'd heard about it. A community of houses built on stilts on the sand flats in Biscayne Bay. Back in the day they had been quite the thing, lots of illegal gambling and drinking, lots of good times for swell people. But hurricanes and bureaucracy had taken their toll, and from a peak of almost thirty buildings in the sixties, the area now only had seven.

"I thought it was off-limits," I said.

"It is," Lenny nodded. "The whole area is now national park. You need a permit to even moor at one. I don't think Alec cares about that." Lenny pointed again, and I looked ahead to see a yellow building with a green roof. It was low-built, despite being high on stilts above the water. Below the deck of the house, a speedboat was tied up.

"Is that it? That his boat?" I asked.

"It is," he replied, dropping the speed right down. The motor put out a low purr, but there was no way Alec could hear it. The rain pummeled the water and the deck and the tender, and cracks of thunder sounded across the bay in a deafening rumble. Lenny pulled the boat almost into line with the house, and cut the motor. We drifted forward and a little sideways, and came in directly under the stilt house. It was some relief from the rain, but not the sound. It was ear-piercing. Lenny used the stilts to pull the tender alongside the speedboat that was tied to the same dock under the house. Lenny grabbed our mooring line and reached around one of the stilt poles and tied us off. We climbed across the speedboat, and held up just under the house, out of the rain. Lenny reached back and pulled out his gun.

"You don't have yours, do you?"

I shook my head. "It's at the shooting range."

Lenny nodded. "Yeah. So I'll go first. Stick close. Visibility is going to be poor."

He looked at me, winked, and then jumped out into the torrential rain.

# CHAPTER THIRTY–SEVEN

**The sun was** falling in the sky but that was immaterial because it shone no light. The gods had grown angry and the clouds were as dark as night. Lenny was right—visibility was poor. Worse than poor. I could barely keep my eyes open to see Lenny right in front of me. It was like standing in the shower fully clothed. We crept up the steps to the deck of the stilt house, but we could have run for all the difference it would have made. There was no sound above the drum band of heavy rain and thunder.

Lenny stopped at the top of the steps and I looked over his shoulder. There was a deck that ran right around the entire house. Unfortunately the roofline only came out about a third of the way, and the pitch of the roof served to do nothing but concentrate the downpour onto the deck. Lenny pointed with a flat hand toward the house, along the side that took our direction toward the distant but invisible skyline of Miami.

We eased across to the side of the house. There was no rush, no dashing through the rain toward shelter. Sometimes there was only so wet a person could get. Lenny pressed himself against the house to get some respite from the rain, and looked at me. I brushed the water from my face and hair to get some sort of vision. What I saw was like standing on the inside of a waterfall.

I could no longer make out the handrail that ran around the outside of the deck, let alone the water beyond. Water ran in little rivulets down the creases in Lenny's face, random and racing to the bottom, where they met finally at his chin before falling from him. He ran his hand through his hair and turned away.

We moved slowly, Lenny edging forward until he reached a door that was about halfway along. He signaled for me to wait, and then he stepped past the door. With his pistol held high in his right hand, he reached back with his left and tried the door. The knob gave a little but not enough. He shook his head, and then he signaled that we would keep moving.

I stopped as Lenny reached the corner of the house, my eyes on Lenny's mane, the red hair gone waterlogged and brown. The rain was collecting in it like a sponge, and without its bounce it had lost its vitality.

He got into a crouch, and then edged his head around the corner to take a look. I assumed that he got low so anyone waiting in ambush would instinctively look to standing height, thus giving him a second to recoil if he saw something he didn't like.

But he pulled his head back slowly, stood and then slipped around the corner. We were now at the front of the house, nearest the Florida mainland, a little over a mile away. Despite not being able to see five feet, let alone a mile, I kept the map in my head to help me keep my bearings. I was edging around the corner when I felt Lenny stop.

I looked over Lenny's shoulder at the wall of wet darkness ahead. There, like a water spirit, I saw a shape appear at the far end of the deck. It emerged like an apparition, not seeming to come from anywhere, just appearing. A dark shape, formless and flowing. A ghost floating above the deck. It seemed to be looking at us, but I saw no face. Then my mind quickly did the recalculations, and the apparition took shape.

A man, standing just under the cover of the eaves, our side of the wall of water. A man wearing a dark poncho. A pointless attempt to ward off the rain. The hood covered his face, and the sides flapped, hiding his arms. The wind blew the shapeless poncho about, making it seem as if the man were floating in front of us, and I felt a shiver go down my spine.

Lenny raised his gun, two-handed grip, feet splayed.

"Freeze, Alec," he said.

He didn't yell it, but somehow the deep resonance of it permeated the white noise. There was no doubting Alec heard him, loud and clear. But he didn't move, he didn't speak. For what felt like minutes but was probably only seconds we stood there, one move from checkmate, waiting for someone to budge.

The apparition budged first. One moment he was floating there, the next he ducked around the corner of the house, gone.

"Stay close," Lenny said over his shoulder. He paced across the front of the house, gun held out in front. He got to the corner and spun around in one swift move, forgoing the get-low-stick-head-around-corner routine.

I took a few quick steps to keep in behind Lenny, and bumped into his back. He didn't turn. Again I looked over his shoulder, along the line of his arm, at the end of which extended the barrel of his pistol. I followed the sight of the weapon to the other end of the deck.

The poncho flapped at the far corner of the house, toward the deep blue, or as it was, deep black.

"There's nowhere to run, Alec," Lenny called. He held the gun steady and took small steps, like a dance move.

One, two. One, two.

We reached the midpoint of the house, and like the other side there was a door. Lenny moved by it.

"Just stay where you are," said Lenny. "Let's talk."

There was no response.

I moved to the door and tested the knob. It was locked, and I wondered if Alec had been waiting on the deck the whole time.

A crack of lightning exploded across the water, like a giant strobe. It lit the side of the house in vibrant color, but everything beyond the wall of rain was just a featureless silver burst. In front of the water wall I saw the poncho had his arm extended toward us.

A gun. Pointed right at us, or more specifically at Lenny.

I blinked my eyes to readjust to the darkness and heard Lenny yell again.

"Drop the weapon, Alec!"

Lenny stopped moving and I stopped behind him.

The rain continued pummeling the roof and the deck and the ocean, and all my senses were focused hard on Alec.

I didn't hear the door behind me open. I felt the earth move, the deck beneath my feet sending the smallest ripples through me, a physical sensation of creaking rather than an audible one. It made me turn back toward the door. Which, as it turned out, wasn't the best move.

I don't know exactly what it was—a plank of wood, a baseball bat—but whatever it was, rather than catching me on the back of the head, it hit me hard on the temple. Whoever had swung it did so with some pent-up energy, because it was out-of-the-park hard.

I heard a loud crack through one ear, a burst of pain, and then the vacant sense of falling, down and down and down, as if I were a giant, and Jack had cut my stalk.

I landed hard on my knees, a temporary position because I had no motor function to hold myself up. My brain had ceased all communication with my body as its internal alarm system shot to *defcon one*. From my good ear I heard a yell, a muffled scream of anguish.

"Miami!"

That wasn't the last thing I heard. As my body flopped forward toward the wet deck, I heard a shot ring out, then another. Perhaps two shots, perhaps one echoing in my mind, bouncing around my skull, in and out of my malfunctioning brain.

Then I hit the deck, a face plant, arms beside me, my cheekbone taking the full impact, as the darkness grew that little bit deeper around the edges of my vision. Then another thud, like I had fallen a second time, or was getting an instant replay in my mind. And then my limited field of vision was filled with another apparition, not my life flashing before my eyes, but a face.

The face of Lenny Cox. Looking at me, the way he often did. That trademark sardonic smile, as if he knew something I didn't know, which was almost always the case. As the darkness bled across my view I looked at his grin, and then up at his eyes.

His cold, lifeless eyes.

And then everything went black.

# CHAPTER THIRTY-EIGHT

**In the movies** people wake from a concussion, shake their heads, and run off after the bad guys, as good as new. It doesn't happen like that in real life. I'd been concussed before, on football fields in college and high school, although not as often as some. Playing quarterback kept the brain injuries to a minimum. But I had seen guys lose their memory of an entire game. I'd seen other guys remember everything, even the hours and days they sat gazing into space afterwards. The brain is mission control, and there is no mission without it. So it takes its sweet time getting itself together. But it also has an emergency system, a life-preserving ability to keep going, to keep moving, even when the circuits are frazzled.

I woke from darkness to near darkness. Not the sense of light, but the feeling of less dark. I lay in place for an eternity. I may have had my eyes open, or they may have been closed. Images began forming in my head, but there was no sense of urgency there. As if somehow my mind had floated out of me, taken stock of the situation, and then returned to tell me that the danger had subsided. After an indeterminable time I lifted my head from the deck, and propped myself against the side of the house. My vision wasn't blurry but my head pounded, a constant source of nausea. I tried breathing deeper but that felt bad, so I tried breathing shallow. That was less bad. I touched the side of my head and felt swelling around eye and cheek and side of my head, soft like a bag of rice. My hair was matted, sticky with congealed blood. I looked around, slowly moving my eyes but not my head.

The rain had stopped. I remembered the rain. Heavy drops still fell from the roof, hitting the deck and my legs, but the deluge had definitely moved on. I wasn't sure how long it had rained. I didn't know what time it was. I didn't know what day it was. I wasn't a hundred percent sure on the year. We had a new president—that I could remember, though I couldn't picture him.

I sat for the longest time, not replaying events or planning movements, just existing, like Lizzy's computer printer taking forever to power up. I finally decided to look along the deck, to move my head. Or maybe it just moved, I don't know. But I looked along the deck and saw nothing. A door, a long wet deck and then misty cloud. Then ever so slowly I rotated my head the other way, bracing against the wood siding of the house. More of the same. Deck, then nothing. And then I remembered the man in the poncho. And then I remembered Lenny.

I glanced down. Lenny lay next to me. He was on his belly, his face side on to where I had been lying for however long. One arm was propped under him, the other lay by his side. I slowly moved my hand to his head. His hair was thick and wet. I looked him over. There were two dark spots on his back. One about kidney position, the other in the shoulder blade. Bullet holes.

My eyes took it all in like a tourist videotaping the art in the Louvre. Capturing the scenery but not really seeing it for himself. Saving it for later, to be processed at another time, in another place. I noticed that one of his shoelaces was untied. The back of his shirt was pulled up a touch, exposing the small of his back. After I'd captured it all for posterity, I refocused my eyes on the mist that hung over the water. And then I cried.

It seemed utterly pointless. Everything was wet already. The rain had come and gone, washed the earth clean and moved on. It was a large ocean and a massive sky and my tears wouldn't fill a matchbox. But there they were. First just tears running down an already damp face, and then sobs that shook my body and pounded my head. For some reason the pain in my skull went away, for just a while. Maybe some kind of chemical reaction, one of those amazing things that our bodies can do. Great gasping sobs across endless water, the sound of my grief swallowed whole by the mist. I played no visions in my mind, no flashbacks of good times or bad times, of words said or not said. Just empty tears and groans.

And then I stopped. Just stopped. Not because I wanted to, not because I felt foolish. But because somewhere deep inside a switch went off. Or perhaps on. I gathered myself, took some deep breaths and felt the pain ebb back into my head. I wiped my face and resolved to move. I didn't know if the man or men who had been there before were still there, but my dinosaur brain said no, so I believed it. I edged myself up the wall and stood on unsteady pegs. Leaned against the wall and patted myself down. Something told me I didn't have a phone but I didn't know where it might be. So I tried the door to the house. It was unlocked. I moved slowly into the room, holding onto the jamb to keep myself upright. The interior was as dark as a cave. There was no ambient light making it in, and nothing to see.

I turned away. Stepped over the edge of the deck and grabbed hold of the railing, and then eased myself around

Lenny and along the deck. I took a long time to make it down the steps to the dock below. The speedboat was gone. So was the tender. I sat on the steps and looked at the water below the house, bereft of ideas and will. Then after some time, a little of both appeared. I dragged myself back up the steps, and around the deck. I knelt beside Lenny.

I didn't want to move him and I certainly didn't want to roll him over, so I reached under him to try his front pocket. He was heavy. The words *dead weight* seeped into my mind and I quickly removed my hand and breathed hard to stop the nausea from erupting. Then I started again, lifting him at the side. I reached in and felt his cell phone. It took some doing getting it out of his wet pocket without turning him right over, but I did it. I sat back against the wall exhausted.

I waited for the nausea to abate to its new baseline of imminent, and then I looked at Lenny's phone. It was a flip phone, an older thing like Lenny. It had literally been through the wash, so I figured the electronics would be shot, but I flipped it open and the little screen came to life, glowing blue. I tried the contacts, found Lucas and hit call. The ring tone was garbled, maybe from getting drenched, maybe because of the distance to shore. The ringing went to voicemail, a robot reciting the phone number. I hung up and looked for something else.

I wanted to call Lenny but his number wasn't there. I found a contact for MB Marina, and I hit it. It rang and rang, and then it too went to voicemail. An Australian accent telling me the marina was closed, try again tomorrow, if they weren't out fishing. I hung up the call and dropped the phone into my lap and looked out toward the mist. I felt very alone, like the last man on earth. No one left, not a man, not a woman, not even a volleyball to keep me company. Then the night burst into sound and the phone buzzed in my lap. I flipped it open. The screen told me it was Lucas. I hit the little green phone icon and held the thing up to my good ear.

"Where the bloody hell's my boat, mate?" I heard him say.

"Lucas," I whispered. I hadn't noticed how dry my mouth was until I had tried to talk. There was a metallic taste on my tongue.

"Miami? Where are you blokes? What's going on?"

"It's Lenny."

"Lenny? What about Lenny?"

I didn't know what to say, and anything that came to mind refused to pass my lips.

"Miami?" Lucas repeated.

"Man down," I said.

"Where are you, mate?"

"Stiltsville."

"Stiltsville? What the—? Which one?"

"Don't know. Yellow. Green roof." I wasn't sure if that was accurate or if I'd imagined it.

"Bay Chateau. Don't move—I'll be there a-sap."

I didn't move. I just sat there and waited. It might have been thirty minutes; it might have been two hours. But I heard the throbbing engine of the boat from the channel behind, and then it dropped low and took its time and then a spotlight hit the side of the house like a trainee sun. The light disappeared under the building, then the whole structure groaned under the weight of footsteps, and the light appeared around the corner of the house. Lucas dropped to the deck beside me. The flashlight lit him from below, his features hollow and dark.

"You all right?" he asked.

I nodded slowly. Then Lucas looked down at Lenny. He put his hand to Lenny's neck, the final gesture. He held it there for ten seconds, but there were no numbers to count. Then he flopped against the railing.

"Oh, Jesus," he said. He looked at Lenny for a moment, maybe taking it in as I had. But there were no tears from Lucas. He got to his haunches, looked at the house and then stood. He stepped past me and in through the door. With his flashlight there was probably something to see. But whatever it was, it wasn't of interest. He stepped back out, and looked at me.

"Nothing," he said. Then he turned toward the city. The mist was breaking and a faint glow emanated from the shoreline a mile away. Lucas watched it for a moment, and then he took out his phone.

"We gotta call the cops."

# CHAPTER THIRTY—NINE

**Rainy days suit** funerals. Lenny's funeral was bright and sunny. A warm wind came in from the northwest, the rain having poured itself dry and moved on. Lenny always walked to the beat of his own drum. He was buried at South Florida National Cemetery in Lake Worth. The cemetery was brand-new, vast open tracts of land. I stood looking across the manicured lawns that in another part of town might have been a golf course, and thought about all that space that would be filled with rows and rows of white military tombstones. It was a suitably depressing notion.

Lenny had requested interment rather than cremation on the grounds that he had already visited the fires of hell. The service was overseen by Reverend Prescott from St. Andrew's in Boca Raton. I'd never known Lenny to attend church, and no service was held in the chapel, but Lucas informed me that the reverend had served with Lenny, so I let it go. Regardless, the reverend spoke eloquently and accurately about Lenny. Often such speeches were performed by clergy who knew nothing of the deceased, and their words rang hollow, however well delivered they were. But Reverend Prescott clearly knew Lenny, and clearly knew a Lenny that most of us, save Lucas, had never met. He captured the essence of a man who had seen the worst that mankind could offer but came out of it expecting the best, and often getting it in return.

The gathering was large. Lenny had that way about him. There were many faces I didn't know, people Lenny had touched on his journey. There were many I knew. Lizzy stood by Ron, his arm around her shoulder as she silently sobbed from beginning to end. An assortment of law enforcement types offered their condolences. Detective Ronzoni stood emotionless at the back, sipping on a bottle of water. State Attorney Edwards stood tall at the front, hands clasped, head bowed. He might have been acting, but he looked genuinely sad. It took me some time to realize that his wife wasn't with him, and more time to notice Deputy Castle, standing in full uniform with colleagues, on the opposite side of the gravesite from Edwards. Perhaps it was a professional thing, but I didn't have the mind to think about it. Lucas stood with me, at the far end of the plot. He was a strong but sinewy man, laconic of attitude and economical in his movement, but even he looked stunted and unsure. After the reverend, Lucas said a few words, mostly anecdotes about Lenny's adventures. I didn't think he was trying to lighten the mood—rather he was speaking about the side of Lenny that he wanted so badly to hold onto, but he brought out a few smiles and choked giggles. After he was done the reverend asked if there was anyone else who wished to speak. No one moved to do so. Lucas gave me nudge.

"Go on, mate," he said, gently.

I didn't really have anything to say, but I stepped around the casket, perched as it was over the perfectly dug hole. I stood at the head of the gathering, faces ranging from serious to morose, all watching me. I didn't want to be watched, I didn't want to speak. I looked at the box that held Lenny. I felt no tears coming, just a malaise and a desire to sit in a dark room alone.

"Lenny was like a father . . ." I stopped and kept my eyes down at the casket. I took a breath, in through the nose, out through the mouth.

"There are a lot of people here today who would call Lenny their best friend. A lot of people. More people than you would think one person could handle, best friends–wise . . . but that was Lenny. He didn't think, he just did. He helped people not because he felt he had to, but because he could. He would say, *what else would I do with my time?*" I looked up at the nodding of heads.

"When you're a kid you're taught that you should go out into the world to find your one and only, your soul mate. Find that person and hold onto them and marry them and have kids and be happy. No one ever mentions the possibility that your soul mate might be a guy with crazy red hair, loud shirts and a fondness for beaches and beers . . . So you run the risk of going through your life not knowing that you have found your soul mate, and that the things you think you should be looking for aren't what you were promised they'd be." I took a shallow breath, just enough to keep things ticking over.

"And you find yourself standing in an open field, on a sunny day, in front of a hole in the ground. And you realize they were wrong—not intentionally—but wrong nevertheless."

I paused and looked at the shiny government-supplied casket, and swallowed hard the knowledge that this was not a dream.

"And you have to deal with the fact that you missed your chance. It was there, and you didn't take it. You missed the chance to tell him that you loved him."

I looked up again at the faces, known and unknown. There were more tears, and I couldn't help but think that wouldn't be what Lenny wanted.

"So let me tell you, each and every one, that Lenny's backstory was murky because I don't think he was of this earth. He was ethereal. More than the sum of his parts . . . he knew stuff, didn't he? Stuff he shouldn't have known, things that his history should have denied him knowledge of, but he knew. He knew where you were going, and he knew where you really needed to be, and he knew what needed to happen in order for you to get there." Again there was lots of head nodding.

"I wish I'd told him a lot of things. I really do. But I also know that he knew. And you know it, too. You know he knew. Somehow, he always knew."

A Marine guard played taps, to the silence that always accompanies it, then a Marine approached Lucas and handed him a folded flag. It was an odd moment, the handing of a flag normally reserved for a grieving family. In a way Lucas was that family, but truth was Lucas received the flag as executor of Lenny's last will and testament. Veterans had the option to donate the flag to the cemetery, to be flown on an avenue of flags on relevant holidays like Veteran's Day and Memorial Day. But Lenny had left instruction that his flag be donated to his local elementary school. That story brought a few smiles and comments of *typical Lenny* when everyone adjourned to Longboard Kelly's for the wake.

Mick opened the taps and put on a spread for the gathered crowd, his famous homemade fish dip taking pride of place. There was an unusual vibe. At such a time folks would normally look to console the family and enjoy memories with each other. But Lenny had no family, so people took to consoling each other, with hugs and laughter, and more than a few beers. Muriel came from behind the bar to give me a bear hug, her tears soaking my shirt. I told her to take five, and I jumped behind the bar and poured beers for a half hour. It gave me something to do, and a chance to chat with people without the physical contact that for some reason I wanted to eschew. I noticed that despite the free beer, Lucas was nowhere to be seen.

After I passed the baton back to Muriel I slowly made my way toward the exit of the courtyard. I didn't want to leave—I just didn't want to be there. I got into the parking lot, my keys in hand, where I ran into Deputy Castle. She was alone, and still in uniform. I got the sense that she had been crying but had waited to do it away from the public eye, and she hugged me hard. I wrapped my arms around her in return. She felt strong and frail all at the same time, and I realized that was just how I felt. When she pulled away, she ran her hand across the bruises on my cheek.

"I want to ask if you're okay, but that seems so stupid," she said.

I nodded.

"I know there's not, but if there is anything I can do, for him. For you." She hugged me again, her hand caressing the back of my head like my mother used to do. I didn't want to talk anymore, and she didn't ask me to. She held me for a long time, and it occurred to me that I didn't want to eschew physical contact at all. I was just scared by how much I craved it. When she let me go she kissed my cheek and dropped her hands to mine.

"If you want to, if you need to, just call." Then she left me to my business and walked into the courtyard.

I didn't know where I wanted to be or why, but I got in Lenny's truck and drifted back to the cemetery, as if I had private words that needed to be said. I wandered in, slipping on shades in the bright afternoon sun. I wasn't the only one with words to be said. Lucas sat on the grass by Lenny's plot. The VA didn't mess around. Lenny was buried and the fresh sod replaced. They hadn't put the tombstone in place yet, so the area looked like ground under repair on a golf course. Lucas saw me coming and nodded on my approach. He had two six-packs of beer sitting beside him. One six-pack was gone. He grabbed one from the second pack, opened it and handed it to me. I sat down next to him and took a slug, and then watched him take two more beers, open them both, and pour one into the ground over Lenny's grave. He sipped on the remaining one.

"Hell of a day," he said.

"One for the ages, just not in a good way," I said.

"You were right, what you said. He loved you, you know that?"

I shrugged. The gesture was unbecoming and unworthy of Lenny's memory. I knew he loved me, just as I had loved him.

"Like a son," continued Lucas.

"I know."

"I read his will."

I nodded and took a sip.

"He left you the business."

I frowned at him. "What business?"

Lucas smiled sadly. "The detective business."

"Seriously?"

He nodded.

"What about Ron? What about Lizzy?"

"I guess he figured you'd look after them."

I looked down the neck of my beer bottle and watched the amber liquid sloshing around inside. I didn't know what to think, let alone what to say. I was taken aback when Lenny asked me to partner with him in the firm, but I had no idea he planned to leave it to me. I wasn't sure I was capable of it. I wasn't sure I was capable of anything.

"He's left a few other things, bits and bobs," said Lucas. "And some stuff for Ron and Lizzy. Most of his money will go to charities helping wounded veterans."

That seemed about right. Then I looked at Lucas.

"What about you?"

He smiled a distant smile. "The silly bugger left me his prime possession."

I frowned again.

"His truck," said Lucas.

"Two trucks," I said. "You could start a car lot." Which made me think of Alec. Which made me think of Lenny, lying on a wet deck in Stiltsville. Which made me angry.

"I'm gonna find him," I said.

"Who?"

"Alec. Alec Meechan."

"He's gone to ground, hey?"

I nodded. "Hasn't been back to his car lot, or his house, according to the cops. I slipped the guy from the taco shop a hundred bucks to call me if he sees any movement at the lot. He said there's been nothing."

"He'll surface. They always do. Somewhere."

"Yeah," I said to myself, taking a sip of beer.

"What about the other two?" asked Lucas.

"What other two?"

"From Stiltsville. There were two other people."

"No, there was just one. Whoever hit me in the head, and the guy in the poncho. One of them was Alec. I can't be sure, but I'm wondering if the other was Drew Keck. He seems to have disappeared with his boat."

"There was a third," said Lucas.

"How do you figure?"

"Alec took a boat out there, by himself, right?"

"Yeah."

"But the other guy, he was already there. But he had no boat. He didn't swim there. Someone took him there, and then left. A third person."

I thought about that. It made sense. The second guy didn't swim there. He was meeting Alec for some purpose, probably something to do with the fact that the sheriff's detective, Neitz, had opened the containers at the port and found the cars inside. And Alec had gotten a call about that the moment Neitz had produced the search warrant.

Alec had a guy on the inside, in the port. I had seen Alec make a payoff to him. After I got back from Stiltsville I gave the description to Neitz and he picked the guy up, and the guy folded like a cheap suit, and told Neitz that Alec was shipping cars back out of the States without inspection, avoiding any customs interference due to the insurance fraud he was committing. Now Lucas had introduced a third person. Someone who wasn't there at Stiltsville but was still in it up to their neck.

"Did you get your tender back?" I asked.

"Yeah," he said, finishing his beer. "They didn't take it, they just set it adrift. Coast Guard picked it up for me."

I nodded and drifted away into thought again. Nothing rational or complete. Just random images, bouncing and colliding in my mind, like a tangle of cables I was trying to unwind. Lucas opened the last three beers, passed one to me and then poured one into the ground. We sat in silence, drinking and thinking, not a great combination. We were out of anecdotes, or at least out of the desire to tell them. They would come, in time. Lenny had an anecdote for any occasion, and we both knew he would never drift too far from us. After I finished my beer I stood and dusted the dirt from my suit. My only suit, for weddings, court appearances and funerals. I hoped I never wore it again.

"Gonna get going," I said.

"No worries," said Lucas. "Same time next week?"

I looked at the fresh, moist sod, and then at Lucas.

"Yeah," I said. "Same time next week."

I made to leave, and then Lucas spoke.

"You find something—I'm in," he said.

I nodded. I expected nothing less. I walked away and got into Lenny's truck. Lucas's truck now. I would arrange to deliver it to him. But for now I just drove. The truck smelled of Lenny, and I felt a storm surge building inside me. I didn't know why, but I drove to the office. Night was falling and the area was deserted. The court precinct didn't do after-hours, and I figured a fair few of the people who worked there were at Longboard Kelly's anyway, toasting Lenny. I stopped in the lot and got out of the truck that smelled like Lenny and walked up to the office. There was no nameplate for us at the front of the building, and no nameplate for us on the office door.

I unlocked and wandered into Lenny's office. His desk sat waiting. The room didn't smell like Lenny. It smelled of fresh paint and new beginnings, as if the world had moved on already. I wasn't prepared for that. Not by a long shot. I clenched my jaw and it was aching before I realized I was doing it. It was giving me a mild headache. Nothing like the one I had felt at Stiltsville, but it was there. The bruising on my face had reached its nasty peak and I looked like I'd been in a car accident. The doctors had shaved a small patch on the side of my head where they stitched me up, which completed the look.

I wanted to do something, to yell, to scream, to sound my barbaric yawp. I sat in Lenny's chair and looked around the foreign room. There was no past, no history, no ghosts. I wanted to find Alec Meechan and make a ghost of him. To put my big pitcher's hands around his neck and squeeze until he was blue and then black and then dust. To calm the red mist I stared at the wall of Lenny's office. The plain, unadorned, fresh wall.

I stood up, stepped over to the wall, took a pace back, and then like a punter trying to win the Super Bowl in extra time, I kicked out with all my energy. I put my shoe into the drywall. It was good stuff, solid and hardy, and I made a dent but not a hole. The second kick made a hole. I kicked methodically, not in a blind fury. I kept kicking until there was a large hole. Large enough for me to reach in and find the wooden box. The box that Sally had sent me.

I pulled it out, breaking away a bit more drywall as I did, and then I sat down at Lenny's desk and opened it. I unwrapped the cloth and held the Glock in my hand. It was cold despite the warmth of the day. Perhaps the air conditioning ducts leaked inside the walls, or perhaps the weapon had been in the hand of the grim reaper before I opened it up. I wrapped it back up, put it in the box and opened a drawer to put it in. In the drawer I found a bottle of bourbon.

I swapped the box for the bottle, closed the drawer, grabbed a chipped glass off the shelf and went and flopped onto the sofa. I poured a measure and drank it down and winced. Bourbon really wasn't my thing. But I'd get used to it. I poured another shot and sipped it slow, but the taste did nothing for me, so I knocked it back quick. I looked out the window, the silhouette of a palm tree dancing lazily in the evening breeze. Then I looked at the bourbon bottle, and I poured a little more.

# CHAPTER FORTY

**When I woke** my eyelids were stuck together and my head felt a familiar dizziness, but at least it wasn't pounding. I opened an eye and saw a gothic vision, Lizzy's face, dark hair and red, red lipstick. I took a moment to consider if I were dreaming, and then she poked me and confirmed I was not.

"Lizzy," I said.

"Did you sleep here?" she asked. I assumed it was a rhetorical question and that the answer was blatantly obvious. I was still in my funeral suit, and an empty bourbon bottle lay discarded on the floor. Good fortune had ensured the bottle ran dry before I was able to inflict maximum damage on myself. I sat up and rubbed my face. Lizzy picked up the bottle and placed it in the wastepaper basket. I noticed her attention was taken by something and I looked at the wall. There was a jagged hole in the drywall. I shot a look at Lenny's desk and saw no box, and then I remembered I had put it in the drawer, where I had resolved to never keep a weapon.

"Are you okay?" she asked.

"Yeah, I think so." I ran my fingers through my hair to comb it. "Some coffee. I think I'll go get some coffee."

"It's okay," she said. "I'll go." She left and I heard her close the outer door. She didn't mention the bottle or the hole in the wall and I was thankful for that. I didn't move from the sofa. A few minutes passed and I heard the outer door open again, and I looked up for my coffee but Ron walked in.

"What are you doing here?" I asked him.

He shrugged. "Didn't know where else to go." He looked at me sitting on the sofa, and then he looked at Lenny's chair behind the desk. He sat in the visitor's chair.

"You sleep here?" he asked.

I nodded.

"You disappeared yesterday."

I nodded again.

Then we heard the door and smelled the coffee. Lizzy came in with three paper cups. She handed me one, then offered one to Ron. Lizzy stayed standing as we sipped our drinks. It was hot and black and tasted like liquid road tar. Just what the doctor ordered.

"What happens now?" Lizzy asked.

I looked at her blankly. "With what?"

She motioned around the room. "Here. This business. It was Lenny's shop. Lenny's gone." She choked a little on the end of the sentence, and then sipped her coffee to recover. "Are we done? Do we all look for work?"

"No," I said. "Business as usual." I didn't really know what that meant.

"How is it business as usual? The business was Lenny's, right? So what happens?"

I frowned at her. I didn't how to word what I was going to say. It didn't feel right, despite what Lucas had told me.

"Nothing happens," I said. "Lenny left the business to me."

Lizzy's eyes widened and she looked at Ron, and then back at me. "He left it to you?"

I nodded. I shifted my gaze to Ron. Part of me felt guilty that I had been given this gift of sorts, and Ron had not. I didn't know why. Did Lenny think Ron incapable of running a business? He owned more suits than the rest of us combined, times a factor of five or ten. He had the business background. He brought in the corporate clients. But he did not own a piece of the business. Lizzy and I both looked at him.

"I don't know what to say, Ron. I don't know why Lenny chose me. You are the one he should have given the business to."

Ron shook his head and smiled. "Did you ever know Lenny to make a wrong move?"

Only one, I thought to myself, but I shook my head.

"No," said Ron. "He gave you his business because you have his soul, Miami. You carry him inside. He knew that you would do the right thing, even when that was the wrong thing. You'd do what Lenny would do."

I shook my head more, but said nothing.

"Besides," continued Ron, "This is not just a gift, it's also a burden. A burden he knew you capable of carrying. One that I cannot."

"What do you mean, you cannot? You know more about business than I ever will."

"It's not about that. It's about knowing the way forward, and doing what needs to be done. That's not me. I succumbed to that before, to stress. I lost a marriage over it. Lenny knew that about me. He knew that not holding me accountable for this place was itself a gift, in its own way."

I took a deep breath and looked at them both. I suddenly felt a great weight on my shoulders.

"So the only question is, do you still need me?" asked Ron.

"Of course I still need you."

"All right, then," he said.

"What about me?" asked Lizzy. She wore a frown, not of frustration, but of uncertainty. She and Lenny had a special connection. Lenny had a connection like that with a lot of people, but none more so than Lizzy. But Lizzy and I were like oil and water. We just didn't blend. You could shake the bottle all you wanted, but eventually we would separate. I figured that was a personality thing, or something more ethereal, well beyond my control. But what I knew was, despite all that, Lenny made her part of his team for the same reason he took me on board. I was a kid in college when we met, a baseball player and a football player and a student of sorts, but Lenny took me under his wing when I needed that most. He could have left it there. But when destiny brought us back together, when my baseball career came to Florida to die, Lenny was there with a new opportunity for me. Not because I couldn't do anything else, and not from pity. But because Lenny could see shapes and patterns that no one else could see. He saw a gothic woman with a snippy attitude and a devout love of God as the glue that held the shop together. He saw an ex-businessman with too much heart to be in insurance as the rainmaker. And he saw a former ball player as the person to sit in his seat.

"What about you, Lizzy?" I said. "I need you more than ever."

She looked at me for a long moment, without a smile.

"Good then," she said. "I've got things to do." She stepped out of the office and back to her own desk. Ron and I smiled at each other.

"So," said Ron. "What's the plan, boss? What are we up to?"

I stood and brushed down my suit pants. I had discarded the jacket during the evening, and now I removed the loosened tie. I stepped behind Lenny's desk and sat down in his chair.

"You met with some guys the other day? Insurance guys?"

"Actually, it turns out it was a personal matter. The guy thinks his wife is cheating on him."

"Sad."

"It is."

"So nothing in it?"

Ron made a face like it could go either way. "That depends. He's got money, plenty of it. Does our firm do that sort of case now?"

"That sort of case was Lenny's bread and butter, so of course we do. The only question is, do you want to do it?"

Ron smiled. "I do. Right now, I wanna be busy."

I nodded. "All right then."

We chatted for a while about other leads, other cases. He said there was every likelihood that if we solved this issue for his insurance guy, he would send a lot more corporate work our way, which would swell the coffers considerably. I told Ron it was his to do with as he saw fit, and to just ask for help if he needed it. He seemed pleased with the plan. After being in jail and then losing Lenny, he looked happy to be focused on the future. There was a knock at the door and Lizzy stepped in. I saw beyond her a guy in overalls.

"Miami," she said. "The sign writer is here."

"Who?"

"The guy with the new nameplate for downstairs. He's going to paint the company name on the glass door."

"Okay." I shrugged.

Lizzy stood looking at me like there was more to say, but I couldn't for the life of me think what that was.

"So what should he write?" she asked.

"What do you mean?"

Lizzy sighed like I was the dumbest hayseed she'd come across that morning. "It's your company now. What is it called?"

I saw her point. We were, had been, Lenny Cox Investigations. LCI for short. But now Lenny Cox was gone. In a few brushstrokes a man in overalls would change everything. Who we were, what we meant. Or not.

"The company is called Lenny Cox Investigations. LCI for short. Tell him that."

Ron smiled, and I might have been seeing things, but I thought Lizzy did too. She turned and closed the door. Ron and I finished up our meeting, and he went off to do his thing. I thought about what my thing would be. I needed some answers, and none were coming. So I needed to find the end of the thread, however tenuous. Something to unravel.

I stood and felt the keys to Lenny's truck in my pocket. I needed to get home and get this suit off, and then I needed to do some boring detective work. I opened the drawer and took out the wooden box and carried it out with me. The front door lay open and the guy in overalls was finishing up. Lizzy nodded at the door. In bold letters it said, *LCI*. In our hearts, and in paint, Lenny would live on. The sign writer asked if it was good and I told him it was great work, and he whistled as he wandered away down the hall. I looked at Lizzy.

She was looking at the newly inscribed door. "That's a nice thing you did, right there."

I shrugged. "We just got all new stationery."

She gave me a half smile, like I was a bit of a lunatic, but she could learn to cope with that. Then the smile disappeared and her face grew frosty.

"Miami, you have to find the guy who did this."

I nodded. I did have to find the guy. And I walked out to do just that.

# CHAPTER FORTY-ONE

**The thread I** had in mind lived in the Biltmore in Palm Beach. I went home and dumped the suit, grabbed a quick cold shower and threw on some shorts and a palm tree print shirt. I felt like me again. I took Lenny's truck and drove to the island and parked down the street from the Biltmore. I wasn't sure what I was hoping to see, but Celia Colfax was my best link to Alec Meechan, so I planned to see if she made any moves. She didn't. I waited and waited and saw nothing and learned even less. But that's the business. Private investigations sound like car chases and tuxedos and sexy ladies, but the reality is more long lonely hours sitting in cars, wading through files and reports and spreadsheets, and dealing with people who make their meager living on the seedy side of the tracks. I wasn't in any hurry. I didn't require constant stimulation. I just waited. I waited until there was a knock on the window of Lenny's truck.

I looked to the sidewalk and saw the mirthless visage of Detective Ronzoni. He signaled for me to wind down the window, but Lenny's truck didn't have power windows, so I had to slide across and wind it down by hand.

"Rice-A-Roni, what brings you here?" I asked.

"It's Ronzoni, genius, and the real question is what brings *you* here."

"The nightlife?"

"It's daytime."

"I just wanted to sit quietly and think. It's been a hell of a week."

"Yeah, well, I'm sorry about Lenny and all, but I've had complaints."

"You persist with that aftershave and that will happen."

He frowned at me, playing catch-up, processing what I said, analyzing it for sarcasm or whatever other filters he used. It was like watching a 1950s computer try to play chess. Eventually he frowned.

"Hilarious, Jones. I've had residents complain about a suspicious old truck parked on the street. This is a good neighborhood, Jones."

I wondered if the complaints were about the age of the truck, rather than its presence. "You on flatfoot patrol now?"

"I know when I smell a rat. What are you doing here?"

"I'm working."

"Who's your client?"

"I'm not at liberty to say."

"If you take Lenny's investigation into your own hands, don't think I won't throw you in the slammer."

"Investigating isn't illegal, last time I checked the constitution."

"I don't give a damn about the constitution—this is Palm Beach."

I had nothing to say to that.

"Leave the murder investigations to the professionals. Let us do our job."

"You're not investigating Lenny. That's Miami-Dade and the FBI. And I am leaving it to them. They're investigating things down there, like professionals. While you hassle law-abiding citizens for where they choose to park."

He gulped, and I got the sense he was getting thirsty. "Let me put it this way then, genius. You move your ugly truck away from here, or I'll impound it."

"For what? I'm not breaking any law."

"Disturbing the aesthetic."

I was impressed by Ronzoni's vocabulary. I wondered if he'd read that in a magazine. But wherever he'd gotten it, he held the cards. He could impound the truck for any old made-up reason, and I'd be stuck. I'd get it out, sure, and he couldn't search it. For that he needed grounds. But he had no intention of doing that. He just delighted in making a home deep down in my craw.

I didn't say anything more. I just slid back across the cab, started the truck and drove away, window down and all. I saw Ronzoni dusting his lapels as I drove away. I pulled out onto Route A1A, and headed down past the golf course, and then I took a left on North County Road, and drove north for a minute or two. Then I cut back around to Bradley Place and parked in the exact spot I had been in five minutes earlier. Ronzoni was gone, but whatever eagle-eyed neighbor had objected to my presence probably wasn't. So I couldn't continue to sit there for however long it pleased me. I had to come up with a plan B. I had to facilitate things, oil the gears.

Deputy Castle had said I should call, should I need anything. So I did. She was on patrol as it happened, and I told her what I wanted to do, and I told her that I was happy for the sheriff's office to tag along, to sit bored for hours with me and then head off and see what we would see. She said the investigation was Miami-Dade's, so the PBSO wouldn't want to tag along unless I found something concrete, but she was happy to facilitate the pouring of the cement. That was her phrase, not mine, but I kinda liked it.

The patrol car pulled up onto the driveway of the Biltmore and stopped right in front of the door. The doorman didn't come out. Deputy Castle went in. She was inside for twenty minutes or so, and then she came out and got in her car and turned the engine on to fire up the AC. I was only about seventy-five yards away, but she called me.

"She's unflappable," said Deputy Castle.

"Celia?" I asked.

"Yes. I told her that we believe that Alec Meechan shot Lenny, and we believe that he also killed her husband. She seemed more embarrassed by what people might think than the fact that we knew who her husband's killer was."

"Yeah, she was pretty upfront about their relationship."

"Well, I told her we knew she was one of the last people to see Alec, and that our office had found evidence that suggested her late husband and Alec were committing insurance fraud and Alec may have killed Will to cover it up. She didn't give me anything to go on with that, so I gave her some sisterly advice."

"Aha."

"I suggested that Dade County Sheriff might want to chat with her, so she shouldn't go anywhere. And then I said, just between her and me, that because Lenny was shot at Stiltsville, and that area is now national park, that the FBI would be all over it, and she might want to go to the ATM and get some cash out. She didn't get it at first, so I told her the FBI had frozen all Will's company assets, and that they might do the same to her personal assets in case Alec was trying to steal from her."

"What did she say?"

"Like I said, she's unflappable. She said Alec had no access, and I said I hoped not. But if he's ever been here, taken documents or anything with him, he might have what he needs. These people are clever."

"And?"

"And nothing. She didn't look happy, but that might have been because she was talking to me. I couldn't tell you."

"Unflappable."

"Exactly," said Deputy Castle.

"Well, thanks for trying."

"If anything does happen, you're gonna call me, right?"

"Yes, ma'am."

"Good. Stay safe."

She hung up, and then she pulled out of the driveway and down onto the street, and she offered me a serious nod as she drove by. I stayed put. I kept my eyes moving: windshield, interior mirror, side mirror, repeat. I didn't want Ronzoni sneaking up on me again. If I saw him I was taking off and he was going to have to pull me over in West Palm, where he had no jurisdiction. I watched the Biltmore. Nothing happened a lot there. I figured at worst Celia would react by going to the bank and pulling out some cash, no harm, no foul. My hope had been the idea of having her cash impounded might jag her into action of some kind, and if she did know where Alec was, or even where he might have gotten to, that she might spill some beans to Deputy Castle. It didn't work, but as Lenny always said, if you don't drop a line in the water, you never catch a shark.

And then there was a nibble. Or it might just have been the current tugging on my metaphorical line. But either way, a conservative silver Mercedes pulled up to the front door and a valet jumped out, and a moment later Celia Colfax got in and drove away. I suspected we were headed for Worth Avenue or somewhere similar, one of the shopping precincts where the local banks liked to congregate. But I was wrong.

Celia headed off the island and north up Route 1. We passed the port where Alec's cars were impounded, and the dock where Drew Keck had polished his boat, then past the turnoff for my new place on Singer Island. We hit traffic in Juno Beach but Celia kept going, all the way into the well-heeled town of Jupiter. Just before the bridge over the Loxahatchee River she cut back along route A1A, the beach road, into an area that was a mix of light industrial and trailer parks. She pulled the Mercedes to the curb in front of a valet station that itself stood in front of a jungle of palm trees, behind which sat a restaurant called Guanabanas. I pulled into a small lot opposite, grabbed an old Patriots cap and dashed across the road.

Guanabanas was popular with both locals and tourists, a warren of stone pathways between copses of palm and banyan trees, and palapa-covered bars. It was a large place that felt intimate because of all the nooks and crannies created by the trees. A few people sat at a bar not a million miles in style from Longboard Kelly's, just fancier drinks, more tourists and higher prices. Plus it was by the water. Which is where I thought Celia Colfax would be. I bypassed the host stand and headed down that way. A string of tables under white umbrellas lined the patio overlooking the water, an offshoot of the Intracoastal that wrapped around the small island opposite. At the end of the row of tables I saw Celia. She wore shades but no hat, and had not yet gotten a drink. She was alone. I didn't want to stand there, waiting to be spotted, so I slipped on my ball cap and retreated to the bar. I took a stool and made sure I could see Celia, and then I ordered a beer. I was looking at her back, over her right shoulder. A waitress appeared and took an order, and then returned to her with a large fruity drink with an umbrella in it. I wondered if that was lunch.

My view of Celia was in the direction of the water, where most people would focus their attention, so it didn't look suspicious that I was facing her. Even so, I took occasional glances at SportsCenter playing on a TV above the bar, and then back to Celia. At the top of the hour I saw SportsCenter restart, and the phone rang at the host stand. I watched the opening of the show on the television, something about college baseball, and then I glanced at Celia. She was gone.

I didn't panic. She might have gone to the bathroom; she might have wanted to wash her hands before lunch or taken a look at the river. Her drink was still on the table. I spun on my stool and looked around the restaurant but didn't see much. I was surrounded by palms and a massive banyan tree. Then I saw her. The waitress was walking her to the host stand, where she handed Celia a phone. The house phone. Celia spoke to someone, half away from me so I couldn't see her face. One hand held the phone to her head, and the other was pressed to her cheek. Then she was nodding, and then she hung up. I watched her return to her table and sit down, and then wave at the waitress. Celia made the universal sign to get the check, miming a scribble on a pad. She was leaving. She wasn't planning on finishing that big drink. It seemed like such a waste. But the question was, why? Then the penny dropped, and I looked back to the host stand.

A young hostess was holding two menus and walking away with a couple who both had skin the color of a fire truck. I slipped off my stool and weaved between the tables to the host stand. There was a phone on the desk, a fancy black thing with

an LCD display and more buttons than Apollo 13. Some of
the buttons had hand-written name tags next to them. Many of
the buttons had specific functions. Such things really weren't
my area of expertise, but I saw one such button that said
Number Recall. I reached over the stand, picked up the
handset and hit the button. The phone dialed, and I got tone. I
looked toward the sunburned couple who were perusing the
menu. The hostess was out of view. Then the phone at the
other end picked up.

"Sharkey's," said a bright voice.

"Hi," I said brightly in return. "Where have I called?"

"Sharkey's," he repeated unhelpfully.

"Where are you?"

"Key Largo, man. Where are you?"

"Jupiter," I said.

"Cool."

"Listen, did you just make a call to here?"

"Nah, man."

"Did anyone?"

"Oh, yeah, maybe. The chick in the hat. She asked to use
the phone."

"Which chick? What did she look like?"

"Like they always look like, man. Blond, big hat."

I bent around the desk to see if Celia was on the move.
"She a regular?"

"Nah. She's been here a few times in the past week, but
that's how it goes. What's the deal, what's this about?"

"Not sure, pal. She called me. Thanks for your time."

"You ever in Key Largo, drop in for a drink."

I glanced back behind the desk. The hostess was standing
there with hands on hips and a raised eyebrow.

"Thanks," I said to the guy on the other end, and I hung up.

I smiled at the hostess. "Wrong number." I didn't get a smile in return, so I walked back to the bar. Celia was gone from her chair. I sat down and finished my beer and then dropped some notes on the bar and headed out. It was time for a road trip.

# CHAPTER FORTY—TWO

**I stopped by** my apartment to collect my two guns and a couple extra shirts. I might be back in a few hours, or not. I didn't know. As I locked the door I made a mental note to give notice to the landlord, and to call some movers. Then I scrapped the idea of movers. I could carry my own damned bag.

It turned out Lenny had a lockbox under the rear seat in the truck, so I stashed away the guns. Lenny's gun wasn't in there, and I remembered that he took it out to Stiltsville, but it wasn't collected by the cops, so that meant Alec Meechan had it.

I drove down the freeway through Miami, and then hit traffic and crawled to Key Largo. It was conceivable that the traffic was going to continue that crawl all the way to Key West, which was no way to arrive in that particular paradise. But I got off and made my way to the east side of the thin slice of a key, and found the restaurant known as Sharkey's. Like Guanabanas, Sharkey's was a local institution, a favorite of boaters who enjoyed pulling up to the dock outside and stopping in for a quiet drink or a bite to eat. I watched some boats do just that. It was a multistory place with decks and a gas pump at the side for the boats. The place was busy but relaxed, the waitstaff brisk but not harried. I wandered over to the bar. A well-tanned guy with wavy hair and a porn star mustache smiled widely at me.

"Howdy," he said.

"Back at ya," I said.

"What's ya poison?"

"What do you have?"

His smile grew. "Lots of good stuff. Craft beers, rum buckets, you name it."

"Gimme something easy drinking."

"Comin' up." He poured me a beer and passed it across the bar.

I sipped and nodded my approval. "Say, were you the guy I spoke to earlier on the phone?"

"Been here since opening, so probably me," he said, wiping down the bar.

"We were talking about the woman who made the call, the blond with the hat."

He nodded. "Oh, yeah, right. Thought you said you were in Jupiter, man."

"I did. I was."

"Got down here lickety split. You must really be keen on this broad. You're not one of them stalkers, are you?" He smiled like it was okay if I was.

"Just keen to chat with her. She took something from a buddy of mine. Just trying to get it back."

The barman nodded in the way barmen do. "His heart?"

"His life," I said.

The barman nodded again as if he understood the metaphor, and I didn't feel the need to explain that it was literal.

"So you said she's not local?"

"Nah, man. Never seen her before this last week. But she's been here a few times lately."

"Does she often use the phone?"

"You know, now that you say it, yeah, she does." He shrugged. "Guess there's still folks don't use a cell phone."

Or don't want calls to be traced to their cell phones, I thought.

"Did she eat, drink?"

"Yeah, drinks I think."

"Credit card?"

"Cash, as I recall."

I sipped my beer. "You didn't happen see a car, which way she came from?"

"I did actually. She didn't come by car."

"No?"

He nodded toward the dock. "She always arrives by boat."

I looked through the restaurant toward the water outside. "That right? You know what sort of boat?"

"Nah, didn't see." He nodded to a couple further down the bar like he had work to do.

"Well, thanks."

"You bet."

I watched the barman pour a couple drinks and sipped at my own. I wondered who Celia was calling down here, and if she was another link to Alec. My bones told me she was. Maybe she was the third person, the one who had delivered the second guy to the house in Stiltsville, if Lucas's theory was correct. The barman wandered back to me and I thought he was going to ask if I wanted another beer, despite being only halfway through the one I had.

"Hey, I just had a thought. If you wanna know about that chick's boat, you should talk to Links."

"Links?"

"Yeah. He handles the gas pump outside. He'd know about who docks."

"Awesome, thanks."

"Yeah," he said, wandering away, picking up glasses as he went.

I finished my beer and wandered out to the dock. There was fleet of motorboats, mostly hybrid craft designed for pleasure boating and a touch of fishing. At the end was a larger vessel, a sport fishing effort with a tower and swivel seat at the back to fight the big fish out at sea. A hose was connected to the tank, filling it with gasoline, and a stocky guy with an unkempt stubble was leaning against the hull.

"Links," I said.

The guy looked at me through squinted eyes. He had wrinkles around his face like dry river beds.

"The guy at the bar said you were the man to talk to," I said as I got to him.

"Uh-huh."

I explained the conversation I'd had at the bar, and the guy called Links didn't move. He stayed leaning on the hull, his face like Monument Valley, changing, but only over the course of millions of years. Finally he spoke.

"I 'member. Never got gas here, though."

"You recall the boat, by chance?"

"Yeah. Boston Whaler."

That was about as useful as saying male Caucasian. Every second boat was a Boston Whaler.

"The small one, with a Mercury 190."

I nodded. I thought that was the engine size, but wasn't completely sure. "You know where it came from?"

"Aha. Smitties."

"Smitties?"

"Yeah."

Apparently I was supposed to know who or what that was, but I didn't. "What's smitties?"

"Boat rental. Down key."

I thanked Links for his time and wandered back inside. I stopped at the bar and asked about the location of what I belatedly realized was called *Smitty's*, and he gave me directions. I left him a healthy tip and got back in the truck and headed south.

Key Largo is the biggest of the Florida Keys, and the closest to the mainland, so for many Floridians it feels just as rushed and crowded as Miami, and the least keys-like. I drove down the Overseas Highway at no more than twenty miles per hour, and was thankful when I got to pull off just before Tavernier at the south end of the key. Key Largo had become famous for the movie with Bogie and Bacall, which itself had been shot on a backlot in Los Angeles. The part I visited now was more backwood than backlot. A travel guide might call it off the beaten track. There were a lot of mangroves, which served to hide a lot more hurricane wire fencing, which always gave a place that penal colony quality that realtors loved so much. The lots were large, the homes small and the yards full of rusted cars and trucks, discarded refrigerators and boats that seemed better maintained than anything.

Smith's Boat Rentals was at the end of a dead-end street, no cul-de-sac, just a clump of mangroves before you hit the water. It was a small tin shed that played the part of an office, and a dock that needed some work but had probably been through more hurricanes than the fences. I parked and took a look down at the boats on the dock. There were only a couple, and on one the cap was off the motor, as if brain surgery were being performed. Each had *Smith's Boat Rentals* written across the hull in small stick-on letters, followed by a serial number.

I walked into the shed. There were two desks, both messy with papers and such, and one man. He was at the desk furthest from the door. A bank of handheld CB radios stood in a charger station on the first desk, alongside a large unit that looked like an old ham radio. The guy was thin and reedy and had dark eyes that seemed to move on springs. He had the kind of angular face that would make a parent push their child behind their legs if he offered the kid a lollipop. I made to walk over to him and he hopped up quickly to meet me beside the first desk, and ended up way too close, for someone I had no intention of kissing.

"Help you?" he said.

"Yes, I think so. I'm looking for a woman who rented one of your boats this week. A blond woman."

"Don't know her."

"I don't suppose you do. But you rented a boat to her."

"No."

"No? You didn't? She was seen in one of your rental boats on several occasions this week."

"You a cop?"

If I were a cop, I was from somewhere a long way away, and I was on vacation. I looked down at my palm tree print shirt as way of explanation, but he didn't seem to get it. "No, I'm not a cop," I said. "Are you Smitty?"

"I don't have time to chitchat with time wasters."

"Perhaps I want to hire a boat."

He looked me up and down. "Don't got any to spare."

I looked him in the eye and he looked at me. Then he shifted his gaze away, and back again. He was a fidgety unit. But he wasn't sharing, so I left. I didn't feel much like saying thank you, so I didn't. I just walked out and sat in the truck and looked at the business before me. It wasn't a fancy operation— in fact I was sure in a thesaurus under antonyms for fancy there would be a picture of Smith's Boat Rentals. I watched a boat returning to the dock from a day out, two guys in shorts and tank tops with a large cooler. More drinking than fishing, I suspected.

I hadn't seen any signage on the highway for the place, so I didn't know how a tourist would get wind of it, and even if they did, I had to think the folks coming down from Maine and Vermont and Ontario would turn tail and run at the sight of the place. So it begged the question, who was he renting to? Clearly the place and the attitude were tailor-made for customers looking to do no good. I could imagine if I were a pirate, this is the place I'd come for a boat. So I got out my new phone and called the closest thing I knew to a pirate.

Lucas answered with a laconic *yeah?*

I explained to him events with Celia and the mystery woman, and my no result at Smitty's.

"Yeah, I've heard of Smitty. A favorite of low-rent drug runners across the Caribbean."

"So how do I find out who this woman is? Any ideas?"

"You say she's had the boat for the week—then she might be reporting in."

"What is that?"

"Most rentals are day rents, so the boats are back by the end of the day. But some places rent for longer periods, and they usually require a radio call each evening to report where the boat will be mooring overnight. That's probably logged somewhere. A computer or something."

"Not sure this guy gets that technological."

"Then a logbook."

I looked over at the shed office. He wasn't going to show me his logbook. But there was more than one way to tack a boat. I smiled to myself at that cunningly clever metaphor, and I thanked Lucas.

"You need any backup?" he asked.

"Not right now."

"If you do, don't be a hero."

"You bet."

I hung up the call and started the truck and drove back up the key toward Sharkey's, to kill some time. The same barman was still there. The guy worked a long day, but he hadn't lost his smile. I ordered some fish and a beer and sat on the deck, overlooking the water. The place was getting busy, folks coming in from a day on the ocean to swap fishing stories and sunburn remedies. It felt like a fine place to while away some time, and I was tempted by another beer or two, but I held off. The barman made me a Virgin Mary that satisfied more than I thought it would, and I watched the water change color and the birds hurry about with last-minute errands, and the night fell. The buzz in the restaurant picked up as I walked out, sad to go but like the birds, things to do.

I drove back to Smitty's. I parked farther up the road by a seaside shack that appeared to be shuttered and walked down to the shed. I wasn't too concerned about any kind of high-tech security, but there were thoughts of guard dogs and shotguns playing in my mind, so I made a wide reconnaissance sweep. I found no dogs, but I did run into an obstacle. It seemed Mr. Smith, if the reedy guy I had met in the office was he, lived on a boat tied up to the dock. I could see a number of other boats had returned from their days out, and Smitty sat on the deck of his own boat, something that looked like a miniature tugboat, drinking from a Solo cup and smoking a cheap cigar that was wafting in my direction. I didn't have much choice but to wait, so I pushed myself against a throng of mangroves and set about that waiting.

Smitty fell asleep in his chair. I wasn't sure if he would spend the night there, but given the look of him, anything was possible. I crept over to the shed and took a look at the door. It was locked with a padlock that wasn't giving way with the tools I had, and not without a great deal of noise. I stepped lightly around the shed, over crushed shell that sounded like a marching band to me. Fortunately the night wasn't silent. Bugs, the slap of water on boat hulls and distant traffic filled the air with a hum of white noise. I made my way around the shed and found one suitable candidate. At the far end of the structure, an old air conditioner hung limply in the window frame. I didn't recall it working earlier in the day. I tested the window above, and found it rusted and salted in place. I lifted the air-con unit up and tried pulling it out, as quietly as I could. There wasn't much give between the sill and the window, and the heavy unit moved only by wobbling it from side to side. The same action also made a grinding screech that would have had the night animals scurrying. I stopped, skipped to the corner of the shed and looked over to Smitty's boat. He hadn't moved and I hoped he was in a rum slumber. I returned to the window and gave it a second effort, lifting and pulling and edging, and the hefty unit eased out. I was hoping it wasn't plugged into an outlet, because pulling it out was going to be easier than pushing it in, and as it kept coming my wish was granted. The unit came free from the window and the full weight fell into my hands and I nearly dropped it, grabbing it at the last second against my groin. I pulled the electrical cord free of the window and a brown ooze the consistency of blood spilled from the air conditioning, running down my shorts and onto my leg. I didn't even want to think about what that stuff was. I just placed the unit on the ground with a soft seashell crunch, and then sat on the window sill. I ducked my head through the window, spun my hips around and flicked my legs over and into the shed.

The office was dark. The moon was only a day or two off being full, but years of grime and sea salt covered the windows and kept the moonlight at bay. I flicked on my small flashlight and made immediately for the desk next to my open window. It was the rear desk from the door, where Smitty had been sitting when I arrived earlier that day. The desk was a sea of paper, haphazardly discarded and spread across the desk. There was no order to it at all. Hand-written notes in a cursive scrawl, computer printouts and Post-it notes, along with receipts for gas and storage and fishing tackle. There was nothing that resembled a logbook. I figured it was possible that Smitty kept such information in his head, but I stepped around to the second desk for the sake of being thorough. Most of the second desk was taken up by the CB radios, the big unit and the handheld units in the charging station. The bigger unit was old, but the handhelds looked like the newest things in the entire place. The rest of the desk was clear. I checked the drawers and found the detritus one always found in drawers, but that was all. I did a sweep across the walls, looking for shelves and such, but I didn't recall any from earlier that day and I didn't find any now. I took a last look across the desk, at the big CB radio, and that was when I saw it.

It was tucked behind the radio unit, against the wall, not so much a hiding spot as a filing spot. I pulled it out. It was a black composition notebook, the kind of thing kids used in elementary school. I opened it and found it divided into four columns by hand. Date, vessel, name and location. I flicked to the last entries, which were about eight pages in. The very last entries were dated that day. There were two. The final one gave the vessel as *2*, written in floral script, name as *Green* with no title, and location as *O/S*. I wasn't sure what O/S meant. Maybe offshore. I moved up to the second last line. Date, then vessel written as *4*, name of *Miss Black*, location *BPK Mar*. I glanced up the list on the rest of the page, and then flicked back a page. All the renters' names were colors. White, Black, Purple, Red, Green. The only notation to have a title was Miss Black. Clearly Smitty didn't get a lot of women customers. At least not alone. About two-thirds of the notations gave the location as O/S. I figured I'd check that with Lucas.

I flipped the book shut and was slipping it back behind the radio when I had a thought. I had no idea where it had come from, and it didn't attach itself to any kind of logic. It was just there, a seemingly random thought, a spark across my mind, the sort of thing we do a thousand times a day. Random but not. Like when you lose your keys, and then a day later you're thirsty, you go to the fridge and see the milk, but you don't want milk, and you don't know why. You think milk is white, and white is a color and orange is a color and you took an orange from the fruit bowl yesterday and didn't have your keys after, so you go to the fruit bowl and find your keys lying underneath a bunch of bananas. It was that kind of thought. I just didn't know if or how it linked to anything. I took the book out again, and flicked open the last page, and then worked back through the dates, to the night Lenny was shot. There was a notation. Vessel *4*, Name, *Miss Black*, Location, *O/S*. Then my mind flipped another switch and I got the idea to go back further. To the night Will disappeared, and there was another notation. Vessel *4*. Name, *Miss Black*. Location, *O/S*.

# CHAPTER FORTY-THREE

**I returned to** Lenny's truck and drove away. I didn't want to be near Smitty's, in case he woke up, or one of his O/S notations turned up in the dark, or the cops dropped by. I figured they were all possibilities. I tried to put the air conditioner back in the window, but it was like putting a hundred-pound square peg in a round hole. I left it facedown under the window, to give the impression that it had fallen out all by itself. No one was going to buy that, especially not a suspicious guy like Smitty, who used codenames in his logbook, but I figured it would mess with his head anyway. I drove into Tavernier and parked in the lot of a small neon-lit bar. I found a gun rag in the lockbox and wiped down my legs. The stuff that had come from the air conditioner was nasty, the closest I would ever come to primordial ooze. When I was done I went inside, ordered a beer and used the bathroom to clean my shorts as best I could. I came out with a wet patch across my groin, and as I approached the bar, a pink guy in a floppy hat smiled at me.

"Have some trouble there?" He laughed to himself.

"No," I said.

"You've peed yourself," he said, looking around for anyone else to enjoy his frat boy humor.

"I don't like to waste time," I said, grabbing my beer and dropping a note on the bar. I walked away and found a table in the corner, away from the speaker that was playing something by some eighties hair band. It wasn't too loud; it wasn't that kind of a place. But I wanted to make a call. I sat and called Lucas. I could hear a distant party in the background.

"Sorry, are you out?" I asked.

"I'm in the parking lot, just enjoying the moonlight. That hubbub's coming from Monty's. Autumn's like spring break for retirees. What's up?"

I told him about the notations I had found at Smitty's.

"So what do you think?" I asked. "O-slash-S."

"Yeah, could mean offshore. That would make sense."

"But that could be anywhere, then."

"I think that's the point. Smitty doesn't want to know where his boats go or what they do. I told you, it's that kind of an operation."

"So if this Miss Black is the third person, and she took the second person to Stiltsville, that means she was out on the night Will died."

"Maybe. Smitty might use Miss Black for every woman he hires to."

"That's a hell of a coincidence. Do you buy that?"

"Nope, I'm just sayin'."

"Well, what about BPK Mar? That mean anything to you?"

I got the sound of relaxed, rhythmic breathing as he thought about it. "Nothing comes to mind. Mar means March in French, or sea in Spanish."

"I'm not sure it's a whole word. There's period at the end of it, like it's abbreviated."

"You didn't mention that, mate." More breathing. "Okay, here's something. BPK down that way, could be short for Big

Pine Key. And if that's the case, *Mar.* might be short for marina."

"Big Pine Key Marina?"

"There's a fishing resort on Big Pine Key, lots of slips and an RV park."

"So Miss Black might be there. Or she could have lied."

"True. Folks often lie about where they are mooring, for all kinds of reasons. Especially the types of folks who rent from the likes of Smitty. But there's a thing about that. People will give a fake spot, but the spot is rarely random. It's usually a place they've been, and as often as not, somewhere they will return to. Either that or it is polar opposite. It's fifty-fifty."

"We'll, I've got nothing better to do. I'm going down there."

"Good. Take a look, suss it out, but don't do anything stupid. Not 'til I get there."

The traffic that plagued the daytime was gone late at night, but the speed didn't improve a whole lot. There were signs along the road to keep the speed down at night or risk hitting wildlife or getting a ticket. I had no desire for either, so I took my time and got down to Big Pine Key inside an hour and a half. Big Pine Key Fishing Lodge was a large plot by the highway, a two-story reception and communal building fronting an RV park. The main building was locked tight for the evening, and a chain had been placed across the driveway into the park, so I stopped on the dark road, down a little, and walked in.

Some teens were watching something on television in a room behind the reception, and two boys played ping-pong. I expected campfires and fishing tales, but as I wandered down the path all I passed were darkened RVs, save the glow of television from within. Air conditioners clanked away to ensure no one's viewing was disturbed by the annoying sounds of wildlife. I got to the end of the path, where an area was dedicated to tent spots, which were all dark and done. No electrical connection, meaning no television, so darkness meant sleep. I cut around the shore to a dock with a series of slips. There were some nice boats, which ruled out Smitty's vessels. A couple looked like the owners were staying aboard. I got to the end, saw nothing and turned around. I followed the shore back the other way, and on the opposite side of the park were more slips. They looked smaller, but still mostly full of boats. There was a row of motel rooms by the slips, and I wondered if these constituted the fishing lodges. I walked the length of the motel and saw lots of fishing boats, some rentals, but none belonging to Smitty. I got to the end of the motel and found myself near the front of the park again, so I cut across and out over the chained driveway, and headed back to Lenny's truck to get some sleep.

I awoke to the sound of my cell phone buzzing. It was Lucas, on approach to Big Pine Key. The sun was hinting at breaking, and the chain was gone from the driveway. Fishermen like an early start. I wandered down to the first dock I had walked past, and saw Lucas motor in. He was in a sharp-looking speedboat with a big engine, and the whole thing looked like a restrained bronco puttering along in the no-wake zone.

Lucas tied up and we shook hands and walked back to the front office. There must be some sort of guild of marina managers because the guy behind the desk gave Lucas a big smile as we walked in. Perhaps they had an annual convention in Hilton Head every summer. Or not. Lucas introduced me and the guy gave me nod.

"We're looking for a woman. Blond, in a boat from Smitty's," said Lucas.

The guy frowned. "Smitty's?"

"Yeah, I know."

The guy tapped on a computer keyboard. "We got a few women booked in, but no solos."

My mind immediately hooked onto Alec, and whether he was here. Lucas must have seen the look on my face, as he placed his hand on my shoulder.

"Go easy," he said, and then he looked back at the reception guy. "What about the boat?"

The guy called to a woman who was selling sunscreen to a customer who looked like she'd walked across the Sahara in a bikini. Sunscreen wasn't going to help her. She was a candidate for skin grafts. The woman behind the desk passed her two bottles to compare and came over to us.

"You seen any boats from Smitty's?" he asked. She looked at the computer, and then at us.

"Not last night."

Lucas nodded. "Thanks."

"But not everyone was accounted for."

"How so?"

"Well, you know. Lots of boats don't get in until late. Some guys like to fish in the dark, for all the good it does. And we close the office at eight, so not everyone's necessarily in."

"You log all the boats?" I asked.

"Of course. The customer gives us the serial number or name. Whichever. And we check them off, morning and night. But we don't keep a record of who isn't there, just any that shouldn't be. And I didn't look specifically for one of Smitty's. I just didn't see one all the same."

"But it's possible it's out, and coming back."

"Could be," she said. We thanked her and she wandered back to sell sunscreen, and I tried another tack.

"The woman we're looking for might have been here a while. A few days, maybe a week. Blond, quite a looker apparently. Wears a big sunhat."

"Yeah, okay. Maybe," said the guy. "A blond came in maybe day before yesterday and filled up with gas. I sent one of my kids down to help her out. But he won't be in 'til later, and honestly, I doubt he'd remember what the boat looked like. She was quite a catch, if you know what I mean."

We nodded and thanked him for his time. Lucas asked if he could borrow a couple camping chairs, and we bought some breakfast sandwiches and carried it all down to the end of the park. The sun had broken and the park was alive. People were lined up at the ablutions block, and trailers were being hitched and the smell of eggs and bacon wafted from more than one RV. Campers were sitting out under awnings, drinking coffee and planning their days. We cut between a couple of tents to a beach I must have skirted the night before. The beach sat on a point, such that we could see every boat that came and went from either dock. We looked directly at the bridge that took the Overseas Highway across Spanish Harbor Channel. The sun was getting higher and the water looking inviting. In other circumstances a day's fishing might not be the worst thing in the world. I didn't really do fishing, in the same way I didn't hunt cows. I liked them both as a food source, but I didn't see either thing as sport. Lucas loved fishing, but again he caught only what he could eat. I guess when you spend part of your life hunting people, as I suspected he and Lenny had in the military, the sport element of fishing was somewhat overdone.

We waited and watched for several hours. We were the only people on the small beach, and our solitude was broken

only by a visit from a key deer. The small deer wandered onto
the beach and watched us, and then stepped just out of hand
reach, I assumed looking for a feed. We had finished our
sandwiches and had nothing to offer, so the deer stayed long
enough to figure that out, and continued on its way. After the
deer left I took a bathroom break and got some sodas and a
couple more sandwiches. I stopped by Lenny's truck and
grabbed the two guns from the lockbox. I put the unregistered
Glock in a holster under my shirt, and tucked my Ruger into
the back of my shorts. Lucas took a nature break after me, and
went and checked his boat, or whoever's boat it was that he
had arrived in.

He came back with a set of field glasses. We took turns
scanning the water, more for diversion than anything. If Miss
Black came back to the lodge, we'd be able to read the make of
her sunglasses from where we sat. I was looking underneath
the highway bridge, and the section of the old bridge that
stood on the northern side of it, when I saw a white boat head
toward me. It wasn't a new boat, but it wasn't ancient either,
but what I noticed most was the driver. Most guys drive boats
by standing or sitting on the back of the seat and looking over
the top of the windshield, wind hitting their face. I don't know
if it was a manly thing, or some long forgotten evolutionary
link to Labradors in cars. But this driver sat low, right behind
the wheel. It occurred to me that a person would do that if
they didn't want their hair blown around, or their large sun hat
blown off. Which was exactly what this driver was wearing. A
wide-brimmed sun hat, like something from an Audrey
Hepburn movie. I passed the glasses to Lucas and he
suggested we get off the beach, where we could just as easily
be seen by the driver.

We stood back in the shade of palms and watched the boat head for the cutout where the fishing lodges were. The sun hat turned out to be straw with a pink band, and the boat, another Boston Whaler, with the name *Smith's Boat Ren* in adhesive letters on it, the *tals* of *Rentals* having peeled away and been given back to the gods of the sea. Lucas and I strode back through the park to the end of the dock where the boat had passed and was pulling into a slip. We watched the woman tie up and walk directly into the motel room opposite. She was in there an hour before a van arrived and she came out and pointed to her boat, and two guys from the van used a trolley to haul supplies to the vessel, and load them up. There was a box of food, cereals and bread and tubs of margarine, and toilet paper and a box of fruits, a pineapple crown sticking out the top. When the guys had finished loading, the first guy returned to the room and knocked on the door, and the woman stood with her back to us, and signed for the goods, and the guy gave her a copy of the invoice and got back in his van and drove away.

The door to the room closed again, for about five minutes, and then the woman stepped out. She was at forty-five degrees to us, looking away toward the front of the park, with her sun hat in her hand. Her hair was blond and wet, as if she had showered, and she wore fresh clothing. Her old stuff must have been in the tote she carried on her shoulder. She fluffed at her hair, perhaps to dry it a little, then turned with her back to us and pulled the door to the room closed. She pulled sunglasses from her tote, and then she pivoted and looked toward the water. She looked in our direction, but not at us. She was looking out toward Spanish Harbor Channel. She pushed the sunglasses onto her nose, and then used two hands to pull the sun hat into place. She waltzed like a runway model to the boat, where she untied the mooring line.

Lucas slapped my shoulder and said *let's go*, but I didn't move. I just stood, half-obscured by palm trees, staring at the woman. A thousand images flashed through my head. Synapses fired and dots connected and my mind painted a picture that made sense but didn't make sense at all. Lucas slapped my shoulder again.

"Who is she?" he asked.

"What?"

"I can see you know her. Who is she?"

I turned to Lucas and shook my head.

"Her name is Amanda. Mandy to her friends. Mandy Bennett. Ron's ex-wife."

# CHAPTER FORTY—FOUR

**Lucas and I** jogged across the RV park to the slips on the other side, and jumped into his boat. I tossed off the lines and he fired her up and pulled away with considerable restraint. I would have accelerated like a bat out of hell, damn the no-wake zone, but either Lucas was more considerate, or he just knew that he wasn't going to lose Mandy on the open sea with the engines that were strapped to the back of his boat.

What I discovered is that it can be quite difficult to tail someone by boat. There is very little traffic to hide behind, so it doesn't take a genius to see when another boat is continuing in your general direction. But Lucas knew how to do it. He hung back, knowing that there weren't a lot of alleys for Mandy to pull down and get away, so he let her choose her channel before committing us to a direction.

She navigated north, under the Overseas Highway, and kept well between the markers and away from any sandbanks or reefs. She was clearly in no hurry. She sat low in the boat and didn't look around. There were no rearview mirrors to look at. She wasn't worried about being followed. We settled in for the journey, wherever it might lead, and followed Mandy through Bogie Channel under the bridge that headed over to No Name Key. After that Mandy navigated on a more northwesterly heading, following the general coastline of Big Pine Key, and then Howe Key adjoining it. Lucas pulled back the throttle and gave her some distance.

"Problem?" I asked.

"From here there aren't many places to go, except the Gulf of Mexico."

I watched through the field glasses and noticed the wake on Mandy's boat die as she reached the northwest end of Howe Key. I told Lucas I thought she was stopping, and he took a look, and then without a word changed direction and headed north across the channel. He slowed right down as the water got shallow and we drifted in between Cutoe Key and Barnes Key. Lucas put the throttle into neutral and the motor spluttered like it was unhappy with that decision, and we floated. He looked across the deeper water to where Mandy lay dormant.

"Has she broken down?" I asked.

"Don't think so," said Lucas. "She appears to be sitting calmly. Waiting."

"Waiting for what?"

"Us," he said.

"She's onto us?"

He dropped the glasses from his eyes. "No. It looks like a predetermined thing. Stop at the top of Howe Key and look to see if anyone is following."

"You think she saw us?"

He put the glasses up to his eyes again. "I don't think she's even looking. She's just floating there. Her engine's still running."

"Can she see us?" I asked.

"Can you see her?"

"Not without the field glasses."

"Well, she doesn't have eagle vision either. Or binoculars."

He watched her for another few minutes and I looked at the water. It seemed pretty shallow.

"We're not going to run aground, are we?" I asked.

"Nah," said Lucas, not looking down. "The draft on this baby is less than three feet, so even if we run aground, we can jump in and push ourselves off."

"Comforting."

"Yeah," said Lucas, as he dropped the glasses. "She's off."

He lowered the throttle and edged forward out in the slightly deeper water. We lost view of Mandy, but Lucas didn't seem too fussed by it. We motored slowly to the end of Howe Key, and then turned about and faced down a deeper channel that ran down the western side of Howe, and onward along Big Pine. But the deeper channel was clear. Not a single boat in view. Lucas hit the throttle hard and drove us forward, and I dropped into the seat I was standing before. Lucas gunned the boat for about a minute and we made more distance than I thought we would, and then just as quickly he pulled the throttle back and we lurched forward as the wake we had created came crashing into the rear of the speedboat and pushed us farther along, like a mini tsunami. As the boat came to rest I looked at Lucas, who scanned the water like a periscope, slowly rotating his body in position. I joined in, looking for the sight of the boat and sunhat. I saw nothing and came to a stop, looking at Lucas and he at me.

"She's disappeared," I said.

He thought for minute, not answering, his eyes doing little jumps as if he were doing a math problem in his head, and then he jumped to action and hit the throttle and spun the steering wheel around and the boat spun on a dime and headed back from whence we had come. We sped north again, then he pulled the throttle back and we stopped once more and he looked across at the top of Big Torch Key. There was no boat.

He was watching the shore. I saw waves breaking. Two set of small breaks coming together at the point of the island.

"See that?" asked Lucas.

"Two wakes?" I guessed.

"Right on," he said, and we moved forward again, not so fast, this time pulling west between Big Torch Key and the uninhabited Water Key to the north. As we passed into more open water I picked up the glasses and looked around.

"There," said Lucas, without the aid of artificial optics. I followed his gaze, due west, and saw the boat and sun hat motoring away from us.

"Yep, that's her," I said. Lucas didn't speed up. Instead he slowed. We just sat in the water, the big motor bubbling away.

"Are we planning on following?" I asked.

"Give it a sec," he said.

I watched Mandy motor away. "What is that key she's headed for?"

"Raccoon Key, if memory serves."

"What's there?"

"Nothing."

I kept watching as Mandy neared the key, and then suddenly she pulled hard left and cut down and back on a southeasterly heading, bringing her due south of us. As she motored I lost her periodically behind several small unnamed keys. As Mandy headed below us Lucas began moving in that direction. There was a lot of shallow water between us, water that Mandy had purposely avoided, and a lot of small mangrove keys that one could easily hit. But Lucas kept it steady if not fast, his eyes locked to the water. There seemed to be some sort of channel, unmarked to my untrained eye, and I just hoped it didn't end in a sandbank.

I should have known better. Lucas guided us out into the wide channel that follows the western shoreline of Big Torch Key. I could see why he wasn't in any hurry now, apart from safety, because the channel was wide and long and handsome and there was nowhere for Mandy to go that we wouldn't see. Lucas let her become a small dot, able to be made out in the field glasses but not by the naked eye, which meant we were the same to her. She followed the channel all the way south past Ramrod Key and back under the Overseas Highway. As she reached the near open water at the south end of Ramrod Key, Lucas sped up so we made up our lost ground. He guided us across to the western edge of the channel, by Summerland Key, so we would be hard to spot against the background of the expensive waterfront homes there. I picked Mandy up in the glasses, and noted she seemed to have slowed again, but she wasn't looking to spot a tail this time. She made a heading toward an island to the south of Ramrod Key.

"I think she's stopping," I said, passing the glasses to Lucas.

He looked through them and spotted her. "You're right. There's a jetty out there."

"What is that key?"

"It's a private island, I think. You can rent it." He dropped the glasses from his eyes and looked at me. "Well, not you, but someone could. Someone rich. Someone like your man Alec."

I wasn't sure that Alec was that rich. Not if my dots were connecting as I thought.

"She's stopping there. Tying up."

He handed me the glasses and held the boat in place. Mandy was tiny in my view, but I saw her walk along a long dock, onto the island, which was surrounded by mangroves and palmetto, and then return with a cart, like a large version of a kid's Radio Flyer. She loaded the cart with the stores from the boat, and then pulled them away. Lucas motored us closer to Summerland Key, and I took a quick look at the houses near us. They were generally large, and generally newer, and reminded me of the waterfront homes back on Singer Island. I wondered if there was an ugly duckling among them, a holdout against the development, the kind of place that made their neighbors cringe. I hoped so.

I watched Mandy make a second run with the cart. No one else appeared to help her. Then she retreated beyond the foliage, to a house of considerable size. I could see a second story above the tree line that must have offered quite a view. I kept watching the vacant dock as Lucas pulled into the man-made channel that cut into Summerland Key. There were a series of boat docks on the channel leading up to big houses. The dock at the first house was empty, the boat perhaps out for the day. Lucas pulled up to it, killed the motor and tied us up.

"Wait here," he said, and he dashed off toward the house above us. I watched the empty dock across the water on Mandy's private island, and in a few minutes, Lucas returned.

"Any movement?" he asked.

"Nothing."

"Good. No one's home," he said, nodding to the house. "Let's go."

He grabbed a cooler from below the foredeck and stepped up onto the dock. I followed, field glasses in hand. We waltzed across the crushed shell and coral yard, to a patio set under some palm trees. He dropped the cooler on the ground and took a chair. The palms swayed in the breeze, making the warm day very pleasant. I took a seat and checked the dock through the field glasses and saw no movement.

"What if the owners come home?" I asked.

Lucas shrugged. "There's a lot of mail in the mailbox, so . . ."

"But what if they do?"

"We were given the wrong address. We're not breaking in."

So we spent the rest of the afternoon in the shade, with a killer view, sharing cold cans of cream soda that Lucas said reminded him of growing up in Australia. We took turns watching the dock on the private island, but nothing stirred. Deep into the afternoon Lucas produced meatloaf sandwiches, which we devoured. He really came prepared.

"So this Mandy, Ron's ex, she was having the affair with Will?" asked Lucas.

"Aha."

"And they met at the yacht club?"

"Aha."

"So it's possible, maybe even likely, that she knew Alec."

"Possible."

"And it's equally possible that she figured Will wasn't going to leave his wife for her, if you're right about their arrangement."

"I don't think he was, no."

"So she could have conspired with Alec to kill Will," Lucas said.

"Maybe. But for what motive?"

"Being scorned isn't enough?"

"Might explain her motive, but it doesn't explain his."

"Maybe they were in love."

"Mandy's version of love involves more money than Alec has, even if he is boosting expensive cars."

"So if she's involved there's more money out there, somewhere."

"There is. And it rests with the second man."

"The second man?" asked Lucas.

"Your theory. Alec was the first man, we now know that Mandy is the third man, and the person who delivered the second man to Stiltsville. That second man is out there."

"How much is this boat worth, the one the other guy was building for Will?"

"Drew Keck? Maybe quarter of a million. Not a retirement fund, at least not at Mandy's level."

"But he had some kind of deal with the dead guy's wife?"

"Celia? She and Drew were certainly up to something when I saw them at the yacht club."

Lucas nodded. "Could she have been paying him to kill her husband?"

"That's what I was thinking. But she can't access the life insurance for years, if ever, without a body. She said it herself: if she wanted her husband dead for the money, a body would have been found."

"Maybe Drew messed up, did it wrong. But he's definitely disappeared?"

"Seems so. Hasn't been seen at the boatyards or at the yacht club."

"So he might be on that island." Lucas nodded across the water. "Regardless, whoever's on that island, they're all equally responsible for Lenny," said Lucas.

"Yes." I thought about that for a moment, and then I thought about Deputy Castle. "Given what we know, the right thing to do would be to call the cops."

Lucas held up his phone. "I got no coverage," he said.

I shook my head. "Me either."

"Well, that's settled," he said. "Let's move out."

# CHAPTER FORTY-FIVE

**With the falling** sun more or less behind us, we motored in silhouette toward the resort on Little Palm Key. The sound of laughter and sundowner drinks floated easily across the water. I thought of Longboard Kelly's, which made me think of Lenny, which made me feel down. Then I thought of Ron, and how he didn't yet know that his ex-wife, whom he didn't want thinking ill of him, had set him up and sent him down the river. That thought made me mad.

From Little Palm Resort we headed due north, and Lucas hit a button and raised the propeller up so it wouldn't hit the bottom, and he pushed us up onto the sand on Picnic Island. It was an uninhabited key that was used by day-trippers, all of whom had headed home for beers and barbecues. We climbed through the brush and sat back from the beach on the other side of the small key and watched the empty dock on Mandy's private island. We sat there until well after dark, the house we were watching doused in light. Lucas used that light as our navigation beacon, and we got back in the boat and headed out without running lights. He took us on a wide berth, east of our target island, and then north until we brushed the south tip of Little Torch Key. We came down toward Mandy's island from the north, on the opposite side to the dock. There were two buildings that we had scoped from a distance, one at center, one east of center of the island. We landed on the opposite end, Lucas using small pulses to guide the boat toward the mangrove-lined shore. There was no beach or landing site on this side, so he turned the engine off and edged into the mangroves. I jumped up onto the bow and pulled us farther in until the boat didn't want to go in anymore, and I tied us up. Lucas went below and came out with a couple flashlights, and, I suspected, his handgun. I checked that mine were in place, and then stood aside as Lucas climbed off the bow and onto the mangroves. He slowly slipped his feet into the shallow water, and began picking his way through.

Fortunately the mangroves were only a few feet deep, and it took us about five minutes to weave our way through the maze of boughs and thick leaves. We stepped onto the coral and limestone that made the island, and pushed through heavy foliage until we reached a clearing. The open space extended through the middle of the island, at the far end of which we could see the lights of the house hidden behind more strategically placed trees. In the foreground of the house was the other building, perhaps some kind of outbuilding, dark to our eyes.

"We'll check the outbuilding first," said Lucas. "Then do a wide reccie of the big house."

I nodded. "Okay."

"You armed?" he asked.

I nodded again.

"All right then. Our main objective is to learn the position of any bogies."

"What?"

"Look for people. We know there's one for sure, Mandy. But there could be three. Alec and Drew might also be here. And we don't assume that's all."

Lucas nodded definitively and marched out, along the edge of the cleared land. He kept his flashlight off, the moon providing sufficient ambient light to see the terrain. We reached the backside of the first building quickly. It was smaller than the house but still quite large. A boardwalk ran between the two buildings. As I reached the first building I realized that it was also a house, up on stilts to offer the best views and protect against a storm surge during a hurricane. We made our way quietly around it, but it appeared uninhabited. There were no lights on at all, and the house lacked that organic vibe that inhabited properties had. I noted a third building that we hadn't noticed before, away from the others. I tapped Lucas and pointed at it.

"This vacant?" I whispered about the house above us.

Lucas nodded. "Caretaker's property. I'm guessing Mandy and Co. didn't want them around." We stepped gingerly up the stairs to the deck. Lucas moved like a ballerina. I wasn't quite so stealthy so I moved slower, and Lucas had done a sweep of the wraparound deck before I got to the top. We peered in through the windows and saw nothing. We didn't want to use flashlights this close to the main house, and the moonlight only did so much, but it was evident no one was home. Lucas tried the door but it was locked, so we retreated back down the stairs. He pointed with his hand at the smaller building. We slowly moved out to it. It too was on stilts, but it clearly wasn't a house. It hummed like a nuclear power plant. I suspected a backup generator. We walked around it, the far side right against the encroaching foliage, like at the warehouse Alec had shipped his cars from. We got to the steps and Lucas pointed in under the structure. It had been walled in to create a room, but it wasn't watertight by any standard. Perhaps where they kept their water toys. There was a standard indoor knob, like on a bedroom door. Lucas pulled a thin screwdriver from his pocket. It was the kind of thing used when working with small electronic components and and it slid into the hole in the knob and flicked the mechanism open easily. The lock was clearly designed to keep wildlife out rather than anything with a high school diploma, and Lucas opened the door and stepped in. I followed and pulled the door closed. It was pitch-black after the full moonlight, and we both flicked our flashlights on.

The room was a storage space. There was some heavy-duty gardening equipment, and the room smelled of gasoline. A collection of cans—paint and pesticide—lined the base of one wall. There was a tarpaulin thrown haphazardly across one side of the room. There were no beach toys, no noodles or boogie boards, no discarded umbrellas. Lucas moved to the back and prodded at something like a deflated weather balloon. It was orange, and tossed aside like a used but never repacked parachute.

"What is that?" I asked.

"Hard to say in this light. Some kind of ducky, or life raft maybe." He shook his head and turned away. "Nothing," he whispered, as he moved back to the door. His light swept the room one more time. "What was that?" he asked, jogging his light across the tarpaulin.

"Nothing, I don't think," I said, but I stepped to it and grabbed a corner and threw the tarpaulin back. It was heavy canvas, like an old Boy Scouts' tent, and it folded over itself with a thud. I played my light over the space and just stood there, transfixed. Lucas saw and stepped over and stopped by my shoulder.

"That fella's dead," said Lucas.

"You think?"

"Years of training, mate. Trust me, a bullet hole in your head will do it, most times."

I glanced at him, his ragged features ghoulish in the half-light. He looked at me and smiled.

"You know that guy?" he asked.

I looked down again at the body. I didn't need to. His face was covered in a thick layer of dried blood, like a mask, but the hair was a giveaway. As were the clothes. He looked like a Ralph Lauren ad, crumpled in the mail, dropped in a puddle, and then shot through the back of the head.

"That's Alec Meechan."

I threw the tarpaulin back over Alec. I didn't feel like I owed him any sort of dignity, but I didn't want to keep looking at him, and I couldn't take my eyes away.

"So they're one down," said Lucas, like it was a mathematical equation, more than a human life. "Still keep your wits about you. Your man has an MO."

"What MO?"

"He likes to shoot people from behind."

I glanced at the tarpaulin under which lay Alec Meechan, with a large hole in his forehead, the exit wound from having been shot from behind. And I thought about Lenny, two shots to the back. And I thought about the discarded raft in the storage room. And about happier times, Amy Artiz's photo of the smiling but tired crew about to leave Nassau on *Toxic Ass*. And I thought about the boat that arrived home, the smiles wiped from the crew's faces. And it all clicked into place.

"Your man Drew is a real piece of work," said Lucas.

I shook my head. "No. He's not. Drew Keck's not even here."

# CHAPTER FORTY-SIX

**We did a** full circle around the main house. It was large, maybe three or four thousand square feet, with a wraparound deck that must have offered views in every direction. If I ever needed to hole up, on the lam, I couldn't think of many better places to do it. We stepped across the boardwalk that ran between the main house and the caretaker's house, back to our starting point near the edge of the cleared land. There was light cascading from one side of the house but not the other. Perhaps the living room lit, the bedrooms still darkened. Lucas outlined a plan and I listened, and then he outlined it again for the dummies in the back. I told him I got it, and he pulled his gun from under his shirt, and I did the same, opening a button on my shirt and removing the Glock from the holster under my arm.

We crept up the stairs, nice and slow. The house gave off slow vibrations, that organic lived-in vibe, and the breeze rustled the mangroves. We got to the top and Lucas nodded, and I nodded back. Then he took off left, toward the light, and I went right, toward the darkness. I reached the corner, with the Glock held forward and ready, and moved around. I found a door partway along. It was a slider that led from a bedroom to the patio. I tested it and it moved a touch, so I slowly pulled it back and then slid in sideways through the opening. I looked around the room. There was lots of dark wood and even more dark corners. I gave my eyes a second, and a four-poster bed materialized. There were clothes on a chair by the bed. I slid the door closed and moved on. The bedroom led out into a small hallway, across which I found another bedroom. It was dark but I checked it anyway, Lucas's words ringing in my ears: *Boldness wins you victory, but caution wins you life.* There was nothing in the bedroom. No clothes, no toiletries in the en suite bathroom. The bed had not been slept in. I moved back out into the hallway and the soft light shining from the living room. I stepped past another empty bathroom, toward the light. On one side I saw the kitchen. It was nice, but unremarkable for the size of the house. I stopped at the corner of the hallway and watched it. Mandy Bennett stood in the kitchen, mixing a margarita. She helped herself to a generous slug of tequila, and padded on bare feet toward the living room. She wasn't wearing yoga gear, but a floral summer skirt and a tight top. Had she looked back toward the bedrooms she would have seen me, the gun pointed at the floor. But she didn't. She was very focused on not spilling her drink. She reached a bamboo-framed sofa and placed her drink on a side table and flopped onto the plush white cushions. There were two matching chairs to the side, and farther on but partitioned off by furniture was an area that looked like a library, where shelves of books and a recliner sat dormant in the shadows thrown from the living room. I waited for a couple of minutes, watching Mandy guzzle her drink and flip through a glossy magazine, not pausing long enough to read any one page. She took another long drink, leaving about a quarter to go, so I figured I'd move before she got up for a refill and saw me standing there anyway.

I stepped softly across the hardwood floor but it groaned anyway, and Mandy flicked a glance to the other end of the sofa just as I arrived there. She said nothing. Perhaps the words had been sucked from her. Her feet were resting on the edge of a coffee table and she dropped them, her jaw matching the movement. We stayed like statues for what felt like the longest time, she staring at me, me pointing a gun at her head.

"Where is he?" I asked.

"Who?" replied Mandy in a soft voice, like she didn't want to wake a baby.

"You know who."

"I don't know."

"I don't believe you."

This made her frown, like she couldn't figure out what she had done to earn such distrust. "Can you point the gun somewhere else, please?"

I left the gun pointing at her. "Where is he?"

"He's here."

I hadn't seen him drift out of the shadows of the library, but I glanced now and saw him. I'd never met the man, but I'd seen photos. If I had to say, I'd suggest Will Colfax was heavier in real life. Maybe it was the stress, but I wasn't convinced he felt any such thing. He was dressed in an Izod polo and Bermuda shorts, and he was pointing a revolver at me. I was no expert on firearms, and one instrument of death pretty much looked like another, but I recognized Lenny's gun. He carried another pistol in his other hand.

"You are one determined SOB," he said, as if he admired my never-say-die attitude.

"You made a mistake," I said. "Trying to set up Ron."

"Ron kind of got caught up in things. Whatever." He shrugged. "Ron's a nice enough guy, but he's weak. He's B-grade, on a good day. And I don't really care who goes down."

"You told me Ron was an accident," said Mandy from the sofa. I realized that I still had my gun trained on her, not Will. I was at the end of the sofa, facing Mandy at my 12 o'clock. Will stood by a bookshelf at my three.

"Don't even think about it," he said, sensing my move. "And Ron was an accident, sweet pea. He got tangled up in events. Not my fault."

"Not your fault?" I spat. "Like Lenny wasn't your fault."

"Who the hell is Lenny?"

"Lenny Cox," I said. The blood was pumping through my head faster than the veins could handle, and I felt them pulsing. I had always prided myself on being cool in a crisis. It was a trait more than one pitching coach complimented me on. I learned a technique, back in college, from a girl I knew. Breathing in through my nose, out through my mouth. It was some kind of monk thing, I heard. It settled my nerves on the mound, that's for sure. And it would have settled my nerves looking at the man who shot Lenny, but the hell with breathing like a monk.

"The guy you shot in the back at Stiltsville," I growled.

Will said nothing in return. From the corner of my eye I saw Mandy's head bouncing between the two of us.

"You killed Lenny?" The pitch of her voice rose as she said it.

"You should have left it alone when Ron got out," Will said to me.

"You killed Lenny?" repeated Mandy.

"Leave it, Mandy," ordered Will.

"What about Alec?" I asked.

"What about Alec?" repeated Mandy, although hers was more of a question than mine.

I looked at Will. "Yeah, Will, what about Alec?'

"Shut your mouth and drop the gun," he spat.

"That's right, Will," I said. "We found Alec in your storeroom outside. He didn't look well."

"Will!" screamed Mandy. "What happened to Alec?"

Will looked at Mandy and yelled. "Mandy, just leave it."

I took my chance. I made to move my aim from Mandy to Will. But Will was faster than I gave him credit for, and he was paying more attention than I figured. He hadn't moved his aim, just his eyes, and he shot them back toward me.

"Move that gun toward me and you die."

I stopped partway.

"Drop the gun. Now!"

I let the gun fall from my hand. It landed with a heavy thud that was swallowed by the room. I wasn't keen on having a murderer point a gun at me, but I calmed myself with two details. One, Will was unlikely to shoot me front on, if his past victims were anything to go by, and two, Lucas was out there, somewhere.

We stood for a moment, Will apparently calm, having grown used to the feel of the revolver, me breathing shallow, trying to look calm but feeling anything but. I glanced at Mandy, who looked chastised. She was giving Will the kind of look that often resulted in wars. I decided that I had very little downside, with a gun already pointed at me, so I poked the bear.

"It was a good plan, Will. Go missing in the middle of the ocean. I figured how you did it."

"Oh, you did, smart guy?"

"Yeah. You brought an extra life raft, didn't you? I saw it in its bag lashed to the transom of your yacht in one of Amy's photos. But it didn't gel until I saw it again, just now, lying in the storeroom with Alec."

"Someone needs to tell me what the hell happened to Alec!" Mandy was unraveling. The whole caper was taking a toll, but there were clearly things that she didn't know.

"Alec's dead, Mandy," I said, like I was talking about the weather. "Shot in the back like Lenny."

Mandy's eyes didn't tear up—they just went glassy and distant, like she was trying to connect dots that weren't even on the same page. It seemed to take considerable effort to look up at Will.

"But the bit that impresses me is you, Mandy," I continued. "You handle a boat around the keys well, but getting all the way out into the Gulf Stream? That took guts."

Will chortled. "She couldn't get out that far. Not by herself. I had to have someone take her to Bimini."

"Let me guess," I said. "Mr. Smith."

Will frowned, which dissolved into a smile. "You are resourceful, aren't you?"

"No more than the cops."

Will snorted. "They think I'm at the bottom of the ocean."

"Do they? The PLB was a nice touch. Let me guess, you jumped into the raft just off Bimini and Alec waited to toss the life jacket with the beacon on it in the water a couple hours later."

"As soon as he heard any movement down below, or the middle of the Gulf Stream, whatever came first."

"But it wasn't enough, was it? The sealer was the blood, and the other stuff on the deck. What was that, brain fluid? How on earth?"

Will nodded at his own cleverness. "Cerebrospinal fluid. I visited my doctor, and he took blood and did a spinal tap. Painful, but did the trick."

"You don't think the doctor will talk?"

"He's got a lot of gambling issues."

"Very clever."

Will smiled. He really did think he was the whole package.

"So you get picked up offshore, taken back to Bimini, then down here."

He shook his head. "Straight back to Miami from the pickup. The weather was going to turn, which suited my purpose."

"Just two problems."

He snorted again. "I don't think so."

"Oh, yes. One, the wrong guy got the blame."

"And got out, and you should have left it there."

"But I couldn't. See, I had a client."

"What client?"

"Michael Baggio."

"What?"

I nodded. "After his partner Keegan got arrested, he saw the writing on the wall, and he came to see me and Lenny."

Will shook his head. "You shouldn't have done that. You should have just let the fag take the fall."

"You set up Michael simply because you didn't like his sexual orientation? Very small of you."

"Those two fell into my lap. I'd been skimming money from the company for years. The damned Internet was killing all the good deals in China. That's why I got involved with Alec in the first place. I had the containers, he had the cars. But Cyntech was going to end, sooner or later. My last finance guy saw it and bailed on me. Then Keegan applied for the job. I could see what he was from the get-go. His fancy suits and that girly laugh. So I knew I had my guy. I just got some key tracking software off the Internet, got his password and started moving the money through his login into my offshore accounts." Will shook his head. "Stupid. Then his other half, Michael, he tries to best buddy me, says he wants to go sailing. Idiot. He couldn't tie his shoes, let alone a clove hitch. So he became my out."

"Except for the second thing."

"What second thing?"

"Alec. He knew the whole plan."

"Alec had a big mouth and was too stupid to know he was in over his head. I told him we were done with the shipments. He should have left the last containers alone. Celia shouldn't have given him the papers to get the containers out but he threatened to expose us. He got greedy."

"So you put a bullet through his head."

"Will," said Mandy. It was the voice of a lost child. Not angry, or sad, just confused. "You said no one would get killed except for you."

"We can still arrange for that," said Lucas.

I had no idea where he had come from, or how long he had been there, but he stood on the far side of Mandy's sofa, in the direction of the kitchen. He was holding his gun in one hand, steady and calm, aimed at Will. Will pushed himself deeper behind the bookshelf. He was totally open to me, but mostly hidden from Lucas. I guessed all that Lucas could see was his shoulder, an area about the size of a coconut.

"You should put your gun down if you don't want your friend to die," said Will. He held his gun close to his body, so his arm wasn't exposed to Lucas, but it meant it would be a very lucky shot to hit me.

"But he's facing you," said Lucas. "You like to shoot from behind, don't you?"

It turned out it was more of a preference than a rule. Will held the gun up to his eyes, looked along the short barrel and fired. It was a hell of a loud sound in the house, nothing else but the distant hum of generators and bugs. It would have been deafening to Will, but I suppose he figured he'd get over it. The round shattered the lamp on the table next to me. It was some kind of a crystal thing, and it exploded around me. I recoiled, curling into a standing ball.

"Will!" screamed Mandy.

"I got five more chances to get it right," yelled Will. "Drop the gun."

I uncoiled myself slowly, my eyes on Lucas. He hadn't moved, his aim still on Will's position.

"You won't get another chance, pal," said Lucas. "It's over. Drop it now, or you're going to meet Lenny at the big house, and he's gonna kick the living daylights out of you."

I waited for the comeback, for Will's snort or pithy remark. But it didn't come. Not right away. Because Mandy jumped up from her sofa and leaped between Will and Lucas.

"Mandy," said Lucas. "Don't."

"You can't kill him. I've got nowhere else to go."

Lucas frowned. He looked worried. I'd never seen him look worried before. Happy, sad, angry. But not worried. It wasn't a good look on him. He didn't want to go through Mandy. I wasn't sure he could, if it came down to it. She wasn't an innocent party, not by a long shot, but she hadn't killed anybody, least of all Lenny. But going through her was the only way this ended well for old Miami. Will was hidden behind her, his gun, *Lenny's gun*, aimed at me. I watched him extend his arm, get a better aim.

I thought about Lenny, and meeting him again sooner that I had planned. We'd cause some trouble together, whether we both ended up upstairs or down. Then I wondered if we would indeed see each other. If he was truly a good man, and I was not. Or the other way around. And who, if anyone, got to make that distinction. And what we could do to change it. To rearrange things. I wished I'd had a backup plan. And then the pithy remark came. Will kept the gun on me but looked at Mandy's back, in Lucas's direction.

"You know why I win?" said Will. "Because I'm a winner." Then he moved his eyes back to reassert his aim. But what he saw was not what he expected to see. What he saw was my backup plan. The kind your mentor makes you get, for situations that you cannot possibly conceive. Insurance of the unconventional kind, tucked away in the back of my shorts, just under my shirt.

I remembered what I had forgotten, and slipped the Ruger out from my waistband and brought it around in a sweeping motion, cocking it with my left hand as it passed my hip, so that when Will looked down his barrel he saw my barrel, and a burst of flame. He didn't see the round flying across the room. That was supersonic, faster than the eye. But he felt it explode into his chest like a heart attack, and he felt his back hit the wall behind him, and then his butt hit the floor as he slid down the wall, leaving a vermillion smudge behind him.

I kept the gun on him, ready to go again. Wanting to go again. I stepped over to him. I think Mandy was screaming, and I think Lucas was holding her back. But I wasn't sure. The sound and movement didn't travel well through my bubble. I stood over Will, his breathing raspy, his chest weeping blood. I looked down at him, ready to say something. But sometimes there are no words. Sometimes the language fails to communicate the meaning. So I said nothing. I just watched Will Colfax, watching me. Then he coughed. Then he died.

# CHAPTER FORTY—SEVEN

**Mandy dispensed with** the margaritas and went straight for the tequila. She sat on the floor of the kitchen, not weeping or wailing, just quietly drinking her pain away. Perhaps she was making plans, mentally going through her rolodex. But after the initial screaming, the shock sank in and she retreated to the kitchen where Lucas let her be.

I was tempted by the tequila myself, but Lucas took me out on the deck, the lights of the houses on Ramrod Key twinkling across the water. He told me to wait on things, that he would call the cops and that it would be better if I didn't have alcohol on my breath, even if it got there after the event. I sat on the deck and watched him collect the Glock from where I had dropped it on the floor. It hadn't been fired, but Lucas said it would be better if the cops didn't find an unregistered gun, so I watched him walk away across the clear part of the island and disappear into the mangroves. He reappeared shortly after, and then came back upstairs. He left everything else as it was, and picked up the phone and called 911. Then he came and sat with me on the deck.

"You throw the gun in water?"

"Nah," he said. "It's a perfectly good gun and it wasn't involved here. You used your registered weapon, which is good. I just put it in a bag and tied it to a mangrove below the waterline. We'll come find it another time."

I nodded but I didn't care. I didn't want it back. It might be insurance, but I felt like I'd already cashed it in.

The Monroe County Sheriff's Office sent a platoon, boats converging on the island from all directions. The Coast Guard turned up and I heard later there might have been a DEA team, but I don't recall speaking to them. Altogether there were too many boots for the job at hand. They taped off the living room, and I answered the same set of questions more times than I cared to. Later the sheriff's deputies took us away on launches, each on our own vessel, and I ended up in an interview room, where I answered the same questions all over again. The Monroe County guys called their counterparts in Palm Beach County. They said they had spoken to Detective Moscow, and that my story checked out. I told them that one of the guns they found on Will was responsible for the deaths of Lenny Cox and Alec Meechan, and that the other was registered to Lenny, and stolen from him postmortem.

As it turned out, the island Will was hiding on was only minutes the other way from Big Pine Key Fishing Lodge, where I had left Lenny's truck. But I didn't drive it home. Lucas did. He left his boat with the sheriff, and one of the deputies promised to transfer it up to Islamorada, where a guy Lucas knew would collect it and return it to Miami.

It was just after noon when Lucas dropped me back at Singer Island. There was no furniture, nothing to eat, not even a fridge. But my old apartment was the past, and this was the future, and it was the looking forward that was keeping me together.

"You driving all the way back to Miami?" I asked him.

He nodded. "Work tomorrow. The kid can't cover for me forever."

"Drive safe."

"Yeah. So, Lenny's, next week."

I nodded. "I'll see you there."

I found that in my absence the power and water had been connected so I took a shower, and then I lay in the middle of the sunken living room, on the shag pile carpet, and fell asleep. My phone woke me. It was Ron, at my old place, looking for me. I told him were I was and he came and collected me. I didn't much feel like being out in the world, but Ron put his hands on my shoulders and looked me in the eye and told me, *it's better this way.* I suppose he knew something about it. Sometimes the very moment you most want to be alone is the moment you most need friends.

Longboard Kelly's was the same but different. I assumed everything was going to be like that from now on, but in the case of Longboards, it was literal. Mick had replaced the stools under the palapa shade. The worn old rickety things were out, and new thick wooden numbers built to withstand a hurricane were in. I wiggled my butt around on it.

"How's it feel?" asked Muriel.

"It will get better with time," I said.

"Just like you." She smiled, passing me a beer. Ron and I toasted with our beers, Muriel with her club soda. Mick wandered into the inside bar. He nodded hi, like it was just another day, and then produced a hammer and banged a nail into the wall, where he hung a photograph. It was framed, a black-and-white shot, but not so old. A portrait of Lenny Cox, sitting under the very palapa we sat under, looking back into the courtyard, the late sun framing his face, his hard skin glowing, a smile on lips and a cheeky glint in his eye. We toasted all over again, and Mick wiped the picture with a towel, and then he retreated into the kitchen.

"He's a big softy," said Muriel.

"I've always thought so," I said.

I sipped my beer and watched the people wander in, the buzz building in the air. Ron turned on his stool and looked at it too, and he smiled. Then he sort of dropped it, and looked at me.

"Do you know what will happen to Mandy?" he asked.

I shook my head. "Not really. The detective in Monroe County said it would take a while to sort out, but he wasn't sure if there was anything she'd done wrong, technically. She didn't know about the murders and wasn't there when they happened, so there's no homicide charge, and they hadn't yet committed fraud with the life insurance, so maybe nothing there either. He said it might turn out to not be worth the effort, with Will dead."

Ron nodded. "I'm glad. She wouldn't do well in jail."

I shrugged. I wasn't so sure.

"But what I don't get is why they were on that island," said Ron. "Why hadn't Will made a run for it?"

"The detective said it's not that uncommon for a perp to lay low not too far from home, somewhere they feel safe, until the wind blows over. He thinks they would have headed for the Caribbean, or maybe South America, sooner or later. He said they'll probably get that out of Mandy, in due course."

"She bet on the wrong horse again," said Ron, sipping his beer.

"She did. And Will pretty much confessed about the embezzlement, so hopefully that helps Keegan out."

"I heard his lawyers are motioning the FBI tomorrow. As long as they get the missing millions back, I think they'll be happy. So that leaves Celia."

"She knew about it, but as Will hadn't claimed to be dead, it's anyone's guess if that was illegal. So she might even still get the life insurance, and not have to wait seven years for it."

"I think they'll fight that. The insurance company will claim he died while committing a crime, and that she was party to the crime."

"I think Celia's up for a fight like that. But she was up to something with Drew Keck, too. I thought he might have killed Will for her, but when I saw the life raft in the storeroom I knew it wasn't that, 'cause I knew Will was alive."

"Drew appeared back at the yacht club," said Ron.

"And?"

"It was the boat he was working on. Will had reneged on their deal to split the profits on the restoration, but Celia was liquidating all Will's leftover assets. I bet that was part of Will and Celia's deal. That's why she could wait seven years for the insurance, because she was selling Will's stuff to finance herself until then. So Drew renegotiated the deal with her, and he sold the boat. Up in Savannah, I heard."

"What was the split?"

"Eighty-twenty his way, is the word on the dock."

"She told him he drove a hard bargain. She was right." I sipped my beer and spun back around to watch Muriel at work.

"So how are you?" I asked him.

"I'm still ticking."

"Good."

"And I'm doing a twilight this week with Amy and Felicity. You should come."

I didn't take my eyes from Muriel. "Nah, I think I'm going to stay off the water for a bit."

"Suit yourself." I felt Ron look at me. "You should probably take a few days off," Ron said.

"Did you?"

"I wanted to keep busy."

"Me too."

"So I guess it's work tomorrow."

I nodded. "We need to find a place for all those boxes of Lenny's stuff."

"Just leave them in the second office."

"How will we work in there?"

"We won't," said Ron. "I don't need a desk much. The sofa's what I prefer. So I'll just crash in your office."

"It's not my office. It's Lenny's." I looked at Ron and he frowned. He was shaking his head.

"No. It's your office. It's your firm. Lenny's office was in an old strip mall. Just the way he liked it."

I nodded slowly and sipped my beer. Everything changes. I wiggled down into the hefty slab of wood I was sitting on. Everything changes, even the things that don't.

# CHAPTER FORTY-EIGHT

**Ron dropped me** back at Singer Island. My bike wasn't there, and I had no food or drink, but I was okay with that. Ron promised to pick me up the next day and take me to find a car. He said it was time to grow up and I couldn't fight him on it. I ambled up to the front door and found two large, long cardboard boxes sitting on my doorstep. There was a delivery note shoved between them, and I had to lift the top one to get at it. The box was heavy. I unfolded the note. It read: *contents, two chairs*, and at the bottom in scrawled handwriting it read: *Happy Housewarming, Sal.* I smiled and shook my head. I opened the door and dragged the boxes inside, and then realized I had nothing to open them with. I took a good while to pick apart the well-glued seams and open the first box. Inside was a deconstructed lounge chair. There were instructions and hardware, and little tools to build it. I had nothing better to do, and nowhere to sit, so I got to work. It took longer than was necessary to put the thing together, but in the end I had a nice new lounger with a cedar frame and blue cushions. The headrest moved up and down, so I could sit up and read, or lay it flat and sleep. With no library to hand, the second option was the better one. Under the headrest were wheels, and I dragged the chair out the sliding door onto the patio. The sun was falling and in my face as I looked across the water at Riviera Beach. I seriously contemplated that nap, but it was too sunny and I had no shades, so I went inside and put the second chair together and dragged it out to its mate.

By the time I was done the sun was still bright but the lower trajectory had taken the sting out of it, so I positioned the chairs to the view and lay down. It was comfortable, and I put my hands behind my head and took it in. It was a real Florida view, sun and boats and gulls. Long shadows reached across the water from the opposite shore like tendrils. It brought a smile to my face, which I felt bad about so I dropped it. I wasn't sleepy. If anything, I was afraid of sleep, and the dreams that would come. I was afraid that my tomorrows wouldn't be as good as my yesterdays, that Lenny was a hole that couldn't be filled, by me or for me. It wasn't a train of thought worthy of such a wonderful view on such a beautiful evening, and it was rightly interrupted by the distant sound of banging. It sounded like my front door, through the sliding back door that I had left open, but I couldn't imagine anyone stopping in on me, since very few people knew I was there. Regardless, I was comfortable and wasn't getting up. Then I heard a call of *anybody home*, and my ears pricked up like a hunting dog. I looked to the side of the house and saw Deputy Castle appear. I wondered for a second if I had indeed fallen asleep, but it all felt real enough.

"Deputy," I said.

"Danielle," she said, stepping onto the patio. She glanced through the open sliding door and saw the empty interior. "You some kind of monk?" She smiled and all the bad things in the world wafted away.

"Just bought the place. Haven't even moved in yet."

She turned and looked at the view. "Nice. You do all right for yourself, for a guy who never seems to wear long pants."

"It's a trademark. I wasn't expecting any visitors."

"Sorry to barge in, but I heard what happened in Monroe County. And after Lenny, you know. The girl behind the bar at Longboards said you'd be here."

I made a note to buy Muriel a drink.

"Anyway, I just wanted to see if you were all right. I completely understand if you'd rather be alone."

"I'm glad for the visit, honestly, but I'm not feeling very chatty."

"With a view like this who needs to chat?"

That made me smile. Then I dropped it. "What about your husband?"

She gave me a wistful look. "I don't have a husband. I have a mistake."

I frowned, not sure what that meant.

"I'm divorced," she added.

I nodded, gently. She was right. Sally's intel was indeed out of date.

"I don't even have a fridge yet, so I can't offer you anything to drink."

She held up a six-pack that she had been holding by her side. "I brought provisions."

"You are good."

"You don't know the half of it."

I didn't know the half of it, but suddenly I really wanted to. Then she held up a cell phone.

"And I have a wide variety of delivery options in my phone, so dinner is on me." Then she made her mistake. She shot me that half smile—part of the mouth, but all of the eyes. And that was that.

"And it looks like there's a spare lounge chair here," she said.

"Just put it together. Hasn't even had a maiden voyage."

"May I?" she asked, handing me the six-pack and stepping around my chair. I watched her move around me. The sun lit her up from behind like a Rubens painting, and the world looked better. Not great, but a hell of a lot better. I smiled. I knew sadness would come, and it might stay a while. But not tonight. I gestured to the lounger.

"It's all yours."

# GET YOUR NEXT BOOK FREE

Hearing from you, my readers, is one of the the best things about being a writer. If you want to join my Readers' Group, we'll not only be able to keep in touch, but you can also get an exclusive Miami Jones ebook novel, as well as occasional pre-release reads, and other goodies that are only available to my Readers' Group friends.

Join Now:
http://www.ajstewartbooks.com/reader

# ACKNOWLEDGEMENTS

Thanks, as always, to all my readers who send me feedback. A huge thanks to Constance and Marianne for their editorial and proofing expertise, and the readers on my inner circle reading team. These books don't happen in isolation, so thank you. Any and all errors are mine, especially but not limited to my fictionalization of life in and around a yacht club. I've frequented more than my fair share, and better people are hard to find. And the Dark 'n' Stormys aren't too bad either.

I've mixed the fictional with the real life. Many places in the book exist. Those with an eagle eye will, for example, notice that Guanabana's in Jupiter is in its expanded form even though the story takes place in spring 2008 and this expanded restaurant didn't open until December 2008. It's fiction, so I get to do that. All real life places are used in a completely fictionalized way, and in no way represent endorsement of my work by them. I may or may not have enjoyed a beverage or two at any number of these places.

# ABOUT THE AUTHOR

A.J. Stewart wrote marketing copy for Fortune 500 companies and tech start-ups for 20 years, until his head nearly exploded from all the stories bursting to get out. Stiff Arm Steal was his fifth novel, but the first to make it into print.

He has lived and worked in Australia, Japan, UK, Norway, and South Africa, as well as San Francisco, Connecticut and of course Florida. He currently resides in Los Angeles with his two favorite people, his wife and son.

AJ is working on a screenplay that he never plans to produce, but it gives him something to talk about at parties in LA.


You can find AJ online at www.ajstewartbooks.com, connect on Twitter @The_AJStewart or Facebook facebook.com/TheAJStewart.

Made in United States
Troutdale, OR
05/20/2025

31527712R00215